Smoke and Steel
A Sapphic Epic Fantasy
Dax Murray

Kraken
Collective

KRAKEN COLLECTIVE

Dax Murray

www.daxmurray.com

Kraken Collective Books

www.thekrakencollective.com

Cover Design: Get Covers

Interior Illustrations by Liz Sauco
Interior Design by Dax Murray
Editor: Ingrid Moon
978-1-958051-81-8
978-1-958051-82-5
978-1-958051-83-2

Kraken
Collective

CONTENTS

Do I even need to say it?

Thank you for believing in me.

Content Warnings

Content Warning List

THIS IS A WORK of fiction; the behaviors, actions, and views of characters should not be conflated or confused with the author's opinions and beliefs. The presence of these darker themes in this work is not an endorsement of them. This list is as complete as the author can make it.

- Consensual Intercourse,

- Violence,

- Murder, Execution,

- Revolution,

- Domestic violence,

- Arson,

- Assault,

- Torture,

- Blood,

- Religious abuse,

- Consumption of alcohol,

- Suicidal Ideation,

ONE

MAR'SAHR'DAN'I ARE NOT BORN; THEY are chosen. That is what her mother—Sumalika mat Qa'taru, Sarhe'Danu of Sua—had told her. Chosen based on strength, wisdom, cunning, and desire. Chosen for their ability to be ruthless, unforgiving, and unfeeling.

In the six years since the violent insurrection at the hands of the Amyrdine Bara and their savitus fighters, Saritrah has not forgotten those words. She turns them over as if they were stones in her mind as General Arishaki moves the pebbles on the parchment, movements deliberate, slow, but coldly calculated. As long as everyone follows his orders, tomorrow they will take back Antalyza from the Amyrdine Bara.

If she can take back Antalyza, she can take back all of Sua.

The cool night wind pricks at her skin, but the glow of the twin moons sets her eyes on fire. The lost princess; six years in exile, six years of biding her time. Six years of sharpening her claws and honing her fangs. Tomorrow will not be her first skirmish, but it will be the most significant. The *sarhe* of Antalyza was loyal through and through to her family, the perfect vassal, the perfect servant to the royal family. Now, she will free him from the prisons the insurrectionists have left him to rot in, proving to the world that she will be a just ruler, righting the wrongs of the world swiftly and decisively.

Distantly, a herd of camels sings into the winds of the desert. "Are the Re'u coming through?" Puzur asks. Young, ambitious, but hopelessly clueless. Saritrah twirls a strand of hair around her finger, willing to let him embarrass himself so Arishaki can step in and prove again why he is the most trusted of her army.

"That doesn't sound like them; that's something else," Harharu replies.

"Aye," General Arishaki says, straightening his back and scanning the horizon. His harsh voice is barely a whisper, but it has the commanding tone required for a leader. Arishaki was chosen from an elite group of women for his cunning and strength to be Saritrah's bodyguard since she was ten summers old. Though the woman was only a few years older than her, he was a better fighter than those with twice his experience. "I don't like the sound of it."

"No, it has to be some merchants or traders. Who else would be here?" Ears pricked up, tail frozen, Yangi glances around the fire, eyes wide.

Saritrah purses her lips. Ashur. It is Ashur. That cursed brother of hers. Her hand reaches for the royal seal, a ring threaded with a leather ribbon worn loosely around her neck. Always next to her heart, pried from the hands of another of her sibling Aishah when she fled the palace the night the Amyrdine Bara attacked. Ashur cannot have it.

"He's getting closer," Arishaki says, both hands brushing the sand, speaking with the dunes. "He'll be upon us within half an hour. From the north."

"Dammit." Saritrah reaches for Katynna, the bladed weapon passed down through the generations, wielded only by the mar'sahr'dan'i; the other item that proves her divine right to the throne and that marks her as the rightful heir to the throne. She pulls the curved blade from the sheath and raises it above her head. "To me! To me! We fight!"

She brandishes it into the night sky, racing towards her stallion, relying on the loyalty of her soldiers to follow her into battle. Fires quickly extinguished, rations hastily eaten—her followers, her believers, her trusted servants rally behind their queen, Saritrah, the next Sahre'Danu of Sua.

She rides toward the gates of Antalyza, the shining city that the Oracle of Yshuld calls home. Of all the people in her demesne that she must protect, the Oracle is the most vital. If Saritrah is their leader, the Oracle is their hope.

She steadies her breath, a trick she was forced to learn before she could walk. She will make it. She will save Antalyza not just from the savage insurrectionists, but from her brother's sharp talons. The glint of gold against the gate distracts her, a flash of light, and then a shadowed figure slips into the desert. A spy sneaking out of the city? The figure creeps along the wall, staying just out of reach of the moonbeams.

But others follow, and the shrill pleas for help that are ripped from the mouth of this mysterious figure alarm her. Not a spy, but someone in distress. Four more figures creep through the gates after it. "Ari, take the lead! There's someone there," she yells, no doubt that he will follow her orders.

"Of course, my princess," he replies. His domineering tone gives way to gentleness and care. He is the only one she has allowed to address her thusly.

The shrill cries continue, interspersed with cruel chuckles. Ashur's soldiers visiting some sort of violence upon a helpless civilian. She leaps from her horse, putting away Katynna, drawing her spear in one swift movement, and stabbing at the predators before they even see her.

Their prey is small, dark hair pulled back, exposing every inch of fear etched in her face, back pressed against the city wall, fingers curled around a dirty gray robe. She is terrified, cowering, weak. But for the brief second that Saritrah glances into the woman's eyes, she sees a golden, radiant light. Power untapped, strength unharnessed, determination hidden beneath fear.

What a waste of potential. And yet, it is her duty to save this woman, even if the woman is too cowardly to save herself. In two graceful arcs, she dispatches the rest of the leering soldiers, sending them to meet Xana. "Hurry back inside," she says, not bothering to look at the woman as she plunges her spear into the sand and then wipes its sharp point on her wrist brace.

"I am not going back in there," the woman says. Her voice quivers, but Saritrah hears just a glissando of defiance in it. A defiance that she can admire, praise, even respect. But not one she can tolerate. Not right now.

"That's an order. Get back inside. Things are about to get violent, and the fighting out here is not something you should have to witness."

"I assure you, I have seen worse."

Saritrahlaughs. This woman looks like she's never seen the outside of whatever walled garden she lives in. What, has she seen the kitchen cat torture a rat? Saritrah turns around. The woman still shakes, but her back is straight, and her chin is high. Just the right combination of fear and defiance for playtime, but a lethal combination on the battlefield. Crossing her arms, Saritrah wonders if she could recruit the woman for something like armor repairs or weapons maintenance. She takes in the rest of the woman's figure, trying to find a place and purpose for her in the army, ignoring the small part of her that wants to take the woman to bed. She wants her for the army, that is all, she tells herself. But once she has been recruited, what fun they could have together.

"Fine. Do as you wish, but I don't like my work going to waste. I saved your life; pay me back by not losing it tonight."

The woman looks out into the desert, a death sentence if she has no supplies. "Thank you, ma'am. I will wait out here until the fighting is over and then go home."

"If I see you out later, I won't be pleased."

"Understood."

Saritrahmounts her horse, enters the city, and only chides herself for not getting the woman's name as she unleashes a fury of lethal assaults on the soldiers she meets inside. She slices her way through the throng; how Ashur acquired so many soldiers is baffling, and yet his numbers are overwhelming. His laugh echoes on the wind, mocking her as she forces her way toward his unspoken call. Haunting her as she races to answer it.

Arishaki—loyal, brave, dependable Arishaki—is already engaging her brother. Blood pounding in her ears, she takes a deep breath. Steady. Steady. You don't win by being reckless; you don't win by being hasty. Squaring her shoulders, she leaps from her horse, lunging at her brother, her sword point slithering toward his throat.

"Ah, sister dearest! I had not expected to see you here. What a delightful surprise! A family reunion. How have you been, love?"

Sister dearest, he would say before wrapping his hands around Zisuthra's throat. How have you been, love? He would say before dragging Zisuthra down the halls by her tail. He never hurt Zisu because he hated her; he hurt Zisu because he knew it hurt Saritrah.

Steady, steady. Don't let him win; don't let him get to you. She swings upward and then back down, quick and ruthless and without aim or method. He dodges easily, just as easily as he had dodged her attacks in the iseru. His smile just as cruel now as it had been when they were children fighting in that arena.

But this is different. She has Katynna strapped at her hip and the royal seal concealed under her tunic this time. She has the power of the mar'sahr'dan'i. She slashes, he dodges, neither getting a hit on the other. But he is clearly winning, no sweat upon his brow, no quiver of fatigue on his lips. Her face is contorted in anger and concentration; his is as tranquil as the glow of Yludi on the full moon night.

Why can't I win? Why can't I beat him? I can't lose, I can't. I have to save our people from him; if he claims the throne, it will be worse than even those brutal insurrectionists.

"Well, this has been so much fun, sister dearest," he says, jumping backward to land on the edge of the city wall and nodding at someone behind, most likely his second-in-command. "But I have more important things to do than to toy with a little mouse. I got what I came here for, but thank you for keeping me entertained." He leaps back over the wall, a silent signal to his troops to retreat.

As quickly as they came, Ashur's army leaves Antalyza. Now all that remains for Saritrah to do is drive out the insurrectionists.

The insurrectionists flee when they realize they are caught between the two warring royals. Their tails between their legs, they are gone before the sun has fully crested the horizon.

As daybreak shatters the bloody night, the isiaq of Anatlyza, an older qatu by the name of Zaakit, summons the Seers of the Temple of Yshuld to celebrate their liberation and meet their saviors.

Hands clasped behind her back, Saritrah takes in the sights of her new prize: The Temple of Yshuld, the patron goddess of Sua. The Oracle, Yshuld's Chosen, resides inside the tall marble walls, attended to by priestesses and acolytes, every comfort given to the one divinely blessed with not just the Sight, but Her Sight. It is the grey-robed novices that patter out of the marble doors first, descending the stairs in the best attempts at dignified waltzes that children can make. Following them are the blue-robed acolytes, those who had survived the grueling instruction of harsh priestesses and decided they still wanted to consecrate themselves to Yshuld.

Saritrah tries not to fidget as the silver-robed priestesses join the crowd around her, impatient to speak with the Oracle and be on her way to her next conquest. But one of the priestesses catches her eye. The woman from last night! Face blank, back straight, the flowing silver robe doing nothing to mask her identity. A runaway priestess?

Before she can wrap her mind around this anomaly, the gold-robed High Priestess floats down the stairs and bows deeply before her. "Our prayers have been answered; the Sahre'Danu has saved us. Let us lift our voices in praise to Yshuld!"

The gathering of Seers fall to their knees and lift their hands heavenward, eyes closed against the bright sun. This show of honor is interrupted by a scream that Saritrah knows all too well. The woman she had saved the night before. Pledged to Yshuld. Part of Saritrah is disappointed; there will be no recruiting. No new bed partner.

She waits for the High Priestess to chastise the wayward adherent, yet the High Priestess does no such thing. Instead, the woman glides across the flowered courtyard to take the frightened woman into her arms. The woman's whispered words carry on the hot breeze. "Child, what has the Goddess shown you?"

"The end, the end..." The priestess paws at the ground, digging her nails into the soil and then pounding her fists, a cloud of dust enveloping her. The sun's hazy rays make the woman seem like a mirage.

The High Priestess draws the frightened woman to her feet, leading, or perhaps dragging, her before Sari.

"Darudan," the High Priestess says, the appellation of royalty only given to a sahre'danu. "Our Oracle is unwell and unable to present herself before you, even though she dearly wishes to be here."

"Unwell?"

The High Priestess does not meet her gaze. "She suddenly became ill late last night."

Is this Ashur's doing? Was he here to assassinate the Oracle? Did he fail and only injure her? No, he wouldn't leave unless he knew the job was done... Saritrah wants to ask the High Priestess for more information, but she seems determined to give no further clues.

"Instead, I would like to present you with Sister Nanshaie, a talented Seer, more than blessed by Yshuld."

Sister Nanshaie curtseys. Saritrah wants to laugh for thinking about inviting this woman into her army, and perhaps to her bed.. But the fear in the Seer's eyes confirms Saritrah's suspicion. She had been running last night to flee Ashur. She must have known he was coming for the Oracle... But why is the High Priestess acting as if nothing has happened? Is the Oracle already dead?

"I am honored to meet you, Sister Nanshaie." Saritrah holds out her hand, but when the Seer touches it, the spark she feels almost stops her heart.

The Seer, eyes wider than they had been the night before, looks straight into Saritrah's soul and somehow stares at something far in the distance. "You will be betrayed; be wary of those you call friends, for their words are naught but lies and their actions naught but subterfuge. I must go. I am sorry, I must go!" She covers her face in her hands and dashes back inside the temple, tripping more than once as she ascends the stairs.

"Forgive her, please, Sahre'Danu. She is young, and the strength of her Sight still frightens her."

"There is nothing to forgive. I appreciate her warning, but I have no need of it. I have Katynna; there is nothing else that I need in order to restore order and justice to the kingdom. All are loyal to me; I am sure she merely misinterpreted what she saw."

"Of course," the High Priestess says, her composure cracking for a fraction of a second. "To show our gratitude, we have many gifts for you."

Isiaq Zaakit joins the congregation as the Seers distribute gold, jewels, and, most importantly, weapons to Saritrah's army. "Darudan, I also would like to offer you and your army medical care. We have several healers who would be happy to attend to your wounded. I believe I saw that my dear friend Ari had a nasty cut."

The general steps forward, gripping the isiaq's hand, laughing. "You worry too much, old friend. I am more than hearty and hale and in no need to see a healer."

"I wouldn't be a friend if I didn't offer, Ari." The isiaq throws his arm around the general's shoulder and pulls him away from the crowd.

"Darudan, there is one more thing." The High Priestess steps closer, far too close for Saritrah's comfort, but she does not take a step back. "The key to your victory, I know what it is. There is nothing that would make me happier than to see you occupy the Kashtu Throne. And I have foreseen the beautiful paradise that you will bring to our nation should you do so. But your victory requires more than just strength."

"Please, speak plainly."

"There is something more you need, something that I can help you find."

"The blade of Katynna and the royal seal are more than enough, but I do thank you. I hope to one day bring about this paradise, but I can do it on my own terms."

"As you say, Darudan."

It has been six years since Saritrah last slept in such opulent accommodations. The cool marble floors, the soft and thick ersu, the silk sheets, and the curtained windows let the cool air in but keep the insects out; such a change from staying in cramped edin'tu and sleeping on thin halersu mats. She had spent too much time luxuriating in the cold pool and had missed her usual practice time with Arishaki.

The general stretches, flexing every muscle in his chiseled body. A body hardened by both battle and training. A body that has lain beside hers every night for the past three years. A body that has defended hers since she was a child and he her servant. Only a handful of years older than her, yet exceptionally more skilled, gifted with a speed and precision she could only hope to imitate, he had been assigned her bodyguard when he was only twelve years old. But he had been her training and sparring partner since before she had even learned her letters.

He had not been allowed in the arena with her, yet he was always just outside of it, waiting. Willing to offer her advice and feedback, as well as to help her wash her wounds and nurse her pride, never giving up on her. He was the only woman Saritrah had ever trusted with her heart. She shared her bedy with many; but only Ari had her heart.

She taps the soft pillow beside her. "Join me, Ari."

He makes one last pass with his spear, wincing at the last second, and then removes his shirt and settles in beside her.

"Are you alright?"

"Your brother may have got me; I will admit to that. But Zaak was making too much of it. It will be better tomorrow."

"Are you sure? Once we leave here—"

"I will be fine." His eyes narrow and annoyance creeps into his voice. "I won't need any medical attention. You worry too much."

"If you insist. I was thinking about what that one Seer said," Sari-trah says, running a finger down his chest, tracing a line around each muscle, watching him twitch with each light touch. She wants to move her hand lower, futher down his body until she can plunge her fingers between his legs and hear him moan as she moves inside of him. But he tenses and she pauses.

"About the traitors?" He asks.

"Yes, about that."

He pushes her hand away, rolling on his side to face her. "Do not worry about it. The soldiers are loyal."

"But—"

He brushes a strand of her gold-brown hair out of her face and then runs the tip of his claw up the side of her ear, flicking the tip when he gets to it. "Don't jump at shadows; fear does not suit you."

"You do not believe in the Sight?"

"I believe that the woman is young, as the High Priestess said, and not in control of herself or her emotions, let alone her Sight."

She rolls away from him, pulling the silk sheets tighter around her body. "Do you think it's Belu? She's always saying she wants fewer duties, she's lazy. Or maybe it is Ditanu; I saw zir talking to—"

"Princess. No. You cannot keep treating everyone like they will turn their back on you."

"But what if they do?"

He rolls off of the *ersu*, letting the sheets fall away as he stands up. "I am going to do one more patrol. When I come back, I hope you are sleeping soundly." He does not bother to put on more than a pair of trousers before walking out.

What if it's him? What if he will betray me? She eyes his drawstring pouch he always has strapped to his belt. . It's small, fits in the palm of his hand. But he did not take it with him. She stares at it, hand twitching, wanting to grab it, to pull on the strings and see what he keeps in it.

Her hand clenches and unclenches, her arm extends and retracts. She needs to know. She has to know if he is the traitor that Sister Nanshaie warned her about.

"All seems well. Why are you still awake, princess?"

Too long. She hesitated for too long. "I think I have too many nerves to sleep," she says, grabbing his hand and pulling it toward her chest, placing it between her breasts. "Do you think you can help me unwind?"

He smiles, but his eyes do not reflect the light. "I am tired, princess. Not tonight." He rolls over, facing away from her, and falls asleep before she can even protest.

TWO

SARITRAH WISHES THAT SHE COULD STAY in Antalyza longer; the fruits—faricot, imquats, dates, and undu—that are offered to her before dawn rival those she had once taken for granted when living in Erzuremei at the royal isi'tu, and the refreshing pools in the Temple surpass the comfort of the ones in her childhood home. Yet, Arishaki ushers her out of the Temple, having already assigned a battalion to stay at Antalyza to help the isiaq protect it against both Ashur and the insurrectionists. A pang of jealousy overtakes her as she looks over her shoulder at the troops now guarding the gates to the city.

They are only an hour into their trek across the Esiri desert when Arishaki calls for a halt. "Is something wrong?" she asks. They should keep moving. They got a later start than she wanted, entirely her own fault, but the high-noon resting time of nialsamsu is still hours away.

"I did not sleep well last night, and the bandages on my wound are loose. I am sorry to cause a delay, princess. I won't be long." He wanders away from their procession. She wants to give chase, but her troops are restless, and she will not give them cause to worry.

Arishaki returns, but he looks worse than when he left, his golden skin dull and the sheen of his fur lacking the usual luster. *No wonder he turned me down last night.*

They are moving again within half an hour, but the sun is not even a quarter of a way into the sky before he requests another stop. She pulls on the reins of her camel, but before she can raise her arm to call for a halt, Ari slides off of his mount.

In one swift motion, she leaps from her camel, twisting in the air to land next to her fallen general. "Ari! Ari, what's wrong?"

He pulls aside his bandage, and the gash across his shoulder is a deadly shade of purple, the center oozing a foul-smelling pus. "Maybe I should have listened to Zaak."

"Belu! Belu, get the medical kit, now!" Not waiting for her medic, she grabs her flask and pours water over his wound; trying to ignore the pained hiss he lets out as the water hits his skin.

"How long do you think you can hold on?"

"I can keep going, Princess, I promise."

"No, you can't! Drink this. Tanit! Set up the edin'tu, get a haler-su. We're taking nialsamsu early."

"But the sun is nowhere near the apex..."

"I said we are taking nialsamsu early! Set up the edin'tu. I did not ask for your input or request that you question me. Do as you're told!" Her words come out with a snarl.

The lieutenant salutes and issues her own orders to the rest of the troops. Leather tents spring up around Saritrah and her general as the sun inches closer to its zenith. She carries him to her personal edin'tu, laying him out on her halersu mat of gaatsu feathers and treated qaboon skin, the skin not having lost a mote of its iridescence or shimmer in the tanning process. He looks radiant; he looks like a sleeping sahru'dane.

"Tu'erebu?" Belu calls from outside of the edin'tu.

"Tu'sala," Saritrah replies. "Come in, hurry!"

The medic pushes aside the cloth entrance to the edin'tu and sets down her supplies next to the general. "What is wrong?"

"His wound... I think it is infected."

Belu takes a quick glance at it. "It is poisoned. It may also be infected, but the primary concern is the poison."

"Ashur... What a monster. It must be imtu'bas venom."

The medic flinches. "I am afraid, Mar'sahr'dan'i, that I do not have the antidote for that."

"Of course! Of course, that bastard would resort to dishonorable deeds like poison! Damn him!"

"Princess," Arishaki whispers, "please, do not let your anger make you lose control."

If he were not ill, she would slap him for that comment, especially for making it in front of a soldier. But she bites her tongue. "I will find the antidote. There's a village nearby, yes? The village Nebu?"

The medic nods.

"I will go get it. Belu, you look after General Arishaki. I'll leave Tanit in charge should the general... I will be back. Take care of him."

The village is small, with only a handful of sub'tu around a central well. But she finds the bu'aru'tu—the healer's sub'tu—easily marked with the crescent moon of Ayndras.

"Tu'erebu?" She calls from the other side of the baputi as if the thick leather flap to the sub'tu is as impenetrable as iron, not caring if she wakes the entire village. "It's an emergency! Tu'erebu?"

"Aye, aye, fine, tu'sala, tu'sala!" the healer calls, his voice carrying the edge of someone reluctant to leave their bed, and while his accent is Suan, their soft vowels hint at Re'u ancestry.

She marches through the baputi, sliding a jeweled ring from her finger and slamming it on the counter just inside, not waiting for the healer to rub the sleep from his eyes. "I need a vial of antidote for imtu'bas."

"I'd love to, especially for that price," he says, pointing to the ring. "But I don't have any, sorry."

"Well, then, come with me. My friend needs treatment. He was poisoned! He's dying!"

"Kit, I'd love to take your payment and help your friend, but there is no helping him."

She clenches her hand. Ari is not dying. Ari can't die. He promised, he promised he'd be there to place the crown on her head. He isn't a liar, he can't have lied, so he can't die! "You need to save him! You need to! I demand it!"

"I don't know who you think you are, kit, but not even the *Bah'en* can stop Xana," he says, invoking the Re'u goddess and confirming Saritrah's suspicions.

She reaches across the counter and grabs the healer by the scruff of his neck, pulling him off of the floor. "I am the *Mar'sahr'dan'i*;

you will not call me 'kit,' and I do not care about your gods or mine. Arishaki cannot die!"

"The goddess of death does not care who you are; she does not care who your friend is," he says, grabbing her hands and trying to pry her fingers off of his neck. "She takes who she wants when she wants. There is nothing I can do to stop her if your friend has truly been poisoned by imtu'bas."

"No! No!" She lets go of the healer and jumps onto the counter, drawing Katynna. The tip of it inches its way to the healer's neck. "If you will not help me, who in this village can?"

The healer raises his hands above his head. "I swear on my life, I swear to *Bah'en*, I would help you if I could, but no one in this village has even a drop of that antidote."

"Liar! Shut up! He can't die! He can't! He promised me, he is loyal to me! He won't die unless I order him to, so there must be some way to save him!"

"Kittu, I am so sorry, but everyone loses someone they love, eventually."

"Shut up! I do not love him. He is my servant, he is my general, he is my..." She does not want to admit outloud that he is the only woman who has seen all of her scars. She does not want to admit there are even scars to show.

"I can accompany you to him and help ease his pain as he passes, but I can do no more than that."

"Tu'erebu, Enlil, are you okay?" Another voice drifts in from outside the tent.

"I am fine, Nazim. I just have a grieving customer." The healer's voice is full of sorrow, and it burns at Saritrah's chest.

"I am not grieving," she says, sheathing her weapon. "Fine. Come with me. Maybe by the time we get to him, you'll remember how to save a life, like healers are supposed to do." She drags the healer out of his sub'tu, glaring at the villagers whom she has woken from nial-samsu with her shouting.

"I'm coming, too," Nazim says, bearing his own spear and flashing his fangs at her. "You hurt our *musalli*, and I will gut you."

She hisses at him but protests no more as she helps the healer onto her camel.

The ride back to her camp is harsh; there is a reason the Suan people do not travel during the sun's apex. But she cares little if she or her companions suffer from sun-sickness; she must make it to Arishaki. She must save her most loyal servant. That is what good sahre'danus do. They save their subjects. She ignores the healer gripping her belt to stay on; she ignores the protests of the healer's son that they are going too fast. There is no such thing as too fast when it comes to saving the life of a loyal bodyguard.

She does not bother to dismount her camel at the entrance to her camp. She rides it straight to her edin'tu, entering without even asking for permission, leaving her two companions to climb down on their own.

"Mar...! You're back!" Belu says, stepping away from Arishaki. "Do you have the antidote?"

Saritrah rushes to Arishaki's side, taking his cold hands in hers, both glaring at and silently imploring the healer to do something as he and his son push aside the baputi and approach. The deathly gray-purple has spread from just the area around the slash to take over his entire torso and arm. "Save him, please," she says.

The *musalli*, his steps hesitant and short, crosses the large edin'tu and sits down across from Sari. "I cannot."

"Belu. Out! Keep everyone away from here."

"Yes, Mar." The lieutenant salutes and exits without another word.

"Save him!" She hisses.

"Kitt—" He says it kindly, but all Saritrah hears is condescension.

"Don't call me that. Just save him! That's an order!" She knows her heart is racing, but she cannot feel anything in her body except the lump in her throat and the stinging in her eyes.

"I wish I could. The poison has spread too fast." The healer says—his full Re'u accent coming out, lines of anxiety etched into his forehead.

"No, that's impossible! He only got the wound last night!" She does not want to cry, so she yells.

"I do not know what else to say; as you can see, it has already spread past his heart. Even if I had an infinite supply of the antidote, it would not be enough. I suggest that you say goodbye to your loved one. I can give him something to regulate his body temperature and dull his pain, or even something to make him sleep and..."

"Do not say it. Do not say what you are about to say if you value your life." Her hand reaches for the royal seal hidden under her camise, feeling the rough grooves in the side of the ring through the fabric. *He promised. He swore on his honor that he would not abandon me, that he would be the one to crown me.*

The *musalli* says something to his son, and the qatu pulls a few bottles from the healer's bag. "This one will help control his fever," the son says, holding it out to Sari. She glares, hands suddenly not knowing how to move. The son says nothing more, continuing to hold out the small glass bottle.

"Fine," she says, snatching it from his hand.

"And this one is for pain. He will need it every three hours." Despite the bite in Saritrah's voice, neither the healer nor his son have said a single word to her with anything but kindness. She hates them for it.

"Fine, fine." She takes it, setting it on the ground beside the first.

"And this one…"

"Don't say it!" She takes the bottle and shoves it into her pocket.

"That last one, it doesn't take a lot. Just a few drops in some water. But with how fast this is spreading… I would do it sooner rather than later. And be careful with it; once you break the seal on that bottle, it must be used within the hour, or it will stop being effective."

Saritrah grabs her own bag, pulling out five gold coins. "Will this be enough?" She already knows the answer. This is more than even the royal physician was paid, and she had the unpleasant task of caring for twelve qitu who tried to murder each other at least once a week. She is not paying the healer for his medicines or his time; she's paying him for his discretion and silence.

"I thank you," the healer says. "*Sen'en'dai, Bah'en'rita.*"

The healer's Re'u accent comes out as he wishes her well in his own language. The wishy-washy Re'u who roam the desert and refuse to offer fealty or loyalty to any isiaq, sahre, or even the sahre'danu. Living on Suan lands yet refusing to acknowledge it;

no sense of loyalty or duty, claiming that they should not have any as they are refugees from another land, another time.

"Ask for Tanit, and tell xir to escort you back this evening. For now, you can use Arishaki's edin'tu to rest. It's one directly next to this on the right. At the center of the encampment, you will find Haruhar. He can provide you with water and rations if you need some."

"You are most generous. Truly, I wish I could do more for your hira'imu."

She bristles at the term. Hira'imu. Life partners. Lovers. Pledged in love. An oath sworn to each other, but an oath that never once mentions loyalty. That is what she has from Arishaki; loyalty, which is infinitely more important than love. "May I ask you a question?"

"Of course, I only hope that I can answer it."

"Your people pledge no loyalty to my family despite the gods demanding such fealty to those they have divinely appointed as rulers. Yet you help me now. Why?"

"I mean no disrespect; but you did threaten me."

She chuckles. "Is that all?"

"No. That is not the full reason. The love in your heart, the love you have for this woman... A woman who can move one so hard-hearted as you surely deserves a dignified death. Maybe, if he had lived longer, he would have taught you to love yourself, too."

She administered the first two tinctures as soon as the healer and his son exited her edin'tu. She hesitates when she grabs the last one.

Should she do it? Should she ask him if he wants it? He has been unresponsive since she returned; she does not even know if he has heard her speaking to him. Sometimes his eyes are open, and he looks around frantically, but otherwise, he is frozen in place. Sometimes his eyes are closed, and he looks as peaceful as when he falls asleep beside her every night.

She sets the last vial down again. If she were to kill him, she would want to do it with her blade. That is how he would want it.

As it stands right now, it is Ashur who is taking his life. She keeps vigil at his side even as the day ends and the twin moons crest upon the horizon.

"I failed you," she says. "If I were worthy of your loyalty and fealty, you would not be dying right now. If I deserved your service, you would not be leaving it. I am unworthy of both you and the people of Sua." She lays her head on his naked, ghost-purple chest, his heartbeat only audible if she holds her breath. "You snuck the wrong mat'sahr'dan out of the palace that night. You should have helped Aishah escape that night! He could have taken on Ashur." She lays down beside him on the halersu, stretching out her legs and entwining them with his.

Outside, she hears her troops chattering over dinner, most likely eager to get moving again, none but Belu and Tanit knowing just how sick the general is.

"He was the rightful Mar'sahr'dan'i. I am just a thief who took advantage of that chaos. You should have helped him; he could have beaten Ashur."

His hand twitches, and she wants to believe it is him reassuring her. She wants to believe it is an attempt at communication and not the spasms of muscles as they die.

Hira'imu. The healer had called them hira'imu. A relationship built on love. What she had with Ari might look like love, but mat'sahr'dan do not know that emotion. It is not taught to them. What she has with Ari is loyalty, respect, trust, understanding, and acceptance. Nowhere in there does love factor in.

But why does the word sit on her tongue right now? What is it clawing behind her teeth, trying to escape her mouth and be whispered into his ear? Why is that the only word she can think of right now, the one word she wants to say to him?

Her heart beats rapidly, as if encouraging his heart to do the same. Her deep breaths an attempt to get him to follow her example. To live, to fight, to persevere. "Please," she says. A word she has never said before. A request. Not a demand. Not an order. "Please, stay, Ari. You promised me. You promised."

His hand twitches again and slowly moves toward her. His thumb brushes against hers.

"Fight, please fight it. If anyone can do it, it's you. Stay with me. Please."

He takes a deep breath, eyes briefly opening. Emerald jewels marked by sharp, vertical pupils. "Prin—"

"Ari! Yes, stay! Please! You need to stay. I lo—" His eyes close and the rattle of death escapes his lips.

She couldn't say it. Not even at the end. And apparently, neither could he.

She does not say a word as she lifts his limp body and carries him into the desert, not acknowledging any of her troops, and they follow her to the unplanned funeral. No one says a word as they dig, taking turns looking out and scouting the area for predators of any variety.

As the gathered mourners finish their task, Saritrah orders them to leave her. Alone, completely alone, she collapses on the sand, imagining it's Ari. "I will see our goal through to the end. I won't fail you. I won't."

She wishes that she could send him away in flames, but only those of royal blood can have the honor and blessing of cremation. If she had married him…

She pulls the ring from under her shirt, clasping it tightly. "I won't fail you."

But he failed her. He betrayed her, abandoned her, and broke his promise. Is this what Sister Nanshaie warned her about? Is this what that cryptic message meant?

THREE

THEY ARE ONLY A FEW days away from Erzurumei, a few days away from home—from the palace, her birthright, her inheritance, her salvation and Sua's. A few days away from the goal she and Ari had dreamed of for the last six years. She wants to keep going, keep pressing forward. It is almost nialsamsu, but if she can just make it another hour, push them just a little more...

"Aye! Mar!" Yangi calls, circling back from his scouting. "Tracks up ahead. Lots of them."

"Ashur... That has to be Ashur. He's ahead of us. While we were celebrating our victory and..." *Mourning our dead...* "He got ahead of us." Weakness. This is what comes from love. Mistakes. She made a mistake trying to save Ari. She made a mistake by not just leaving him there to rot. A mistake that might cost her the throne.

Nothing for it now. "We press ahead. We will set up nialsamsu in an hour but for now, press ahead."

She pretends that she does not hear the groans some of her troops make, pretends she does not see their faces fall and their shoulders sag. She has no patience or time for weak soldiers. If they cannot push through a little longer while marching, they will not make it through the upcoming battle.

"Hey, Mar... I don't think these are tracks from Ashur; they are not orderly at all," Belu says as they approach the marks in the sand.

"No, these aren't his army. So who—?"

The bandits, hiding over the top of a dune, descend.

"Formation! Get in formation!" She raises Katynna, signaling their strategy. But instead of rushing to obey, they fall apart. They race forward, not even in any sort of order.

"Formation! Get in formation!" She tries again, but no one can hear her now over the shouts of the bandits. She has more soldiers, but the bandits have more discipline.

If Arishaki were here... they would listen to Arishaki.

But he's not here.

The largest of the bandits shoves his way through her soldiers to engage her. He smirks at her. *He probably does not even know who I am. But he will learn.*

He knows how to leverage his weight, not needing any effort at all on his downward swings. He slashes randomly, relying on gravity and luck to do the work for him. But she is fast, more clever, and prepared.

The bandits engage in battle only long enough for their second group to swoop in, scoop up as many packs and bags as they can, and scurry off with their stolen goods. Despite her own skill and her soldiers' overwhelming numbers, the bandits make off with over half of their edin'tus, most of their dried meats, and almost all of their water supplies. While they did not manage to steal any camels or horses, they did kill enough of them to hobble her army's progress.

"Badly done!" She shouts at her troops as they nurse their wounds, watching the bandits disappear again. But they do not listen.

What is wrong with them? Or is it me? Am I not worth listening to?

She hears Sister Nanshaie's words again. Is someone here a traitor?

She allows her troops to rest for the night and decides not to break their camp until the sun has crested the horizon. But as she calls for order, she is ignored. They carry on with their chattering and banter as if they do not even hear her.

Her frustration mounts. She clenches her fist, a weight on her shoulder as she recalls all of her failures. She takes a deep breath, waiting for Ari to place his hand on her shoulder and whisper that it will be fine, that everything is well. These are just stumbling blocks on her way to the throne. But he will never again do that. She calls out once again, imagining that she is Arishaki this time, imitating his cadence and tone.

Still, they disregard her commands. She has led them through countless battles, fighting side by side, and yet now they choose to ignore her.

As the rays of the twin moons illuminate the camp and the desert sands cool, she gives up. She marches through the camp, glaring at her disobedient troops. In the privacy of her edin'tu, she cleans her weapons, pushing out all the memories of her and Ari doing this together.

She does not sleep, she does not want to crawl into her cold haler-su and find it empty. She does not want to awaken to another dawn without Arishaki. She stays up until the sun crests the horizon.

"Let's get moving," she shouts to her troops as she marches through camp. "Pack up. We're going."

The soldiers' eyes shift towards her as she shouts. One says, "No, we're still tired, Mar. We want to get going, we do, but we have not even recovered from Antalyza. We've barely had a break. Can we at least scout for some food first?"

Not one of her troops has ever talked back to her, and yet…

"Ashur's troops have more than one advantage over us now. If we do not get there soon, he will claim Erzurumei for himself. Do you want to live in a Sua ruled by that monster?"

"Heh, maybe. Does he let his troops at least rest?" The voice of the disobedient soldier is snide, loud enough to be heard but soft enough to be denied.

"Who said that?" She draws her spear from her back.

No one responds.

"Who? Who said that? I demand that you answer me, or you will all be held accountable!" She glares at her troops, searching for a face that has guilt written across it. No one even moves. Is this what Nanshaie meant when she said someone would betray her? Did she mean the entire army? All of her soldiers? "Fine! Fine. We will rest until after nialsamsu. But then we leave. I expect everyone to have reconsidered their behavior and be ready to march. If you are not, you will be left behind."

She returns to her edin'tu. She wants to throw things; she wants to scream and claw out the eyes of every single one of her soldiers.

Which one is the traitor? Which one is sabotaging her efforts to get to Erzurumei? Which one set the bandits on them? Which one has convinced the rest of her troops to run amok and be so disobedient?

One of them has to be a traitor. One of them has to be working either for Ashur or the insurrectionists. How much are they being paid? How much are they being bribed to betray her?

She's a good leader; Arishaki would not have stood behind her if she were not worthy of being followed. She's worthy of loyalty and respect; she is. She is. The only reason one of her soldiers would have to betray her is money. Is this what Nanshaie meant?

As they set out after nialsamsu, she realizes what she needs: another general. There is no one that she can trust as much as she trusted Ari. But she needs someone to at least take care of the minor details. She mulls over her lieutenants: Tanit, Ditanu, Belu, and Harharu. They had not been amongst those who disobeyed her when taking out the bandits, and they had all started packing up before she had even ordered it, anticipating her orders before she issued them.

She falls back. She did not spend one-on-one time with each soldier and does not know everyone's strengths and weaknesses the way Ari had. But someone in her troops must. She needs to figure out who that is and appoint them. Someone the troops feel they can get close to and confide in a way they would never feel comfortable confiding in a ruler. Yes, that is the problem.

"Tanit! Here." She holds up her hand and gestures Tanit to the front.

The qatu approaches, falling in next to her, and Saritrah does not miss the hesitation in xir face. "Yes, Mar?"

"I need a new general. Who do you recommend?" She keeps her face neutral, matter of fact, not wanting anyone to see the storm raging in her mind.

A thousand emotions pass across the qatu's face. Saritrah wishes she could decipher even one of them. She scrutinizes the lieutenant's countenance, hoping for even a hint, a glimpse, into the inner workings of one of her troops.

"Ditanu or myself."

"Interesting. What is your rationale?" If it were anyone but Tanit, Saritrah would be put off by the confidence. But Tanit has more than earned the right to request a higher position.

"Ditanu is experienced in far more fighting styles than most people even know exist. She is calm, logical, but approachable. While I am not the best fighter, I worked side by side with the general on strategy and can identify shifts in battle before they become an issue."

"Not Puzur? Yangi?"

"Puzur is well versed in many areas, but his skills are better suited to the backlines, organizing, training, and recruiting. Yangi is definitely a sight to behold... on the training field. But he cannot keep his head in an actual battle. It does not matter how often he wins sparring matches nor how soundly."

Saritrahwants to laugh, acknowledging the faults of Yangi. But she must maintain an appearance of neutrality. "Harharu or Belu?"

The qatu bites xir bottom lip. "They both have exceptional leadership skills, and I think one day they could take on more responsibilities. They are still too green right now, though, and need more experience. But with time, I believe either of them could rival the general in talents, if given the right learning opportunities."

Saritrah's ears flatten and she hisses. "No. No one can rival Ari." She kicks her camel forward; no need to even bother finishing that conversation. No one can compare to Ari. They are right to idolize him, but she wonders if they respect him more than they will ever respect her. Or maybe they did not respect him enough if they think they can ever ascend to his level of skill and prowess.

Four

Without better alternatives, Saritrah appointed both Ditanu and Tanit. It took two experienced and capable qatu to fulfill the role that Ari had filled all on his own. Her irreplaceable general.

She stands tall at the top of a dune, and in the distance, the royal isi'tu juts into the sky; the tallest building in all of Ahnlisen, proof that the Suan people are unrivaled even if the rest of the world cannot comprehend their culture. It sparkles in the morning sun, and at night, it glows in the light of the twin moons. Made with marble and granite quarried from the far north and laboriously transported through the harsh Esiri desert, it is graceful without harsh angles, intricately carved with elegant filigree, and inlaid with emeralds. Its windows are all of sea-blue stained glass, set so well into the stone that one cannot even see the seams. It has stood for longer than even her family has ruled. It dates back to the founding of Sua. Some say it goes back further, that the Suans found it and made it theirs. But those people are wrong. They cannot fathom that the people they label as uncivilized could build such a structure.

But it was always meant to be hers, and tomorrow it will be. Tomorrow, she will take it back, the final item of her inheritance.

She imagines what the people in that city are doing; it's almost nialsamsu, but city-dwellers do not adhere to the tradition as much as others might; they have no need. They have awnings, and sturdy roofs, and a fountain on every street corner. But for six years, they have lived under the thumb of the insurrectionists; what tragedies have since befallen them? She's heard that those belonging to the mashr'i class had their assets seized and are now forced to work among the people they once managed, forced to do the demeaning labor that should be reserved for the kinatu'i class. Upending the natural order.

If a qatu cannot claw and fight their way to the top, they deserve to be in the dredges. Perhaps, strangely, the insurrectionists are another manifestation of that. They relentlessly clawed their way to the top. They had no qualms with slaughtering her siblings like livestock.

She had been one of twelve qitu. The ruthless infidels had brutally eliminated all of the royal descendants except for her and Ashur, and they would not have hesitated to kill them as well, had the opportunity arisen that night.

And Aishah. They had not struck down Aishah, but they would have, if Saritrah had not killed Aishah first. His death, the death of the Mar'sahr'dan'i, was still laid at the feet of those ghouls, however. But she slew him and in doing so, the title of Mar'sahr'dan'I passed to her.

She retraces her steps to the camp, hoping to find her troops check-ing their armor, sharpening their blades, and stretching their mus-cles. She finds them doing no such preparation. Even her newly-ap-pointed generals are reclining on their worn halersu and gazing at the stars.

"Troops!" Her voice carries across the sea of sand, loud enough for anyone nearby to hear. A risk, but it is not as loud as the din her troops are making. "I have some words to say."

Only her generals and lieutenants rise; no one else even acknowl-edges her presence.

With allies like these, she does not need enemies. Traitors, all of them. Nanshaie was not wrong about betrayal in her ranks; she was wrong about the number. "I said order! Tomorrow, we will re-claim Erzurumei! Today, I need your attention as I explain the plan."

"They aren't listening," Tanit says.

"Why? What is wrong?" she asks as a high-pitched flutter rings out across camp

"I could not say, Mar."

"Who's that, the one with the flute?"

"I am sorry, Mar, but I do not know his name."

"Even better." She strides into the throng of qatu that are sup-posed to make up her army but have instead decided to have a party. She snatches a flute from the hands of one of her shoulders and breaks it over her knee. "Up. On your feet."

He hesitates for only a second, but it is still too long. She grabs him by his neck and drags him to the center of the camp, holding a dagger to his throat. . "If any of you says another word, he will pay for it!"

The camp quiets. Her troops have never dared to look at her like this before, but she does not care. Like they fear her; like she is some monster. Tomorrow, she will take her capital back or die trying, and if they are content to die, then they shall, but her hands will not be the ones covered in blood when they fall.

"Now that you are listening, I would like to go over strategy for tomorrow because, unlike you, I would prefer to come out of the battle unscathed. Ditanu will cover the cavalry formations and lines of attack, and Tanit will cover the infantry movement. I have assigned Belu to instruct and prepare our long ranged—"

"Can we do this tomorrow, Mar?"

She presses the knife into the young soldier's neck. "Who said that? Who is questioning me?"

"Mar," Tanit says, quiet enough only for Saritrah to hear it. "They are overworked, they are spent. They've had far too many days of hard and long marching with dwindling rations and little rest. If you explain a plan now, they will forget it by tomorrow."

She lowers the knife. "Fine. We do not march today. Go hunting, get us meat if you can or stay in camp and see to the weapons. Tomorrow morning, we will discuss strategy, and after nialsamsu,we march. We march to the capital, attack and reclaim our nation."

She storms off to her edin'tu and flops onto her halersuEven though she and Ari technically each had their own, they always shared a halersu together. The freezing nights of the Esiri desert never bothered her before. But without Arishaki next to her, suddenly, every inch of her skin feels exposed and frozen.

Her soldiers do not complain the next day when they are roused; they do not protest as they march through the desert with the ferocity and speed of a desert storm. And they make no complaint while Ditanu and Tanit explain their orders. No one says a word as the cavalry advances into the city, clearing the way for the rest of the army, and there is no objection as Saritrah leads the infantry past the gates, spears and swords raised. They are once again the obedient, well-trained army, dedicated and loyal to Saritrah's cause.

But what she finds on the other side of the city walls frightens her.

It's a trap, she realizes. The cavalry had cleared the way, had invaded the city from all sides, and yet the insurrectionists met them with more soldiers than she would have thought possible for such a small and radical movement.

But that is not what has her frightened.

She looks over her shoulder. Advancing, far too quickly, is Ashur's army. She thought that her army had managed to pass his; that her mad dash across the dunes had meant she would arrive here well before he could. But he has been here all along. Hidden. Waiting. And now he has her surrounded. Her army is caught between two enemy forces.

She scans the melee for her generals, inexperienced but already in the largest battle of their careers. Ditanu atop her warhorse, and Tanit, camel now abandoned, leading a battalion up the stairs to the entrance of the isi'tu. Impossibly, they had the advantage. But General Aziru, confidante and loyal servant of Ashur since birth, was advancing from the east while Ashur charged in from the west.

Ashur had always been one to let others weaken his prey first. He was content being second place to Aishah. Aishah would beat everyone else down, and Ashur would come in and land the final blow. Aishah might get more points for landing more hits, but Ashur was never one to work harder than he had to. And today, he is letting the insurrectionists pick off Saritrah's army, whittle it down so he can swoop in and take her out.

He slices through two of her battalions with ease, striking riders from mounts and separating heads from bodies without hesitation.

"Sister dearest!" He raises his spear, waving it in a mockery of greeting, blood clinging to the point. "Imagine finding you here. But, oh my. I haven't seen your lover yet. Where is he? It would be rude of me not to greet my sister's mate." He laughs, the harsh cackle that rattles on the wind and causes every hair on her body to prickle. "I mean it, sister dearest. I have something I want to tell him." His warhorse takes two steps back before rearing up and lunging at her, his spearpoint sneaking towards her heart.

She leaps from her mount, rolling as she hits the ground and almost getting trampled by camels, horses, and falling infantry soldiers. Struggling to find her footing, she shoves aside other fighters, reaching for her spear.

It is not there, though. She reaches for her other scabbard and withdraws Katynna. It is meant to be ceremonial, but the blade can still slice skin and draw blood.

"I hate an unfair fight," her brother says, leaping from his horse, feet landing firmly on the ground. "So that's where the sword went. Did you scavenge it that night? Or did you steal it from Aishah's dead hands?" He circles her, spear held, but not brandished at her, as if truly desiring a conversation.

"I killed him." She holds Katynna up, both hands firmly gripping the hilt, feet wide.

"Sister! Tsk tsk! That's not very nice."

"Oh, shut up, Ashur. It's mine now. That's how it works." She bounces on the balls of her feet, waiting for him to strike.

"Yes, it is. And so I shall have to kill you, I suppose. Shame, you were my favorite." He yawns, making a show of covering his mouth with one hand, before raising his spear in a lazy challenge. "Perhaps you can tell me where the royal seal is while bleeding out?"

Hissing, she makes the first move, cutting Katynna to the side and back, slashing at any opening she sees, only to be blocked and deflected.

"Six years and no improvement. Shame. I would have thought that Ari had taught you a thing or two."

The sun rises on the horizon, the battle having lasted the night, and the brightness brings tears to her eyes. Blinking, she tries to follow his movements as he swerves, the sun now at his back.

"You know, sister dearest, I realized I can't really fault you for killing our eldest brother." Quicker than a sandstorm starts, his face is next to hers, the tip of his spear under her chin. "I killed our youngest sister on the way out that night. Thought it would be better she die quickly at my hands and not be brutalized by those insurrectionists."

Zisu. Zisuthra. The youngest of the royal qitu. The only one Saritrah cared about.

"How dare you!" She skitters away from him, leaping onto a fence. "She was the only one among us who wasn't corrupted by Sumalika!"

"She was the only one weak enough to escape Mother's notice, you mean? If she had been left alive and somehow gotten the throne, Sua would be even worse off. She wasn't fit to rule, and you knew that."

"She would have been far better than you!"

"Do you have the power of prophecy now? You say that with such conviction. Or did the Oracle tell you that when she rewarded you?"

Saritrah grits her teeth.

"Or was the Oracle indisposed? Or was she perhaps looking a little purplish when you saw her?"

He poisoned her.... She died as painfully as Ari had.... He had killed the Chosen of Yshuld, a holy figure even the insurrectionists refused to harm. The traitors who killed the entire royal family respected Yshuld, at the very least. But her brother had committed a crime against the very goddess that blessed their family's reign.

She needs to kill him. He needs to pay, if not for the sake of her throne but for his insult to Yshuld. She shakes her head to clear it, and as she glances around the city-turned-battlefield, she realizes how few soldiers remain on standing wearing the vibrant blue sash that marks them as one of hers. She's losing. But so is he.

He follows her gaze. "Dammit." He lowers his spear. "Tell you what. Join me right now. Together, we can take those bastards out. That's what matters, right? Getting revenge for our family? Getting Sua out of the clutches of these traitors? I will make you my second-in-command. You will be my top advisor when I sit on the throne. You have my word, join me now and you will live."

"No," she says. But she wants to; some dark part of her wants to join him and lay waste to those wretched insurrectionists, tear out their throats, and fry their livers for celebratory feasts. But he just admitted to killing Zisu. And that is the worst crime anyone can commit. "Retreat! Retreat!"

Ditanu and Tanit pick up her cry, and they flee back into the dunes as the sun sets..

As she races across the sands, she wonders who in her army sold information to Ashur. For the way he was prepared, he had to have known something.

He knew! Their camp has been ransacked. At the center of it is a spear, piercing the ground with a red sash tied to the top, a crimson stain on the amber sands. Her own edin'tu has been shredded, and the few personal items she had are scattered or buried in the waves of the Esiri desert. He knew where they were camped, and he made sure they were trapped in that battle long enough for his spies to do their business. Whether or not they found what they were looking for doesn't matter; the message he is sending her has been received.

He is the one with the more legitimate claim to the throne. He is the one most deserving of wielding Katynna and holding the royal seal. He is the one who should bear the title of Mar'sahr'dan'i.

But more than that, someone in her troops is a traitor. Possibly more than one. The words of the Seer echo so loudly in her mind that she wonders if Ditanu and Tanit, standing sentry behind her as she inspects the site, can hear it, too. She wonders if everyone can hear Ashur's laugh every time the wind blows, whistling through the crevices of the distant buttes.

She yanks the spear out of the ground, breaking it in half over her knee, and shreds the red sash with her claws. If Ari were here, he would be giving a speech right now. Chastising the troops for their poor performance while encouraging them to do better, motivating them for the next battle, and building their determination to do better.

She has no idea how to do that, though. All she wants to do is shout at them. Is this why they do not listen to her? Ditanu and Tanit are attempting to direct them to salvage what they can, and assigning watches and hunting groups. She did not even need to ask them to do that. Is she really that useless? Is she really that incompetent? Was Ari the real leader of her army, and she simply the figurehead they gathered around?

She gazes back at the isi'tu, the sparkling jewel of Sua, so tall that it can be seen from mitu away. The diamond at the center of an oasis. It should be hers. But she is not strong enough to claim it. The people, her people, are depending on her to deliver them from the wickedness of the insurrectionists and protect them from the wiles of Ashur. But she can do neither.

Five

S HE TAKES HER FATHER'S HAND AS he leads her under the waterfall, through the cave, and then down the slippery rocks to the iseru, that hidden arena under the palace where she is expected to fight, maim, harm, and battle her own siblings. To make them bleed, scream, cry, and limp away in shame. The winner will take the ultimate prize; the right to call themself the Mar'sahr'dan'i.

It is not her first time, but it is Zisu's. Only five years old, she must now pray to Yshuld that none of her siblings swing too hard, strike too swiftly, or kick too forcefully. While it is frowned upon to outright kill your siblings in this match, there is no punishment for those who do. Their mother was once one of fifteen, after all. But by the time she took the throne, she was the only of her siblings alive.

It is Saritrah's flaw, her weakness, the thing that will prevent her from claiming that title; her affection for her sister. Instead of striking down her siblings tonight, she will act as a bodyguard to Zisu. The contest for the throne is not a private affair, with many of the mashr'i attending fights once a month, putting money down on who they expected to win. But those placing bets expect more than monetary profits if they win their bets.

Zisuthra. The youngest mat'sahr'dan, debuting tonight at the iseru. And Saritrah has appointed herself as Zisu's guardian. Zisu takes after their mother, and even though she is only five years old, everyone expects her to grow into a great beauty. If she has the privilege of surviving that long.

Saritrah, Zisu, Anenlilda, Rahbani, Tudiya, Alaparos, Ashur and Aishah are scheduled to fight this evening. Zisu clings to Saritrah's other hand as they continue their descent, slipping on the slick rocks and fighting for balance as she hops over puddles before they emerge at the entrance to the amphitheater. Anyone who is anyone is sitting in the crowds, waiting for the Sahru'Dane to tell the Sahre'Danu that he has brought another potential champion for her to assess, for her to judge, and for the people to determine if she is worthy of calling herself the daughter of the Sahre'Danu, if she is worthy of being a mat'sahr'dan.

Saritrah had volunteered to be the first challenger, but as her father bows before her mother, Aishah materializes before them, his head already severed from his body, his hand still bent backwards from where she broke it on the night of the insurrection, his teeth already missing from where she punched him at the very last tournament in the iseru.

The crowds disappear, their cheers replaced by the laughs of Ashur, suddenly occupying their mother's throne. "Sister dearest, you still wish to protect her? She's dead."

She turns to look at Zisu, her chestnut eyes dull, her ochre fur lusterless, her tiny hands clammy. "No. No!"

She lifts her sister into her arms, her body limp, and runs back to the entrance, but the tunnel has collapsed. She turns, searching for the small doors that lead to the medical chambers. But they are gone, and standing where the entrances should be are a dozen different Aishah's; different ages, different sizes, but all wearing the identical sneer he reserved for those he saw as lesser.

She runs into the stands, and each step she climbs seems even farther from the top than the last one. She ducks into a servant's door at the end of a row, but Ashur is waiting for her. She turns around, only to collide with Aishah. They are everywhere; everyone. She cannot save herself; she cannot save Zisu. She clutches her sister to her chest and screams.

Someone is caressing her face, someone with calloused but warm hands. She opens her eyes, expecting to see Ari, expecting him to understand where she just was—when she just was. But she couldn't save him, either.

The tattered remnants of her army amble away from the capital, hungry, thirsty, injured, and tired. She does not tell them where they are going, though. She does not dare give any information that a spy might run off and take to Ashur when she is not looking. He must have some sort of network along the roads; she could easily stop at a village and every one of the residents eager and willing to race off once she is gone to inform him of her whereabouts.

He knows now she has Katynna, and from the way he ransacked their camp, he probably guesses she has the seal.

The only option she has right now, without heading into the Erid desert, is to lay low while she and her troops lick their wounds and nurse their pride. There is an isiaq that she believes will allow them to do just that. Isiaq Etana.

Etana had once been a close friend, perhaps too close, to Sari, and even on the days when Saritrah was sure to lose in the iseru, Etana would still bet on her. Etana was one of her mother's most loyal vassals, but she was also one of Saritrah's most loyal friends. A friend that could offer shelter, supplies, and possibly fighters and arms.

They make their way to the large encampment, arriving shortly before nialsamsu, and Saritrah is thankful she will not have to contend with grumpy troops. She sends Ditanu into the encampment to request the isiaq's permission to enter.

"Sari? Is that really you?" The effervescent leader of the Susan'i clan does not bother to open the gate to her domain, instead vaulting over it and landing softly next to Sari. "I knew you made it out alive, but never did I think I would see you again. What is all of this?" The isiaq's orange-spotted tail flicks, head tilted to the side, as the few surviving soldiers amble to the gates.

"We tried to take back Erzurumei."

"Ah. And they were prepared?" Etana bites her lip.

"Somehow. Yes. And Ashur was there, too. I would like shelter and food for the night while my troops recover. Ashur stole all of our supplies, too." Saritrah's face burns in shame, admitting to so much weakness, so much incompetency. Etana is the legendary warlord who drove out the Re'u from the aburru region. Telling Etana about this failure, she who should be more cunning and clever than all others in the Suan lands, is just another dagger in her pride.

"Is that all?" Etana asks, arms crossed, eyebrow raised.

"I would not turn down a pledge of troops or arms on the day I return to exact my revenge."

Etana tosses her head back in laughter, loud but musical. "I bet you wouldn't. First, let's get you and your troops some food, then we can discuss more. Welcome to Eluuti." The isiaq throws her arm over Saritrah's shoulder and leads her past the gates.

Etana's domain is sprawling, and the former warlord has transformed her army's encampment into a village, complete with aqueducts and an irrigation system for keeping crops and livestock. There are many edin'tu, but they have all been reinforced into more permanent dwellings, more akin to the sub'tu seen on the Erid steppe. Many of her soldiers now have children, and look like they have not picked up a spear in years, let alone trained with one. But many of them do sport the red welts on forearms and chests that speak to learning the art of iron-making and steel-forging. If Etana cannot provide suitable troops, Saritrah may convince her to turn those ironworkers from spade makers into swordsmiths.

Etana leads her to a large sub'tu at the center of her base-turned-village, inviting her and her generals to take a seat at the large round table at the center. "We have had a wonderfully fruitful year, and I would like to share with you the bounty of the Susan'i."

It is not long before Saritrah and her troops are feasting on ripe vegetables, juicy meats, and sweet fruits. "Pears?" Saritrah says, taking one from a bowl at the center of the table. "I have not had one of these in..."

"Six years, I imagine," Etana says. "It took us a while to figure out how to properly grow them. But what we make off them—well, the money—has allowed us to experiment in many other areas. My goal is to become entirely self-sufficient."

"In the middle of the Esiri?"

"If the Re'u can do it, anyone can. The difference is that I hate riding on camels." Etana claps Saritrah on the back. "Eat it! Don't just stare at it!"

Saritrah bites into the fruit; the perfect amount of sweetness and tang. "This is amazing. But why?"

"Why? I am guessing you are not asking about water supply and soil quality."

"No. Why are you raising animals? Planting harvests? No one here looks like they have seen battle in ages."

"I got tired. The insurrectionists won, Sari. Fayn couldn't oust theirs, and if you and Ashur can't take them out here, well." She gestures before her, a hint of a smile on her lips. "But look at my people. Look at them."

Saritrah glances around the sub'tu, the other tables filled with Etana's qatu. They are out of fighting shape, but their eyes sparkle, their ears pricked in amusement, and their tails swishing in joy.

"We work hard, we cooperate, just as an army. But we don't leave behind the weak; we don't force the injured to endure. We don't have to rely on battle and pillage to fill our stomachs. It's quieter, yes, but I find that it suits me now. And it suits my army, too."

"You sound just like the insurrectionists, all that talk of looking out for each other, even the weak..."

Etana shrugs. "Maybe. Perhaps. They might be on to something."

"That's treason. Careful."

"Fear not, Mar. I am still and will always be your loyal vassal. I just think there are ways you could improve Sua, and maybe the insurrectionists have a good idea or two you could incorporate. Look at your own troops right now. They were defeated and demoralized, but look what the food is doing for them."

She knows what her troops are doing. Behaving badly. Laughing and shouting when they should be reflecting on their poor performance and scolding themselves for how they shamed and betrayed their mar.

"Speaking of being your loyal vassal," Etana whispers, running the tip of her claw down Saritrah's arm. "I would like to invite you to share my halersu tonight. Like we used to."

Saritrah's stomach twists. Ari flashes in her mind. But he betrayed her. And besides, Etana and she had been intimate long before she asked Ari to share her halersu. "We'll see." But she already knows that she will. Etana is loyal, Etana knows her. And Etana knows how to make her forget about everything else, if only for a little while.

"You need to leave," Etana says, waking Saritrah from an uneasy sleep. "Now."

"What? What do you mean?"

"Ashur's men are on their way here," Etana says, throwing Saritrah a clean camise. "You have maybe an hour to be on your way. I let you sleep as long as I could."

"What do you mean?" Saritrah blinks, the sun searing away the nightmares.

"I had to. I had to tell him you were here."

"You betrayed me? You had to tell him? What the fuck does that mean, Eta? What was all that nonsense about community and cooperation if you are on his side? What about *what we just did?*"

"I'm not on his side, but he could destroy me. In exchange for leaving us alone, there are certain... favors I provide him. Food and lodging when he comes through, information, and—"

"Oh gods no, don't tell me," Saritrah says, sliding her feet into the leather sandals.

"No! Oh no, not that, but I knew he would find out you were here, and I knew he would know if I didn't tell him, and I can't—"

"Your people are more important than your Mar'sahr'dan'i. More important than me, what we had... What we shared..."

"That's not it. Don't say it like that."

"You're a traitor. Why did you even bother to tell me? Wouldn't it be better for you to hold me here until he arrives?" She buckles her belt, pulling it too tightly. She does not want to think about what she was using the belt for just a few hours ago, but she glances at the red stripes across Etana's back.

"You've seen my people now. We aren't fighters. We couldn't hold you here if we wanted."

"Well, I hope you all rot."

"Sari, don't be like that," Etana says, grabbing her hand. "I didn't have a choice. This is the best I can do. You can 'steal' our camels and pillage our food stores and be on your way. All of my people will swear that you forced them to. Just don't come back."

"Fuck you, Eta," Saritrah says. She storms into the sub'tu that Etana had set up for her troops, calling for them to rally. But most of them ignore her, rolling their backs to her.

"Mar, many of them are still not recovered," Ditanu says, pulling her hair back and tying it tightly. "May I suggest we stay another day?"

"We can't. Ashur's on his way. We don't have time."

Ditanu touches the sheath at her waist. "How long?"

"An hour."

She bites her lip. "Do you think we can leave some behind? Come back for them later? Let them hide here?"

"If they stay behind, they are deserters, and if I see their faces again, I shall strike their heads from their bodies."

"I will do my best to rouse them. Leave it to me."

Half an hour passes, and when Ditanu and Tanit meet her at the gate, it is with only five dozen soldiers. "Where are the rest?"

"They all ask for permission to retire; they would like to live out their remaining years in peace, here."

Saritrah spits. "Cowards. Fine. We don't have time. But I swear, in Yshuld's name, if I see them again, any of them, they are dead."

Etana's voice bangs around in Saritrah's mind. "I knew he would find out you were here, and I knew he would know if I didn't tell him—" There is a traitor in her army, and even Etana can see it. Someone in her army sold her out to Ashur. The question is who?

She raises her arm, calling a halt, hoping they are far enough away. They rode all the way through the last part of *nialsamsu* and still kept going. It's almost dark, and she wants to keep going, taking advantage of the falling temperatures before it gets too cold. But sees that the few troops who have remained loyal, or at least seem to be loyal, are truly struggling. She is stifling a yawn herself.

She checks the packs on the camels and horses; at least Etana was true to her word. They have some supplies again. Food and enough materials to make serviceable edin'tus. "Unload, we will rest here. Four hours. No more."

"Mar, may I speak with you?" Puzur runs up to her, out of breath, and collapses to his knees. "It's important, please."

She crosses her arms. "You may."

"Thank you, Mar. I saw someone... someone who..."

"Say it. Just say it."

"I think one of the soldiers betrayed us."

She swears under her breath. "Follow me." She leads him away from the group. "Who?"

"Yangi. I think Yangi sold us out."

"What makes you believe that?"

"I am sorry, Mar, I should have said something earlier. The day before we attacked, he disappeared for longer than he should have while scouting. He came back and said he got lost, but that's not like him. And then at Etana's, he just disappeared without any reason at all."

"Did he join us? Or is he at Etana's?" She turns away from Puzur, her hand instinctively reaching for her royal seal hidden under her camise.

"He's with us."

"So, we aren't safe here. Excuse me, I am going to talk to Yangi. Thank you, Puzur, for your loyalty. I am promoting you, don't make me regret it."

"Thank you, Mar, you won't regret it, I swear."

She marches to the encampment. She has maybe sixty soldiers remaining in what was an army of over 3000. Dead or deserted. It is not hard to find Yangi at the center of it all, tending a fire while showing off sleights of hand and tricks. "Yangi. Here."

He claps Harharu on the shoulder, springs to his feet, and skips toward her. "Yes, Mar? What can I do to help you?"

"You will tell me who you are, first off. Second, you will let me search your belongings."

"Excuse me? Is there a reason for this?" His confusion at her request seems genuine, but she cannot take the chance.

"We have a traitor, and you've been named. Give me your satchels."

His hand shakes as he unties it from his belt loop and hands it over to her. Before she can open it, he dashes away. "Tanit! Don't let him escape!" Her general leaps onto a camel, racing toward the traitor and spearing him in the knee. He falls into the sand, bleeding and unable to run.

Saritrah opens the pouch. A tiny copper coin sits among other personal effects. Etched into the coin is the flower of the imquat fruit—the savitus. The symbol of the insurrectionist army.

That Seer was right. "Ditanu, when Tanit drags that traitor back, I want him executed. I will also be searching the personal belongings of everyone else in camp."

"Mar?"

"Rodents breed, and I need to make sure there are none among us. Gather everyone."

While Ditanu and Tanit carry out their duties, she contemplates checking Ari's satchels. They have been tied to her own belt since he passed. She wants to look inside of them; she wants to see what personal effects he carried, but that feels like a violation of his trust, even though he broke his promise to stay by her side.

In the end, over half of her troops are discovered carrying items bearing an image of the savitus. None of them deny it when directly questioned. Yangi had not just sown discord, he had turned hearts against her.

She executes them and urges the two-dozen remaining loyal troops to follow her, leaving the bodies to rot in the sands. But one thing puzzles her. They were loyal to the insurrectionists, so why did they betray her to Ashur? Or are there more traitors in her midsts? Ones loyal to Ashur, but far better at keeping their cover?

Nanshaie had said she would be betrayed. But the High Priestess Ia... The priestess had told her that she knew the key to her victory and could help her get it. Saritrah wants to reclaim her throne on her own, under her own power, and with her own strength. She does not want whatever this key is; if it is not an army of a thousand loyal troops, then she does not and will not even consider returning to Antalyza with her tail between her legs and begging for help.

Six

WITH THEIR DIMINISHED NUMBERS, SARITRAH CAN MAKE the supplies last longer, but they are still not as well-stocked as she would prefer. She returns to camp after catching several small pieces of game, but not enough for everyone. She has tried to lead the troops, but even though they claim they are loyal, she wonders why they still follow her. She is a failure in every way imaginable. She would not follow herself, if she were in their place.

As other hunters return and add their own game to the fire, she tries to speak with her troops, to converse with them as Ari used to, to ask their thoughts and learn about their lives. But they do not laugh while she sits with them and do not chatter back when she tries to joke with them. The words are stilted, stiff, and lacking any sort of emotion as they answer her questions.

What am I doing wrong?

As soon as she departs from the fire, she hears the laughter start, Tanit cackling the loudest. This is why royalty are not meant to interact with those they rule. The gulf is too great.

She is about to retire for nialsamsu, tired of looking at her troops' gaunt faces and dull eyes, but someone races into their camp, breathless, on a horse that has no business being driven so hard. "Help! Help! Mar'sahr'dan'i! I come to beg your help."

She recognizes the rider from Susan'i clan at Eluuti, one of Etana's people.

"Mar, please," the rider says, nearly falling off of their horse. "The isiaq humbly requests your aid. General Aziru attacked Eluuti shortly after you left. He has destroyed almost everything we have built and is holding the isiaq hostage. We gave up our arms years ago and request your assistance in driving Ashur's soldiers out again."

Tanit approaches almost silently. "Mar, this is probably a trap."

Saritrah bites her lip. She would have guessed as much on her own. Someone wants to draw Saritrah out to either catch her or kill her. It could be either Ashur or the insurrectionists. She does not put it past either of them to lie about who they are or what they are doing. Perhaps it is the insurrectionists wanting to take revenge on her, having not heard from their spies in several days now and assuming the worst.

The quiver on the lip of the Eluuti rider is hard to ignore. It is the same quiver, the same eyes, the same expression that Zisuthra had before she was forced into a match. Pleading for help, uncertain if the plea was even heard; uncertain if the plea was even worthy of a response. If Etana really is being held hostage by Aziru... If Ashur is cruel, then Aziru is a monster. What he did... What he does... Even if it's a trap, even if she hates Etana for the betrayal, she hates Aziru more. And she will take any opportunity presented to her to deny Aziru his fun.

"Troops. Break camp. We are going back to Eluuti."

"Sari, I told you not to come back!" Etana says when she sees Saritrah at the gates. The rider had lied. Saritrah rides into Eluuti to find it quiet; everyone is just waking up from nialsamsu.

"But you sent—" She looks over her shoulder, searching for the rider who petitioned her for aid. "There was someone you sent to me."

"I swear I did not, and I will not let you in here again. I've accepted your abandoned troops as my people, and they do not want to see you, and nor do I. Leave. Do not come back."

Wasted days, wasted resources, wasted energy. But something is wrong; the rider is missing, and while both Ashur and the insurrectionists are conniving, they are not petty. They are not pranksters. This is a trap; it just has not yet been sprung.

"What shall you have us do, Mar?" Tanit asks.

She came all this way, with the intent of saving Etana. She paces in front of the gate, hand touching the royal seal through her shirt.

"You said you believed that this was a trap. I did, too. So, where is the attack?" She asks her general.

"I do not know, Mar. And that scares me."

"We wait. I do not want to leave Eluuti undefended against whatever attack is sure to come."

The words barely leave her lips when the battle cries echo across the dunes. From all sides, cavalry units advance. Once again, she is trapped. Prey awaiting slaughter. Her heart races as she spots the distinctive banner at the head of the charge, a symbol she knows all too well. General Aziru.

The cavalry advances, more than half a dozen battalions advancing on all sides, utterly surrounding them and Eluuti.

Etana returns to the gate, face whitening when she catches sight of the forces coming to destroy her would-be communal paradise. "Go. Go Sari," she screams. "Just run!"

"But…"

"Go, and please, if you have ever had an ounce of feeling for me, remember what you saw here. Consider what we tried to build here. Remember us."

Some of her troops did not return, and she has just a dozen remaining soldiers. A dozen in what had once been a grand army meant to take out the insurrectionists and restore order to her nation.

She is so incompetent that she has to run and hide now. She chides herself for returning to Eluuti; she tells herself it was because she wanted to take out General Aziru. She pretends it was not because of lingering sentiment for Etana.

Etana, who is now dead.

From atop a dune, Saritrah had lingered for half a second, long enough to watch Ashur's army, under Aziru's command, swarm Eluuti like wasps and obliterate it.

She is a terrible leader; this is why everyone betrays her. This is why no one will remain loyal to her. There is something fundamentally broken inside of her, some part of her that makes her incapable of inspiring loyalty and unworthy of what loyalty she does have from the handful of people who still believe in her.

She reaches for Ari's satchel, both wanting to open it to see what he keeps inside, but hating herself for doubting him even after death.

She unties it, weighing it in her hand. The cold of midnight strengthens her resolve. She peers inside, moving aside buttons and bits of string and twine to find it. Buried at the bottom, worn and tarnished, sits the token of the insurrectionists, their emblem inlaid in bronze.

Even Arishaki. At the end, even Arishaki had betrayed her. Nanshaie could not have foreseen this level of betrayal. Why is there no one who will remain loyal to her?

There is nothing left for her. Nothing except a cryptic promise from the High Priestess of Yshuld.

Seven

"Again, I want to offer my thanks," Zaakit says. The sun is low on the horizon when Saritrah and her dozen soldiers arrive at Antalyza, but Zaakit does not let the lateness of the hour stop him from throwing together a welcome feast for the Mar'sahr'dan'i in the courtyard of his isi'tu. "But tell me, what has happened to the rest of your troops?"

"They were traitors," she says, not able to meet Zaakit's eyes, instead taking in the splendor of the miniature isi'tu that the isiaq lives in. It does not match the grandeur of her childhood home, but the emerald and topaz gems set in the sparkling marble flooring speak to the wealth that Anatlyza has managed to hold onto despite the insurrectionists' rallying cry of plundering the wealthy to feed the lazy. "Deserters."

"And what of General Arishaki? Where is he?"

"You should not be worried about him; he was also a traitor." She crosses her arms, glaring at the leader of Antalyza, daring him to challenge her.

"You executed him?" Zaakit puts his hand on his chest, jaw slack.

"No. Ashur did. That is not the point. I must speak with the High Priestess."

"Ah, you shall. But the High Priestess and many of the other Seers are in seclusion."

"Then get them out of seclusion."

"I cannot do so; their seclusion is at a retreat in the desert."

"Then fetch them," Saritrah hisses through gritted teeth.

"I cannot." The isiaq folds his hands in apology and bows again to Sari. "They do not tell me where they go for these retreats. They are very secretive about them, and I do not question them."

"Why?"

"The Oracle passed away shortly after you left, and they have been on this retreat to find the next Oracle and initiate the grey-robes as acolytes."

"When will they return?"

"I have no idea, but I, too, am anxious for their return. It has been almost two months since they left. My daughter, Gemeti, is among the novices who hope to return as a blue-robed acolyte. She has shown small traces of Sight. I hope that Yshuld further blesses her."

"Two months? It's been that long?" Has it been that long since Ari was poisoned? Only two months since he broke his promise and left her alone? No, he broke his promise long before that. Two months since she saved Antalyza... and only failure since.

"You mean it's been that short? I wasn't around when they last picked a new Oracle, but the last time they went out to initiate novices into their blue robes, they were gone for six months."

"I can't wait that long!" She throws her napkin down on the granite table. "The High Priestess made me a promise. I need to speak to her! Now!"

"Whoa, Mar, I understand you're anxious to talk to her—" Tanit says, placing a hand on Saritrah's shoulder.

"I am not anxious!" Saritrah rises to her feet, knocking over her chair. "I am in need of her. Where are they? Where is this temple?"

"Sari, as I said, I do not know," he says, holding his hands up. "I would tell you if I could."

"I guess I'll just have to go find them." Saritrah places her hand on the hilt of Katynna, glancing at the setting sun. She can search all night if she must, if she can just get Zaakit to tell her in which direction the Seers set off.

"Saritrah, you're a mess," Zaakit says. The isiaq abandons his food and goes to Saritrah's side, putting an arm around her shoulder, a too-familiar gesture. "It's clear you haven't eaten well. Stay here for a few days, eat, sleep. If they haven't returned by then, well, I won't stop you. But you can't go searching for them now. It's the middle of Fe'annarhi. The summer sun will kill you if you don't take at least a day to recover. You were marching too hard."

Some part of her knows that the isiaq is right. She lost two of her soldiers during their mad dash across the sands. She has only ten people remaining loyal to her. She cannot risk her own life right now. That would be handing the lands over to Ashur for sure.

"Fine. But if they do not return within the week, I will go looking for them."

"And you will have my blessing and my aid. But you are too precious, Mar'sahr'dan'i. Too precious to become a casualty of the Esiri."

The silver-robed priestesses of Yshuld invite Saritrah and her followers to lodge at the temple again, and Saritrah wastes no time in taking advantage of their cold pools and soft sheets. She wanders the temple, admiring its similarities to the isi'tu in the capital where she grew up. The cool marble floors, imported from the northern cliffs of Janeuq, elaborately etched and speckled to create gorgeous mosaics. The tall pillars, sculpted at the ceiling into the shapes of flowers and inlaid with gold. The fountains that adorn the intersections of the corridors, rimmed with stained glass and amber. The beauty of the Temple of Yshuld remains unspoiled by the wars and battles that have scarred the Suan lands for years.

What this temple lacked, however, was the thunder of metal meeting metal and the pounding of firm feet racing through the halls. The Seers have no need for armed guards; instead, they wear soft silk slippers lightly lined with the hides of the graceful fa'leen. The halls of the temple are filled with the whispers of robes, not the clanking of armor and growling of nobles that rang in the corridors of the royal isi'tu.

She is admiring the sandstone sculptures in an atrium when a barefoot but veiled Seer rushes past her, hood pulled low, sprinting to the fountain in the middle. The Seer splashes water over her face twice before collapsing to the ground in tears. "Why me? Why, Yshuld, why am I so cursed?"

Saritrah backs away, wishing that she, too, were barefoot and could slip out easily without being heard. But the Seer's sobs drown out the clanking of her armored sandals.

She enters the main temple, uneasy as more voices echo down the corridor. More voices than she has heard while staying here previously. Another priestess passes her as she ambles back to her temporary chambers, this one wearing the blue. "Excuse me," she says, turning around to catch the priestess's attention. "Is the High Priestess back?"

"Oh! Yes, we all just got back! Do you like my robe? It's so much softer than the gray ones! Oh, are you a dali'e, miss? Have you traveled very far to be here? Do you need to commune with Yshuld? I can help you with that now! Do you need my help? It is the responsibility of all acolytes to help the weary who journeyed here for holy worship!"

"I appreciate your offer, but I am here to speak with the High Priestess."

The newly raised acolyte crinkles her nose. "Why?"

Saritrah crosses her arms. The High Priestess can't be more than 50 summers, hardly old. But novices were raised from grey to blue robes during their 22nd summer, so she cannot fault the acolyte for her comments.

"Oh!" The acolyte covers her mouth with both hands. "I mean no disrespect! She has Yshuld's favor, and it is far beyond our mortal limits to know the workings of the goddess."

Saritrah rolls her eyes. "Where is she?"

"Oh, I do not know. We just got back. She might still be in the entrance hall."

Saritrah turns on her heel and marches away from the acolyte, not caring if it is rude to ignore the further offering of help.

The light of the candles catches on the golden robes of the High Priestess, giving the appearance that she herself is a mirage on the sands. Her eyes meet with Saritrah's almost instantly, and Saritrah cannot help but feel like the High Priestess has seen inside her very soul and found it lacking.

Yet the priestess disengages from the crowd around her and gestures for Saritrah to follow her. Silently, she accompanies the High Priestess to an antechamber behind the main sanctuary, but another priestess accompanies them, too, saying nothing.

"Sahre'Danu, you honor us with your presence." The High Priestess gestures to the gaatsu feather pillows on the floor.

Saritrah sits down, all the while glancing at the silent Seer that has followed them into the room. The Seer's facial markings are strange, or perhaps she has faint scars. But her fur is neither the dark browns of the Esiri desert nor the red-orange commonly found in the Erid steppe. Her fur is darker, with hints of auburn on her tail. And yet, she has an air about her that makes Saritrah want to rip off her clothing and learn every secret she is keeping.

She does not sit, but lurks in the doorway. The High Priestess does not acknowledge the strange qatu at all. "I was informed by Zaakit when we returned that you were here, but I had thought that I would have to seek you out. I am honored that you were so eager to speak to me that you sought me out."

"I wish to speak with you about this key to victory." Saritrah does not want to play games of polite conversation and underhanded compliments. She needs information, and she does not need it wrapped in golden cloth.

"Right on time, although I wish you would have come sooner. It would have saved you so much heartache."

Saritrah's chest tightens. She does not wish to discuss her feelings with the priestess. Especially not with other onlookers present. "Well, I would like to speak alone."

"What? Oh. Tinanna. Yes, you can speak in front of her."

The strange qatu does not blink or acknowledge that she is being spoken about. Saritrah takes a deep breath, ready to repeat her request. Or rather, make sure that the priestess understands that it is a demand.

"Tu'erebu?" The person on the other side of the curtain does not bother to wait for the reply, pushing aside the heavy silk. Still barefoot, still veiled, the sobbing Seer enters the priestess's chambers.

The High Priestess rises and bows. "Oracle, how may I serve you?"

Saritrah jumps to her feet, her heart pounding. The Sahre'Danu bows to only one person, and so Saritrah does so.

"Will you be moving my items tonight?" The Oracle's voice is quiet, strained. As if she is holding back tears. It's Sister Nanshaie, Saritrah realizes. Sister Nanshaie is the new Oracle. The alluring qatu is now forever out of reach, Sari thinks to herself. Perhaps before, she could have forsaken her vows to join Saritrah's army. But now, she is Chosen. And yet, she believes being Yshuld's representative is a curse?

"Yes, some novices should be there packing your personal items. But the chambers of the Oracle are already furnished much better than the ones you had as a priestess. They should be done shortly, and you may get settled in. Have you bathed already?"

"Yes, I have. But I—" The oracle fidgets, shifting her weight from one foot to the other.

"You have been called. No more tears. No more doubt. You are Her Daughter."

The Oracle bows, touching her thumb and forefinger to her forehead, and exits. Tinanna raises an eyebrow, looking at the High Priestess. "Yes, please. Follow her. I shall select a new guard for her soon. For now, though—"

The strange qatu bows and slips away far more silently than should be possible.

"She is a guard? Not a Seer?" Saritrah asks.

"She is both. She came to us far later in life than most of our novices. I assume she had lived on the streets for some time, but she showed strength and dexterity beyond what is normal. Not long after that, the Oracle, the previous Oracle, informed us that Tinanna was blessed with Sight, yes, but her purpose here was greater than that, and requested that she be trained, that her skills would be needed one day, and her destiny was to avert catastrophe. She has been guarding either the High Priestess or the Oracle since."

"I see. She certainly looks as though she is capable of taking out any threats." Saritrah again wonders what muscles and scars might be found beneath Tinanna's clothing.

"She is capable, and she has done so on many occasions. We are eternally grateful that the goddess has blessed us with her. This is such a grand day," the High Priestess says, taking a seat again, eyes sparkling. "We have a new Oracle, and the goddess blessed over a dozen of our novices with the Sight. Our order continues to grow. And now the Sahre'Danu is here to start her journey and save our land."

"What is it that I must do? How do I get my throne?"

"I will tell you after nialsamsu. I must get the new acolytes settled in, and there are other things I must attend to if I am to explain this properly to you. Meet me at the sanctuary a quarter of a sun after your rest."

The sanctuary is the only room in the temple that has a solid door. It is made of granite and requires three guards and the use of a rope system to open. The sanctuary is round, with feather pillows creating rings around a pool at the very center. Positioned at the heart of the pool is a raised platform, upon which the new Oracle rests on a chaise. A sheer curtain shields her from view.

The high ceiling and glass roof provide a stunning view of the sky during the day and the stars at night. There is no other illumination in the room.

The High Priestess and Tinanna are at the edge of the pool, both standing tall, hands clasped in front of them. Saritrah wonders if the Oracle is expected to swim to her platform or if there is a walkway on the other side, or perhaps the Oracle never leaves that tiny podium.

"Child, daughter of Sua, savior of our realm, and protector of our people; Sahre'Danu Saritrah, I welcome you to the seat of the Oracle," the High Priestess says.

Saritrah bows to the Oracle, but is unsure if the High Priestess is expecting any obeisance from her. It does not matter; she would not give it, anyway. But she is rankled by the fact that the High Priestess does not even dip her head. "What have you to share with me?"

The High Priestess hands Saritrah a piece of parchment. The parchment is old, but remarkably thick and with little texture. Painted at the center is what looks like a city; a large one, with not just one soaring spire, but dozens. More than dozens. A skyline filled with spires spiraling up to near-impossible heights. Above this skyline is the sun. No, there are markings on it; it cannot be the sun. A stone? The color of the object resembles the vibrant yellow-orange of the sun, yet it has a slight divot at the top and mysterious symbols etched onto it. Symbols she has never seen before. "What am I looking at?"

"Paradise. That is paradise. And I have foreseen it many, many times. A paradise that has been prophesized for centuries, now on the precipice of existence."

She looks at the parchment again. "And the object above it?"

"That is the Heart of Aodhe."

"What does that mean? What is it?"

"It is a source of power, enough power to build a grand city with little effort. Enough power to keep irrigation systems running, to melt and forge iron without fire. It can create a world where hard labor is not needed, where food can be stored without fear of spoilage indefinitely, enough power to remake our sands into fertile fields and plentiful pastures."

"But how does that help me with the insurrectionists? Can it be used as a weapon?"

"Is that what you care about the most? Not the power to free your people from want or need?"

"I care about freeing my people from the bloody insurrectionists."

"Yes, Sahre'Danu. Well, the Heart of Aodhe will also grant you the power to obliterate them." The High Priestess hangs her head, not meeting Saritrah's eyes.

"How?"

"That..." The priestess pauses, glancing over her shoulder at the Oracle. "That I do not know. But I have foreseen the Heart in your hands and the paradise that will come once you have it."

The Oracle rises from her chaise, taking two steps forward, almost touching the sheer curtain that separates her from the rest of the world. "But I have foreseen a terrible calamity if you do not obtain it. If the Heart of Aodhe falls into the hands of others, disaster most severe will strike." Her voice is different now. There is no hint of the fear or sorrow that Nanshaie had at the pool, nor any of the determination she had the night of the attack. It is almost as if someone else now resides in Nanshaie's body.

The High Priestess bites her lip. "We shall not let that happen. We will keep you and the land that Yshuld cherishes safe."

"And how do I get this Heart of—" Saritrah points at the parchment.

"Aodhe. The Heart of Aodhe. We will need to find it." The High Priestess takes the parchment from Saritrah's hands, rolls it up, and slides it into her pocket.

"It's lost?" *Great, this is going to be a waste. They just want someone to do their errands.*

"It is in the City of Bec."

This is indeed them trying to trick me into doing their errands. "And where is that?" She crosses her arms, shifting her weight to the side.

"We do not know." The High Priestess shuffles her feet.

Saritrah rolls her eyes and turns on her heel, her tail slapping the High Priestess's legs. "Let me know when you find it, then."

"Wait! No!" The High Priestess grabs her arm. "You must be the one to find it. It is the only way. It is my—it is our only hope."

"Why? Because that's what you saw in your visions?"

"Because your journey will end here, otherwise," the Oracle says, voice reverberating across the sanctuary, assaulting her from all directions. Both the voice of Nanshaie and the voice of a divine being; a command, a promise, a threat.

Saritrah looks between the High Priestess and her guard. Tinanna displays no emotion, but the High Priestess appears terrified—eyes wide and pupils small—and in awe, jaw dropped, hands over her heart.

"Very well. I will tell my troops. When do we go to this Bec city? Do you even know what direction it is in?"

"We will leave tomorrow. But your troops are not to come with us," the High Priestess says.

"What do you mean? I need them," Saritrah scoffs.

"This is a journey you must take without them. We cannot risk betrayal."

Saritrah's stomach drops. Her troops number less than twenty, but they are loyal troops who have remained so—*are* they loyal, though?

She tells them she wants to celebrate and leads them a short way out of town. Tinanna, an unasked-for but silent shadow, trails behind her as she and her troops walk into the desert. Perched on Tinanna's shoulder is a tawny falcon, not native to Sua, and certainly not suited for survival here. When Saritrah asks about it, the strange qatu shrugs.

She has a few large bottles of wine and one now-empty vial of Re'u medicine. Medicine that is meant to ensure someone dies painlessly, swiftly, and silently. A relief from what would otherwise be a painful and slow death.

"Why can't we just celebrate in town?" one of the fighters asks.

"I do not want to disturb the Seers or the townsfolk with our carrying-on. I know how loud some of you get." Saritrah tries to keep her voice light, jovial, and free from hesitation.

Tanit laughs as Saritrah calls for them to halt and tosses the bottles of wine into the sand. "All this for us, Mar?"

"I reward loyalty. Help yourselves." She lets out a slow breath, hoping none can detect the wavering in her tone. Loyalty rewarded.

And they do. They pour the poisoned wine into the flasks, taking deep gulps. But Saritrah does not touch it, and she is glad that Tinanna does not attempt to partake in the festivities.

It is Ditanu who curls up first, dropping to the sand and clutching her heart, mouth moving but no words coming out. Then Harharu, and Belu...

"Mar, something is wrong..." Tanit says, rubbing her stomach. "Who gave this wine to you?"

The concern in Tanit's voice, the worry in her eyes... Genuine concern, and not and hint of suspicion that it might be Saritrah behind this massacre.

"You didn't drink it yourself, did you?" Tanit collapses, pawing at her throat, eyes growing cloudy. A single scream pierces the cold night air while her loyal troops die far more painfully than she had hoped.

When she is sure that they have all perished, she lets out her own scream. "I had to," she says as Tinanna approaches. "I had to. But it was supposed to be painless. The healer who gave it to me said it would be quick and painless, but they all died in agony..."

Tinanna helps her dig a shallow grave, helps her bury the people whose only crime was loyalty, and heads back with her.

The Oracle is waiting for them, face pale and eyes watery. "You... But why? Why did you do that?" She somehow already knows what Saritrah did, like she witnessed it herself.

"You told me that I could not bring them with me. I could not take the chance that one of them would tell Ashur where I was going or why."

"They could have stayed here! They could have stayed with us until you returned!" Tears streak the Oracle's face, but she does not move to wipe them away.

"I cannot trust anyone; they all betray me."

"I wonder why!" The Oracle jabs her finger into Saritrah's chest. "And it was too old. It goes bad after a few days, even if sealed. That's why they died in agony!" The Oracle nearly trips on her robes as she spins around and races back into the temple, face buried in her hands.

She had told no one where she was going or what she was doing. But of course, the Oracle knew.

A blue-robed acolyte wakes Saritrah up far earlier than she is used to. But she dresses quickly, packs lightly, and meets the High Priestess at the stables outside of the city gates. With her is Tinanna, and, to her surprise, the Oracle. If either the Oracle or Tinanna had told the High Priestess about Saritrah's actions, the High Priestess does not comment on it.

"Where are we going?" Saritrah asks.

Tinanna, falcon on her shoulder, hands Saritrah the reins to a camel and then unhitches the reins to another camel, burdened with plenty of supplies. The Oracle is already sitting atop a camel holding a parasol, face covered in a long sheer veil.

The High Priestess, swapping her long gold robes for a gold blouse and skirt, says "First we will be finding Namu. She belongs to the Ishme caravan. She knows where the City of Bec is."

"And where is Namu and these Ishme?"

"I do not know, but the stars will guide us." The look on the High Priestess's face is one of ecstasy, her eyes large as she gazes toward the horizon, her smile vibrant in the dawn's first tendrils of light. The High Priestess mounts her own camel and pulls the reins to the pack camel beside her. "We should have enough supplies to get us to her caravan. "They will allow us to restock before we then make our way to the City of Bec, wherever that shining city may be."

She kicks her camel, and Tinanna and the Oracle do the same. Saritrah looks over her shoulder, the sun now illuminating the Temple of Yshuld, bathing it in radiance. The home of the Oracle; the one qatu that the Suans revere more than the Sahre'Danu. Yet now, both are heading into the unforgiving Esiri desert without a true plan. What would Arishaki say?

It doesn't matter. He is dead; he betrayed her. She can only hope that these Seers do not join her long list of traitors. She kicks her camel, catching up with the Seers, the silent Tinanna, the ecstatic High Priestess, and the Oracle, whose hands are white and shaking as she clutches the reins.

EIGHT

"Please, call me Ia. We are away from the Temple, and I rather enjoy the freedom it is giving me," the High Priestess says, taking a drink from her worn leather flask and shivering.

Saritrah considers what Ia has said. "Then you may call me Sari," she replies. She is no longer the leader of an army, no longer the warlord Saritrah. She is still seeking her throne, but it feels wrong to call herself Saritrah now. "Why are we going to your friend again? And when will we get there?"

Ia deflects again. For two weeks, she has claimed she is following the stars, and they are leading her to this mysterious friend, Namu, who knows the way to the City of Bec, but Ia will not divulge any more information. But the entire time, she has been giddy, her voice at times breathless with anticipation, her hands trembling as she would speak reverently of the paradise that awaited them at the end of this quest.

Still, her excitement does not mean she lets her guard down; and she guards her secrets well. She will not tell Sari how she knows this friend, how this friend knows where this lost city is, or how they even know that this lost city exists. Not a single word about this city.

A city that, until two weeks ago, Sari had never even heard of. Aside from her teachings in combat arts, she had some of the best professors from Khidima Alam instruct her on every possible subject. Yet she cannot recall a single thing that might be tangentially related to this forgotten city. The history of Sua spans back to the conquests of the now-fallen Isadoran Empire across the Avon River and into Ku-Aya and Nin-Imma; causing those populations to flee south. But before that, there was nothing but wilderness in the area. How could there be forgotten and lost cities? She can't help but feel that she is chasing a legend.

Dusk creeps in. They approach an oasis, where Ia tosses some coins into the chest at the foot of the statue of Meria, whose acolytes maintain and preserve the Esiri water sources. "I need to consult the stars now," she says, wading into the water without removing her clothing.

Sari dismounts and rummages through the packs for some dried meat. While Ia is occupied, she decides she might get an actual answer from the Oracle. The Oracle spreads out a blanket on the sand and plants her parasol beside it. The stars are bright overhead; she has no idea why the Oracle bothers with the parasol, but she holds herself back from asking. She needs information. Sari offers her a bit of the jerky. "Hungry?"

The Oracle shakes her head. "I am fine."

The two have barely exchanged any words, and only converse when Sari initiates. The Oracle has been as withdrawn and forlorn as Ia has been wild in ecstasy.

"More for me," Sari says, sitting down in the sand next to the Oracle. "Do you know where we are going? Ia has not been very forthcoming with her information. And, honestly, I am only here because of what you said."

"You do not trust Ia?" The Oracle does not look up when she speaks, wrapping her arms around her knees and hugging them close to her chest. She does not look like the regal and divinely blessed Seer that Sari had seen at the temple, nor the determined but frail woman she had encountered attempting to flee from Ashur's army. She looks almost like a regular qatu, resigned to a harsh trek across the Esiri.

Sari tries not to let irritation creep into her voice. "I did not say that."

"Yet you do not deny it." While she looks normal, she speaks still with the cadence of one who has knowledge that is denied to others. She is, despite appearances, still the Oracle.

"I just want more information; I sacrificed a lot to—"

The Oracle whips her head to face Sari, eyebrows raised. "That's what you call it? You call murder a sacrifice? Ten qatu died in agony and you call it a sacrifice. You lost over 3000 soldiers in the span of a month and you call it a sacrifice. You killed your eldest brother, too. Was that also a sacrifice?"

Sari sighs. "That's not what I mean. I just want more information."

"I cannot give it to you. I trust Ia, though. She can be..." the Oracle pauses, looking to the stars as they unleash their first light, one of the moons rising above the dunes to illuminate the water. "Eccentric. But she means well. I want to believe in her vision of paradise."

"But you do not?" Sari swallows down the lump in her throat; she has already joined this strange adventure. This is not the time to let doubt win.

"My premonitions are always of disaster. And despite coming along, I have a terrible feeling that something unfortunate will happen on our journey." The Oracle's gaze stays fixed on the stars, and Sari glances up at the sky, her eyes finding her favorite constellation: the crown. The pinnacle of it being the pole star. The whole sky rotates around the coronet in the sky; and soon that will be her. The sky, the world, everything in Erid and Esiri will rotate around the crown; around *her*.

"Always? But your premonition of me obtaining the Heart of Aodhe... You did not see disaster for that."

"The goddess has both cursed and blessed me. Blessed me with the Sight, but cursed me with nightmares. I cannot escape it." She tears her eyes away from the sky, closing them tight and shaking her head before resting her forehead on her knees.

"But what you saw of me—" Sari glances at the night sky, wondering what it is that the Oracle sees among the stars when she consults them. What Ia sees. What any of Yshuld's children see when they consult the stars.

"I saw what happens if you do not obtain it. I did not see what happens if you do. It was Ia who foresaw your triumph." Her voice trembles, and even though Sari lacks the Sight, she sees dark flames flash across her vision and the smell of burning flesh invades her nose.

"I see. Before you had said someone would betray me. Did you see how many? Or who?"

"It does not work like that. I do not control my visions; they control me. I am at the mercy of the nightmares. They choose what to show me; I cannot make demands of them. The woman—the woman in my visions, it is she who chooses what to show me. I knew only that you would face betrayal."

"The woman in your visions?" This is the first time Sari has heard of this. She has spoken to few Seers in her life, only the ones that took up residence at the royal isi'tu as advisors to her mother. None of them ever spoke of a woman in their visions.

"She's always there. She looks different every time, but she's always there. Always forcing my eyes to gaze upon tragedy." The words come out forced, as if they are torn from her mouth.

"But what if you try to change it? What if you knew who it was in my army, and you told me, and I removed them? That would have been a tragedy averted." Sari is thinking only of herself; she has to know, however, if there was some way she could have prevented her failure. If only she had had the knowledge, if only she had—

"It does not matter. It always comes to pass. My visions are always true. And Ia will not be getting the happy reunion she believes she will get. I see sorrow, loss, and blood."

"Have you told her?"

"There is no point. Excuse me." The Oracle rises to her feet gracefully, and marches—a little too quickly—to the oasis, entering the pool without looking back.

Sari's chest squeezes. This is why the Oracle had tried to escape Antalyza. She was not fleeing Ashur, but a fate of endless torment set upon her shoulders by a goddess. For the space of a heartbeat, she had admired the Oracle, without knowing who she was or who she would become. The nerves and determination for one so small and frail to run away...

But she has no room in her life for sentiment, let alone for someone like the Oracle who has given up on her own powers, who has resigned herself to fate rather than fighting back. She will not allow herself to have affection for the Oracle. She cannot risk it, not again. Not after what happened with Arishaki and Etana. That doesn't mean her heart does not quicken when she watches the Oracle wade back out of the water, robe clinging tightly to her skin.

The tranquility of nialsamsu is broken by the shrill screams. Sari bolts upright, hand reaching for the hilt of Katynna, scanning the area for the threat. The Oracle is stumbling in the sand, running from something that Sari cannot see.

"She's here, she's here! I can't get away from her. What do you want?" The Oracle collapses, hands over her head.

Tinanna lifts her falcon from its perch and then releases it before looking across the dunes, squinting. Sari draws Katynna, her feet spreading to a guard position. "I don't see anything," she says.

"Bandits," the Oracle says. Sari whips around, and Tinanna is pointing due north toward the shimmering dark spot on the horizon. Bandits, closing in on them fast.

Ia breaks down their camp, frantically packing everything she can before scooping up the Oracle's bedroll and parasol, too. Sari squares her shoulders. She will not run from this; she is a warrior, and she would much rather fight than run.

The bandits approachriding in a uniform fashion, as if they have military training. This is not the haphazard approach of people intent on chaos but the methodical advancement of a skilled battalion. But they bear no insignia; they have no banners or flags to declare allegiance to isiaq or sahre.

"Sari, come!" the Oracle cries. "We must go!"

"I will stay and fight!" They are too organized. If she runs now, they will follow. This is a mission for them, not a random attack of opportunity.

Tinanna grabs her hand and pulls her; too strong for a simple bodyguard.

"Fine," she says, running to her camel and kicking it into motion.

They dash away, Sari looking over her shoulder every few seconds. They ride for half an hour, not breaking speed or slowing, before Ia holds up a hand. "I think we are safe. I think we've outrun them."

The falcon cries, returning from wherever Tinanna sent it, and lands on her forearm. She nods.

"I'm going back. Stay here. Those weren't bandits." Sari needs to know who they are; the pounding of her heart is all the evidence she needs to know that enemies are on their tail.

Tinanna tries to cut her off, her camel stepping in front of Sari's.

"No, I am going back." Sari dashes off, wishing she had a fresh and rested camel. But she still makes it back to their former camp quickly.

No sign of the bandits. But placed in the sand is a solitary coin, glinting under the sun's rays. Deliberately left, sitting on top of a mound where Tinanna's sleeping mat had been. Set there to be discovered. The coin is large, solid iron, and engraved with a symbol she has never seen before; but one that looks like a dagger piercing a caged heart.

These were not bandits; these were organized professionals. But what were they after? Were they sent by Ashur to find her? Or someone who had heard that both the Oracle and High Priestess were away and hoped to find a ransom? She examines the sands, seeking clues in the hoof prints. They were not being chased; but this coin is a sign. They will try again. Whatever they are after, they will continue to seek it another day.

She pockets the coin and returns to the Seers.

Sari does not speak of the strange coin to the rest of her companions when she returns to them. Without waiting to hear Sari's report, Ia insists that they press ahead, promising that they will stop early in the afternoon since they have now ridden through nialsamsu.

"She is my mentor," Ia says, finally deeming Sari worthy of hearing the information. "She is the one who recognized my Sight for what it is and brought me to the Temple of Yshuld. She is the one who trained me, who taught me, who molded me into the priestess I am today."

"But she left?"

"The goddess called her away. It seems that the reason was for her to protect the map to Bec against those who might steal it. She holds it now, safely hidden in a caravan."

"She joined the Re'u?" Sari would rather avoid any run-ins with the nomadic qatus that swear no allegiance to Sua nor sahre.

"No, they are a Suan caravan. For the most part."

The hesitation in Ia's voice is enough to let Sari know that Ia is only being partially truthful. "And she has a map to this lost city?"

"Yes, she does. Or, she should. I have not spoken to her in years. I hope she still remembers me."

Sari lets out a heavy sigh. "Does she know anything else about this city? Or what the Heart does?"

"The City of Bec was a paradise!" The priestess pulls on the reins and steers her camel around to cut off Sari. "A paradise of wisdom, civility, learning, innovation... But it will pale in comparison to the paradise that you are destined to create, Sahre'Danu."

"What happened to it? Why have I never heard of it before?" Sari rolls her eyes and tries to maneuver around the priestess now blocking her path.

The priestess slumps in the saddle, hand over her heart. "It was destroyed."

"They must not have been so great if they allowed themselves to be destroyed, nor so noteworthy that their legacy crumbled into sand."

"And that is why it must be you who builds the final paradise, Sahre'Danu. It is you who has the strength to ensure that it will never fall. You are the one who can wield the Heart of Aodhe to ensure that the new paradise birthed never dies."

"If you have a map to the City of Bec, and know what the Heart can do, why in all of these years has no one tried to use it? What of my mother? Could she not have done so? Or her mother? Or my great-grandfather?"

"We have been waiting for the one chosen by Yshuld, and She chose you; She showed me the vision of you wielding it. Its power can only be controlled by an heir of Kyna, which is more than just a matter of blood. It is also a matter of spirit."

"Heir of Kyna? Who?"

"I think it is time we stopped for the day," Ia says. Her smile is almost too wide, and the spring in her step as she dismounts seems out of place for one who is normally so dignified. She practically skips as she goes from camel to camel removing the edin'tu, humming some unknown tune as she sets them up.

The Oracle, however, is far too pale, and her shoulders sag under the weight of some unfathomable terror. Tinanna sets up a perch for her falcon, expression unreadable.

These Seers are all hiding something, all carrying something that they do not want Sari to know. But Sari has no choice but to hope that she will see the knife coming when one of them raises it against her.

Ia consults the stars. Between the detour they took to avoid the bandits and the movement of her mentor's caravan, they are several days away still, and their supplies are running low.

"I shall go find us some game," Sari says as evening draws near.

"I will go, too," the Oracle says, rising to her feet and fanning herself. Sari wants to protest. The Oracle is small, not at all trained in combat, and unfortunately prone to screaming and pointing at apparitions that only she can see.

"Is that wise? We cannot risk you getting hurt," Ia says.

"I am going." Her shoulders squared, her back straight. She again reminds Sari of the version of her she had met when Ashur attacked Antalyza. Determined, spirited, not letting her size scare her out of what she wants. *If only she could always be like this.*

Ia crosses her arms but goes back to her business once the Oracle pulls a knife from her belt. Sari does not agree with this, but if the High Priestess is fine with the Oracle possibly being killed, well, that is not her problem.

"What was it like to grow up in an isi'tu?" the Oracle asks as they leave the safety of the firelight.

"It was what one would expect of a qatu household, nothing like you would find in Janeuq or Garcelon, if that is what you are asking. There was no pampering or lazing about."

"You had so many siblings; you must miss them all very much."

"Not Ashur."

"Well, no, you are correct. But aside from him, you must miss the rest."

Sari hisses. This chatter will scare away any prey. "I miss Zisuthra. But I did not get along with the rest."

"That is sad. I do not have siblings, but I always wondered... I grew up in the Temple, mostly, and I suppose the other novices were like siblings, but I know it's not the same. Why did you not get along with your siblings?"

"We were encouraged not to." Sari shrugs. She had one thought that the iseru and the events that took place there were common knowledge. But as she had raised her army, Arishaki had told her that most of Sua did not know. She stopped talking about her upbringing because she hated explaining this part of it to people.

"What? By who?"

"By everyone. Siblings are rivals. Our ascension to the throne depends on their subjugation." Sari does not know why she is telling the priestess this. She hates talking about; it makes her feel weak. But the words come out, harsh and clipped, but spoken all the same.

"What!? That's terrible." The Oracle clapped both hands over her mouth.

"Why is this shocking to you? Were the other novices not your competition? Everyone knew the previous Oracle was over three hundred years old, well past the age most Oracles live to. Those fellow blue-robes were all potential thieves who could steal your seat."

"You see betrayal and treachery around every corner. What a horrible way to live." There was pity mixed with disdain in the Oracle's voice. If the Sahre'Danu were not sworn to protect the Oracle, Sari would consider letting some wild beast claim her while they hunted.

"Is it? It just makes sense. If I anticipate the betrayal, I can make it out alive." *But you did not anticipate it with Arishaki.* She takes a deep breath, not wanting to follow those thoughts to their conclusion.

The Oracle halts. "You predict betrayal, and then you behave in ways that encourage it."

Sari spins on her heel to face the Oracle, jabbing her forefinger into the priestess's chest. "You predict disaster and do nothing to avert it. Are we so different, Oracle?"

"Nanshaie. Just Nanshaie. And that's different. I told you that." Her eyes widen, holding Sari's gaze for half a second before narrowing into a challenge. There is ice in Nanshaie's words, a source of strength that Nanshaie has tapped into only once before, to Sari's knowledge. A strength she wants to encourage, cultivate, and help Nanshaie grow. But now is not the right time. She turns away from the Oracle, not glancing behind her to see if anyone has perhaps followed them. "Was Ia the High Priestess when you arrived at the Temple?"

"Yes," Nanshaie says, almost jogging to keep up with Sari. "But she had only just been called a month before I arrived."

"Has she always been so eccentric?"

"Perhaps. I must admit, I didn't think much of her at all until she started paying attention to me. Giving me special attention, I suppose, when she was not supposed to."

"She made it sound like she's been like a mother to you since you were young." Sari raises a hand against the low sun, searching the dunes for any clues of nearby prey.

"I don't think she knew my name before I shed the gray and donned the blue robes. That is when she started mentoring me. Before that, I was invisible to her, as all the grays are."

There is more to it, Sari can tell. The pain that is braided into Nanshaie's voice is evident, an unhealed wound. One that she must mend soon if she is to be of any help in their quest. Sari points to a small copse of rocks and then creeps towards it, motioning for Nanshaie to do the same. They kneel down behind the largest boulder.

The braying of a beast startles Nanshaie. "That's a fa'leen," Sari says. "Perfect. Here." She hands a long length of rope to Nanshaie and climbs up on top of the boulder.

"What am I supposed to do with this?" She holds it in front of her, squinting at it.

"When the fa'leen approaches, toss it. You'll want the loop at this end to go around its neck. Do you think you can do that?"

"I can try." Nanshaie gulps. "I hope."

"You're the one that volunteered to come along." Sari wants to touch her, reach out a hand and set it on her shoulder, like Nanshaie is a sparring partner and she is helping her learn a new combat skill. But that is not what either of them are here for.

"Well, to be honest, Sarhe'Danu, I was hoping just to watch. I didn't think I would be doing anything." A smile almost reaches the corners of Nanshaie's mouth, and for a second, Sari wonders if Nanshaie can ever forgive her for what she's done. But she silences those thoughts as quickly as they spring to her mind; she's done nothing wrong. She's only ever done what she had to do. There is nothing to forgive.

"It's Sari," she says, laughing. "I helped you out once before; tossing a rope is the least you can do to repay me."

"I had rather hoped that night that I would never see you again," Nanshaie says. "I didn't predict this."

"Does this mean meeting me isn't a disaster?" Sari says, extending a hand to Nanshaie to help her to the top of the boulder. The Oracle hesitates before smiling and clasping her hand with Sari's.

"Stay here," Sari says. She holds her finger to her lips, and then leaps to the next boulder. It's more than one fa'leen, it's a whole herd of them galloping across the sands.

Sari points to one that has a limp, and Nanshaie nods. Her tongue peeking out, eyes set and determined, she swings the rope and tosses it.

To Sari's surprise, the toss is true, and the prancing fa'leen is pulled back from the rest of the herd. Sari leaps down onto the captured animal's back and slices its throat in one swift movement. Nanshaie leaps from the boulder, rushes over, and helps Sari slide a blanket beneath the animal, wrapping the neck tightly to prevent blood from dripping as they return to camp.

"I cannot believe I did that." She is breathless, a wild energy almost tangible around her, her eyes wide.

"I also cannot believe it," Sari says. "But well done. Next time, you can be the one holding the knife."

"Oh," Nanshaie says, smile fading. "That, no. I do not think I could."

"You brought a knife with you."

"Yes, but I did not think you would ask me to use it. I only have it to get Ia to leave me alone. I could never kill another living being." The way her eyes dart to Sari's face and then back down to the fallen fa'leen tells Sari all she needs to know: Nanshaie will never see Sari as anything but a murderer. One she will tolerate, for now. But after their quest?

Sari sighs. "You could be strong if you wanted to be," Sari says. "You could have fought off those soldiers if you wanted to. You could train like Tinanna. You might be small, but that does not mean you have to be weak."

"Who says I am not strong? Do you determine strength only by how many foes you kill?"

"That's not what I—"

"There is strength in keeping a sword sheathed just as much as there is in wielding one."

"No, you let others pick your battles for you. You let me kill this fa'leen, and you let me kill those soldiers. There is no strength there."

The spark of connection that Sari had felt dies, their levity fading away, now cold in her chest where she thought warmth might take root. She can't let anyone in again, not after Arishaki. And she especially cannot let in a coward who lets others do her work so that her hands remain unstained.

"The Masayaf oasis is just ahead," Ia says, pointing to the north. "We should be there in an hour, and these tracks are fresh. Soon. I will get to see Namu again soon. We must hurry!" Ia kicks her camel, not bothering to see if the others are even behind her. But her jubilant cries are cut off by Nanshaie's screams.

Sari sighs. Ia turns around, lips pursed, and dismounts. "What's wrong?"

"They who bring the snow, they are coming," Nanshaie says, her voice taking on an otherworldly echo. "They are coming, and with their oaken sword, they shall cut a path of destruction."

"Who is coming? What destruction?" Ia asks, grabbing Nanshaie's shoulders.

The Oracle pays no mind to Ia. "The wine they fill the chalice with shall turn to blood and stain the sand."

"Nanshaie, who? Who are you talking about?" The High Priestess shakes her mentee, eyes wide.

The Oracle collapses, fingers raking through the sand as she screams. "I don't know! I don't know! I don't want to know! I don't want to see these things."

"What did you see?" Ia asks, voice still wild and harsh, sitting beside Nanshaie. Tinanna takes a seat on the other side of the Oracle, running her hand up and down Nanshaie's back but offering no words to accompany her gesture.

"I saw blood, and people dying, and so much..."

Ia's shoulder's sag and her face softens. "No, I am sorry. You do not need to continue. I ask too much of you." Ia pulls the sobbing Oracle into her chest, letting her cry, stroking her hair and whispering words of comfort.

Sari shifts uncomfortably, scanning the area for any threats, listening to the wind for any sign of predators, feeling the sands for any vibrations that would warn of an oncoming army. But there is nothing, just Tinanna's falcon circling above.

"Come, we are almost there," Ia tells Nanshaie. The Oracle nods and climbs back atop her camel, wiping her eyes. Tinanna offers her a flask, but Nanshaie refuses it. They ride in silence for the next hour; even the High Priestess has lost the spirited lilt in her voice.

Ia looks to the night sky, taking a deep breath. "Over the next dune. They are just on the other side of that dune."

As they crest the dune, they see the sprawling caravan. Or what is left of it. The edin'tus are slashed, the supplies scattered, the animals gone, and the members of the Ishme caravan are stacked in a pile, dead.

"No," Ia says, both a firm denial and a question. "No. This..." She flies down the dune, racing into the wreckage.

Sari lets Nanshaie and Tinanna go ahead of her, not wanting to be caught unawares from behind. Whoever did this might still be here.

The High Priestess does not bother to tie her camel to a post or lead it to the trough of water. She immediately starts pulling bodies from the pile, screaming. "Namu!"

Tinanna wanders the scene, poking at tarps and bed piles, lifting the canvas from the fallen edin'tu. Sari walks around aimlessly, not sure what to look for. There are no survivors here. Another casualty of the desert, of the lawlessness that has descended in the Esiri and Erid since the insurrectionists took over. Her mother had her army combing the desert, keeping their people safe from would-be bandits and opportunists, keeping the trading caravans and merchants protected from the plundering Re'u. This, whatever it is, would not have happened if her mother were still on the throne. This would not have happened if Sari herself were on the throne.

This should never happen.

Her ruminations are broken by a whistle. She looks over her shoulder, and Tinanna is waving everyone over. Ia cries, "Did you find her? Did you find Namu?"

Tinanna shakes her head but lifts a pole up and tosses the canvas under it aside, revealing a qatu missing an ear and half of her tail. Nanshaie hurries over, checking the pulse. "She's alive. Barely. Can someone fetch me some water?"

Without a word, Sari marches back to their camels. This is not what they need right now. There's no one else around for days. What are they going to do with a half-dead qatu? A mouth that needs food and water, a body that needs rest and sleep, a traumatized mind that will need coddling. They need to find the map; this qatu is a distraction. She yanks a flask out of a bag and fills it with water, a precious resource that will be wasted on a qatu that will just delay them and end up dead anyway.

Her stomach drops when she gets close enough to the barely alive qatu to make out the facial features. A face she knows, or knew, so well, six years ago. A face she could stare at for hours, a face Sari wished she would never see again if it meant that this qatu was safe. Zisuthra. Her sister.

"How?" Sari can manage no other words and falls to her knees. "How is she alive?"

"I do not know," Nanshaie says. "Her injuries..."

"I thought she died... Ashur said..."

"You know her?" Ia asks, a little too pointedly, her eyes skipping between the two royals.

"I would know her anywhere; she is the other half of my heart." A word wells up in her throat, one she couldn't say even to Arishaki, not even at the end. But she feels the urge to say it now, to declare that she loves Zisu, her sister. But even now, she can't. Not even when she might be torn from her, too.

Tinanna snorts.

"Who is she?" Ia asks.

"My sister," Sari says, taking a step towards her. "Zisu. But how?"

"Sari?" her sister says, barely audible, eyes opening slightly.

"Yes, I am here," Sari says, crawling to her sister and taking her hands. "I am here. How?"

"I hid," she says. "When the bandits arrived. I hid. But..." She grimaces.

"Take it easy," Nanshaie says, handing the flask to Zisu.

Sari shakes her head. "I mean that night... Ashur said..."

"Yes, he tried. But I always was good at acting," she says, trying to laugh, but she ends up coughing up the water.

"Did you notice anything about the bandits?" Ia asks. "Did anyone here know who you are?"

"No, Namu found me wandering the desert. But I never told her or anyone else. And the bandits, they all had a chalice embroidered on their shirts."

"Nanshaie," Ia asks, tone demanding. "What did you say earlier? About destruction and wine?"

"I don't remember everything, but 'the wine they fill the chalice with shall turn to blood and stain the sand,' or something. It was not my words; it was the woman's."

"Bringing snow and bearing oaken swords. Well. No matter," Ia says.

"Do you know something?" Sari asks.

But Ia does not respond.

Nine

Tinanna releases her falcon into the air and then searches the ruined encampment methodically, starting at one end, taking apart ruined edin'tus and putting them aside once satisfied they contained nothing. Nanshaie does her best to keep Zisu comfortable, but Ia is relentless in her interrogation of what happened with the bandits. When she obtains a satisfactory answer from Zisu about how long ago the bandits left and what direction they took off in, she demands that Sari accompany her to chase them down.

"They have the map," she insists. "They have it, and if we let them go, you will never get the Heart of Aodhe, and our chance at paradise will be lost forever."

"We need to stabilize Zisu first," Nanshaie says, carefully crushing herbs. "I fear there is internal bleeding, and she needs proper care from a trained healer. Care that I cannot provide."

"If we let the bandits get too far, we will never be able to find them," Ia says. "We need the map."

Nanshaie sets down the bowl and wipes her brow. "We have not searched all of the encampment. It could be hidden in a box they did not find; we have no proof the bandits took it!"

"They would have; it is what they were after."

Sari is only half paying attention until that moment. "How do you know they were not after my sister? How do you know they were not sent by Ashur or the insurrectionists after hearing a rumor that there is still a third mat'sahr'dan alive?"

Ia shoves her hands in the pockets of her light skirt, lips pursed. "They were after the map. Trust me."

Sari laughs. Trusting people is the best way to get killed. Tinanna drops something metal, the clank reverberating through the dark encampment.

"I..." Ia says, drawing out her words. "I saw it in a vision. A long time ago. Only now do I realize what I saw. But they were here for the map."

Zisu coughs, opening her eyes for the first time in half an hour. "Sari?"

"I am here," she says, racing back to her sister's side. "We will get you to a healer, I promise. Don't leave me. I can't lose you twice."

"I'm dizzy, very dizzy."

"I know, I know. We will make it better, I promise."

Ia stomps away, grabbing her camel. "I am going after the bandits. I need that map. I suggest you accompany me if you wish to see me alive again."

Sari searches Zisu's face, looking for any clue as to what she should do.

"If you are content to let Sua fall to ruin because you got sentimental over one qatu—" Ia chides.

"She's my sister!" Sari growls.

"Is she worth more than every other qatu in Sua?" The frantic, joyous energy is gone from Ia, replaced with a surliness that could rival the worst of Sumalika's temper.

Sari stands up, scowling. "Fine." She glances back at her sister, who has drifted off to sleep again.

"If you leave now," Nanshaie says, voice laced with prophecy, "she will die. She will."

This makes Sari hesitate. She glances between the Oracle and the High Priestess. Each offering different prophecies. Ia is right; she's letting sentimentality distract her from the mission. She needs the map; she cannot let her feelings for one stop her from saving all her people. Even if that one is Zisu. She is a ruler, she needs to think like one. She grabs her camel and follows Ia.

Despite not being asked, Tinanna joins Ia and Sari, taking off into the desert and leaving Nanshaie to look after Zisu. Sari hopes that the bandits will not loop back around.

"Ia," Sari says. "We need to make sure we only take out the actual bandits, but if they are members of an Erid clan, we must leave them alone."

"No, we take them out no matter what!" Ia snarls.

"The tension with the people of the Erid steppe was already high when the insurrectionists took over; if I am not careful, I will take the throne of a divided Sua. We cannot upset the isiaqs or sahres of the steppe, even if they have the map!"

Ia does not respond, leaning forward and urging her mount faster. The bandits did not attempt to cover their tracks after they got about a mitu away, and the trio was able to catch up quickly. They caught the bandits unprepared, making their own camp.

"Kill them," Ia orders, her voice full of metal and fire. "All of them. No survivors."

Tinanna tilts her head to the side.

"No witnesses. No one can know. No one can guess." Her tone leaves no room for argument.

Ia has no sword or spear of her own, just like Nanshaie—relying on others to do the work for her; including killing. Sari has no qualms with killing, but something about it being at the behest and orders of someone else rankles; her fur stands on end. The fire in Ia's voice is one she recognizes, not as one of practicality but of revenge. This is not truly about ensuring Ashur or the insurrections do not hear of their plans.

Knot in her stomach, she still races into the camp, spear in hand.

Tinanna is elegance where Sari is efficiency, Tinanna's thrusts and swings land perfectly, dispatching bandit after bandit, piercing the embroidered chalice over each knave's heart precisely. Sari catches herself more than once pausing to admire the way Tinanna fights, something in her chest stirring.

The oddest thing, though, is the sheer number of lohyue among them. Most bandit gangs in the Esiri and Erid are entirely qatu, but a stray lohyue from Janeuq or Qaewi can occasionally be found among their number. But these bandits easily have more than two dozen lohyue in their ranks.

Foes defeated, Ia trudges across the blood-red sands, searching each victim herself, not letting Sari or Tinanna even attempt to help. "Bastards," she repeats again and again as she rips off clothing, slashing the already dead bodies with her claws.

When she finally finds the map, she collapses into the sand, clutching it to her chest and screaming into the night sky. "It will be worth it, Namu. It will be. We will defeat them, and this world will be destroyed; our world will be remade. I will see you again, Namu. I will. I will."

They found the map, but Namu is nowhere to be found among the bandits. Her body was not at the ruined encampment, either. Sari wonders how Ia can believe she will ever see her mentor again.

They pillage the bandit's camp, taking what they can carry as well as the camels, which could easily be exchanged with a healer for treating Zisu. Provided Zisu is still alive.

How many people, qatu and now lohyue, has she killed to get the Heart of Aodhe? For a future she can't even fathom, one promised by a priestess who just ordered a massacre for revenge yet spoke of a paradise free from violence and conflict. A priestess willing to chance the death of her sister.

When they near the camp, Sari leaps from her camel and stumbles into the edin'tu that Nanshaie has set up. "Is she—"

"She's alive. But we need to get her to a healer."

The way Nanshaie runs her hand over Zisu's forehead as she checks for a fever, the way she measures out tea leaves into hot water with precision and care, the way she glances at Zisu with brows knit in concern and lips down-turned with worry... All speak of a compassion that Sari can only imitate.

All are clues that one could easily use to decide that Nanshaie cares more for Zisu than Sari does. All clues that Sari is not worthy of Zisuthra's love. Sari may have spent their childhood protecting Zisu, but so far, all she has done is abandon her to a near-stranger.

But a sahre'danu has no need for sentiment, not for a sibling; that was her flaw as a child. And not for a partner, for that is a distraction from her responsibilities. Especially not for a partner like Nanshaie, someone unable to even wield a sword, or even the silent and strong Tinanna who keeps her secrets behind closed lips. Arishaki could have been an adequate consort, but Nanshaie would fail at even that. Tinanna might have been adequate, if only Sari could speak with her.

Love is weakness; it gets one killed and is a vulnerability to be exploited in an act of inevitable betrayal. Not even Zisu or Nanshaie can be counted on not to betray her. If Arishaki could, then anyone can.

And yet she sits beside Zisu, combing her loose hair with her fingers, wondering at each scar on her face and the lopped-off ear. And yet, she speaks to Nanshaie. "Maybe the curse is not truly a curse. Zisu lives. You made sure of that. You changed the future and averted the disaster."

"There is still a shadow following her." Nanshaie turns away from Sari, tail twitching. "She is not out of danger yet."

Nialsamsu is upon them, and although Sari is anxious to get back on their journey and find somewhere to get Zisu medical aid, they must rest. But when they awaken again in the afternoon, Zisu is not the only one who needs healing. Tinanna is heaving, vomiting, and clutching her chest in pain. She waves off every attempt from Nanshaie at assistance and keeps scanning the area as if she, too, has had some terrible prophecy of the future.

"We need to go. I have spent the past few hours examining the map," Ia says, ignoring the illness of her bodyguard and fellow Seer. "I know how to get there. I know which stars we must follow."

"We should find a clan or caravan," Nanshaie says, gesturing to both Zisu and Tinanna, lying on their bedrolls.

"We will. We will find one on our way, I promise. I will not let anything happen to either." Ia's assurances do not appear to sway Nanshaie, who refuses to move from her spot.

Sari withdraws Katynna. "I shall hold you accountable for that."

"Of course, Sahre'Danu." Ia does not flinch away.

Sari makes a cart for Zisu to ride in, pulled by the extra camels they now have. "Where is your falcon?" She asks Tinanna.

The Seer says nothing but glances at the sky. Sari shrugs. It is not her problem.

As they set out, Zisu does perk up enough for conversation. "How did you get out?" Sari asks her.

"Ashur thought he had killed me, and the insurrectionists did not touch me, either. I overheard them say that I was already dead. And I thought I was. But my retainer found me after and helped me escape through a servants' door."

"Iltani helped you after Ashur… ? Is that how you lost half your tail and your ear?"

"Yes, that was all Ashur."

"Bastard."

"He tried to make it quick, he promised me quick and painless." She pulls down the scarf around her neck.

"That means nothing," Sari says, scowling.

"I don't want to know what the insurrectionists would have done if they thought I was still alive. Anyway, Iltani snuck me out of the isi'tu and gave me some food and water, and told me to run."

"She didn't go with you?"

"No, she didn't. I don't know where she is now."

"So you just wandered?"

"Until Namu found me. I never told her who I was. She just thought I was another orphan, another parentless waif. What about you?"

Sari grimaces. Not a story she wants her sister to hear. Not a story she wants to tell within earshot of Nanshaie. "I fought my way out. Arishaki helped."

"Arishaki… The few words I heard about you, of course. He was always mentioned, too. Where is he?"

Sari grimaces. Another story she does not wish for anyone to hear. "He passed away. About three months ago."

"Oh, I am so sorry. He loved you so much, you know. I always thought you two would—"

"Well, we won't," Sari snaps.

"Sister, I did not mean to upset you."

"Of course, you didn't," Nanshaie says, joining them uninvited. "Sari knows that. You have both had very hard lives."

Ia also joins them. Sari wishes she could be alone, truly alone, with just her sister. But Ia interrupts them. "Yes, but you two are so lucky to be alive," Ia says. "For before the year has passed, you shall witness the dawning of a new paradise."

While Tinanna has recovered from her passing illness, Zisu has taken a turn for the worse. A week after they left the abandoned caravan, Zisu slips into unconsciousness and they still have not come across anyone capable of lending aid. They have been following the stars, with Ia swearing that they are bound to come across a clan or caravan while they continue their journey to Bec.

But Sari is having none of it. "No, we must detour. She could die!"

"Detour where?" Ia asks as they break down their edin'tus after nialsamsu. "Any detour would be days away. We must keep going."

"No. I will go no further unless we—"

The falcon screeches, circling overhead. Tinanna points to the west, where a large caravan is slowly approaching.

"We have to see if they have a healer," Sari says.

"Those could be more bandits or an army."

"No, it's a tribe of Re'u," Nanshaie says, no one questioning how she could possibly know this. "They will be able to help us."

"Re'u? No. They can't be trusted," Ia says. "They have no respect for the law except for the laws of the desertThey could swindle us or rob us."

"But Zisu will die! We cannot let her die," Sari says. Having been willing to let her sister die once on this journey, she is not willing to risk it again. She cannot risk it again.

"No, what if they are violent?"

"Not all of the Re'u are violent," Nanshaie says. "Most of them are not, especially if you do not attack first."

"You want to risk that these are peaceful?" Ia asks."We could just ask them for assistance and offer them payment. This does not have to be complicated." Nanshaie runs a hand through her long hair. "If they are violent, then we fight."

"But what if they do not have anything that is helpful? We will have wasted our time." Ia rolls her eyes.

"What do you mean?" Nanshaie asks.

"They do not even believe in the Tuyude, let alone worship Yshuld. They cannot be trusted, especially not their medicine. They are not as educated as we are."

"They will help us!" Nanshaie says, stomping her foot, tail straight and fur raised. "We just need to ask!"

"No," Ia says. "There are too many risks. We must keep going at all costs."

Tinanna raises her hand to her heart, breathing deeply. She nods but says nothing.

"But—" Nanshaie says.

"They won't listen," Sari says. "We should get going."

"You're giving up?"

The words are a slap in the face. "No. I'm being realistic."

TEN

Nanshaie's screams pierce the silence of the desert. Sari opens one eye, searching for the Oracle. Nanshaie stumbles out of her edin'tu and dashes towards the camels, hitching one to another, and then taking off with both, not a single word or backward glance.

"What the—" Sari says, crawling out into the camp. "Where is she going?"

Ia and Tinanna join Sari; Ia squinting in confusion and Tinanna stone-faced.

"I'm going after her." Sari makes sure her spear and Katynna are both strapped tightly to her belts before mounting her camel and giving chase to the Oracle. Nanshaie is making in the direction of the Re'u. Is she disobeying the high priestess? Is she going to get medicine for Zisu? Another case of this stranger being more willing to sacrifice for Zisu than she is. *Some sister I am.*

The ride is no more than half an hour, and the Re'u are just settling in for their own mid-day rest when they arrive.

"Nanshaie, wait!" Sari calls, chasing after the Seer as she enters the Re'u camp.

"Hello," she says. "*Sen'en'dai. Nanshaie etta. Yshuld'eni. Ose lu. Ose lu pehn.*"

"Of course," one of them says, the soft accent clashing with the harsh desert. "Him get. Artaxerxes."

"*Lu e tan,*" Nanshaie replies.

Sari had studied many things; the mat'sahr'dan all receive robust educations, even those like Zisu, who are not expected to survive to adulthood. But none of them had learned the delicate Re'u language. It was thought beneath them, and if any of the Re'u did wish to speak to their rightful ruler, they should do so properly in Suan. Yet Nanshaie can speak this language. Not easily; she pauses and cannot form some of the more complex vowel sounds, yet she came in here willing to speak to them on their terms. For Zisu.

An elderly qatu approaches, walking stick in one hand, the other clutching a bag. "I am Artaxerxes. Told Yshuld-blessed is here for assistance from *pehn*. Blessed by Yshuld, but also by the Bah'en."

"I do not understand. I am sorry. One of my traveling companions is sick. We believe she has internal bleeding."

"Is qatu behind?" The healer points at Sari.

"No. This is my bodyguard. Zisu is another acolyte. We were on a holy retreat to commune with the desert, and she was injured."

"Ah," the healer says, but the way he raises his eyebrow belies his acceptance of Nanshaie's assertion.

"Bring here?"

"She is too sick. Otherwise..." She glances over her shoulder again. "Much too sick."

"Is well. Ride with you."

"Yes, we have an extra camel, too. And you may keep it after, as payment. In addition to whatever else you may need." Nanshaie touches her thumb to her sternum and then make a circular motion.

"*Sen'en'dai, rita.* Ready. Go now?" Artaxerxes points towards the camels, and Sari helps him mount the camel. "Thank you, Princess."

Sari holds back a hiss. No one here should know who she is, and yet...

Only Ia and Zisu are at camp when they arrive with the Re'u healer.

"Where were you? Where did you go? Thank Yshuld you are alive, I have been beside myself with worry!" Ia cries, embracing Nanshaie tightly.

"I am fine; please let me go." Nanshaie struggles to disentangle herself from Ia, panic heavy in her voice.

"You are my own heart! I raised you as a daughter and you go running off!" Ia steps back, her tone turning stern.

"*Sen'en'dai.* I am Artaxerxes." the healer says, interrupting the reunion. "The Bah'en-blessed said there is illness?"

"Bah'en?" Ia says, finally relinquishing her hold on Nanshaie.. "Oh, yes. Zisu. She is in that edin'tu."

Sari follows the healer, briefly wondering where Tinanna is. As she enters, she finds Zisu huddled on her side, vomit in the sand, and bile running down her cheek.

"Oh, *rita.*" The healer sets down his bag and touches Zisu's forehead. "*Rita, osi. Osi, rita.*"

Artaxerxes sorts through his pouch, pulling out vial after vial, inspecting each before putting it back. "What are those?" Sari asks.

"Medicine," he says, continuing to consult the labels and prod at Zisu.

"From where?"

"Some, make. Some from Qaewi or Janeuq. Some even from Sua, when not fight."

"What is that supposed to mean?"

"Truth. Not double meaning. Sister, yes?"

"She is my sister. How do you know?"

"Guess. But everyone knows how mar'sahr'dan'i look," he says with a laugh. "Re'u do not be fooled easily, even when other qatu want to."

"I see."

"No," the healer says. "Not yet. But you will."

Sari is about to ask him what he means when Nanshaie enters. "Is everything alright? Will you be able to cure her?"

"Yes, Bah'en'rita. Acolyte will be well," he says, opening the stopper to a vial and pouring the contents into Zisu's mouth. "Acolyte will need one week rest."

"One week?" Ia asks, joining them. "We have to be on our way; we cannot stay here for a week for her to convalesce."

"Then die," Artaxerxes says. "Acolyte will die."

"Can she stay with you?"

"No, no."

"Name your price. We have gold, jewels, food, camels. What do you need?" Ia asks.

"Re'u head north. If acolyte comes, could not say when will be back. Acolyte become Re'u."

Ia rubs her chin, looking at Sari.

"No! No, Zisu... I lost her once. I do not want to need to find her again."

"I will go with them," Zisu says. "I miss Namu and traveling. I do not want to go back to the isi'tu."

The healer frowns, brushing a stray hair out of Zisu's face. *"Rita mah bah. En'danu'i, kron y."*

Tinanna walks in, her falcon perched on her shoulder, hand over her mouth.

"Bard'i! Liars!" Artaxerxes says, pointing to Tinanna. He jumps to his feet, surprisingly spry. Grabbing his stick and satchel, he says to Nanshaie, "The Bah'en'rita needs better bodyguards."

Before he storms out, he spits on the ground in front of Tinanna. "Bard'i!"

Nanshaie and Sari both trail after the healer, but he climbs onto the camel on his own and disappears into the desert.

"She is still going to die. I took action on the vision; I tried to change it. But the shadow still clings to Zisu."

The next day, a caravan passes them, one that is planning on staying in the area for at least the rest of the month of Qorarhi. They did not say no when Sari asked them if they would look after Zisu for a while.

"I might decide I like it with them," Zisu says, lingering on the edge of the camp the caravan has set up, splayed out on her halersu. "I might decide to stay with them."

"But I can't protect you if you are with them," Sari says, lying on her own halersu next to her sister. "Once I am done in Bec, I will get you and bring you home. We can make sweets together at night again, and you can have your garden and fill it with all the flowers you want. We will have all of the isi'tu to ourselves."

"Will I have to fight again?" Zisu says, not meeting her sister's eye.

"What? No, of course not. Why would you ask that?" Sari props her head up on her elbow, searching her sister's face for any hint at her meaning. Zisu has always been better with words than Sari, each question hiding a dozen more.

"You would do away with the iseru?" Her voice rises, a breathy excitedness taking over that Sari hasn't heard in too many years.

"What do you mean? It's tradition. It would be my qits that would be in the *iseru,* unless you would challenge them with your own."

"What if you have a qit that is like me? One that does not want to fight? Would you force them, like our mother forced me?" Zisu rolls away from Sari, covering her face with her arms.

"It won't be like that," Sari says. The idea that any of her qits would not want to fight unsettles her. But then again, her mother had probably thought the same thing—Sumalika would have none know that any of her qits were not as strong as she was. But would Sari force a qit to fight? "We need the iseru. How would we know who would be the next sahre'danu?"

"Janeuq and Garcelon just pick the eldest." Zisu rolls back to face Sari again, her eyes narrowed.

Sari laughs. "And look how that turned out for them."

"Or maybe you could pick the smartest, the one that does the best in school. Or have just one competition, just one fight. One that is voluntary. There must be another way."

"Come on, Sahre'Danu," Ia says, sneaking up behind the sisters with three camels in tow. Behind her, Tinanna and Nanshaie are already mounted on their camels, bags packed. "We will be back soon. But for now, we must be going." The priestess hands a set of reins to Sari and then another to Zisu.

"Well. Goodbye," Zisu says. Still refusing to look directly at Sari. "When we see each other again, you'll be a proper ruler."

"Goodbye?" The high priestess says. "What do you mean?"

"I thought that—" Zisu starts, her brows knit and her voice shaky.

"She's joining the other caravan until we complete our mission," Sari says, her tone leaving no room for argument.

"No. She comes with us." Ia throws her shoulders back, chin high. "I have foreseen it."

"But it is too dangerous. She is still recovering." Sari looks past Ia, silently pleading with Nanshaie to say something; to provide her own prophecy, to countermand the high priestess. The Oracle shakes her head, looking down.

"The Sahre'Danu and her heir must both seek the Heart," Ia says, her gaze shifting to some realm that only she can see, her voice escaping from the desert to inhabit some otherworldly plane. "And the paradise the Sahre'Danu will build shall be like a dream."

Sari helps her sister onto a camel, eyes never leaving Zisu's face. She's so pale, so thin, a soft breeze could blow her away. But there is no arguing with the high priestess, especially if the Oracle will not back her up.

"You are doing the right thing," Ia tells her, pulling ahead of the rest of the party. "You get the Heart, and then when you return, your sister will be able to rest and recover; you shall be able to give her the life she deserves. She's had so much loss, but you shall be able to make up for it."

"I hope so," Sari says, remembering the way Zisu's dark green eyes had been fading into a pale brown.

"The world you shall build, Heir of Kyna, will be one without poverty; a society of knowledge; full of artistic expression, creative works, music, literature, and freedom for everyone to live the life they choose without fear of homelessness or hunger."

"That does not sound like paradise to me," Sari says through gritted teeth.

"Because you have not had the chance to think things through, but when you see the Heart of Aodhe, you will understand."

"What does that mean?" Sari grips the reins as if they were a spear; tight and firm.

"The Heart has the power to make manual labor unnecessary. It can build houses out of nothing, and it can install irrigation systems without effort. Everyone shall be free from want, free to spend their time pursuing their dreams."

"If this paradise is about freedom, where does a Sahre'Danu fit in? How can I be an absolute ruler if my people are not subject to my laws and edicts?"

"You are so young. I forget that sometimes. The lines on your face speak of an age older than your years. You have much to learn, young Sahre'Danu. But one day you will be remembered as the Heir of Kyna, remembered for ushering in the darasra'tu. The stars have told me as much. You shall bring about the great reordering and bring eternal paradise to the land. Tomorrow, in Bec, your prize awaits you."

"There it is," Ia says. It is dusk, the last rays of the sun disappearing behind the dunes, the two moons rising in the east.

"I don't see it," Sari says. "All I see is sand." A lost city? Where are the buildings? Or the ruins of them? *Ia has to be crazy,* Sari thinks. Absolutely crazy. She glances at Zisu. Her sister has managed to keep up, but she has not made any recovery. Zisu, eyes half closed, shrugs, and leans to the side.

"Between those two buttes. That is the entrance." The High Priestess grins, her tail twitching at the end.

"How do you know?" Sari asks, pulling on her reins, bringing the camel to a halt, and dismounting to catch Zisu before she falls from her saddle.

"The stars told me. See that one right there? The one that does not twinkle, the red one. It points the way." The high priestess does not even glance behind her; she keeps riding, eyes never wavering from the spot in the distance.

Sari rolls her eyes, glancing at Nanshaie and Tinanna. Neither of them show any sign of disbelief. If they trust Ia... "Let us be to it, then" Sari says. She climbs on Zisu's camel behind her, wrapping her arms around her now-sleeping sister. Kicking her camel, she flicks the reins and races down the dune after Ia.

As Sari catches up with the High Priestess at the bottom of the dune, she sees a smudge in the distance. Heat? A herd of fa'leen? Or people? Another caravan?

Ia halts, but Sari climbs off the camel, handing the reins to Ia. "Watch Zisu."

She sneaks ahead, glancing back once to make sure her sister is safe. The closer she gets to whatever it is in the distance now between them and the buttes, the more her hair stands on end. The fur on her tail prickles. No. These are bandits. She pulls out her spear, ready to skewer them, and darts across the sands.

She lunges in, heedless of the dangers. She strikes at one of them before noticing their thin, leather tabards. These bandits bear the embroidered chalice symbol. Once this is over, no more asking. *I am demanding that Ia tell me more about who these people are.* She stabs one of them right through the symbol, pulling out her spear and stabbing another. Tinanna joins her, pulling out twin daggers, leaping from her camel, and skittering to the ground.

"Be careful," Sari shouts. "I think there are more of them some-where!" There are too many riderless and packless camels in the chaos of the fight. Their riders must be somewhere. Sari cannot figure out where they might be, however.

If Tinanna heard her, she says nothing. But Sari is used to the si-lence now. The only answer she gets is the screech of the falcon as it flies past her, clawing at the face of another combatant.

Without saying anything, Ia joins the fray. She has only a dull spear as a weapon, stolen from her mentor's caravan. Her movements are jerky, she stabs without precision, and her thrusts lack strength. Sari darts between Ia and an oncoming blow, determined to keep the reckless, stupid priestess safe. "Get back!"

But it's too late; the enemy combatants have now surrounded them from all sides. Sari's heart races as she searches for Zisu. Did Ia leave her back with their camels? Or is she here, now also trapped? She doesn't see Nanshaie, either. Perhaps both of them are safe.

Ia shouts at the attackers in some language that sounds nothing like Suan or Re'u, nor any other language Sari can place. They shout back at her in the same tongue and grab the high priestess, pulling her away from Sari.

Sari tries to fight her way back toward Ia, parrying lashing swords and stabbing spears. Ia's spear is knocked from her hands and she cowers on the ground, protecting her head with her arms. Sari pushes harder, faster, more frantically through the crowd, desperate to make it to Ia.

But she is too late. The attackers grab her arms and drag her to her feet. With a dagger pointed at Ia's throat, the rest of the attackers retreat. They drag her away with them, disappearing so quickly that Sari knows there will be no catching up to them no matter how hard she rides.

Without Ia, Sari has no idea what to do next. She had let Ia take leadership of their group based on her knowledge. However, she does not believe that Nanshaie will have a similar amount of knowledge, and she knows that the Oracle has even fewer leadership skills. She's proven more daring and courageous than Sari could have guessed, but not enough to be able to continue the quest.

"Let's retreat to the east, set camp, and figure out what to do from there," Sari says. Neither of her Yshuldi companions complains or questions her choice, and she knows that Zisu won't. Sari wants to chase the bandits, but she also wants her sister safe. Nanshaie had made the right choice by staying behind during the battle, but Sari is still too agitated by the disaster to properly thank the Oracle.

"What shall we do now?" Nanshaie asks as they finish setting up their edin'tus.

"I do not know. I have no idea who those people are. Do you?" Sari breaks the stem off of a faricot and bites into it, not caring that it's not even fully ripe. The sour tang does not distract her from her irritation.

"No, I can only guess." Nanshaie pulls her shawl off and places it over Zisu's shoulders. The younger qatu smiles up at the Oracle and nods.

Sari looks at Tinanna, but the priestess keeps her silence, staring into the distance, breathing slowly.

"I suggest we sleep," Sari says. Without another word, she enters her edin'tu and curls up on the halersu for an early evening, hoping to hear her sister whispering for permission to join her like they did when children, and knowing that she won't.

It is not Nanshaie's scream that wakes her unexpectedly, but the high shriek of a falcon. *More soldiers? Did they find us?* There are dozens of them on the horizon. Sari curses, drawing Katynna. "Nanshaie! Nanshaie, take a camel and ride away from here with Zisu!"

The Oracle does not object, and neither does Zisu, as Nanshaie enters the edin'tu of the youngest royal.

Sari nods to Tinanna, and they brace themselves.

It is not the strange soldiers with the foreign tongue and chalice symbol that greet them, but General Aziru, Ashur's second in command, leading a force larger than Ashur had had in Erzurmei. *How are there so many? Is Ashur here, too?*

She swings, stabs, and parries as the soldiers surround her and Tinanna. But her strength is still low from the battle they just retreated from.

"There you are," General Aziru says as he makes his way through the throng of his army. "You've not been the best sister."

Sari does not dignify his jab with a response. She keeps holding the line, waiting until she thinks Nanshaie has had a long enough lead to get away.

She swings at him as he gets closer, hoping to slice his head from his body, but her blade strikes metal. What the heck? Wearing metal in the desert is a death wish, why and how does he have metal armor under his tunic?

He darts in, spear raised high. She dives and rolls, but his spear smacks Katynna out of her hand.

He is faster than she is, and he spins around, catching the weapon before it can even strike the sand. Raising Katynna about his head, he cackles. "Oh, Ashur will be so happy to have this." He waves it in the air, and his soldiers fall back. "Your brother has granted you one last chance to join him. He does not wish to quarrel with you. You can come with me now and join him."

"Never," Sari growls.

"That is a shame. You may leave here then, unharmed. Your brother grants you this last mercy out of respect for you and your prowess in battle. But if you should ever cross paths with him—or me—again, we will not hesitate to strike you down." He turns around, racing away from them without another word.

Sari lunges towards him, but Tinanna blocks her way.

"I need that! I need my blade back," Sari shouts, pushing Tinanna to the side. "I can't claim the throne without it!"

Tinanna grabs her again and pins her to the ground.

"Get off me! I need to get it!"

Without releasing her, Tinanna points to the east, where Zisu and Nanshaie continue their retreat.

"Oh. Nanshaie," Sari says. "You're right."

Tinanna gets off of Sari, nodding. Sari touches the royal seal still secured under her tunic. Ashur can't claim the throne without both Katynna and the royal seal. She can't claim it, but right now, neither can he.

Eleven

Tinanna and Sari drag themselves, exhausted from their battle, back to Nanshaie and Zisu.

Tinanna extends her hand as she dismounts, and her majestic falcon swoops down from the sky to land on her outstretched arm. The falcon deposits a small object into Tinanna's open palm before soaring to its perch on the back of the camel. Tinanna brings the object up to her face, examining it, turning it over in her hand to inspect every facet of its surface.

Sari leaps off of her camel and falls to her knees, screaming into the sand. "I am useless! If I cannot even protect a priestess, how can I protect an entire nation from its enemies? From insurrectionists? I am useless. Who would be loyal to me? No one!"

Nanshaie scoops up a fistful of sand and lets it slip through her fingers, glancing at Zisu sleeping beside her, undisturbed by Sari's storming.

"Do you have something to say?" Sari asks her. "Did you foresee this? Where were your premonitions of disaster this morning? You couldn't have warned us that Ia would be captured?"

Nanshaie squeaks as she takes a deep breath, her eyes glistening.

"It's too late to cry now," Sari says, crossing her arms.

"Stop it!" Tinanna says, storming over to Sari and slapping her. "Stop it right now!"

Sari's jaw drops. Tinanna's voice is a gust of wind through embers—harsh, yet with a subtle, grainy texture that adds depth to her words with the hint of a clipped accent, her vowels elongated.

"Stop feeling sorry for yourself! And stop taking it out on Nanshaie!" Tinanna glares down at Sari, still wallowing in the sands.

"I am fine, Tinanna," Nanshaie says, wiping her eyes with the corner of her shawl.

"No, Sari needs to pick herself back up and do what she says she will do and stop complaining."

Nanshaie and Sari turn toward each other, their faces etched with disbelief. The hairs on the back of Sari's neck stand on end, her tail swishing in anger. She takes a deep breath, searching for sharp insults to hurl at Tinanna.

"We need to move," Tinanna says, staring to the west, interrupting Sari before she can stab back. "I am being—We are being followed. We need to move."

"How do you know that?" Sari says, brows arched, and arms crossed. "Is it Aziru?"

Tinanna does not speak again, her hand reaching toward her chest and coughing.

This is the first time the priestess has addressed her at all, but Sari can still tell she is omitting something. Regardless, she packs her belongings quickly, waking a too-lethargic Zisu and placing her in front of her on the camel, and they take off. The camels sway beneath them as they journey deeper into the desert, leaving Sari with nothing to do but to stew in her anger and drown in her worry for Zisu's deteriorating condition.

The Seers and princesses dash through the night, not even pausing as the frost of midnight sets in and the nocturnal predators awaken. None pause to scan the sands for venomous qaboons or stinging al-paburus that creep through the darkened sands. They continue their journey without rest, pushing on into the early morning light.

Sari wishes to get Zisu as far away from their foes—known and unknown—as she can.

Tinanna brings her camel to a sudden halt, her hand falling away from her chest as she gasps for breath. "I think we're safe now," she manages to say, her voice ragged with exhaustion, before nearly toppling from the saddle.

Nanshaie does not wait for permission to be given from Sari. She leaps from her camel and unties her packs, setting them out neatly on the still-cool sand and gathering what she needs to make camp.

Sari hisses, helping Zisu down from the camel. "Can you set up your own edin'tu?"

Zisu nods. "I don't want this," she whispers, glancing at Nanshaie. "I know we have to respect the Oracle, and she seems kind enough, but I don't want to be here."

"I know," Sari says. "I want you near me, but not like this. But Ia said she saw you coming along…"

"But I don't have to," Zisu says, grabbing Sari's hand. "Ia is gone now. You haven't even told me what this is about. It's just been danger and running. I want to go home." Zisu releases Sari's hand and takes a step back, leaning against the camel for support and taking a ragged breath.

Home. Sari does not know where home even is for Zisu. She can't mean the isi'tu. That was more of a prison for Zisu than a palace. Does she mean Namu's caravan? Which has been annihilated… "I know, but once this is all over, we shall make a new home. A better home. And we can do it together."

Sari pulls her sister into her embrace, closing her eyes and imagining it. Her own version of paradise.

Zisu clenches at Sari's camise, and Sari can feel the tears escaping her sister's eyes dampening the fabric. But then Zisu shoves Sari away. Sari stumbles back, catching herself just before falling. "No, Sari. I don't want that home, either. One made from violence? Built on anger? No."

"So you want whatever it is Ia spoke of?"

"I don't trust Ia. And you shouldn't either. Her words may be the truth, but it's a twisted truth." Zisu turns away and busies herself with untying her packs from the camel.

Sari wants to say more, to argue with her sister. But the knot in her stomach tells her that if she keeps pushing, she'll lose her sister before they even get a chance to get reacquainted with each other. She has no idea what Zisu has been through, no idea what she has experienced since the night the insurrectionists stormed the palace. And Zisu no longer knows the cause of every scar Sari bears. They both need time.

But the anger in her chest needs an outlet. Now.

Sari turns and marches toward Tinanna. "I need answers," she demands. "Both of you have been keeping secrets from me. Who were those soldiers back there? And why are they following us? The insignia on their tunics does not belong to any sahre or isiaq that I know of."

"I think," Nanshaie says, flinching. "I think they are members of another religious order. But I'm not sure."

Sari does not miss the fact that it is Nanshaie answering the question she had aimed at Tinanna. But she is willing to overlook it. This is the closest she has gotten to an answer. "Another order? Who? Qor? Barhd? What are they after?"

"I heard Ia say something about other sages seeking the artifacts," Nanshaie says. "I never asked for details, however. This was before we left, so I did not think it would be related."

"Artifacts? Multiple? There is more than just the Heart of Aodhe? What else is there? Did you know about this, too, Tinanna?"

Tinanna stands with her arms tightly crossed, leaning against an outer pole for the edin'tu she just finished raising. Her falcon rests on her shoulder. She glances at it before looking back at Sari, scowling. She does not say a word.

Nanshaie interjects again. "But I think I have heard of this religious order from elsewhere. They were supposedly involved in the downfall of the monarchy of Fayn."

"Do you think they are working with the insurrectionists?" Sari's hand clenches, gripping a phantom spear.

"I cannot say," Nanshaie says.

Tinanna's breathing heavily, focused intently on tying two leather straps together to raise her edin'tu, not even glancing at Sari or Nanshaie.

"Then how do you know anything about it?" Sari raises her hand above her eyes as the morning sun continues its ascent, bathing the dunes in shimmering warmth.

"Our vows include not divulging anything said to us by dali'e in confidence in the temple. People travel far to our holy places, and we honor that sacrifice with silence. I have broken my oath too much already." Nanshaie looks down at her feet, hands behind her back.

Sari throws the spear into the sand and screams. "Why does everyone keep secrets from me? You expect me to keep you safe!" Sari shrieks as she pulls the spear from the sands and drives it back in again. "But you withhold vital information from me!" She hisses and runs a hand through her hair. "I am going to scout the area. If I don't come back, well, just forget about me."

She does not even glance at Zisu as she leaves the camp that Nanshaie has just finished setting up. The rebels who overthrew the Fola family years ago might somehow be involved. She's suspected that the insurrectionists in Sua might have had outside help. She clenches her fist, not wanting to count the number of enemies on her list now.

She realizes too late that her spear is still at their camp. All she has is a dagger. Not even Katynna. Regardless, she cannot allow herself to return to camp empty-handed. She would not be offering any caught game as a token of contrition or remorse, but as a way to show her strength. They need her, and that means they must give her full honesty. No more hidden truths, no more obscured motives, no more evasive answers that reveal nothing.

She needs them to know that she is worthy of trust; worthy of...

She halts at the top of a dune, glancing at the two tall buttes in the distance, the entrance to the lost city of Bec. But is she worthy? They did not witness her string of military losses, but what accomplishments of hers have they witnessed? Within the span of a day, she lost one of the items she needs to claim the throne and allowed the High Priestess to be captured and taken.

Her tail switches and she takes a deep breath, collapsing to the sand. She is a failed pretender to the throne. She does not deserve loyalty. Tinanna and Nanshaie's loyalties lie with Ia, as they should. She runs a hand through her hair, pulling back and securing it with a loop of leather.

Tinanna had said that the soldiers with the chalice symbol are part of some religious order. This religious order was somehow involved in the downfall of the Fayn monarchy. She closes her eyes, trying to remember what the professors of Khadima Alam had told her about those events. Was one of the temples supporting the rebels? Which one was it?

And people from that order were now here in Sua, possibly supporting the insurrectionists... And after the Heart of Aodhe. Does this mean that the insurrectionists know of her plans?

She slams a fist into the sand, ignoring the heat as she flexes her claws. Is that why they attacked Namu's caravan? They wanted the map to Bec... Or perhaps they were after Zisu and then found the map? It is only decades of practice that keep Sari from screaming in frustration. There are still too many questions. Did Ia suspect that there would be forces waiting to ambush her at the entrance to the City of Bec? If so, why request that her army be left behind? If she'd had her troops—disloyal as they may have been—she might have been able to keep Ia from being stolen.

Zisu had complained that she didn't know what exactly was going on. Sari can't even give her sister an answer, not knowing herself.

"Found you," Zisu says. "May I help?"

Sari springs to her feet and spins around to see her sister, a spear in each hand, ambling towards her. "You should be resting."

"Nanshaie made a tea for me that has helped a lot," Zisu says.

Sari squints. "Has she made this tea for you before?"

"I don't trust Ia," Zisu says this as if it should answer Sari's question.

"Nanshaie, has she made this tea for you before?"

"No. She could not. I do not think you should trust Ia." Again, Sari gets the feeling that there is more to Zisu's words than she says.

"If this tea is so helpful, why hasn't Nanshaie—"

"The Oracle is the only person in the land with more authority than a sahre'danu," Zisu says, testing the tip of the spear before handing it to Sari. "And yet she does not know how to wield it. Odd, is it not? That even she acquiesces to the High Priestesses edicts?"

Sari blinks. Her sister might not be much of a fighter, but she was always the first to pick up on the subtleties of court politics. "Yes," Sari says, adjusting the leather grip on the spear. "It is odd. But we should catch lunch first."

She has never hunted game with her sister; she had never hunted game at all until she had to flee on the night of the insurrection. But, before that, she had hunted. It just so happened that her prey was her siblings. That attitude and those skills had easily translated into the ability to hunt animals in the desert.

But Zisu had been taught how to hunt by the hunters of Namu's caravan. Actual hunting. Her movements as they track a herd of fa'leen are as graceful as those of their quarry; fluid but still efficient, meant to blend in with the desert, to sway like the large leaves of the trees found at an oasis, to have the shape and look of the common flora.

It is Zisu who gets the first kill, and Sari cannot help but beam as her sister slices the throat of the herd leader—a clean, effortless slash of her dagger, perfectly hitting the vein. She admires her sister's dexterity as she grabs the fallen fa'leen and rolls out of the way from the rest of the galloping pack, protecting her prey from unnecessary damage.

Perfectly executed. Her sister is not one for violence, but she is built for survival.

"Are you always so cold?" Zisu asks as they prepare the fa'leen to be carried back to camp.

"What do you mean?"

"Distant from everyone else, and sometimes violent. You do not let people get close to you, even when they want to," she says. "I understood it when we were children, but now I see you doing it to Tinanna and Nanshaie, who don't seem like they deserve it."

"What is the point," Sari says, plunging the spear's tip into the sand and then wiping it off on her tunic, "if they will just betray me?"

"It's understandable to sometimes feel apprehensive and doubtful about those around us," Zisu says.

Sari shrugs.

Zisu bites her lip as she ties the hooves of the fa'leen together. "I can't imagine what the past few years have been like for you."

"They've been hard. Full of nothing but betrayal."

"Be that as it may... consider that you might not be giving those around you the chance to prove their loyalty. You constantly anticipate negative outcomes, displaying a lack of trust in others and just assuming the worst."

"Zisu, you had the same childhood as me. Can you really fault me for assuming the worst?"

"I am just saying... If you don't take action to prevent negative outcomes, you may unintentionally contribute to their occurrence." Zisu stands back up, offering a hand to Sari. "Come on, it's almost nialsamsu. We should get back to camp."

Nanshaie is   waiting, wringing her hands and   sitting outside Zisu's edin'tu when they get back. She rushes up to them. "Oh, I am so glad to see you looking so well," she says as she pulls Zisu in for an embrace. "Remember what I said..."

"I remember," Zisu says, a smile playing at the corner of her lips. "I'm going to rest now. Sari?" Zisu raises an eyebrow at her sister.

"Of course, I can get the meat prepared. Enjoy your rest," Sari says, barely hiding her scowl.

"Did you fight with your sister, too?" Nanshaie says, crossing her arms and raising an eyebrow.

"We had a difference of opinion, that is all."

"May I ask what about?"

Sari rolls her eyes and sets to work on preparing the fa'leen, Nanshaie taking a seat beside her to assist. "She seems to think my behavior is the reason people betray me."

"She has a point. You foresee disaster everywhere, and then you do everything to encourage it."

"That's amazing," Sari says, laughing. "Consider what you just said and apply it to yourself."

"Fine!" Nanshaie says, throwing her knife into the sand and jumping to her feet. "I keep trying to be kind, to show you trust and understanding. And you throw it back in my face every time. I have no reason to trust you after what you have done, what I know you have done, but I am trying. I don't know why, but I am. And you rub sand in my face!" She stomps her foot and storms into Zisu's edin'tu without another look at Sari.

Sari waits for Nanshaie to come back out, to apologize, or at least offer to have a discussion. But minutes become hours, and the only noises that come from the edin'tu are the soft whimpers of an Oracle trapped in the throes of an inescapable nightmare.

Twelve

SEVERAL DAYS OF SCOUTING AND SPYING reveal that the army that stole Ia has split into several camps and are surrounding the entrance. "We need to find another way in," Sari says as dusk falls. "If we sneak in, get the Heart of Aodhe, and get out, then maybe we can use the Heart of Aodhe to take that army and save Ia. Because I can't take all of them out on my own."

Tinanna nods.

"I wish we could do something more," Nanshaie says.

"You're doing more than enough," Zisu says, laying a hand on Nanshaie's shoulder.

Tinanna plucks a dagger from her belt and etches something into the sand.

"Do you have something more to add?" Sari asks, scrutinizing the drawing. Does Tinanna not know how to write, either?

"Oh, did you find that?" Nanshaie says, sitting next to Tinanna. "Is it guarded?"

Tinanna shakes her head.

"What's going on?" Sari asks, frustration dripping in her voice. Can the Seers communicate without words somehow?

"There's another entrance. Not as heavily guarded. I think we can sneak in there," Nanshaie says.

Tinanna nods, stabbing the ground.

"Pack up, then. We're heading out."

Her companions are ready to go within half an hour, and Tinanna leads them to a distant plateau, pointing to a small crevice, wide enough for their camels, but only single file. There are no soldiers in the area, and Sari wonders if they should leave the camels or if the camels might be found by patrols and tip them off.

"We're going to have to leave them," Nanshaie says, dismounting from her camel and removing her pack from it.

Sari whirls around to face Nanshaie. "How did you—?"

Zisu laughs. "You give away more than you think you do." She grabs her own supplies and pats the nose of her camel affectionately.

Sari shakes her head and wonders if they will have enough water and food for whatever lays ahead of them. But she squares her shoulders and leads the way into the small crevice, relishing the drop in temperature as they leave the scorching sun behind them.

The crevice widens the further they go in, and a strange illumination comes from plants growing out of the walls.

"Did Ia ever tell you what this city looks like?" Sari asks, wondering how much further they had to go. Surely this cave did not go on forever?

"No, why?" Nanshaie says as she takes a cloth to her forehead. It's cooler inside, but the trek is arduous and Nanshaie is clearly not used to the effort.

But just as Sari is contemplating calling for a halt and a discussion to reevaluate their plan, the crevice ends abruptly, and the view before her steals her breath away.

Sari steps aside, spreading her arms out at the view. Below them, a city rises out of an underground lake. A dome surrounds it, holding back the sand above them. The city does not look ancient; it looks far newer than Erzurumei. There are no collapsed buildings or decaying structures, no crumbling houses. No scattered debris.

If it were not for the empty streets, Sari would think this to be an opulent and wealthy city. More than a dozen of the buildings rise higher than the central spire of the isi'tu, all made of marble, with a central spire rising twice as high.

If this is the paradise that Ia wants to bring about, Sari understands now why she spoke of it so reverently. The Heart of Aodhe will give her the power to create a city like this? *Better* than this? Her people could live in security and safety...

She grabs Zisu's hand and squeezes it. Her sister could live here. A peaceful place where Zisu could thrive; where she could be sheltered from violence and war. Zisu meets her eyes and returns the smile, but it does not reach her eyes.

"There," Nanshaie says, pointing to the tallest spire. "The Heart of Aodhe has to be there."

"How do you know?" Sari asks, again suspicious of all the information the Seers have been withholding from her during this quest.

"I can feel it. Can't you?"

Sari closes her eyes. There is a whisper, a slight tug pulling her in that direction. But the city is so vast that she cannot pinpoint it. "What is that?"

"It means you are the Heir." The words come from Nanshaie's mouth, but it is not her voice.

"I don't understand," Sari says, looking at Nanshaie. The Oracle's eyes are blurry, and a glow comes over her whole body. Sari stumbles a step back.

"What?" Nanshaie asks, shaking her head. "I'm sorry. I don't know what just happened."

Sari raises an eyebrow at the Oracle, but thinks better of saying anything to contradict her.

"So, how do we get down there?" Zisu asks. "And will we have to swim to get to the city? I'm not the best swimmer."

"Let's keep going," Sari says, surveying the paths before them. "And we can find out."

At the edge of the cliff, there is a series of platforms and walkways leading down into the depths. The platforms are adorned with intricate carvings; symbols that look like the fluid script of the Suan language but occasionally have the sharp angles found in the Janeuqi or Garcelonian alphabets. Despite having the best education one could acquire in Sua, neither Zisu nor Sari can read the writing.

As they descend, Zisu marvels at the breathtaking sights around her, racing ahead and clapping her hands, tugging on Sari's wrist to keep up with her. Bioluminescent plants line the walls of the cavern, and Tinanna plucks a handful, holding it up so that Nanshaie can pause to better inspect the symbols on the stone as they near the bottom of the cavern. The air is crisp and clean, filled with a hint of floral fragrance. The underground lake glistens, reflecting the lights of the city above

A marble bridge stretches before them, leading them over the lake and to the entrance of the city.

"Do we continue on?" Zisu asks, her eyes still wide and taking in every inch of the city looming before them. For a second, Zisu shimmers, a strange double-vision of her both standing tall and her vanishing into smoke. Sari rubs her eyes, convincing herself that it's just a trick from the glowing flora. Something is off, but it's a side effect of the strange plants.

But when she glances at Nanshaie, a worried look is written across the Oracle's face as she too squints at Zisu. "Maybe we should take a break," she says haltingly, swinging her sack off her shoulder and rummaging through it for a flask.

Tinanna saunters to the edge of the pathway and places a hand into the lake, the ripples stretching out until the lap against the walls of the city. Seemingly satisfied after a moment, she cups both hands together and draws the water to her lips. Sari waits, scrutinizing the silent seer's face for any signs of distress. But she simply nods, wiping her mouth with the back of her hand before dipping her own flask into the lake and filling it.

"How will we find our way to the center?" Zisu asks. "Do we have a map?"

Nanshaie shakes her head. "Ia might have. But this is a different entrance than the one she had wanted to use."

"Have some jerky. We will make it, but you need your strength." Sari hands her sister some strips of dried fa'leen meat, suddenly wishing she had left her sister somewhere safe. This lost city *should* be abandoned, deserted and empty. No threats should be lurking in its streets; no nightmares waiting in dark alleyways. And yet she cannot shake the image of Zisu vanishing before her eyes.

With no sun, no moons, and no stars in the sky to mark the passage of time, Sari allows them to rest for as long as she can before urging them all forward.

The bridge is sturdy, wide enough for several caravans to cross at once. She cannot fathom how this much marble was quarried and brought here; how much time must have gone into constructing it. It stretches before them, on and on; a marvel of engineering.

"This must be several mitu long," Nanshaie says as the reach the midway point. Sari looks over her shoulder, glancing back at the series of walkways and platforms that had allowed them to descend, the creeping vines shimmering like stars. She wishes they could have brought the camels, but there is no way they would have made the descent.

"How has this stayed hidden? How do the professors at Khadi-ma Alam not know of this?" Zisu mutters, running her hand along the edge of the bridge, letting her fingers trace the strange writing in stone.

But Sari does not care how long the bridge is, nor how it was made, and certainly does not care whether the haughty academics know of it. She cares about the Heart of Aodhe; saving Sua from the insurrectionists and her brother. It is her only option left; the only way she can claim her throne and secure safety for her people. For Zisu.

Finally, they reach a grand entrance guarded by colossal statues.

"What are those?" Zisu asks, skiping the last few fitu across the bridge and inspecting the statue of a six-legged creature with a head not just on the front but also on its tail.

"I don't like it, whatever it is." Sari pulls Zisu away from it and stands in front of the towering doors. "Do you think we need a key?"

Nanshaie shakes her head, opening the gem-embedded doors with a slight push. Sari takes a deep breath, pulls out her spear, and steps inside, anticipating an attack and instead finding an elegant atrium filled with a fine mist. The atrium is brimming with lush foliage, a waterfall, and a stone path without a single crack. It's gorgeous but eerily silent. No birds, no insects, and no breeze to stir the leaves. Just plants and mist.

"How can this possibly exist here..." Zisu whispers, tracing a finger along the edge of a frond. "It is like time simply stopped."

"It doesn't matter," Sari hisses. "We must keep going. Get in, get our prize, get out. This isn't a vacation."

Zisu's shoulders sag. "Fine."

"Something's wrong," Nanshaie says, holding up a hand.

Sari barely has time to dodge as soldiers rush at them, materializing from the mist—appearing before them as if they sprang into existence; lethal and new. Sari draws her spear, taking a defensive position in front of Zisu. "Here," she says, shoving the hilt of one of her swords into Zisu's hands. "Use this."

Zisu does not argue, but holds the sword before her and squares her shoulders like she is back in the iseru.

Tinanna draws her knives and throwing stars, taking aim and letting the blades embed themselves in the leather armor of these phantom fighters.

The soldiers are vicious, attacking with a ruthlessness that borders on madness. As Sari plunges her spear into the chest of one of the attackers, she notices that the soldier's eyes are bulging, iris and pupils mere pinpricks.She catches glimpses of her companions fighting back as she spears soldier after soldier. Tinanna is like a dancer as she leaps across the atrium, tossing bladed stars and circles at their foes, slashing them across the neck without ever nearing them. Before meeting Tinanna, Sari had only read about such weapons. Now, she hopes she will never be on the other side of Tinanna's aim.

Zisu fights like a hunter, not a soldier, but she downs their enemies with the same efficiency. Next to her, Nanshaie lashes out without strategy or planning, but there is a fury in her movements, and her foes die just the same.

Without sun or stars, she cannot say how long their battle lasts, but she lets out a feral cry as a soldier stumbles towards her, already bleeding and battered. She grips her spear with both hands and does not hesitate to pierce the soldier through the heart, letting it sag on the pole before she pulls her spear free again.

"I think that is the last of them," Sari says as the atrium once again goes silent.

Nanshaie leans against a tree, panting and out of breath. "I hope so."

"Where did you learn to fight like that?" Sari asks her as she wipes the blood off of her spearpoint, not wanting to think about why the blood smells old.

Nanshaie blushes. "I have been watching you... In the morning... and in the evening."

"Watching me?"

"I am sorry," Nanshaie says, covering her face.

"You're injured," Sari says, seeing the gash on Nanshaie's forearm. "Let me help you."

Nanshaie flinches away, pulling back. "I can tend to my own wounds. You have more important things to worry about."

"No, please, let me help you." Something tugs at her heart; a feeling she has not experienced in years. A memory of Zisu's first night in the iseru—the anguish at watching her return to the rooms bleeding and bruised. For some reason, she cannot tolerate the gnawing in her stomach as Nanshaie presses a rag against the cut on her arm.

Nanshaie relents, sitting down. "I promise I was not trying to spy on you. You just look... I don't know the word for it. But watching you as you do your exercises and practice. It's beautiful."

"I have never had my fighting called beautiful before," Sari says, pouring water from her flask onto a strip of cloth and carefully cleaning the area around Nanshaie's wounds, her cheeks burning as her fingers brush across Nanshaie's soft skin. "Fierce, fiery, ferocious, feral... I think feral is my favorite."

Nanshaie laughs. "You might be feral, but your fighting is completely at your command. Controlled and deliberate." Their eyes meet, and Sari is reluctant to break her gaze away.

There is no sun in this buried and forgotten city, and it is not long before they lose all sense of time. They creep through the emptiness; Sari refusing to let her spear out of her hand as she glances around every corner, waiting for another ambush by those strange, unsettling soldiers.

"I can't keep going," Zisu says, hands on her knees and bent over. "I'm sorry, I just can't."

Sari bites her lip, not sure if she should push to keep going. They have no camels with them, and the further they go into the city, the farther away the glimmering spire at its center seems to be. She has had time to determine how far she can push Nanshaie, and Tinanna's energy has never been a problem. But her sister; she can't bear the thought of Zisu struggling. *Why had Ia insisted on her coming with them?*

"Can you go a little farther? I promise we will try to find a resting spot soon," Sari says, squeezing her sister's hand.

Zisu takes a deep breath and nods.

They pass through a series of gates, and Sari is overwhelmed with the change; the buildings in the outer ring of the city may have been gorgeous, but these are breathtaking. Each is etched with gold and silver, thousands of lines like a flowing river and tributaries spanning the entire height of the buildings. The stone itself seems to sparkle, and many of the buildings have gems along the corners. The windows are clearer than any glass that Sari has ever seen and stronger. No matter how hard any of them try, the glass does not break.

"Guess we will have to set up a camp outside," Zisu says after attempting to break into another building. "But there's no sand here and almost no breeze."

"But there still might be other weather patterns we would need shelter from," Nanshaie says, biting her nail. "And after what happened at the city entrance, I do not feel safe outside."

Tinanna says nothing, pulling a piece of dried meat out of her pouch and handing it to the falcon perched on her shoulder.

Sari curses under her breath. If only Ia hadn't gone and gotten herself captured. Ia would likely know how to navigate this sprawling, silent city. Sari stares up at the large dome holding the sand at bay, an artificial night sky lacking any sources of guidance. No stars, no moons, no smidgen of light to the east to announce the impending arrival of dawn. The twinkling of the city spires is the only means of charting a path.

"I understand, but I don't think we have a choice," Sari says. "Let's keep going and see if we can find something that at least provides a little shelter."

Sari's eyes widen when she spots a building with a large patio and an awning, the perfect shelter for them to rest. "Will that do?" she says, pointing it out to the others.

"That will do," Zisu says, and they make their way toward it. "The tables and chairs," Zisu says, putting her hands on her hips. "I bet we could at least re-arrange them to make a little more shelter."

"Let's get to work," Nanshaie says, smiling at Zisu and setting her pack on the ground.

Sari still is not entirely convinced of their safety. "Let's scout the area," she says to Tinanna. The other Seer gives her standard nod and withdraws a dagger from her boot.

Sari does not want to let her sister and Nanshaie out of her sight, but she trusts that they can hold their own for at least a little while. She draws a sword and marches into the city, Tinanna silent beside her but just as alert.

As they search the area, Sari can't shake the feeling that they're being watched. She glances over at Tinanna. "Do you sense anything?" she asks.

Tinanna shakes her head, but there is uncertainty in her eyes.

"Something feels wrong." Sari tightens the grip on the hilt of her sword.

Sari takes a step into an alley; there are no glowing plants lining it, and the darkness is inexplicably consuming. She takes another, then another, and the sound of a pebble skipping across stone echoes from all sides. She takes a hurried step back, more scared than she had ever been when fighting in the iseru. She makes it back to the safety of the eerily illuminated streets, but a low growl reaches her ears.

"Did you hear that?" she asks Tinanna, her heart pounding, utterly convinced that whatever lurks in the shadows will send her quickly and painfully to meet Xana in the afterlife.

Tinanna does not even acknowledge Sari's question; she stares into the alley as if she can see whatever lurks in its depths and is issuing it a challenge.

"Let's go back." Sari takes another step away from the alley, but she still feels like she is too close. "Come on, we need to get back."

Tinanna stares into the darkness a moment longer, and then her shoulders sag. She lets out a deep breath and nods.

They make it back to camp without any further unsettling encounters and find a suitable shelter has been set up. Zisu and Nanshaie make quick work, and Sari has never been more relieved to see a an edin'tu. "I'll take the first watch; you sleep."

"You didn't find anything out there?" Zisu asks.

She cannot bring herself to tell Nanshaie and Zisu what she experienced. "No, it's safe."

"Then you should rest, too." Zisu sits down and pats the ground next to her.

Nanshaie stares at her, expression unreadable. Sari hopes that whatever visions the Oracle may have, they do not involve some monster lurking in the shadows of the city. She does not want to be called out on a lie.

Reluctantly, Zisu gives up her insistence that Sari rest with them, and her companions drift off into sleep.

The whimpering sound startles her, and she leaps to her feet instinctively before realizing that the sound is Nanshaie having a nightmare. She pulls back the shawl that Zisu had affixed to the entrance of their shelter, but Nanshaie is not the one having a nightmare; she isn't even asleep.

"She won't wake up," Nanshaie says, holding Tinanna's hand as she thrashes, sweating despite the lack of any desert heat.

"Silla," she mumbles. "Silla…"

Perhaps it is because she is sleeping, Sari thinks, but as Tinanna mumbles and cries out, she swears she hears the hint of a Re'u accent.

They set out again without further incident, taking careful stock of the dried meats and water supply—no one is too keen on drinking from the fountains they find at the crossroads or attempting to eat the plants they find surrounding those fountains.

Sari reassures herself that the growl she had heard was just her imagination; they run into no more adversaries and hear no more signs of other life. Even as she tells herself that, however, she can't help peering down every dark street and alley, sure she will see a monster lurking in the shadows.

"It's as if everyone vanished at once," Zisu says as they turn a corner and find a pavilion that looks like it once served as a gathering spot for large groups of people to enjoy meals. There are no signs of any conflict driving people out or disaster forcing people to flee. Sari silently agrees with her sister. But if they are gone, where did they go?

Being far from the threats of siblings and parents, Zisu has grown into a curious qatu, asking questions that might better be left unsaid. She is not frightened of the eerie emptiness but intrigued. "You should have been a scholar," Sari replies, dragging her away from her inspections of a strange structure abandoned on the street.

"Mother never would have let me go to Khadima Alam."

"I know, but Mother is not here anymore," Sari says, smirking. "You can do whatever you desire."

Zisu chuckles. "True, true. I think I would like that."

"First thing we do when we get back to Erzurumei," Sari says, throwing an arm over her sister's shoulder. "Find you a good tutor."

Zisu beams, her eyes lighting up as she nods. *This is what I am fighting for,* Sari thinks. *This is why I have to beat Ashur.*

She extends and retracts her claws as she leads them further into the deserted city, trying to keep the image of Zisu wandering the gardens of the University of Khadima Alam in the front of her mind. But the image is destroyed repeatedly by thoughts of Ashur and his plans if he takes the throne.

She won't let that happen; she will take the throne. Ashur will not rule Sua as a tyrant and the insurrectionists won't destroy it with their weakness and chaos. She will be the firm and steady hand Sua needs.

They come to a fork in the road they are on; both paths seeming to lead away from the glittering spire at the center of the city. She halts, again wishing she had a map. "Nanshaie, do you which—"

"She's here, she's here. She was here!"

"Who? Is Ia here?" Sari asks, withdrawing her spear and whirling around.

"The sky... The sky is on fire," she screams, falling to her knees and pointing toward the still-dark dome. "I don't want to see this! Don't make me watch; please don't make me watch this!" Nanshaie covers her face, and then peaks between her fingers. "Oh no, not again—" She bolts back to her feet and dashes away from the group, turning down a dark alley.

"Stay here," Sari says to Zisu, and chases after the terrified Oracle.

Although she is as panicked as a startled fa'leen, Nanshaie still moves with an otherworldly grace as she dodges obstacles that only she can see, fleeing dangers only she can sense.

But Sari is still faster. She catches up to Nanshaie, grabbing her by the shoulders and pulling her in. The Oracle's heart is beating so fast, so fiercely, that Sari can feel it in her own chest. "You are safe," she says, running her hand down Nanshaie's back.

"The kahbush'a! So many of them everywhere! And the sky, this city... How is it still standing?" She pulls away from Sari, staring up at the spires and towers, jaw hanging open, eyes wide. "What just happened? Where did the old woman go?"

"What old woman?" Sari asks, taking Nanshaie's hand, afraid that the Oracle will run away again.

"She's always with me. Always in my dreams, and even when I am awake, she stalks me, a shadow two steps behind me that I can only see when I am not looking."

The Oracle pulls her hand away and takes off down the street again, hands reaching for objects that are not there. "The Council could not stop them."

"What council?" Sari says, jogging to catch up with Nanshaie. At least the Oracle is heading back in the direction of Tinanna and Zisu.

"The attacks," Nanshaie says, as if it is the most obvious answer, coming to a stop next to Tinanna but seeming unaware of her presence." We were caught in the crossfire between the Blodheimr Hjart and the Araelta."

"The what? What's going on?" Sari glances at Tinanna, hoping the other Seer can fill her in or at least decipher what the Oracle is saying. Right now, she is not Nanshaie; Yshuld's representative walks before them wearing the face of Nanshaie.

Tinanna halts, face pale, fur standing on edge.

"Do you know what she's talking about?" Sari asks.

Tinanna doesn't move, her eyes fixed on Nanshaie, muttering about something only she can see.

"Kyna tried to stop it, but she was injured. Isolde tried to revive her, but—"

"Who is Kyna? Who is Isolde?"

"Aodhe was destroyed."

"Nanshaie! What is going on?" Sari grabs her shoulders again, shaking the Oracle.

"This is a dream; this is all just a beautiful, heart-wrenching dream. Escnea is gone. It belongs to the kahbush'a now." She collapses onto the ground, sobbing. "You cannot let Ia get the Heart, Sari. She cannot have the Heart of Aodhe! She is not who she claims to be!"

Zisu stoops next to Nanshaie and pulls her into her arms. And some part of Sari wishes she could be the one comforting the frightened seer.

Their food supplies are running dangerously low, and the gnawing sensation of hunger is an ever-present agony.

Nanshaie does not mention her vision, and Sari is too afraid to ask about it. Instead, they focus on finding sustenance that they can be assured is edible.

"The soldiers. They might have food," Sari says, as she rolls up her halersu and pulls out the last of her cheese, tearing down their camp after their brief rest.

"What do you mean?" Zisu asks. Sari can't help but notice the hollows under her sister's eyes. Those weren't there when they found her, were they? "We haven't seen any soldiers since we arrived."

"True, but they had to have supplies somewhere if they were living here. And if we can find their camp or their base—"

"That sounds too dangerous. I thought we've been trying to *avoid* them, and I was considering us lucky not to have met any others," Zisu says.

"I think it is a good plan," Tinanna says, and Sari once again catches it—that faint accent she heard when Tinanna was crying out.

"Would you like to scout together?" Sari asks, hoping that the usually silent Seer will speak again, rather than nod or shake her head. If she says one more word, Sari can be sure of it.

But Tinanna shrugs and plops a date into her mouth. "Fine, I'm going to go scouting. Maybe I'll find something else that we can be certain is edible."

As she creeps down the narrow streets, she tries to keep her mind focused on her task, to keep her senses fixated on her surroundings. But her mind will not cooperate and her thoughts are intruded upon with doubt and questions about her companions. Over and over, a soft voice tells her that she cannot trust them.

It makes no sense for a Priestess of Yshuld to have any hint of a Re'u accent. The Re'u have their own gods, their own culture, and their own religion, entirely separate from most of Ahnlisen. They would never send one of their qits—Sighted or not—to worship a goddess they do not believe in.

And the way Tinanna fights, it is far more fluid, more lethal, than any basic self-defense the Temple might teach their acolytes. And it is much fiercer than Re'u hunting.

The priestess might have some modicum of Sight, but Tinanna did not grow up in the Temple of Yshuld. What is a woman with a Re'u accent who fights like a warrior doing in a temple?

Sari turns another corner, another empty but pristine street. There are not even any rodents, let alone debris to entice them. Sari has never had to resort to eating rodents for dinner. Even when her army numbered in the thousands, their supplies were never so diminished that vermin remained their only option. She made sure her troops never went hungry.

Troops that are now dead because she believed Ia's promise. Troops that she killed, thinking the sacrifice would be worth it, executing her own soldiers at Ia's insistence.

Nanshaie said that Ia is not who she says she is. But if she is not a high priestess of Yshuld working to put Sari on the throne with the help of the Heart of Aodhe, who is she?

Sari wants to punch something, kick something, beat something until there is nothing left. She believed a lie, and now the few people who are in her care might starve in a ghost city, including Zisu.

And Nanshaie... Nanshaie is also more than she seems, even if she herself does not realize it. Her courage, but also her kindness... Her kindness to Zisu, and even occasionally to Sari, even if Sari knows that she does not deserve it. Not after what she has done.

She halts, suddenly unable to breathe. Her chest tightens, and she wants to do more than stab and kick. She wants to scream. Her eyes water, eyesight blurring.

What I have done...

Every face—twisted in agony and rage. Every body—writhing in pain and terror. Every person she *murdered* at the behest of someone she barely knew. And for a power she did not understand, a power she did not even know of before that stranger had told her about it.

What kind of ruler would she even be if she could be...

She bites her tongue. "No. I cannot get distracted. Not now. I need to find food and water. Not now. Please, not now."

She closes her eyes, forcing her breath into a steady rhythm, forcing her lungs to obey her. A trick she learned long ago in order to survive the iseru—she glances around her, giving names to objects she's never seen before, listening for any noises that could anchor her, any smells that can reorient her.

Then, she *does* hear something. The faint sound of rushing water, not a familiar sound to one who has lived so long in the desert, but one she welcomes. She freezes, not moving a muscle, not even breathing, trying to locate the source. She looks down at her feet. The sound is somehow beneath her. An underground lake or river this far down? If it's running water, not still water... It might be drinkable.

But how to get to it? There is a disc in the street further down, and as she approaches, the sound grows louder. She runs her finger around the circumference and it wobbles slightly. "It can be moved," she says. It's far heavier than she could imagine, but there are two small inlets that she can squeeze her fingers into. She grips it as best she can as she pulls it away, a cool mist rises up from the dark hole. Without a second thought, she jumps.

Instead of an underground lake, she finds herself in a narrow tunnel that stretches before her. Water runs through it like a river, with sturdy walkways on either side. The sides of the tunnel are the same glimmering stones of the city's streets, and along the edges, glowing silver offers enough illumination to see by.

Carefully, she crouches down and dips an empty flask into the cool, rushing water until the flask is full. She sniffs it, expecting the musty smell that is present at all of the fountains they've come across. But it smells as fresh as the water at the Masayaf oasis. She laughs; maybe this is part of the underground river that feeds the Masayaf.

She pours the water back out in front of the silver veins and sees no signs of pollution. She bites her lip. She's still suspicious that it might not be safe, but she would rather risk it herself than let anyone die of dehydration. She fills the flask again, closing her eyes before taking a sip.

There is no foul taste, no strange texture, no odd sensations as she swallows. It's as pure as she used to drink at the isi'tu. She takes another tentative sip, and again waits for any signs of illness.

She fills up the remaining flasks she has with her. If there is something in the water that kills slowly, she will know by the time she gets back.

She pauses. It's as pure as the water at the isi'tu. But back then, she had others to taste everything for her, and even as commander of her army, she was never the one to risk death. Someone else always took the risk of poison or contamination. She was too important to be the one at risk.

Why does she feel differently now? Why shouldn't it be one of the others that takes the risk? It can't be Zisu; she doesn't want it to be Zisu. But why does she think that it is her responsibility now?

No time to worry about that. If there is running water, there might be life. Rodents at the very least might have a nest down here.

As she makes her way through the dark tunnel, a low rumble echoes off the walls—she's never heard a sound like it before. *Are there rapids ahead? Or a waterfall? Or could it be an animal?*

She tries to reassure herself that even if it is a creature, it's meat—potentially food. But the fur on the back of her neck stands on end. She stands still, body tense. She cannot pick up any hint of another creature nearby. The ground does not vibrate with footsteps, and there is no waft of air through her fur that would indicate movement or breathing. There is no smell in the air to give away another presence.

The growl in the alley on that first day, and now this. She wants to be the fierce and fiery warrior Sua needs her to be—that Zisu, Nanshaie, and Tinanna need her to be, but every instinct tells her to run. So she does. She races back up the tunnel, searching for the hole she jumped through.

Just as she gets there, something on the ground catches her eye. Ears pricked listening for danger, she takes a tentative step toward the object on the ground, slowly plucking it from the ground. It's heavy in her hand: a ring with the royal seal emblazoned on it. But more than that, it has Ashur's personal crest on it engraved on the inside.

There is only one person who would have this ring, and it would be Ashur himself.

Sari wishes they had brought the camels with them; they would have been a source of food. But drinkable water is better than nothing, and Tinanna had found a building that had a cache of canned goods. After much debate, they agree to try it. They risk a small fire in the middle of the street to boil the water and cook the food; whatever enemies might still lurk in the streets might know their location, but they are too thirsty and hungry to go on without it. "We will be at the spire soon," Sari says, poking the embers. "We should sleep once more before we go, though."

"I am going to patrol," Tinanna says, not even the faintest hint of an accent.

"Oh! Can I come?" Zisu says, leaping to her feed. "Can you show me how to use those spinny circle dagger things? I want to learn!"

Sari bites back the urge to tell her sister no; she wants her sister here, where Sari knows she is safe. But nowhere in this ancient city is safe, and Tinanna is competent.

Tinanna looks Zisu up and down before nodding and handing her two of the throwing stars. Zisu bounds after her new mentor, leaving only Sari and Nanshaie to stare into the flames.

"I feel like I am holding you back," Nanshaie says, arms wrapped around her knees. "I interrupt your sleep; I cause you needless worry. Even Zisu contributes more than I do. I do not know why Ia asked that I come along. I cannot even properly help you with finding food."

"But you have been able to warn us of much danger," Sari says, not able to deny that Nanshaie has contributed a lot of strife to the mission.

"And what came of that? I warned you, but it changed nothing. It altered nothing. It did not help at all."

Sari pokes the fire again. This is why her troops didn't listen to her; she doesn't know how to relate to others. "Your Sight has never helped anyone?"

"No. I foresaw death when I was four and before that, a dozen smaller tragedies. My family and my village thought I was cursed; I was kicked out while I was still just a qit. No one in the village would take me in."

There are many things that Sari wants to say. Love is not something that parents need to give their qits; it's not something the qatu should bother with at all. The calla might cling to it, taking up the habits of the lohyue, but the qatu of Sua are fierce and feral. "What did you do?"

"I nearly died in the desert, but I was found by a priestess who recognized my Sight and took me to the Temple. Ia was assigned to care for me while I recovered, and then she became something of a mentor."

Ah, it makes sense now. Ia might have been a mother-figure to Nanshaie. No wonder she trusts the High Priestess.

"I thought Ia loved me; she protected me from the other gray robes who bullied me for my nightmares and screaming. But—" Nanshaie buries her face between her arms.

"But she is not who she says she is." Sari leans back and looks up at the dome. When they trekked across the desert, Ia kept saying that the stars would show her the way; there were no stars here, however.

"Yes." Nanshaie looks up again, wiping her tears on her arm. "Am I her pawn? What role did she want for me? Why did she lie to me? Did she ever love me?"

Love is not something you should aspire for, Sari wants to say. But there is a small voice in the back of her head asking a similar question. *Why isn't anyone loyal to me...* She bites her lip and says nothing.

The silence is heavy, but Sari does not know how to lift it, so she lays down.

"What was it like growing up as a mat'sahr'dan? Living in the beautiful isi'tu?"

"Terrible," Sari says without thinking.

Nanshaie straightens, knitting her brows. "What do you mean? Did you not have all the time to play and do whatever you pleased?"

"No, it was training and fighting. And I was never strong enough to both win the fights and protect Zisu."

"Fights?"

"The Sitnu," Sari says, frustrated that she has to elaborate for Nanshaie. "In the iseru."

"I do not know what that is. I am sorry," Nanshaie says, looking away.

Sari hesitates, wanting to explain to Nanshaie, wanting to open up about the torment she endured in the arena. But she's already been too open with Nanshaie. She needs to be strong; she does not want Nanshaie to think any less of her, to think that she is weak. "Never mind, I am going to try to sleep." She rolls to her side, not wanting to see the hurt she knows will be in Nanshaie's eyes.

"No!"

Sari rolls her eyes and flips back over, ready to scold Nanshaie.

But Nanshaie's hand shoots up in the air, looking frantically in all directions; eyes wide. "A kahbush'a! It's coming."

"A kahbush'a? Nanshaie, those are myths. What are you talking about?"

"No, it's real," she says, voice shaking, ears pricked straight up. "It's coming."

"I don't hear anything," Sari says, sitting up and holding her breath, not wanting to miss any sound. "There's nothing." She leaps to her feet and taking a few steps outside of the shelter.

Claws tear into her back—agony and fire down her spine—and she is dragged out into the street by a giant beast, the roar echoing down the empty streets and drowning out her screams.

Saritrah hits the ground with a thud, her back a mess of torn flesh and blood scraping against the cold stone street. She gasps for air, her mind racing as the massive kahbush'a looms over her, raising one of its long limbs for another strike.

Nanshaie grabs Sari's spear, swinging it at the beast. But the attacks only enraging the creature further.

"Toss it to me!" Sari shouts, struggling to stand, hoping that the beast standing between her and Nanshaie is the only one.

Nanshaie nods, hurling the spear over the creature's back.

Sari catches it, grunting as the movement further aggravates her bleeding wounds.

Nanshaie grabs a stick from their campfire and throws it at the kahbush'a. The flames catch the creature's attention, but it does not even flinch in pain.

Sari grits her teeth, ignoring the pain in her back, and lunges forward, thrusting the spear with all her might into the kahbush'a's thick hide while it is distracted by Nanshaie.

But the spear's tip merely breaks off. She tumbles to the ground, her ankle twisting painfully as she falls. Wincing, Sari scrambles back, realizing with a sinking feeling that they have no hope of defeating this monstrous beast in direct combat.

"Nanshaie, we have to run!" she shouts.

The kahbush'a lets out an earth-shaking roar, its red eyes locked on the two women. Sari grabs Nanshaie's arm, pulling her away from the advancing creature and they flee down the ancient streets, the thunderous footfalls of the monstrous kahbush'a shaking the ground behind them. Her back burns with agony and her ankle pulses with intense pain, but she pushes that aside, focused solely on putting as much distance between them and the beast as possible.

Sari looks over her shoulder. The kahbush'a's massive tail whips back and forth, shattering a glass window in one of the buildings as they race past.

"We can't outrun it!" Nanshaie pants, her voice trembling with fear. "It's too fast!"

Sari's mind races, searching for any possible escape. There has to be something they can do, some way to lose this relentless predator. She scans the area, looking for anything that could help them. "The broken window... If we can loop back around, or get past it somehow—"

Nanshaie nods and removes one of her bracelets, tossing it at the beast. The monster distracted; Sari and Nanshaie run back towards it, slipping behind it and leaping through the jagged glass of the building. Sari hits the floor hard, shards of glass embedding themselves in her skin, but she holds back her scream.

"We have to keep moving," she says, her voice strained, grabbing Nanshaie's hand and pulling her up.

The kahbush'a roars and slams its massive paw against the wall, but the building does not move or shake. Sari grabs Nanshaie's hand, and they race down the dark corridor. The thuds of the creature bashing itself into the wall still echo behind them.

"Up there," Nanshaie says, pointing to the faintly illuminated staircase at the end of the corridor. Sari nods, the pain in her ankle and back becoming unbearable. She cannot ever remember an injury this painful, not at the hands of Aishah, or Ashur, or even her father. But she focuses on the only thing that matters right now: survival.

Survival, and hope that there is not another one of the creatures chasing Zisu and Tinanna.

They climb flight after flight of stairs while the monster throws itself against the building, but Sari does not feel safe stopping yet.

"I can't go any…" Nanshaie says as she collapses.

Sari does not protest, for once, her mind does not fill with insults, she does not begrudge Nanshaie's lack of strength, she does not feel completed to call her weak or mock her, the way her parents would do when she would fail to keep up during training. She puts one arm under Nanshaie's knees and throws her arm over her shoulder. She carries the Oracle up the rest of that flight of stairs and when they get to the landing, she searches for a safe room to set down the fatigued priestess.

"This should be safe for now," she says, setting Nanshaie down in a chair and then bracing a shelf against the door to the room. She closes her eyes and listens for the thudding, but it's gone. Has the creature given up on getting inside and gone somewhere else? She finds a window and peers outside. The creature is scaling the building, its thick claws digging into the hard stone walls, leaving deep gouges in the otherwise perfect exterior.

There is no escape; this is how she will die. She could not save her people, she could not save herself, and she will not be able to save Zisu and Nanshaie. Ia led them into a trap, and she wishes she knew what the High Priestess's ultimate goal was, but it's too late to ask.

"Nanshaie," she whispers, not sure how to convey what she is sure the Oracle has already seen.

A flash of silver distracts her; something small whizzes by the window—small and fast and aimed directly at the lumbering beast.

Whatever it is hits the beast in the middle of the jugular, somehow piercing its skin, purple blood oozing out of its throat and down the side of the building.

"Nanshaie, I don't know what just happened but—"

"—Tinanna," Nanshaie says without leaving her spot or even opening her eyes.

Sari looks out the window again, and that's when she sees them—Zisu and Tinanna standing on top of an adjacent building.

THIRTEEN

A S THEY APPROACH THE TOWERING SPIRE at the heart of this beautiful, terrifying city, Zisu stops to wonder at it, mouth hanging open in awe.

"I've never seen anything like this. Not even the isi'tu compares. How do you think they did it? The panels of stained glass are so large... Oh! And look at these engravings running all the way up... How long do you think that took?"

"It doesn't matter," Sari says, checking the point of her spear one more time. "The people who did it are dead, and no one even remembers their names."

"Do you think, when you are Sahre'Danu, that you could have something like this built?"

Sari looks at the spire again, taking in the details this time. The stone is so finely placed that she cannot even see cracks, and the gold ribbons that spiral around it and upwards appear to be one long string. "I'll see." She wishes she could promise her sister more than that.

She does not know how to handle this moment. If she were a general, Tinanna, Nanshaie, and Zisu her lieutenants, and the spire a town she was about to seize, she would give a speech about loyalty, dedication, and honor. But she left her army behind, and this is not a siege. She knows she should say something, though. But what?

They survived the soldiers at the gate, they survived the lumbering kahbush'a, they survived the arduous journey through both desert and deserted city. But the last time she gave a speech to soldiers under her command...

She had killed those soldiers, and a dozen times during this journey, her overconfidence, her impatience, and her anger had almost killed *these* companions, too.

What could she possibly say to them? What words could she utter? Their goal is within reach;, they have made it to the spire at the center of the city and within it lay the object that will grant her the power to take back Sua from the insurrectionists who are trying to destroy it and protect it from her brother who seeks to subjugate it. Will it be worth it? Worth all that she gave up; all the deaths she caused...

"Well, let's go then! I want to see what's inside!" Zisu claps her hands and rushes to the towering, glass doors, pulling on the handles with both hands.

Sari sighs; as much as she loves Zisu, she would be a terrible lieutenant, and a worse soldier.

"Be careful!" Sari shakes her head and follows Zisu, spear ready if there are any strange soldiers. It's been just as lifeless the last few days of their travels. The nightmare creature, defeated by Tinanna, had proven edible. But while they were grateful for a reprieve from their hunger, none of them were eager to encounter another one. Thankfully, they hadn't.

But Sari does not believe this city is done tormenting them yet.

She steps inside and shivers. The center of the spire is almost entirely hollow, with a giant purple tree planted right in the middle. The ceiling of the spire extends all the way up, culminating in a magnificent pane of stained glass. The spire's walls are lined with bookshelves, laden with countless tomes and volumes of knowledge, while on the edges of the space, a spiral staircase winds up to the upper levels. The awe-inspiring sight of the spire's interior is enough to leave Sari spellbound. She cranes her neck, noting that each level of the spire has numerous doors; thousands of rooms that could be hiding the Heart of Aodhe.

"It's a library," Nanshaie says, approaching the purple tree and setting her bag on the desk to its side. "Or a university? It reminds me of Khidima Alam."

Zisu sprints to one of the shelves, pulling books off at random and flipping through them.

"You've been there?" Sari asks. The sparkling university, one of Sua's greatest jewels and long considered the best university in all of Ahnlisen, was once extremely selective in whom they would admit as students, as well as whom they let visit. Zisu had always wanted to attend one day; and Sari would see to it that she did, when all of this was over. But Sari herself has hoped to at least visit; she could spend a year learning about historical battles, weaponry, the art of forging iron into steel, and learn from some of the greatest minds in the land about politics and law. The university used to be exclusive to those of sahre'danu, sahre, or isiaq lineage. But the insurrectionists had changed that; now, it is open to almost anyone with enough intelligence and determination.

"Only once," Nanshaie said, words tinged with sorrow, tracing her finger along the edge of the desk. "With the previous Oracle. It was just a few days, but I wish I could have stayed there."

"Oh, tell me more!" Zisu says, rejoining them, clutching a tome. "I want to go there so badly. I want to learn to be an orator! I want to recite all of the great epics! I will write one myself one day about this adventure."

"We should move," Tinanna says, hand hovering over her belt. "We need to find the Heart quickly."

"Where should we start?" Nanshaie asks.

"Up," Sari says. She does not know why she believes it is at the top, but something is tugging her that way. She wonders if the Seers' visions feel even a little like this mysterious sensation in her chest. "We go up."

"Can I take this one with me?" Zisu asks flipping through a book.

If it were anyone else, Sari would have scolded them. But she merely nods and beckons for her companions to follow her. Zisu places the book in her sack and scurries after them.

The stairs go on forever, and their progress is slow. Nanshaie constantly asks for breaks, apologizing profusely. "Of course," is all Sari says to the Oracle every time she asks. "If you need a break, we will take one."

Each break, they find a small room on that floor and relax. Nanshaie chooses a book from a shelf, finds a table to sit at, and attempts to read the strange script, Zisu taking a spot next to her peering over her shoulder.

"Can you actually read them?" Sari asks as they settle in for another break. This room is more like an alcove; barely enough room for the four of them, with just one desk and two chairs. She spreads out her feet before her on the floor and pulls out her flask of water, taking a long drink before passing it to Nanshaie.

"Not really. Some of them I can understand a little bit. I think this one is just a long complaint about some copper merchant. But look at them!" She holds up one of the large tomes. "They are so well preserved! The parchment is nearly perfect, and there is not even a single ink splotch! No running ink or faded words. Even the ones that are illuminated, the colors are still vibrant."

"Everything in this city is so perfect, almost like a dream," Zisu says, eyes still focused on the book that Nanshaie has in her lap.

Nanshaie jerks her head up. "Because that is what it is," she says, her voice once again sounding like it belongs to someone else, somewhere else, or some time else. "A beautiful dream."

Sari tries to push the unease from her mind, pulling out a strip of jerky to distract herself. "We should get going."

"Oh, yes. I am sorry," Nanshaie says, setting the book back on the shelf. Zisu runs a finger down the spine as if reading the embossed title.

Sari slings her bag over her shoulder again and stands up, checking to ensure she did not drop anything.

"Wait," Nanshaie says. "There's one over there I want to look at. There's something about it—"

Sari rolls her eyes, her patience finally wearing out. "We don't have time. We can come back later." She opens the door to the alcove and steps out into the open staircase, glancing up and down the hollow center of the spire while waiting for Nanshaie to follow.

A low, guttural growl reverberates through the spire, a rumbling that sets Sari's fur on end. Another echoes it before a chilling howl pierces the air.

"Run!" Sari says, drawing her spear and looking up and down the spiraling stairs again, searching for the source.

The Oracle does not respond. Sari glances over her shoulder, and Nanshaie has the book open in her hands, eyes rapidly moving back and forth over the text. "Nanshaie!"

"She won't move," Zisu says, pulling on the Oracle's elbow.

Sari bites her lip. "Zisu, stay there with her. Close the door and barricade it if you can. Tinanna, with me."

Tinanna pulls a dagger from her belt and nods. It only took a few seconds for the kahbush'a to appear while Sari was distracted. Where it had come from, Sari can only guess, but it is now halfway up the purple tree at the center of the spire.

It has the clever eyes of the qatu, with long, thin ears and a lashing tail. It moves with the agility, the grace, and the dexterity that is only found in the felinesque race from Sua, leaping from branch to branch. But most unsettling of all is the intelligence it possesses.

In one swift movement, it leaps from the tree and lands on all four in front of them.

But it does not pounce on them immediately; its eyes are focused, assessing and appraising them with unnerving patience, and its claws extend and retract like it is considering its actions. The cleverness behind its eyes is nothing like the wild hunger of the kahbush'a they had previously encountered and it unnerves Sari.

She tries to take a deep breath as she squares her shoulders and bounces on the balls of her feet, but she regrets it; the creature smells of day-old meat that's been left in the heat. It hisses at them, and in that hiss, Sari swears she hears her own name.

It knows me. She cannot figure out why, but she believes it nonetheless; *this creature is intelligent, and it knows who I am.*

Sari steadies herself, feet in position to lunge at the beast and strike the steel point of her spear into its eye, hoping that she can at least incapacitate it.

She narrows her eyes, assessing the kahbush'a's movements. Tinanna moves silently beside her, her daggers held at the ready. The kahbush'a growls and crouches low, muscles coiled and ready to spring.

"Now!" Sari shouts, lunging forward with her spear.

The beast reacts with lightning speed, twisting away from the strike and landing on all four with a poise that is distinctly qatu. Sari curses.

Tinanna darts in, her daggers slicing through the air. But the kahbush'a parries the attack with a swipe of its massive paw, knocking a dagger from Tinanna's hand.

Sari thrusts her spear again, aiming for the creature's flank. It howls as the steel tip pierces its side—*at least this one has a thinner hide than the one that chased us through the city*—then whirls around and sinks its teeth into the shaft of the spear.

Sari grits her teeth, struggling to yank the spear free without breaking it. The creature stares at her as she struggles, and its eyes once again look far too sentient, too patient, too calculating.

Tinanna rushes in, a dagger in one hand and a rope in the other. She leaps onto the beast's back, pulling the rope around its neck and yanking hard. The kahbush'a thrashes, releasing Sari's spear.

Sari stumbles back, gasping. The kahbush'a roars, rearing up on its hind legs. "It's neck!" Tinanna screams as the monster's head is pulled back, exposing its jugular.

Sari grabs the dagger Tinanna had dropped. She's not as skilled at projectile weapons as she is with a spear, but it will have to do. She squares her shoulders and hurls it, praying to whatever god will listen that her aim is true.

The dagger finds its mark, and brown-red blood sputters from the kahbush'a's neck, staining the pristine marble floor and splattering on the glimmering walls and shelves.

Sari swallows. "I really hope that there is only one of these things in here."

Tinanna releases the rope and leaps back down, tail flicking. She pulls her dagger from the creature's throat and shakes her head.

"Well, we should return to the others," Sari says trying not the look one last time into the eyes of the beast.

They stalk down the narrow corridor quietly, but before they can knock on the door, Nanshaie screams.

"Zisu!? Nanshaie!" Sari pulls on the handle, but the door won't open.

"I'm fine!" Zisu says. "But Nanshaie... I don't know what happened. She was reading a book, and then she just screamed and fainted."

Zisu unlocks the door and slides the large desk out of the way, letting Sari and Tinannan in. Nanshaie is sprawled on the floor, mouth open and eyes closed; the book she had been reading still open on the floor beside her. Tinanna rushes to her side, setting her head in her lap, and gently runs her hands through Nanshaie's hair, stopping to stroke just behind her ear. For the second time, Sari wishes she had thought to offer comfort to the Oracle first. But she pushes aside the traitorous thought.

The Oracle speaks without opening her eyes or acknowledging the presence of anyone else. "This city is a dream, the memory of a place that long ago fell into decay and ruin, obliterated when caught in the crossfires of the war between the Araelta and the Blodheimr Hjart. The fall of Escnea was merciless; their paradise torn apart by the greed of others. Elpace, Bec... All gone."

"What does that mean?" Sari asks, knowing already that she won't get an answer.

"She won't say anything else," Zisu says, not looking up at Sari. "She's just been saying that over and over while she read the book, and then she screamed... I think it's a line from the book she was reading..."

Sari picks up the book, squinting at the pages as she leafs through them, hoping something will stand out to her. But nothing does.

"The old lady showed me, she told me. What Ia has seen... Ia did not see the future; she saw the past before... before the war." Nanshaie says, this time her voice more her own. But she is still on the floor, Tinanna's fingers still

There's too much information for Sari to comprehend, to sift through, to analyze. Too many names she does not recognize in what Nanshaie is saying, but the one thing that stans out to her is that Ia was wrong about something. She has to stay focused on the only thing that matters. Getting the Heart and getting out with her companions alive. "Where does the Heart of Aodhe fit in? Is it even here? If Ia lied—is the Heart even here?"

Nanshaie rolls over, turning away from Sari and burying her face in Tinanna's camise, sobbing.

Sari grabs Nanshaie's shoulder, trying to roll her back over. "I need to know!"

Tinanna shoves Sari, glaring at her, before scooping the distressed Oracle into her arms again.

Sari needs to punch something, stab something, kill something. "Fine. I'm going to make sure the way ahead is clear."

She flicks her tail and leaves, not caring that her sister is calling after her. She takes the stairs two at a time, her tail swishing as she runs up the tight spiral. At each floor, she loops around the hallway, listening down the corridors and then dashes up to the next floor, searching for more of the beasts, listening for any sound that is not her own heart or footsteps.

She loses count of how many floors she climbs, she isn't even sure she knows what floor her companions are on or if she would know it if it weren't for the remains of the monster. But she doesn't care. She can't get the image of Tinanna and Nanshaie out of her head. Their closeness, the protectiveness Tinanna has for Nanshaie. A protectiveness that isn't borne of duty or loyalty, but something else. Something Sari does not want to consider.

Her thoughts are abruptly interrupted by the horror she finds as she reaches the top of another flight of stairs. Scattered across the floor are the tattered remains of leather armor and ripped clothing, all the distinctive reds and yellows of Ashur's army. Yet she smells no blood, sees no torn limbs, and they had heard no wails of the dying. There are no remains to tell the tale of what tragedy befell these soldiers.

She picks up one of the yellow sashes; badges and embroidery denoting the many acts of bravery that this officer carried out in the name of Ashur. A warrior this decorated would not have gone down easily, and would not have abandoned the rest of the troops to an ugly demise.

Not only is Ashur here, but something else is, too. Something possibly something far, far worse than she already suspects. She has too many questions: why is Ashur here, how did he find it, what does he know, and how does he know it? And most importantly, what else is here with them?

As much as she hates him and his soldiers, anyone who fight to defend a Sahre'Danu, deserves a proper end. These soldiers—wrongly—believed they were defending a rightful monarch. And whatever fate met them here does not seem like it was anything honorable.

Her ears prick up, all of her fur standing on end. Something does not feel right; the way the air moves through the spire is unnatural; something that prickles across her skin and settles in her bones; something screaming at her to *run*. She leaps over the railing and onto the tree, skittering down its branches, something in her mind screaming at her that she needs to run, she needs to flee. She's a warrior, a feral and fierce fighter. Fleeing should not be in her repertoire.

She leaps from the tree, over the railing, and down the hall, entering the room with her companions, and slams the door behind her.

Nanshaie recovers but refuses to say anything more about whatever she learned or saw. She shoves the tome she had been reading into her bag, claiming it is too important to leave behind.

They carry on as if nothing had happened. But Sari does not warn her companions about the torn clothing she had found earlier, a mistake she only realizes in hindsight.

"What is this?" Zisu says, picking up a torn leather bracer and sniffing it. "What happened here? This is Ashur's standard." She runs her finger along the pyrographed seal on the edge of the bracer. "What is this doing here?"

Nanshaie shivers, grabbing Tinanna's hand and pulling her close. "Don't ask questions you don't want to know the answer to. Let's just keep going."

But three more levels up, they find something even worse.

"Oh my gosh," Zisu says before vomiting.

The hallway and corridors are littered with destroyed armor and shredded clothing. But this time, there are tufts of wet fur and deep claw marks etched into the walls and floor, the otherwise elegant library now desecrated by something horrific.

"I want to go home, now," Zisu says, still clenching her stomach and dry heaving.

"No, we have to keep going. Pretend you don't see this."

"I can't pretend I never saw this, Sari! What if whatever happened to these... What if at the top... We can't. I won't," Zisu says through shaking sobs. "I don't care what the High Priestess said! I can't be here!"

You have to be willing to give up everything; you have to be ruthless. That is what their mother had drilled into them. Do not love people, do not cherish items, do not value anything more highly than you value securing and holding the title of Sahre'Danu. To do otherwise was to have a weakness that could be exploited.

Zisu is my weakness, she always has been.

She can turn around, she can lead them out of this haunted city, she can give up on the Heart of Aodhe, and she can learn to live under either Ashur's reign or the insurrectionists' rule. She can keep Zisu safe from whatever might lurk at the top of the spire. She can give up everything to keep Zisu safe.

Or she can continue on and make the world safe for Zisu. "We keep going. Come on."

Nanshaie tilts her head to the side and glances between Zisu and Sari.

"Something wrong?" Sari asks, raising an eyebrow.

"Ia might have lied, but..." Nanshaie closes her eyes and takes a deep breath; her voice laced with a hint of a strange echo. "But Zisu is here now, and we must press forward. We cannot let Ashur get the Heart."

"Right," Sari says. "Let's go."

They press forward, but the closer they get to the top, the more oppressive the air feels; something crawls across Sari's skin, like the strange sensation before a sandstorm. But they keep moving.

They reach the top; a massive observation deck enclosed on all sides by crystalline glass with a beautiful, massive wrought-gold telescope taking up much of the center of the platform. But just past it stands a tall, cloaked figure.

She does not have to guess who it is. She recognizes his scent immediately.

"Sister dearest," Ashur says, throwing back the hood, holding the Katynna in one hand and his own blade, Rasabu, in the other. "I did not expect to see you, but I probably should have." He sheaths both blades and pulls a stone out of his pocket. She does not need to be told what it is: The Heart of Aodhe. It is unlike any gem she has ever seen before, smooth but multi-faceted, opaque but radiating light, and shimmering as if it were carved from the night sky. "Is this what you were after?"

Sari grits her teeth, not sure what she wants to do first: steal back Katynna, snatch the Heart of Aodhe from his hand, or smack the grin off of his face.

"And who are your companions? Is that our sister I spy behind you? If I had known you were both coming, I would have had my soldiers dress more appropriately."

"Give me the stone, and I won't slaughter you here and now," Sari says, ears flat against her head.

"You never want to take time to exchange pleasantries, do you? You need to learn diplomacy, sister dearest. You haven't even told me how it is that you came to find Zisu alive. I'm dying to hear that story."

Sari readjusts her grip on her spear and calculates the distance between her and Ashur, wondering if he is still as strong as he was on the day they attacked the capital, or if he also lost some weight while making the journey here. "Shut up."

"Well, if you won't be polite, it is my job as your older brother to make a good example." He claps his hands. "My soldiers will make you quite comfortable. They always do their best to make sure my honored guests never have to lift a finger again."

Footsteps echo up the stairs behind them. But they aren't footsteps, more like pounding. Sari whips around to see not an army of qatu, but a horde of kabush'a racing up toward them.

But they all have red and yellow sashes. She glances back at Ashur. "Oh my gosh, what—"

"Isn't this gem amazing? I've made my soldiers stronger, faster, deadlier. I've heightened their instincts, sharpened their claws, and worsened their bites." He tosses the Heart into the air and then catches it again.

The Heart can transform qatu into kahbush'a...

Heedless of the danger, Sari lunges at Ashur, hoping that Tinanna and Zisu can handle the monstrosities on their own and that Nanshaie can at least stay out of the way.

She hurtles towards him, the smooth wooden shaft familiar in her calloused hands. Her eyes narrow as she faces Ashur, waiting to see if he is willing to let the beasts kill her rather than taking that honor for himself.

"Let's play, sister dearest," he says and draws both Katynna and Rasabu, parrying her thrust before the point of her spear can even make contact with him.

She shuffles backwards, regaining her footing and balance, bracing for his attack.

He lunges at her, both blades slicing close to her face. She barely has time to raise her spear to counter. Her tail lashes back and forth, ears pinned against her head as she grits her teeth, she shoves him away.

He circles her, ignoring the growls and hisses of his soldiers as they battle her companions. "Is that all you've got, little sister?" Ashur taunts, his blades a blur as he blocks her incoming attack. "I expected more from the so-called Mar'sahr'dan'i."

Sari says nothing, her jaw clenched tight as she pivots and thrusts her spear toward his midsection. Ashur dances back, laughing. "Still as reckless as ever, aren't you, dear sister?" he taunts. "You never did have the discipline or the patience for leadership."

"Shut up," she growls, taking a quick second to wipe the sweat from her brow.

"Half your soldiers were reporting to me this entire time," he sneers. "You're a pathetic excuse for a leader if you couldn't even see the traitors in your midst."

A growl rumbles in Sari's throat as she feints left, then whirls right, the steel tip of her spear leaving a shallow cut along Ashur's bicep. He hisses, yellow eyes narrowing. She remembers all the tokens of the insurrectionists she had found in her soldiers bags. Were they to throw her off the scent? Distract her? Lead her down the wrong path? She tries to clear her head, to focus on the present. But he won't let her.

"And look at you now," Ashur continues, his blades clashing against Sari's spear once again. "Reduced to scraping by with a handful of followers. You're nothing, Sari. Just a feral beast playing at being a leader."

"Shut up!" She takes a few steps back, almost losing her balance.

"You think you can defeat me? You're nothing but a monster, sister dearest. As soon as Zisu realizes the truth, she'll leave you, too."

Sari's vision blurs with unshed tears of rage as she launches into a relentless offensive, her spear a whirlwind of flashing steel. But her anger has made her sloppy, her strikes growing wilder and more erratic with each failed attempt to strike Ashur.

He cackles, batting away her attacks with almost lazy ease. "I was born to lead, while you were born a disappointment. Surrender now, and I may show you mercy when I take the throne."

Gritting her teeth, Sari is forced back onto the defensive, her spear a blur as she desperately tries to deflect the punishing onslaught of Ashur's blades.

She takes a deep breath; she doesn't have to defeat him. Not right now. She just has to get the Heart of Aodhe from him and escape with Zisu, Tinanna, and Nanshaie alive. She doesn't have to prove anything to him. This is not the iseru. *This is not the Sitnu, we are not in the iseru. I don't have to win, I just have to survive.*

Sari sees an opening and grazes the tip of her spear across the leather halter that secures the Heart of Aodhe to his belt; it clatters to the floor and rolls away from them. Sari dives, grabbing it, terrified that it will shatter. She pulls it to her chest, clutching it tightly. *Victory!*

She steadies her breathing, focusing again on her surroundings. The roars of the kahbush'a have ceased, and from the corner of her eye, she spots Tinanna pulling a dagger from the throat of one of them. *We've won.*

Her moment of celebration is shattered when Nanshaie screams. She pounces to her feet and whirls around. Ashur is holding Nanshaie, a dagger digging into her neck. "Give that back, sister dearest."

"Let her go!" Sari shouts, voice cracking.

"Oh? Do you care about her? Tsk tsk. What would mother say?"

"Let her go, or I'll use it!" She holds up the Heart of Aodhe, but she has no idea how to use it or if she even can.

"That's cute, sister dearest. Very cute. Now give it back, and I won't slit her throat." He presses the knife deeper, drawing a drop of blood.

"That's the Oracle, if you kill her…"

"If I kill her, another will be found. And I can make sure the next one is loyal only to me."

She knows her brother; he will do it. She takes a step forward, and he wraps his hand tighter around the knife.

Tears are welling in Nanshaie's eyes, but she does not say a word, not even mumbling a prayer. Sari drops the Heart to the ground and kicks it toward Ashur. "Release her!"

One hand still holding Nanshaie's wrist, he picks up the Heart, laughing. "Oh, that's interesting. I did not know our parents raised such a failure. You don't just care about her, you—"

"Release her! You promised!"

"I promised she would die if you did not give back the Heart. Nothing more than that."

Both Tinanna and Sari lunge at him, weapons raised. But there is a flash of light, and the room fills with smoke. As it clears, Ashur, Nanshaie, and even the bodies of the slain beasts are gone. There are no claw marks on the ground, no scattered books or shredded clothing; it is as if no quarrel took place, and Ashur had never been here.

Sari runs to the window, leaning out and gazing at the expansive city, searching the streets for any movement.

Asher's laugh echoes in the wind.

Sari turns back to Tinanna, who is clutching a bloody arm. "You're hurt."

"It's nothing," Tinanna says, gritting her teeth. "Just a scratch. I'll be fine."

"Was that done by Ashur?" Sari asks, she crosses the room in a leap, and pulls back Tinanna's hand. The wound is deep, the edges turning purple. She does not need to wait for Tinanna to answer her. This wound was made by Ashur's blade. His poisoned blade.

"I'll be fine," Tinanna says again. "Let's just get out of here and find where Ashur went."

"No, you need medical attention!" Sari insists. Some part of her is screaming to just leave Tinanna here, leave her to die. To move on, get Zisu to safety, find Ashur. Tinanna was the one careless enough to get hurt, and Sari should not have room in her army for someone weak enough to fall. But even as the thought crosses her mind, her stomach lurches. She can't leave Tinanna behind. She can't. "That's poisoned, and it's fast-acting. We need to find you a healer."

"She's right," Zisu says. "Ashur does not let his prey live, just one scratch..."

"This wasn't from his blade, one of the kahbush'a did this."

"That is probably worse," Zisu says, shaking her head.

Tinanna stops dead in her tracks. "Fine," she finally says and turns away, stumbling but not letting Sari help her.

"We need to get back out of the city and find a village that has a competent healer," Sari says, picking up Nanshaie's bags.

"It took us days just to get through the city..." Zisu mumbles.

Sari glares at her. "We should move more quickly then. Come on."

Saritrah watches with concern as Tinanna stubbornly refuses her help, the wounded woman's steps growing more unsteady with each passing moment. She exchanges a worried glance with Zisu.

Tinanna says nothing, her jaw set in a hard line, but Saritrah can see the strain in her features. Gripping her bags tightly, Tinanna leads the way out of the spire, Saritrah and Zisu flanking her on either side in case she falters.

As they descend the winding stairs, Sari's mind races. Ashur has the Heart of Aodhe, Nanshaie is in his clutches, and now Tinanna is gravely injured, poisoned by one of those nightmarish kahbush'a creatures. She curses under her breath, wondering how everything has gone so wrong, so quickly.

Sari grips Tinanna's good arm, supporting her weight as they make their way back through the eerily quiet streets of Bec. Zisu walks ahead, clutching Nanshaie's belongings tightly, her head swiveling warily for any sign of more danger.

"We need to move faster," Sari says, her brow creased with concern. "The poison is spreading." She can see the sickly purple hue creeping up Tinanna's arm, the wound oozing a dark, viscous liquid.

Tinanna nods, jaw clenched, and forces her legs to move faster despite the obvious agony it causes her. "I'll be fine," she grits out. "We have to find Nanshaie and stop Ashur."

"We will," Sari promises. "But we cannot do that if you are too sick to fight."

The journey back through the city feels interminable, every step a struggle against the growing weakness in Tinanna's limbs. Sari can see the beads of sweat on her companion's brow and the tremor in her hands. "Izmyri," Tinanna says as they stop once again on their way out of the city. "I think they will have someone who can help…"

"That's days away," Zisu says. "And we have no idea if the camels are even still at the entrance…And even with camels…"

Sari's brow furrows as she weighs her options. Every moment they delay is another moment Ashur gains distance, slipping farther from her grasp, and making who knows how many more of his monster-solider hyrbrids. But the thought of leaving Tinanna behind, injured and poisoned, sits ill with her.

She glances at the wounded woman, who is fading quickly. Tinanna has proven herself a capable fighter, her skills with blade and stealth far surpassing what one would expect from a temple priestess. But even as she allows herself to think of Tinanna as a trusted ally for just a moment, doubts resurface. How much of what Tinanna has told them is truth? Like the others, she is hiding secrets, guarding something she does not want others to know.

Can she really trust any of her supposed allies? Sari's grip tightens on the hilt of her dagger as her gaze flicks to Zisu. Her own sister has secrets now, the circumstances of her life these past years a mystery still. A heavy sigh escapes her lips. Everyone has deceived her to some degree, even Arishaki.

Tinanna sways on her feet And Sari reahes out, grabbing her arm to steady her. As much as she longs to give chase after Ashur, to rescue Nanshaie and wrest the Heart of Aodhe from his grasp, she cannot abandon an injured companion. Not when Tinanna may still prove a valuable ally in the battles to come. Steeling her resolve, Saritrah loops Tinanna's uninjured arm around her shoulders.

"Izmyri it is," she says through gritted teeth. "But we cannot afford any delay. Every second brings Ashur closer to his goals." *And my demise.*

Their camels are not there at the entrance when they finally make it out of the city and the cave that led to it, but Zisu disappears for an hour, telling Sari she knows where to find some. Sari has no strength to argue with her sister and sets up a small camp for herself and Tinanna, washing her wound and forcing her to eat.

When Zisu comes back, she somehow has three healthy and well-fed camels, a large pack of dried meats, several canteens of water, and a stern warning for Sari to not ask questions.

They do not pause, they do not take breaks; Sari keeps pushing, hoping the camels do not collapse from exhaustion as they exit the crevices in the plateau. Hours pass, and the sun sets, but they keep going.

Not long after sunset, Tinanna falls from her camel and fades into unconsciousness. Sari throws Tinanna over her own camel in front of her, balancing speed with not jostling the priestess off of the camel.

"We're still days away," Zisu says. "Is she going to make it?"

Sari does not answer her sister; she does not know how to. They do their best during breaks to try to keep the priestess hydrated, but Sari is afraid that before her journey is over, none of the priestesses she set out with will be alive.

The walls of Izmyri finally come into view, a welcome sight after days of hard riding across the unforgiving desert. Sari urges her camel onwards, her jaw set. Beside her, Zisu keeps pace, her own mount loping steadily over the sand.

They pass through the city gates, the clopping of hooves on cobblestone replacing the muffled footfalls in the dunes. Sari scans the cramped streets and bustling market stalls, searching for any building bearing the symbol of Aydras, patron goddess of healers. She needs to find a healer, and quickly.

At last, a modest establishment with a swinging sign catches her eye. Sari pulls her camel to a halt outside and slides off. "You there!" she barks at the innkeeper loitering by the door. "Where is the nearest healer?"

The man raises an eyebrow, his brows knitting. "Well, now, that's no way to ask for help, miss."

Zisu dismounts gracefully beside Sari. "Please forgive my sister," she says with a smile. "We've had a difficult journey. Our companion is gravely ill—could you point us towards a skilled healer?"

Sari shoots her sister an impatient glare but says nothing as the innkeeper considers them shrewdly. Finally, he jerks his thumb down the street. "Kalarah's place is two roads over. Can't miss the green door with the Aydras sigil carved in it."

"Thank you," Zisu says.

Sari pulls Tinanna from the camel, cradling the unconscious priestess in her arms. "Get us rooms here, Zisu. And the camels taken to a stable. I'll be back."

Saritrah strides through the crowded streets of Izmyri; her jaw clenched as she clutches the unconscious Tinanna in her arms. The city's sights and sounds blur around her—the bustling market stalls, the chatter of passersby, the rhythmic clop of hooves on cobblestone. Her singular focus remains finding a healer who can save the priestess's life.

She lets out a sigh of relief when she finally spots the healer. She forces the door open with her shoulder and hurries inside, not bothering with any greeting.

A middle-aged woman looks up from where she is tending to a patient on one of the larger beds. "How can I help you?" she asks, wiping her hands on her apron.

"My..." She struggles for the right words. "My friend. I think she has been poisoned."

The healer's brows knit as she takes in Tinanna's sickly appearance. "I see." She gestures to one of the empty beds. "Lay her there. What can you pay, miss... ?"

Saritrah's fists clench. Of course, the woman would ask about payment—healers rarely worked for free. But Saritrah has nothing of value to offer. "You may call me Damkina," Sari says, easily giving a false name. "My companion is Tinanna.But I don't have anything to pay you with," she admits through gritted teeth. "But please, you must help her. She's dying."

The healer's expression turns skeptical. "I see. And what makes you think I should provide my services for free?"

The healer's gaze flickers between Sari and Tinanna, considering. Finally, she sighs. "Very well. Lay her down, and I'll see what I can do." She gestures to one of the empty beds again. "But understand, I expect fair compensation once she's on the mend."

Saritrah nods tersely, relief warring with frustration as she lays Tinanna down on the bed. She can only hope the healer's skills will be enough to counteract the poison coursing through the priestess's veins. As Kalarah begins her examination, Saritrah steps back, her fingers tightening around the royal seal that hangs from her neck.

"Just hold on, Tinanna," she murmurs. "Don't you dare give up on me now."

"That necklace looks like it would pay for my services."

Sari freezes, wondering if the healer even knows what Sari is holding, and if so, if she suspects who Sari is.

Izmyri... Izmyri... Wasn't this one of the first cities to fall to the insurrectionists? Wasn't it one of the insurrectionists' early bases of operation? Their headquarters until they had taken the isi'tu? And Tinanna specifically requested to be brought here... "This is nothing of value," Sari says. "An old family heirloom, but the metal is cheap, and the stones are imitations. The only value it has is sentimental."

"If you cannot pay me," Kalarah says, putting an ear to Tinanna's chest, "then perhaps you can compensate me by helping me out."

"I only know the basics of first aid," Sari says.

"But you look strong. There's some wood out back. Chop it up for me. I'll need to boil some water."

"Very well," she says and turns towards the back door. Sari hesitates for a moment, a flicker of doubt crossing her features. What if Tinanna doesn't make it?

Shaking her head, Sari pushes the thought away and stalks towards the back of the healer's modest home. Her jaw is set, anger simmering just beneath the surface at having to perform menial labor in exchange for the healer's services. The rightful heir to the throne of Sua; chopping wood.

The chopping block sits in the small courtyard, stacked with untidy piles of firewood. Sari seizes the axe leaning against the wall and hefts it in her hands. With a grunt of effort, she swings it down, cleaving a thick log in two with a satisfying thunk.

As she works, her mind churns, anger and frustration fueling each swing of the axe. She is royalty, the one true heir to the Sahre'Danu. Her birthright has been stolen from her—first by the revolutionaries who overthrew her family and now by her wretched brother Ashur.

The memory of Ashur's mocking laughter echoes in her mind, stoking the flames of her fury. She can still see him clearly, basking in the power of the Heart of Aodhe. The way he had taunted her, mocked her...

Saritrah's grip tightens on the axe handle until her knuckles turn white. A low growl escapes her throat as she hacks at the logs with renewed vigor. One day, her brother will pay for his treachery. For stealing her birthright, for daring to claim power that is rightfully hers. Aishah had the most wins during the Sitnu when the insurrectionists attacked, he had been the heir. But she killed him. She took his life and with it she took the right to claim the throne. Ashur would have to kill her before he could ever be the rightful ruler. And he will pay for trying... and what he did to Zisu, both in the iseru and out of it.

Yes, Ashur will suffer for his crimes. She will see to it personally, watching as the life drains from his eyes while she wrenches the Heart of Aodhe from his grasp. And then... then she will finally take her place as Sahre'Danu and restore order to Sua.

But first, she must deal with the Araelta and this shadowy organization called the Blodheimr Hjart. Nanshaie's cryptic ramblings had hinted at their involvement in the downfall of the ancient civilization—the same cataclysm that had robbed the world of the Heart's power in the first place. If Sari is to wield its might and usher in a new era of peace and prosperity, she must eliminate any who would dare stand against her.

Sari brings the axe down in one final, vicious stroke, splitting the log clean in two. Her chest heaves with exertion, a bead of sweat trickling down her brow. Her path is clear now. First, she will find a way to heal Tinanna and rescue Nanshaie from Ashur's clutches. Then, she will hunt down the Araelta and the Blodheimr Hjart and destroy them utterly, leaving no threat to her reign.

Finally, when all her enemies lie crushed at her feet, she will claim the Heart of Aodhe as her own and take her rightful place on the throne of Sua. A cruel smile tugs at the corners of her lips. If even a fraction of the power Ashur displayed is true, she will be unstoppable. And this time, she vows, no one will stand in her way.

Saritrah shoulders the bundled firewood and heads back inside, her mind fixed on the path that lies ahead. She is the true heir—and she will stop at nothing to claim what is rightfully hers.

Zisu is sorting through Nanshaie's belongings when Sari arrives at the inn. Her sister had secured them a large enough room with two beds. A meal was already waiting for Sari on the table, although it seemed to have grown cold.

"You took awhile," ZIsu says, not looking up from her examination of the ceremonial robes that Nanshaie had, for some reason, brought with her. She is tracing her fingers across the beadwork and embroidery; a dozen sunbursts interlaced with sickles done in a rainbow of colors.

"I had nothing with which I could pay the healer. I chopped wood for her, instead."

"Well, this robe would cover it," Zisu says. "It must have taken a hundred hours to make. Why did she bring it with her?"

"I couldn't say," Sari replies, sitting down at the table across from Zisu. "Does she have anything else interesting?" She feels a little guilty going through her companions belongings. But before she had been taken, she had been vague and cryptic. Maybe the answers to some of her questions would be inside one of the bags.

"Just this book, but she had taken it from the tower." Zisu hands the tome to Sari. "I've marked the pages she was reading before... Well, you can see what she was trying to read."

Sari opens to the marked pages, but the script is not one she recognizes. "Can you make any of this out?"

"No," Zisu says, finally looking away from the ornate robe. "But I have seen it before. Namu, she was one of the elders in the caravan I joined. She had some books with this language, I think."

"Namu was the one Ia was looking for. Did she ever say anything to you about Araelta? Or whatever that other name was?"

"She might have, but I do not recall. It sounds a little familiar. I was not close with her, however."

Sari flips through the pages of the book, looking for any words that might be familiar. "What were the names that she had been saying? While Tinanna and I were fighting?"

"Escnea? Elpace? I can't recall." Zisu moves next to her sister, looking at the book. "I think I recognize these words, however." She points to a few near the bottom of the page. "Do you want to try to translate it?"

Sari nods. "At least until Tinanna recovers."

Fourteen

S HE IS SCRUBBING THE DISHES—HANDS PRUNED and knuckles aching, but glad to be out of the sun—when she hears footsteps outside over the howl of the wind.

"Tu'Erebu?" The voice outside is soft and inquisitive but firm. Her heart sinks. It's not Zisu. Zisu was supposed to be back from her errands hours ago

Kalarah is not in, and Sari hesitates, unsure if she should answer it. But another voice, gruff and commanding, shouts through the canvas partition. "Tinanna! Kalarah!"

More than one person? How did she miss that? She sets down her dishrag and pulls aside the sturdy fa'leen-hide baputi to admit these visitors, ready to pull the dagger from her belt if necessary.

"Tu'sala."

A handful of people push past her, scanning the sick beds for Tinanna. None of them wear any insignia of Yshuld, nor do they appear otherwise affiliated with any other temple. They do not even have an Izmyri accent.

Tinanna has been unconscious since they arrived, but she finally stirs when one of these strange qatu sits beside her and places a hand on her cheek. "Love, are you alright?"

Tinanna coughs, spitting up blood, but nods.

"Why did you leave? You said you were safe there, we—"

A tall qatu with long gray fur clears his throat.

The qatu sitting with Tinanna blushes, and pulls a shawl tighter around her shoulders, but not before Sari notices the embroidered sativus flower on the qatu's tunic. The sativus flower of the insurrectionist army.

The healer steps back inside, the wind howling past the baputi in a cry of agony. A sandstorm is coming, a fierce one. "Ah, you have arrived just in time. She has been quite sick; from what I can tell, she met the wrong end of a poisoned blade. But there is much more news than that," the healer says, glancing at Sari. "Excuse me, Damkina, would you mind giving us privacy? I wish to speak to my patient's family privately."

Her family? Tinanna has family? How does Kalarah know that? And why does her family wear the symbol of the insurrectionists? Sari swallows and nods, drying her hands and stepping outside into the oncoming storm, her anger more intense than the wind's. She'd risked nearly everything to get Tinanna to safety, and yet her supposed family are potential traitors. The only thing she can think to do is chop more wood, imagining each log is an insurrectionist's neck.

Kalarah, at the very least, suspects that Sari is wealthier than she lets on and has charged even more than first quoted for the antidote that Tinanna still needs to receive several times a day. She again pointed to the ring that Sari tries to keep concealed under her tunic, and Sari again made a counteroffer. This time she offered to catch meat while Zisu stays behind to help clean and sanitize the medical instruments.

The sun is low in the sky, and a grazing fa'leen herd has stopped by an oasis. Determined to catch at least two before the herd scatters in alarm, she crouches behind a large yardang, waiting for the herd to dip their heads toward the water, her mind swirling with questions.

Is Tinanna a Re'u? A priestess? An insurrectionist? One qatu had mentioned Tinanna was safe at the temple, and questioned why she left it. Safe from what? Or from whom?

Kalarah had also called them family, and yet none of the potential insurrectionists have a Re'u accent, and Tinanna's accent has only become more pronounced.

And worst of all, despite being called family, none of them have offered to help with payment.

She slowly pulls out her spear, ready to pick her mark and strike, careful to not make any noise that would alert the finally quieted fa'leen, wishing for the calm of the Esiri to infect her own too-loud mind. If Tinanna is an insurrectionist, then her enemy is also Ashur and Ashur might be higher on the list of enemies than Sari is right now. If they currently share an enemy...

She does not finish her thought; an unsettling odor drifts across the sand. Something alive; something that smells like a predator—aggression and determination and perspiration. But she has

seen no signs of smilodons; the only other predator she can think of
that would be hunting at this time. She inhales again; this time,
the scent is mixed with something else, something metallic. Not a
something—a someone.

Her fur stands on end, reacting to every movement of the air
around her. With a burst of energy, she twirls on her heels, springs
to the top of the yardang, grasping her spear tightly in her hand, and
launches it at the stalker. But this lohyue with shimmering copper
skin is unnaturally dexterous, with long legs and lightning-fast reflexes; they dodge the spear with ease and keep running, not even looking
back to see who their attacker might be.

Sari hisses, pulling a dagger from her belt. Lohyue are usually slow,
clumsy, and awkward. But this one dashes off, almost at galloping
speeds, towards Izmyri, unconcerned with Sari.

Insurrectionist, solider for Ashur, or member of one of the mysterious ancient orders; it does not matter. Something in Sari's gut tells
her that the lohyue is not here to wish anyone well. She leaps onto
her camel and chases after the preternaturally lithe lohyue. Yet even
on a mount, Sari cannot keep up.

Her heart races as the lohyue vaults over the city wall and soars
from rooftop to rooftop, evading her pursuit. Sari dismounts from
the camel and scales the wall, landing on an awning. But Sari cannot keep up with the strange lohyue's determined flight. No lohyue should have this much agility; no creature without a tail should
be this adroit.

Sari's stomach churns when the lohyue dives from a rooftop and
through a window to Kalarah's hut. Tinanna is not the only patient
inside, but something in Sari's gut tells her that Tinanna is this suspi-

cious lohyue's target. It should not concern her, especially if Tinanna is affiliated with the insurrectionists—why not let this strange lohyue do Sari's work for her? One less betrayer for her to bury.

She hesitates. But what if Zisu is back? What if Zisu is in there now? What if Zisu is the actual target?

Sari dives into Kalarah's hut, rolling as she hits the ground. The lohyue has a hand placed on Tinanna's chest. Zisu is nowhere in sight, and Kalarah is also missing.

The lohyue leans forward with a smirk, not noticing Sari's presence. "Did you think you could stay lost?" The voice is otherworldly, reverberating and forceful but with a hint of malice and mourning.

Sari reaches for her hunting knife, tackling the lohyue and pinning them to the ground. "Stay away from her!"

As soon as she has the knife to the lohyue's neck, she realizes what she's done. She could have let them take out Tinanna... Why is she saving her instead?

"Get back, kitten; you don't know what you are messing with," the lohyue says, shoving an elbow into Sari's abdomen. Sari loses her balance, rolling off the strange attacker.

The lohyue bounces back to their feet, eyeing Tinanna once more, not even sparing a glance back at Sari. Their knife poised above their head, ready to plunge down into Tinanna's chest. But the qatu springs out of bed and staggers away, spry and dexterous despite her illness.

The bags under her eyes and the loss of color in her fur give her the appearance of a phantom, but she assaults the lohyue with a flurry of solid punches, claws raking across the lohyue's face and tearing away their veil, Tinanna is somehow still lethal even when on the edge of death herself.

Their eyes are too large, too far apart; their nose is too long, too pointed; their neck is too long; their skin too luminescent, and their ears are too small. Despite it being death to wear metal in the desert, the lohyue wears a thin copper circlet around their head, resting right over their brow.

Sari leaps to her feet again, eager to plunge her knife into the attacker's heart, but they skitter back, staggering out of the hut, and are gone, leaving behind no hints of their identity.

Tinanna gasps, collapsing to the floor and clutching at her chest. "Thank you," she says between wheezes.

Sari has too many questions for Tinanna, if Tinanna is even the priestess's real name... if she even is really a priestess. Sari scowls at the familiar stranger on the floor. "I do not even know who you are. Why are you talking to me?"

She marches back to the inn, leaving Tinanna still sprawled on the floor. Zisu is asleep in the bed, and Sari collapses next to her, confused and lost. She dreams again of battles in the iseru, of stabbing her siblings, of choking them, of watching their blood stain the sands red.

She dreams of running from isiaqs and sahres that eye her with lust, running from the laugh of her parents' advisors as they bet on the likelihood that she or one of her siblings will die that night. She dreams of running from insurrectionists and her hands on her brother's throat before she flees the isi'tu.

She dreams of Zisu, sobbing at Ashur's feet.

The sun is too hot even for Sari, and yet she strikes the stone on the steel tip of her spear, refining it again to a point. Tinanna is almost recovered, and she had hoped to have some sort of plan by now, and yet she has none. Her hopes that the book would give her some clue proved unfounded; she could not read the letters, and she was not a linguist, so her attempts to decipher it were wasted. Even with Zisu's previous exposure to the language and her sharp mind, they could not make out any useful information.

She does not even know why she is still here waiting for Tinanna to recover. Tinanna is not who she says she is; Sari is not even sure Tinanna could give her a straight answer if she wanted to. Her strange visitors and the snippets of conversation she overhears have only solidified her suspicions that she is allied with the insurrectionists. Even if she is not one of them, she must be giving them some information. She thinks of all the times she watched Tinanna whisper to her falcon and then send it flying. How much do they now know of Sari's plans?

She does not know why it matters so much to her that Tinanna might be lying about her identity. Something Nanshaie had said long ago tugs at her mind. Sari never gave Tinanna a reason to trust her, so why would she? Why would she tell Sari who she is or what her affiliations are?

It doesn't matter; what she needs to do is find Ashur, kill him, get the Heart back, and save Nanshaie. She strikes again at the hot metal, smoothing out a chip, and then plunges it into the bucket of water. Miramis mar Amata, the blacksmith of Izmyri, has agreed to let her use the forge and supplies in exchange for Sari teaching her how to make steel. She had not realized how limited the knowledge was, apparently a closely guarded secret of the sahre'danus and their weaponsmiths.

But even though she wonders if the smith might be an insurrectionist and might turn these skills against her, she cannot leave an entire town without the knowledge to make weapons that could repel Ashur's forces. She hated Ashur right now more than she hated the insurrectionists. They, at least, would not have threatened the Oracle.

"Hey," Miramis says, stepping out of her edin'tu, pulling up a seat beside Sari. "Let's talk."

Sari nods, glancing away from her work for only a second. Miramis is tall, her fur stripped around her arms; darker and lighter shades of gray. But her fur is thin, and it's not hard to see the burns and welts dotting her skin. Her long hair is worn loose, but it still has the choppiness of someone who has had to make several impromptu haircuts. She's a skilled smith, but a careless one.

"I know your name is not really Damkina." The smith leans back, eying the clear and cloudless sky.

Sari opens her mouth to refute Miramis, but is cut off.

"I know who you are, Saritrah," Miramis says, tying her long blue-black hair back and wiping sweat from her forehead. "And I think you know who we are. Thank you for saving Tinanna."

"Is that all?" Sari says, testing the edge of her spearpoint.

"Well, yes."

Sari is used to silence, used to sitting in it even if it makes others uncomfortable. But this is not silence; this is Miramis asking a question. *Why did you save her?*

"She's a good fighter." The only answer she can think to give.

"Is that what you care about? Is that what you respect?" Miramis would have been a formiddble isiaq, or maybe even a sahre. She has a talent for asking one question while meaning to ask another.

Still searching the steel for imperfections, Sari replies, "I suppose. She was a valuable asset to me, although I guess it would be more apt to say she was valuable to me while being your asset."

"Interesting way to put it. She's not 'our' anything. She might work with us, but she doesn't belong to us. Anyway, she told me that Ashur has some weapon?"

"It's not a weapon, at least, I don't think it's meant to be..." Sari recalls Ia saying that it has the power to bring about paradise, the power to grant her the throne. Then she recalls the way Ashur had used it to turn soldiers into beasts. "But it can be used as one."

"And he's planning on using it?"

"Most certainly. He takes any advantage he can get and will make the most of it. Did Tinanna tell you about the lohyue that tried to kill her?"

"That was not a lohyue. That was an *Ástfriður.*"

"I didn't think they ever left their islands." The spearpoint is complete, not a single imperfection. Yet Sari still turns it over in her hand, examining it, refusing to look away, refusing to look at Miramis.

"They rarely do."

"That explains why they were so nimble," she mumbles. At least one mystery has been solved. "Do you know why they wanted to kill Tinanna?"

"I can guess, but I am not at liberty to share my speculations." *If my mother had Miramis as an advisor, the insurrectionists never would have stood a chance.* Sari laments that this armsmaster would not be swayed to her cause, wondering how many bright minds and persuasive speakers had been tricked into allying with the insurrectionists. If they were all have as sharp as Miramis... But then again, they weren't fighters. They could likely not prove themselves on the battlefield, and so they never would have come to the attention of her mother in the first place.

"But she told you who I am? She was at liberty to share those speculations with you?" She sets down the spearpoint and reaches for her polearm.

"She said you wanted the power to create paradise. If that is your goal, then welcome to our cause." Miramis picks up the spearpoint, holding it up to the sunlight and angling it in different directions.

"No, don't play those games with me. You lot cause nothing but unrest." She unwinds the thick leather laces securing her worn spearpoint.

"Is that so? Aside from the assassin after Tinanna, have you seen any unrest here?"

Sari thinks about her time so far in this village. In many respects, Izmyri is similar to Eluuti; farming with irrigation, communal division of responsibilities, care for the elderly and disabled, and when one cannot outright purchase something that they need, there is always room to barter or trade. No one is hungry, and no one is left without a sub'tu to keep safe from the elements. But it looks nothing like Bec—it is not any sort of paradise. She remembers the Susan'i clan; Etana and her plea to remember what they had tried to build. "But people must still work and toil."

"Aye, but this is just the start. This is the first blossom of a savitus flower; it will take time to reach full bloom."

"But when it does, will it not then wither and die?"

"Maybe, but wouldn't it be fun to at least try?"

"Well, your savitus flower is about to be trampled by my brother."

"Possibly. Aren't you going to try to stop him?"

Sari sighs. She has no army. She has no plan. She has no direction and no leads. "I can try. I have nothing more to go on than a book I brought back from the city. And I can't read it."

"Your parents did not teach you to read? Only to fight?" There is no condescension in Miramis' words, more like sorrow. Pity.

And Sari cannot stand pity. "No, I know how to read. The issue is that it is written in a language I do not know."

"Is that so? We might have someone who can translate it. What language?" Miramis leans forward, setting the spearpoint back down on the table between them and resting her chin in her hands.

"It does not look like any modern language." Sari opens a cannister of oil, dipping her fingers into it before running them along the leather laces.

"That should not be a problem. Kegan is good with obscure languages, even ancient ones."

"You would help me?" Sari tries to hide her scowl. Why would the insurrectionists help her? This has to be a trap.

"Would you help us? To stop your brother?"

Sari sets the leather laces down, stretching them out straight and flat, and leans back, tail twitching, appraising Miramis. A common enemy. "So, we work together to stop him and then what? Go back to being enemies? You hoping I don't then use the Heart myself?"

"Maybe, but you'd be hoping the entire savitus forces don't execute you right after."

Sari still wants the throne, and she still wants the Heart of Aodhe and all that it promises. But right now, what she wants even more is to see Ashur dead. She wants Zisu safe. She wants Nanshaie safe. If it means lying to the insurrectionists, well, she is fine with that. Right now, the insurrectionists are the lesser of three evils. Right now, she does not need loyalty, she has no room to be that picky. She just needs allies. "What if I renounced the throne?"

"Excuse me?"

"You heard me. What if I gave it up, renounced it like the princess in Fayn gave up her throne. She wasn't executed."

Miramis scratches her chin. "Why would you do that? What is bringing about this change of heart?"

"I want Ashur dead. He stole something from me that is more precious than the throne... If allying myself with you lot is what it takes... I'll do it."

"Huh. Tinanna said you were a weird one. Keep that spear sharp. I'll talk to some of the leaders and let you know what they say." She springs to her feet and is gone again.

"I have come with an answer from the Amyrdine Bara," Tinanna says, not bothering to ask for permission to enter Sari's room at the inn. A room that she had told Tinanna was hers, too. But the qatu, her loyalties now in the open, refused to share a room with Zisu and Sari. Zisu had seemed disappointed with this answer, and even offered Tinanna a hug.

Sari sets down the tome on the desk, turning around in the chair and taking in Tinanna—still pale, still too thin. It shouldn't concern her, it shouldn't worry her. But it does. "And that is?"

"They will ally with you to stop Ashur. But you must prove yourself by beating their toughest fighter." Her words are formal, stilted and stiff.

An interesting test; when they had taken over Sua, they had promised an end to violence as a means of social mobility. No might fighting to establish dominance, no more battles between isiaqs and sahres to control territory. And yet, that is the kind of test they are offering her. A test she can respect, a test she can accept.

"I can do that. But first," Sari says, rising to her feet and crossing the room. "You owe me answers."

"I owe you nothing." Tinanna says, turning away from Sari and pulling aside the baputi to exit.

"I saved you!" Sari grabs Tinanna's wrist and pulls her back into the room.

"You did the right thing." Tinanna twists her arm, forcing Sari to release her grip. "Why should you be rewarded for doing what is right?"

Sari grits her teeth, tempted to reply that she is the mar'sahr'dani, her word should be law. That might have worked while Tinanna was masquerading as a priestess, but now it would be pointless, potentially counterproductive.

"I am Tinanna. Is that not enough?"

"You know what I mean," Sari growls. "Just answer the question."

"What is going on?" Zisu steps into the room, her hair and fur still wet from her visit to the bathhouse, eyes wide when she recognizes Tinanna. "You should not be out of bed!" She grabs Tinanna's hand and leads her to the bed, placing a hand on her shoulder and forcing her to sit. "Let me get you some water. Have you had any food today?" Zisu flutters to the basin of water and fills a glass.

"We were just discussing our next steps." Sari leans against the desk, one hand resting possessively on the tome.

"What do you mean?" Zisu plops down next to Tinanna and hands her the glass of water, still surreptitiously checking for signs of illness.

"Taking out Ashur," Tinanna says.

"And what about Ia? And Nanshaie?" Zisu's tail flicks as she looks between Tinanna and Sari.

"That depends." Sari taps the book with her claws. "I need to know a few things first."

"Ia isn't one of us," Tinanna says. "And neither is Nanshaie. Nanshaie is who she says she is. Ia, I do not know."

"Why should I trust you on that?" Sari's tail twitches, ears flattening against her head.

Zisu bites her lap, clasping her hands together in her lap and staring at the floor. "What is going on?"

"Tinanna is one of the insurrectionists. I would not doubt if she has been planning something this whole time."

Zisu jerks her head up to stare at Tinanna. "Is that true? That can't be true. You wouldn't— You're a priestess."

"Fine," Tinanna stands, clasping her hands behind her back and pacing across the cramped room. "I am a priestess, I do have some

Sight, and I was not being deceitful when I took the vows. I did mean it when I promised myself to Yshuld."

Tinanna's accent creeps into her voice, her words strained both with emotion and memory. "I was born to the Re'u, but I left when I was a child to take a job."

"How young? What job?" Zisu leans forward, still sitting on the bed but precariously close to the edge.

"Maybe five or six summers. The job was dangerous."

"You were still a qit! Why did you leave?" Zisu's ears are pricked forward, hanging on Tinanna's every word. Sari rolls her eyes. She does not want to know whatever ghosts Tinanna has in her past. All she needs are fighters who can help her take out Ashur. She does not need specters from the past pursuing them, too.

"It was not really a choice."

"You were forced?"

Tinanna shrugs. "By circumstances, yes. It doesn't matter, though. I was good at my job, my employers kept me fed and clothed, it paid well, and it seemed better than any alternative."

"What did you do?" The concern written on Zisu's face surprises Sari, her voice holding a measure of affection that is more than familiarity.

Tinanna shakes her head. "It is better if you do not know the details. Suffice it to say, I was taught how to handle weapons at a very young age, and my training involved fighting the other recruits, sometimes to the death."

Zisu places a hand over her mouth. "Just like the *Sitnu.*"

"The what?"

"How we pick the Mar'sahr'dan'i." Zisu's face reddens as she says it. Sari wants to cut her off, not reveal that secret. For some reason, she does not want Tinanna—or Nanshaie—to know about this part of her life. She shakes her head, but Zisu is not paying attention. "It's a tournament, I guess you could say. That all the other isi-aqs and sahres can come and watch. Sometimes they fight, too. But it is also entertainment for them; the qits fighting, sometimes to the death."

Sari crosses her arms, and looks out the window, avoiding Tinanna's gaze.

"I had no idea. Has it always been like this?"

"I think so. Sumalika—Mother—was the best, that's why she was Sahre'Danu and..."

"And why all of her siblings died young." Tinanna sighs, shaking her head.

Sari does not want to be here, in this room, with her sister spilling these secrets so easily.

"Were you good at it?" Tinanna's eyes are trained on Zisu, assessing her thing and wiry frame.

"Hardly. But I was clever, in the end. And Sari helped me a lot."

Sari's face is too hot. It must be the sun still streaming in the window.

"Fascinating. The Re'u do not teach their qits much about Sua, and my employers thought our time was better spent learning to wield weapons."

"What did you do? What was your job?"

"I can't answer that."

Sari snorts and rolls her eyes, biting back a sarcastic response.

"Then why did you leave?" Zisu tilts her head to the side, her tail flicking with curiosity.

"They assigned me a job that I did not want to do." Her mouth hangs open, her lips moving as if she has more to say but stops herself. She looks between Sari and Zisu, searching for something in their faces. Sari recognizes the look; a painful memory clawing its way free.

"So you just quit and went to the temple?"

"No, there is no quitting. They kill deserters." She turns away from them, staring out the window.

This piques Sari's curiosity. An organization that trains qits from a young age to be living weapons and kills anyone who tries to leave. She can only think of one line of work that would operate like that. A mercenary organization that is not afraid to carry out assassinations.

"Then how did you leave?"

"I was attempting to carry out my mission but was caught. I honestly did not want to carry it out. Maybe I let myself get caught. The person who caught me gave me the option to join Amyrdine Bara. They helped me."

"How did they help you?" Zisu is enthralled by Tinanna's tale. Sari just wants to poke holes in it.

"They got me into the Temple of Yshuld. My former employer isn't without all scruples; they don't enter religious houses. I would be safe there. In exchange, I gave the Bara information now and then and pulled some strings where I could. Only a handful of the savitus know about my actual past. Please do not spread this information."

"You're trusting me and Sari?" Zisu asks the question that Sari has been holding inside.

"Don't make me regret it. I've been trying to atone for all the destruction I caused ever since."

"What is there to atone for?" Zisu again tilts her head to the side; she has never been one to confront the destructive nature of the Suan people head on. Sari has always protected her from it as much as she could. The one pure thing... The one innocent person that Sari has been fighting for her whole life...

Sari laughs at her sister. "You have not changed. You still want to believe the best of everyone."

"It's far less stressful than mistrusting everyone." Zisu's words are like sharpened claws against Sari's skin.

"She murdered people, Zisu. That's what she's not saying. She killed people for money."

"That is not true. It can't be. Right?" Zisu shifts back into the bed, eyeing Tinanna with trepidation. When Tinanna says nothing, Zisu closes her eyes. Sari shifts her weight to the balls of her feet, ready to sprint after Zisu if her sister decides to run. Instead, Zisu swallows and stares back at Tinanna, hesitation gone. "It doesn't matter. You were taken against your will. It is what you were raised to do. Why do you have to make up for that? You were just doing what you needed to survive."

"I still did wrong." She won't turn around, her gaze fixed on something outside the inn.

Sari balls both hands into a fist, her claws drawing blood; she cannot take it anymore. "You want to say you are done committing violence? That you want to atone?" She advanced toward Tinanna, shoving her against the wall and jabbing her in the chest. "And yet you aligned yourself with the Bara as you call them! The insurrectionists! Do they not have to atone? They murdered half of my family, as well as the guards at the royal isi'tu, and anyone else who stood against them that night!

"Sari... Stop it... . please." Zisu grabs her arm and tries to pull her away from Tinanna.

"No, Zisu. This woman breaks bread with the people who tried to kill you! They are also violent and take life, and you are now aligned with them. How is this any different?"

"Sari, it does not matter now! Leave her alone." Her voice quivers and Sari knows if she were to turn to face her sister, she would see the tears welling in her eyes.

"She asks a good question," Tinanna says, averting her eyes from both of the royal qatu. "There is no perfect answer, and the lives that they took are ones they will have to answer for when they meet Xana in the afterlife. But they took lives in an attempt to make a better world; I took lives for a paycheck."

Sari wants to keep yelling, keep fighting, keep instigating. Keep holding onto the anger that she has no idea where else to direct. But it is slipping through her fingers like sand. "And how will you know when you have atoned? How will you know when you have done enough to earn redemption?"

"I won't." Tinanna looks Sari square in the eyes. "I'll just keep trying until I die and hope that when I do, it was enough. But there are some things you can only ever try to atone for; you don't get to decide for yourself if you were successful."

Sari hates the honesty, the vulnerability, the openness with which Tinanna is laying herself bare. She hates that it is making her reconsider her own actions. Like Tinanna, Sari had been raised to fight; raised to cut down foes and execute those who betrayed her. That was the place of the sahre'danu. That was the position she was born into. She had no reason to atone for the lives she took, no need for redemption. She did not have a choice; her ruthlessness was necessary to keep her people safe.

She takes a step back, letting her hands fall to her side.

"You said that they kill you if you leave," Zisu says. "How do they do that?"

"They track you. Like the one the other day. They'll keep tracking you, sending someone after you to finish you off." Tinanna places her hand over her heart. "And they are very good at tracking."

"They would not have come after you if you stayed in the Temple..." Sari says, taking another step back. "Did Ia force you to come along? Does she know? She let you leave the Temple knowing—"

"She did not force me, and she did not know. I chose this."

"You chose to leave safety? Why?"

"I want to atone. I cannot do that in the confines of the Temple."

"You want to atone, so you chose to follow a mat'sahr'dan into the desert. You chose to protect *me,* the enemy of... Oh." Sari sits down again, the faces of her former generals flashing before her eyes. "They needed someone else to keep an eye on me. I slaughtered what spies they still in had in my army."

Tinanna takes a deep breath but does not deny it.

"Well, thank you for answering my questions." If nothing else, Tinanna had done that. She closes her eyes and takes a deep breath, disappointed to see Tinanna still standing before her when she opens them again. She does not like the answers Tinanna gave her. But that doesn't matter. She still needs the insurrectionists' army. "I hope whoever the insurrectionists want me to fight will be ready."

"Oh, I am. We should take this outside, though."

"But you are still recovering. You need to rest." Zisu says, still concerned for Tinanna even as she admits she joined the quest under false pretenses. She cannot bring herself to say it, but Sari finds that she is also concerned for Tinanna's well-being.

Tinanna smirks. "Let me know when you are ready."

The sun has set, and Sari makes Zisu swear that she will stay put. Stay at the inn, do whatever she pleases with her time but stay inside. Do not venture out, do not follow Sari.

She has agreed to meet with Tinanna in the desert; outside the city walls and when Yludi is at its zenith for the night. The larger moon is high in the sky, the lesser moon of Gali trailing behind it, and Tinanna is waiting.

The village of Izmyri sits atop a high plateau, a few wooden bridges connect it to adjacent buttes where farmers will let their livestock roam without fear of predators easily making a meal of them. It is on one of these adjacent buttes that Tinanna is perched, feet dangling over the edge as she watches the moons chase each other across the dark sky. Rather than her usual leather, she is dressed in a short, simple silk dress with cap sleeves and a golden robe cinched at her waist. The glow of moonlight reflects off of TInanna's dark fur and for a second, Sari wonders if she is looking upon Aydras, goddess of the twin moons and healer of wounds.

But goddesses do not leave their divine realms, certainly not to possess the bodies of those pledged and sworn already to a rival. Yshuld, goddess of the sun, would never allow someone favored by her sister Aydras to enter her temples.

"You came," is all Tinanna says as she springs to her feet and leaps across the chasm between them, landing just at the edge of the plateau.

"Of course," Sari says. Her heart races; Tinanna is still far too beautiful in the moonlight. She's seen her fight, but it is with a sinking feeling that she realizes she might know how to fight, but she is not trained the way Tinanna has been. Tinanna was taught more than just fighting, she was forged into a living weapon.

Sari learned how to fight *her siblings*. Hers was not a general education let alone an advanced education in the art of one-on-one combat. She was a tactician in the iseru, but in the classroom she was a strategist. Logistics, resources, management of arms and securing supply lines was where she excelled.

She was trained to lead armies, to be the commander on the battlefield, not the foot soldier. She joined her troops in battle, but before the insurrection, she never would have done so. Her mother would ride onto the battlefield to rally the troops, and she toppled her fair share of opponents, but she was always surrounded by trusted warriors who she could count on to have her back.

And Sari would have had the same had she ascended to the throne.

She knows how to fight Ashur. She knows—knew—how to fight Aishah and the rest of her siblings. She learned their weaknesses, their quirks, their foibles. But she has only studied Tinanna with admiration, not with an eye toward tactics.

She swallows and draws her spear.

"No," Tinanna says. "We fight without weapons. Pure cunning and strength."

Sari tosses her spear to the ground and removes the daggers from their sheaths, throwing each one into the sand next to her. "As you wish."

Sari waits for Tinanna to do the same, but then she realizes that Tinanna arrived unarmed. She is still weak from the poison, recovering from an assassination attempt, and distrustful of Sari. And she is either reckless enough or confident enough to show up to this fight without any weapons. She focuses on Tinanna's arms, her abdomen, her legs, looking at every muscle for signs of Tinanna's first move.

"The first one to pin the other to the ground for five seconds shall be the winner." Tinanna clenches and unclenches her fists, and Sari ignores the heat rising between her legs as she admires Tinanna's biceps. Or, she tries to ignore it but some part of her keeps imagining herself pinning Tinanna to the ground and then letting her hands explore the assassin's body, relishing in whatever she might find under the silk dress.

Tinanna's eyes sparkle with starlight as she spreads her legs and bends at the knees, drawing her elbows into her sides, preparing for the battle. Her movements are halfway between the grace of a dancer and the brawn of a brawler; she would be at home in a rowdy tavern or an elegant performance.

Sari wishes she could quiet the rambunctious thoughts racing through her mind, but even the grounding techniques she had learned as a qit are no use. This fight determines her future, but she cannot keep her focus where it should be.

Tinanna counts down from five, and the final number has scarcely left her lips when the first blow strikes Sari in her stomach.

She staggers back, but quickly regains her footing. She skitters to the left as Tinanna's second unarmed strike glances just to the right of her ear, the speed of her fist as loud as a whizzing arrow. Sari grins. Tinanna is fast, but her speed cannot make up for her lack of mass.

If she can use that speed against Tinanna, she will have a shot at winning. They circle each other, Sari letting Tinanna get a few punches in as she further assesses the strength of the assassin. She watches for the tells before the fists fly.

She dodges and feints, waiting for a sign that Tinanna's stamina is faltering, but Sari realizes her own heart rate is rising all while Tinanna's breathing remains just as steady as it had been before they started.

She is incredible; stamina and speed where Sari is strength and steel. The moons continue to soar through the sky, the stars silently observing the battle.

Tinanna spins on the ball of her left foot, her left elegantly rising like a dancer from Janeuq, extending impossibly high. Sari reels back as pain ignites in her cheek. She catches herself and grits her teeth before lunging forward, hoping to Tinanna while she is still mid-twirl.

But the other qatu is already ducking, her knees and hips bending; back still straight as her hands briefly touch the ground to slow her momentum.

No taunting, no insults. Just quiet determination, her mouth set in a hard line as she rises again and beckons for Sari to try again.

It does not matter how hard she tries, the few blows she does manage to land seem to have no effect on Tinanna. Just as she believes she has learned Tinanna's quirks, the other qatu changes strategies. How many different styles of fighting did she learn? How many teachers did she have? Sari tries to identify them; some ancient styles dating back to before Garcelon, before Tsvetokrasa, some styles might be recent meldings of two opposing techniques, attempts at shoring up the weaknesses of a style while giving extra flare to the strengths.

But Sari could not say with certainty. What she can say is that Tinanna is nothing like any of her previous opponents and she wants her. She wants her loyalty, she wants her beside her. She wants her to take the place of Arishaki at her side.

And she cannot ask that of Tinanna if she does not win.

How can she ask her to swear loyalty if she cannot demonstrate she is worthy of it?

The muscles in Tinanna's legs tense again, and Sari is ready. Tinanna lifts her right leg and Sari ducks, one arm reaching out to grab Tinanna's left leg, ready to pull her to the ground.

But even as her fingers lace around Tinanna's calf, she realizes her mistake. Tinanna twists mid-spin and comes crashing down on Sari, her hands clutching Sari's shoulders while her knee jabs her in the abdomen.

The assassin pins her to the ground, sand filling her mouth and mixing with the blood. Her head is too close to the edge of the plateau, and if Tinanna wanted, she could toss her off the cliff and no one would know what happened to her. But she doesn't; she leans forward to whisper in her ear, counting down the seconds to Sari's defeat.

But even as Sari relaxes, accepting her loss, her hands reach up to stroke Tinanna's cheek and the other qatu lets her.

"Are you ready for a second round?" Sari says, a finger twirling around a stray strand of dark hair.

Tinanna's face, usually an expressionless mask, flickers between confusion, doubt, curiosity, and then mischief, a levity lifting the corners of her mouth. She nods and lets her own hands explore Sari's body.

They bite, they claw, they let themselves enjoy both pain and pleasure at the others hands. Sari relishes in the touch, the brief connection with this other fighter. She forgets that this started as a battle for resources, a political fight to secure an alliance. She forgets all the other times she's engaged in intercourse to further her own cause or strengthen her position. There is just the night sky and this powerful warrior beside her, on top of her, underneath her, inside her... This other warrior who might be the only other person who could possibly understand her like Arishaki had.

The large sub'tu at the center of Izmyri used to be the sahre's home. But the insurrectionists have remade it into a seat of communal governance; it is where everyone meets to discuss the running of the village, where they distribute information that everyone needs to know, and hear the complaints or questions of other residents. It is here that Sari now sits, around a central circular table, to discuss the threat that Ashur poses.

She had lost to Tinanna, the sweetest defeat she had ever experienced. But she had not proven herself worthy of being followed into battle, yet they were still willing to ally themselves with her. Or was it the other way around and they were willing to let her join them?

"Our scouts have not seen nor heard any reports of large armies or even caravans moving about that area," one of the insurrectionists says, pointing to the map on the table, now marked with the location of the City of Bec. "We've asked some of the Re'u who frequently pass through that area, and they have seen no one. This leads me to believe that he is still in the ruins of the city."

"That makes sense. It's a wonderful place to hide his forces," Miramis says.

"Tinanna?" another says, voice laced with concern.

"It makes sense; however, I told you already of the strange magic," Tinanna says.

"Magic?" Kalarah says, squinting. "Wait, I heard rumor that people in Fayn were claiming to have magic now."

"That's the rumor I heard, too," Miramis says. "Not many, but a few. I thought it was superstition and fear with a dash of disgraced nobles trying to spread or encourage rumors to make people distrustful of Sharidan and Saoirse."

"It is real," Tinanna says. "Or at least, Ashur's is. Sari?"

Sari leans forward. "From what I saw, the Heart of Aodhe has magic, and he was able to use it to turn his soldiers into kahbush'a. Normal weapons are ineffective against them. If you want to advance on the City of Bec and take out his army, you're going to have to rely on more than just numbers."

"We can pull troops from other cities, provided you promise your army will not swoop in to re-take the towns and villages," Miramis says, raising an eyebrow.

"I do not have an army," Sari says, crossing her arms and refusing to look at Miramis or Tinanna, tapping her foot on the ground.

"So, you cannot even join your troops with ours? Where did your army go?"

Sari laughs. "Well, half of them apparently were insurrectionists, and the others loyal to Ashur."

"So what happened to them?"

"I executed them." She fans her face with a hand, suddenly overheating. When no one says anything, she says, "They were traitors." Her stomach turns over and she is afraid that her dinner will come back up. A strange feeling takes root in her chest, squeezing her heart and tightening around her lungs. Why does she feel so uncomfortable admitting this?

"Your family is really bloodthirsty," Miramis says, face twisted in horror. "Did no one ever love you growing up?"

Sari's heart races, eyes wide as she analyses the emotions on Miramis' face; nose crinkled in disgust, jaw dropped in shock, and eyes wide with pity. Pity: the last thing she wants from her enemies. She can feel the harsh eyes of every insurrectionist at the table appraising her, all judging her and her actions and finding her lacking. "Mat'sahr'dan are not to be loved; they are to be trained into weapons."

"Well," Kalarah says after several moments of silence. "It is a good thing that you are no longer a mat'sahr'dan. Now you can learn what love is."

Miramis clears her throat. "Right. Back to business. Since you no longer have an army to lead, we will assign you one unit of ours. You know your brother's fighting style best. Before we leave, you will brief everyone on it."

"I understand," Sari says, face as hot as sand at noon.

"We will be keeping an eye on you. So do not get any ideas."

"Of course. My only ideas are taking out Ashur."

"Good. Kegan is on their way here and we are hoping they will be able to translate the book you brought back. Perhaps this will give us some clues on what to expect when we arrive at Bec."

"Who is Kegan?" Sari tries to put steel in her voice, but it comes out as weak as bronze.

"A linguist and code-breaker from Fayn." Miramis shuffles papers on the table and clears her throat.

From Fayn. Working with the insurrectionists. So one of the rebels that overthrew the Folas family and tore the crown from King Cian's head. Sari holds back a hiss.

"How soon will they be here?" Tinanna asks.

"Only a few days, but we are also waiting for more troops to arrive before we move out."

FIFTEEN

S ARI HAS BEEN SEARCHING FOR TINANNA SINCE DAWN, wanting a rematch, if only for her pride. Or, so she tells herself. She wants a rematch so she can win this time. Not because she is still buzzing with energy, with need. She enjoyed her night with Tinanna, but that's all that it was. All that it can be. After they take out Ashur, they will be enemies. There is no way she can convince Tinanna to join her. Not after she lost so succinctly to her.

But the qatu is not at the Kalarah's, nor the inn, nor the communal sub'tu; she has vanished.

Sari supposes that the qatu was trained to disappear and not be found, so if she does not wish to be found, she won't be. But Sari is not about to let that deter her. She steps beyond the Izmyri gates and takes in a deep breath, analyzing the scents on the wind.

She double-checks that she has her weapons and flasks and steps into the Esiri to find her quarry. Tinanna knows how to step lightly, not leaving even the smallest divot in the sand to mark her passing, not making a single sound that would give away her location. But

Sari is also trained in stealth, having mastered the art of running and hiding from isiaqs and sahres that wanted to spend time with a mat'sahr'dan; or more accurately, hiding Zisu from them.

She, too, can *walk* with total silence; but now she fears that her thoughts are so loud that any can hear them. Thoughts of what it means to be a family, thoughts of what it means to love someone and have that love returned, thoughts of what a childhood outside of the isi'tu might have been like, free from the fighting, free from the fear.

The way the insurrectionists looked at her, like they had no idea, as if it was not common knowledge that the Mar'sahre'dan'i was determined by the Sitnus. As if they did not even know that the Sitnus existed at all, and that the war now between Ashur and Sari is just another round in a match they started over twenty years ago. The insurrectionists had no idea that they had stumbled into the middle of the iseru.

The scent of saffron and cardamom tinges the air, and Sari pauses to locate the direction. East. Tinanna is to the east. No longer caring for stealth, Sari sprints towards her target, but when Tinanna comes into view, Sari gasps and pushes herself to run faster.

The qatu is sitting in the sand, hunched over, holding a knife to her chest, tip pointed directly at her own heart. "Tinanna! Stop!" Sari races toward the spy-insurrectionist-priestess, determined to stop her before she does something that can never be undone. She kicks the knife out of Tinanna's grasp, the weapon spinning in the air and landing far enough away to be out of reach.

"Why did you do that?" Tinanna's voice is as harsh and dry as the sand.

"You were going to hurt yourself!"

"I was going to free myself." She clutches at her chest, face twisted in anguish.

"From what?" Sari scans the horizon, wondering if there is some threat on the way.

"From the Siúlóir Scáth. From Silla."

"Who?" But the first two words echo in her mind, reminding her of whispers she would overhear when attending to isi-aqs and sahres—whispers of killers they would like to hire. Assassins, expensive ones. Ones that had made more than one attempt on Sari's life... and Zisu's.

"My former employer. It's the only way to be free of them forever. They will find me, no matter where I go."

Sari blinks. This has to be a dream. Tinanna has been nothing but calm and stoic, a silent but strong companion, a steadiness on this journey that had been grounding. The qatu before her is a mess of tears and agony, the torment that had been locked away finally break-ing free. It is unnerving, and Sari hates the tiny piece of her that wants to reach out and tell Tinanna that she understands, the tiny piece of her that is always looking over her shoulder for Ashur. "There has to be another way to free yourself from them."

"They put a cage around my heart, and I want to be free," Tinan-na says. "I'd rather die than still be living in their chains. I'd rather die trying to free myself than live the rest of my life searching the shadows. They'll find me again. We might have chased off one of them. But more will come. More are coming."

"We'll find another way," Sari says, not sure why she feels com-pelled to comfort this enemy-ally. "I promise."

An energy has been building in Sari for the past day, energy that buzzes under her skin and she can't release. It gnaws at her stomach, claws at her heart, and snaps at every thought she has. It is well past dusk, and the Esiri is freezing. But Sari decides that the best way to release this energy is to take out her aggression on the local wildlife. She grabs her spear, puts on an extra tunic for warmth, gently kisses Zisu's forehead, and leaves the safety of the village gates.

She treks down the winding path from the plateau and stalks across the desert slowly, heading north, following the scent of a smilodon, a large predator that will surely provide a challenge. But the scream that slices through the silence dashes her hopes of making a catch. Someone stupid enough to approach the animal unprepared or a lone traveler beset upon by marauders. The screaming continues, frantic pleas for help.

Sari does not care about the circumstances; she's not out here to rescue people; she's out here to hunt. But then again, maybe this is an opportunity. If the idiot really is being attacked by the smilodon, then the idiot is a marvelous distraction while Sari takes aim. She races towards the screaming, heedless of anything else.

Her guess is correct. Her prey swipes and claws at the face of a low butte, attempting to scale it and reach the frightened qatu atop it. Sari smirks. Maybe idiots can be useful after all.

Sari moves stealthily, her lithe form hugging the side of the butte as she inches forward. Taking a deep breath to steady herself, Sari raises her spear, the smooth wood cool to the touch. She carefully aims, positioning the spear and then stepping forward and releasing it. The spear lodges itself right between the shoulder blades of the smilodon. The predator stumbles and falls, its massive form crashing to the ground in a shower of sand and rocks.

"Oh, thank you!" The qatu on top of the small butte leaps down, landing badly and rolling. "I am—" The qatu stands up, brushing off her tunic and skirt and Sari wishes that her spear were not currently embedded in the smilodon, for she wants nothing more than to skewer the qatu standing before her.

"What the hell are you doing here?" Sari shouts at Ia, springing toward her and grabbing her by the throat. The priestess is bruised, with smudges of blood on her torn tunic, chunks of fur missing, dry and chapped lips, and red eyes.

"Wait, listen!" Her voice is hoarse, raspy with dehydration.

Sari tightens her grips, her claws digging into the priestess's neck ever so slightly. "You lied to me. You manipulated me. You've had an ulterior motive this whole time, why should I listen?"

"Because I am loyal to you!" Ia says, pawing at Sari's hands, but her own claws are worn. broken and ineffective.

"Like hell you are. You are no priestess! You are no devout follower of Yshuld! You belong to some blasphemous—"

"Belonged! Used to! Not anymore," Ia gasps out, weak fingers trying to pry away Sari's hands.

"What does that mean?" Sari leans in closer to Ia, and the qatu tries to lean away, but the butte is right behind her. Sari loosens her grip on the qatu's throat slightly.

"I used to belong to the Araelta. I believed in them, that they could bring paradise, but now I see it's you! They manipulated me, they lied to me, but I know now that you are the truth! I was kidnapped by the Blodheimr Hjart for being an Araelta, but the whole time I was locked up all I could think of was how strong and capable you are. I fought my way back out of there just so that I could kneel at your feet and offer my unwavering fealty."

Sari releases Ia, letting her drop to the hot sands, and takes a step back. "Then do so," she growls.

The priestess collapses, burying her hands in the sand as she leans forward and prostrates before Sari. "Sahre'Danu, I pledge to you my life, my love, and my loyalty. I am your vassal, your servant, your soldier. I renounce all other leaders, forsake all other ties, and pledge forever more to serve only you."

Sari bites her lip, mulling over Ia's words, weighing each in her mind but still unable to calculate their worth.

"I have a gift for you, if you will have it." The priestess' eyes are wide, pleading and blood-shot.

"Where is it? Don't get up." Sari shoves the priestess back to the ground before she can scramble to her feet, not willing to let her pull any trick.

"My bag, my bag over there, next to the—"

Sari kicks over the carcass of the smilodon and hoists up the bag. Long, thin, and heavy. She tucks it under her arm and jerks her spear from the predator's back, holding it out to point at Ia. "What is in the bag?"

"Your inheritance. I do not know how you came to lose it, but I brought it back for you."

Sari peaks inside the bag. Katynna. Her doubts about Ia rise again. "You stole this back from Ashur? How? I thought it was the Blodheimr Hjart that kidnapped you?" Sari raises an eyebrow.

"Yes, but they are—"

"Working together." Sari lets out an exasperated sigh and scowls. "Ah. I see."

"Yes, Sahre'Danu. And I know where they are now, and how to catch Ashur unaware. What else can I do to prove my loyalty to you?" Her words sound earnest, desperate but sincere.

Sari grins. She once again has everything she needs to get her claws on the crown. She can use the insurrectionists to help her take out Ashur, and once the Heart of Aodhe is hers, she'll be able to ascend. *Funny,* she thinks, *that they will be the ones to hand it back to me.*

Sari frets the whole way back to Izmyri, glancing every few seconds at Ia—the way she limps, the way she cradles her wrist, her sallow skin, the fur missing from her tail, the scabs on her ears; Ia needs medical attention. She spent who knows how long wandering the desert, searching for Sari. She risked her life to escape her captors, she took on untold dangers to prove her loyalty. For that, Sari believes her. And she will not let Ia die now that she has completed her quest to reunite Sari with Katynna. She needs food and water and Sari will get it for her..

Kalarah is as attentive to Ia as she had been to Tinanna, taking her to a bed and making her sip salt water before allowing her to eat anything solid. Over and over, Kalarah reassures her that Ia's wounds are superficial and she can't have been wandering in the desert for long. But Sari won't leave the High Priestesses side; her most loyal follower. Her only true believer. She must protect her.

But when the sun rises, Ia shakes Sari awake. "There is no need to stay here. I am sure you have other business to attend to, Sahre'Danu."

"When did I fall asleep?" She looks around; Kalarah is busy already checking on other patients.

"Not too long ago, Sahre'Danu. I know you have far more important business. Please take care of it."

She nods. Zisu is most likely sick with worry, and Tinanna is not here, so she must be off on her own business already. "I will be back later to check on you."

She marches to the inn, head high, shoulders back, the swagger of royalty, the confidence of a warrior queen. But neither Zisu nor Tinanna are at the inn, so Sari heads to Miramis' shop.

"Are you sure we can actually trust her?" Miramis asks after Sari informs her of Ia's return.

The skeptical tone in Miramis' voice makes Sari hesitate, but only for a fraction of a second. "Yes, she wants to help us now."

"What makes you so sure? You wanted to tear her stomach open and spill her guts into the sand not too long ago."

"She explained what happened, and I believe her." She cannot very well tell the insurrectionist that the reason she trusts the High Priestess is because Ia has promised to help her harness the power of the Heart of Aodhe in order to secure her throne. But she can think of no plausible lie, she has to hope that Miramis will not prod any further.

"She's telling you that Ashur isn't in the City of Bec; he's in some ancient and run-down fortress from the days of Ku-Aya, and that his army is completely depleted. She claims these Blodheimr Hjart allies of his have now abandoned him, so we can go in there with only 200 soldiers and wipe him out, and that this Heart of Aodhe that he has... is not a threat to us?"

"Exactly," Sari says, fighting to keep the confidence in her voice, but as she listens to Miramis repeat back what Ia had told her, she realizes how unbelievable it sounds. "But who knows how long it will be before he can regroup? That's why we need to leave now. We do not have time to wait."

"I do not mean to be disrespectful," Miramis says, crossing her arms and swishing her tail. "But this Ia woman sounds like she's spinning tales to lure you into a trap. And you want us to follow you into it."

Despite the protestations from Miramis, the Amyrdine Bara follow Sari and Ia out of Izmyri the next day; Ia leading them not south to Bec, but toward the delta of the Alleghenaie River.

"There," she says after several days of hard riding, trudging over towering dunes and more than once, they must hunker down in between two buttes to wait out a sudden sandstorm .

At the center of the river delta is a small island, and situated on it is a crumbling fortress at least several hundred years old. Not so old as to be forgotten even by history like Bec has faded from memory, but old enough that even though the historians can name who it belonged to, they know not much more than that. The stones are a gray-brown clay more likely to be found far to the north, and the harsh angles of the exterior speak to the fact that once, long ago, Esiri was not so prone to raging sandstorms. The pointed roof suggests that once, rain had been plentiful. Once, Sua had not been a desert.

"Your prize awaits you, my queen." Ia appears at her side, standing tall and proud, all traces of her harsh journey and horrific ordeal erased.

Saritrah grins and gives the order to seize it.

Sixteen

WHILE THE FORTRESS LOOKS IMPOSING FROM a distance, as Sari rushes towards it, doubt about her course of action burrows into her chest. Her feet splash in the cool water of the Alleghenaie River, the shock bringing the clarity to her mind that she has lacked for days now. There is no way an army could be hiding in that fortress. There are no archers in the windows nor sentries at the gates. It looks utterly abandoned.

Did Ia lie to her? Or did Ashur learn of her plan and find a new place to hide?

Her forces advance past the outer gate without any opposition, their spears and swords clutched at the ready but with no foes to strike or skewer. The sound of their footsteps echoes through the empty space; she spies no other divots in the soft clay ground, no signs of anyone else stepping foot on this islet.

"This is too easy," Tinanna says, her tail twitching as they enter the fortress itself, Sari throwing open the wooden doors with unnecessary force. The air inside is heavy with dust and the scent of mold. Empty cobwebs cling to the corners—abandoned even by the spiders. The only sound is the clanking of swords being pulled from sheaths. Despite the neglect, the fortress still stands, though. "Why is there no one here?"

"Ia had said his forces were dwindling," Sari mumbles. "Maybe they have abandoned him entirely." They reach the second floor, still no signs of life.

"Or maybe they are all—" Tinanna's words are cut off by a low growl echoing down the stairs. A kahbush'a barrels toward them, head thrashing back and forth. The stairs rumble with each step the monster takes.

Sari takes several steps backward, assessing the beast. Its fur is matted with dried blood, and large patches are missing, exposing oozing and festering wounds.

This beast has already seen several battles and lived. A flash of gold at the creature's neck—she recognizes it. A medal of honor affixed to a red and yellow sash, worn like a collar.

The beast halts, still half a floor above them. It's piercing amber eyes are too intense, too intelligent, too calculating to belong to anyone except General Aziru.

"They've all been transformed into monsters." Bile rises in her throat—soar and acidic—as she tightens her grip on her spear.

For some reason, her heart aches with grief as she takes in wild beast that had once been Sua's greatest military strategist, one of her mother's most trusted advisors. His reward for loyalty, determination, and prowess—a slow descent into monstrous madness. She brings her hand to her forehead, a sign of respect for warriors killed in battle, and raises her spear. "You deserved better," she whispers. She hated him, hated him for choosing Ashur over her, hated him for the ways he abused her on the nights she lost in the iseru, and hated him for even glancing in Zisu's direction. But this? What Ashur had done to him is worse than he deserved.

It is a trick of the light; it has to be. But she swears the beast nods in acknowledgment. "We cannot fight on the staircase; retreat to the lower level and prepare to attack it," she shouts to the troops.

The soldiers retreat down the stairs, and Sari glances one more time at the general-beast before drawing back herself.

The ground trembles as the beast resumes its charge, its strained growls a cruel mockery of human speech. Sari skips the last two steps, skidding on the damp floor and using the momentum to turn and face the beast again.

Rearing on its hind legs, the kahbush'a swipes at her, long claws barely missing her face. She skitters back, and troops rush past her, weapons raised.

The beast spins again, its gnarly tail sending troops to the ground. Each swipe, each swing, each lunge of the general-beast causes the ground and walls to tremble. Cracks in the walls become large fissures.

But it does not matter how many soldiers land a blow or a strike to the beast's hide; it keeps attacking, and Sari wants to shut her eyes against the chaotic scene—never has she seen such terror and hopelessness in the eyes of soldiers. It is not because the savitus fighters are cowards; she is sure that some of the fighters with her here today are ones that stormed the isi'tu. No, they are not cowards.

But they are fighting a monster that no warrior could even imagine challenging, let alone winning against. A monster that should not exist.

The former general swipes again—the intelligence of Aziru still lurking in the depths of the creature's mind—eyes now locked on Sari, tracking her, studying her, goading her. Sari leaps at it, spear before her, aiming to strike the vulnerable spot between its broad shoulders. But she misses—too low and too slow. The creature's jaws snap down on her hand, tooth piercing through flesh and bone.

Before she can even fully process what has happened, the beast howls, releasing her hand. She stumbles backward, falling to her back, gasping for breath. Her spear lies on the floor, trampled and now broken. She looks down at her hand; too much blood. She can't feel it at all and there is so much blood.

She tears off a length of her tunic with her teeth and wraps her hand in it, biting her lip, wishing she had some alcohol. Why hadn't she considered that Ashur would have more beasts? Ia had assured her again and again that he was all but defenseless, that he had few soldiers remaining. But one kahbush'a is worth a dozen soldiers. He doesn't need an army anymore.

She tries to ball her hand into a fist, but her fingers will not move. Without the use of this hand, she cannot properly wield a weapon; perhaps she will die before infection can even take root in her hand. She does not have a choice but to fight, even hampered. She must; she grits her teeth and pulls Katynna from its sheath.

It is difficult to hold the sword steady in her hand, requiring more force from her thumb to keep it balanced. She slashes wildly, recklessly, distracted by the extra effort it now takes to brandish her weapon.

The creature lunges at her again; its lips curled up in a mockery of a smile, its black teeth a threatening promise. Adjusting her grip, distracted by the exertion, she leaves herself open to attack. The creature seizes the opportunity and lunges at her again.

There is no dodging this attack. No rolling out of the way, no ducking to the ground. She closes her eyes for half a second, bringing Zisu's face to her mind, waiting for the claws to rake her chest. She opens them again, and instead of seeing her death, two daggers fly through the air, each embedding themselves in one of the monster's eyes. The creature rears up, pawing at its head and howling in agony. Tinanna swoops in, another knife in her hand, and rolls under the creature before hurling the knife up at its jugular.

An assassin—Tinanna had been trained not in how to use weapons, but how to be one. A weapon that had just saved Sari's life. A weapon that Sari needed as her own—a weapon for a sahre'danu to wield.

Even as she thinks this, she recalls all of the times she stood between Ashur and Zisu, every time she stepped in to save her sister while her sister cowered in a corner. Is this how Zisu felt? A strange mix of gratitude, relief, and admiration?

But underneath all of that is shame; anger at herself for being so weak and so pathetic.

The beast-general is defeated, but the ground is littered with fallen soldiers, and the air is heavy with the scent of blood and sweat. Too many losses for Sari's liking—too many losses to face Ashur if he has even one more kahbush'a at his beck and call.

Her chest heaving with exhaustion, she takes a moment to catch her breath. Tinanna, Ia, and Zisu rush to her side, their faces etched with concern.

"No, there are others hurt worse than I was," Sari says through gritted teeth as she unbandages her hand.

"There are plenty of medics," Ia says, opening her pouch and grabbing a bottle of alcohol. "There's only one of you."

Sari does not protest as Ia pours the liquid over her wounds—it is agonizing, but she will not show any more weakness. Not in front of the troops—and not in front of Ia, and especially not in front of Tinanna. She cannot bear any more shame today. "We must be quick. Ashur must know we are here by now."

Miramis approaches, splattered in blood, but none of it appears to be her own. "It is not as bad as it looks. Many of the soldiers are unconscious, not dead."

"Have the medics carry the wounded outside, those who can still fight, will fight. We must press on." Sari barks out the order as if she were still leading her own troops, as if these are her loyal warriors fighting to put her on the throne. She realizes her mistake too late. "That is what I suggest, anyway."

"No, we need to retreat. He hasn't sent any more of those monsters, but who knows how many wait for us if we keep going? We don't have the forces to take out even one more of those nightmares," Miramis says, wiping black-red blood from her sword and testing the point.

Sari hisses, both at Miramis for contradicting her and at pain in her hand as Ia continues to clean it. "But he might get away!" She snarls again, hating the feeling of being defied. "We have no way to know where he might go next; this is our only chance! We have to take him out! Now! We can't let him..."

She had not meant to shout, but suddenly too many eyes are on her, judging her. Despising her. Glares and curled lips that whisper to their companions.

She does not want to hear this muttering, their mistrust.

"...is she even competent with a weapon..."

"...why did Miramis agree to this? She's mad, I heard she..."

"...no wonder half her troops turned savitus..."

No sense of loyalty. These troops have no sense of duty or trust for their leader. She is leading them; they should be trusting her; they should be confident in her abilities. Sari looks at her left hand, though. *Who would trust a leader who gets injured like this?*

And besides, she does not need loyalty from them. They are pawns. She has Ia, Ia is loyal to her. That is all she needs.

"We need to keep moving," Ia says, hand resting on Sari's shoulder.

"You're right. Let's go. Follow me if you wish save Sua from a tyrant!" She marches toward the stairs, not waiting to see who will follow her.

They encounter no more monsters as they continue their ascent. But the silence is almost as unnerving. There is a saying for those who live in the Esiri; *you are never alone in the desert.* Yshuld is always there. But this is not the desert. The silence could mean anything; goddess or monster.

"I'll go first," Sari says, gesturing for everyone to stay behind her. She climbs the final few steps with no one beside her. The temperature drops the second she places her foot on the floor. She is in the center of a large room, doors spaced out along the walls, a bright and burning chandelier above her illuminates the room far better than it should.

"Thank you for showing up on time for your execution, dearest sister."

She whirls around; Ashur is reclining on an ancient throne of copper and stone. Nanshaie stands to his right, hair a mess and robe soiled with dirt and blood, manacles clapped around her ankles, chains fastened to the dais.

Sari raises her sword, closing the gap between her and Ashur. "I am not here to die," she says, hoping Tinanna can hear her, hoping she understands the meaning.

She takes another step, just a few more inches and she could slice off his nose. *Why isn't he attacking? Why doesn't he seem worried?*

Before she can ponder it any further, the sword flies out of her hand, drawn away from her and toward Ashur. He catches Katynna and shrugs. "Shall I execute you or Zisu first?"

"You can't have Zisu!" She has no weapons but her claws and strength. A dozen troops join her, and Tinanna and Ia come up on either side to flank her. No, she is not without weapons. She has Ia, and potentially Tinanna.

"Really?" Her brother drums his claws on the arms of the throne. "Ia, there you are."

Ia does not acknowledge him, but Sari steps in front of the High Priestess. "You can't have her, either!"

He continues to lazily tap his claws, a random pattern. "You never were clever, sister dearest. Ia, my love. Thank you for bringing Sari and Zisu here. Will you fetch Zisu to me? And summon the rest of my council, too."

Ia bows to Ashur. "As you wish." And then she is gone, vanished from the room as if she had never been beside Sari.

Her mouth will not move. She has a thousand curses that she wants to unleash on her brother, on Ia, and on herself for being so damn stupid. She had let herself trust someone again. She had let herself believe that she had what it takes to inspire loyalty. *What a fucking idiot I am.*

"Shall we attack?" Tinanna whispers.

A bright red light fills the room and Sari reflexively closes her eyes, but just as quickly as the light fades, and Ia is back, an unconscious Zisu cradled in her arms. "Perfect, my love. And my council?" Ashur looks his sister up and down, appraising her as if she were meat.

And she probably is... He will feed her to his kahbush'a. She imagines her claws digging into his eyes, she imagines biting into his flesh and tearing him to shreds. She is the smilodon and he is a helpless gaatsu, and she will pluck every single one of his feathers before throwing him into a stew.

"On their way." Ia bows again to Ashur before standing at attention on his left, flanking him with Nanshaie. Where Nanshaie looks scared and beaten, resigned to her position, Ia is standing with her back straight, proud of her station. Zisu is still in her arms, but Ashur flicks his wrist in Zisu's direction, and she vanishes like Ia had earlier.

"You traitor!" When she is done roasting Ashur, she will tear out Ia's throat and leave her for the vultures.

"She picked the mat'sahr'dan most capable of ruling, dearest sister. I am sure you understand. Now, it's time to meet the rest of my council." He pulls out the Heart of Aodhe from his pocket. Smoke engulfs the room; the air tinged with the smell of burning flesh and rotting meat, and a dozen kahbush'a step out from the midst of it.

She howls, extending her claws and lunging at Ashur. He might be powerful, but his weakness has always been his pride. It makes him slow; it makes him unalert. A claw grazes his left eye before he can raise his hands to defend himself. Only one eye, but that is all she needs to throw off his sense of depth.

He roars, one hand reflexively covering his wounded eye as blood drips down his face. His other hand reaches for Katynna, brandishing it wildly. "I will disembowel you, you filthy cur."

"Aww, am I no longer your dearest sister?" The fog in the room is still thick enough that she has trouble making out his silhouette as he rises from his throne and backs away from her. The rampant shouts of soldiers and the violent howls of the kahbush'a are just background noise—as indistinct as the cheering of the crowd in the iseru.

For that is where they are. The iseru. It does not matter that they are in a crumbling fortress far from Erzurumei. It would not matter if they were far to the north in Tsvetokrasa, or across the sea in

Fayn. They are in the iseru. They have always been fighting each other in the iseru. They have never left it. They cannot—will not—leave until the winner of the Sitnu is declared and Sumalika has an official heir for her crown. Sua might be naught but ash and debris, and they will still be in that underground arena trying to kill each other while their parents count out the diams.

Ashur's other weakness is his lack of stealth. She hears him behind her; others might not recognize the faint patter of his wild gait, but she does. She ducks before her own sword can slice through her. He staggers forward, and she comes behind him, a kick in his back sending him sprawling to the ground.

Katynna clatters across the stone floor. She could chase after it, try to find it amidst the chaos, or she could pounce. She is upon him before he can even get to his hands and knees. She slices her claws down his back, relishing in the sound of his stifled screams. He thrashes wildly beneath her. "Get the fuck off of me, you mutt!"

He bucks back and forth, and she struggles to keep him restrained beneath her. But he gets the upper hand, dislodging her. She is not quick enough to prevent him from pinning her down.

He punches at her wildly, grabbing her hair and trying to lacerate her face. "You fucking bitch! You harlot!"

She gets an arm free and punches him just below the nose. "You ass!" She brings up her knee, rolls him off of her, and kicks him again. "Fucking bastard," she snarls as she places a foot on his neck. "You do not deserve to live."

"The sahres only ever backed you because you were good in bed!" His voice is strained as both of his hands clutch her ankle, trying to force her off. "That's all you were ever good for! Don't you dare think you are any better than me!"

"You are a nightmare. No one ever backed you because they knew you were a sadist!" She grinds her heel in harder. "They knew they would one day find themselves on the wrong end of your claws." The fog and mist are lifting, and as she stares down into her brother's eyes, she notices that Katynna is only inches above his head. She snarls at him as she picks it up. "It ends today, Ashur. I win." She raises the Katynna high above her head, ready to skewer him upon it. But he grins, laughing while he pulls the Heart of Aodhe out of his pocket. "Well, it looks like I'll have to take a rain check on your execution."

The stone pulses with a crimson light. She braces herself; she will cut him down before he can do anything else. She brings the sword down, aiming right between his ribs. But her sword passes through him as if he were made of mist—embedding itself in the floor, and then he is gone; all that remains is his mocking laughter echoing on the stone walls.

The pungent smoke dissipates, and the howls no longer reverberate across the room. Not only has Ashur vanished, but the kah-bush'a are gone, too.

"Fucking hell." She pulls on her sword, but it does not budge. She pulls again, and still, it does not move. The fortress shakes and then lurches. "What the—"

Tinanna seizes her hand. "We need to go. This place is about to collapse!"

"But my sword!"

"Leave it!" Tinanna says, pulling her away from Katynna.

Seventeen

"We can't leave without Zisu and Nanshaie, we have to find them first!" She can't let Nanshaie stay in the clutches of Ashur any longer, and she is terrified that her brother will kill Zisu as soon as he can. "We have to get out of here," Tinanna says, grabbing her arm and pulling her to her feet. "The fortress is collapsing around us! We will be trapped if we don't get out."

"No," Sari says. "I need to find Zisu!" She wrenches her arm free of Tinanna's grasp and runs towards the door behind the now-empty throne, dodging falling stones.

As she bursts through the door and finds a long and branching system of corridors, her heart pounding, her ears catch the sound of a familiar voice shouting in the distance. Without a moment's hesitation, she sprints towards the source of the sound, her footsteps echoing through the winding, narrow stone corridors of the ancient building. Her eyes dart around, trying to catch a glimpse of her sister through the dimly lit passageways, her mind racing with all the possible ways she could fail to save her sister again. "I'm coming, Zisu!"

She keeps snaking through the maze, following the sound of her sister crying until she comes upon a large door. She presses her ear against it, confirming that it is Zisu crying on the other side of it. "Zisu! I'm here! Stand back!" She kicks the door, but it does not even rattle on its hinges. It's made of solid wood, the kind that can only be found in the most northern reaches of Ahnlisen—it shouldn't be this far south. "Hold on! Stand back, Zisu!"

Her foot connects with the wooden door with another loud thud, the sound echoing through the empty hallway. Undeterred, she kicks the door again. The old hinges, once solid iron but now orange with rust, finally give way under the relentless assault, and the door falls to the floor, sending up a cloud of dust. "Zisu! Zisu!"

Sari's heart sinks as she sees her sister lying on the floor, bruised and unconscious. "We need to get out of here quickly. Can you walk?"

The moment her sister opens her mouth, all that can be detected is a subtle, whispered breath. She shakes her head. Sari, filled with terror, lifts her sister up in her arms. *This is my fault... This is all my fault.*

She races back out, hoping she remembers the way; the fortress is a maze, and she has little time to navigate it again. She clutches her sister close to her chest, straining to hear the exhale of breath, hoping to feel the rise and fall of Zisu's chest. She needs to get Zisu to a healer and then she needs to find Nanshaie, if she's even still here.

The floor shakes, sending both to the floor, Zisu landing badly and crying out in pain.

The sound of a falcon's cry echoes in the hallway. "Hold on!" Tinanna races towards them, bending down and picking up Zisu. "Come on, we need to get out. We have Nanshaie already."

Sari does not reply. She gets to her feet again and takes off.

Only a handful of them make it back to Izmyri. Miramis waits anxiously at the gates to see if Ashur is following them while Sari finds Kalarah. Kalarah is not optimistic, and while the savitus keep watch at the gates day and night, Sari keeps vigil at her sister's side.

She cannot join the watch. While the healer did a better job at treating her mauled hand, she lost the top knuckles of two of her fingers to infection and she may never regain feeling in what remains of those fingers. She is not proficient enough at using a sword or spear anymore to be of help to the savitus fighters. She will have to relearn how to fight, how to hold a sword and spear and keep it balanced in her hands .

And Sari wishes she *could* fight. She has so much rage pent up inside her that needs release, so much anger that needs to be directed. Why does everyone betray her? Why do people promise her fealty only to forsake her? Arishaki, her troops, and Ia. And Tinanna was never even loyal to begin with. Sari wonders if Tinanna even knows how to be loyal.

Why did she believe Ia? Even the savitus fighters warned her not to. Why didn't she listen to Miramis? Was she too eager to hear those sweet words that she ignored the warning signs? What signs were there, though? What did Miramis see that she didn't? What did the other savitus notice that she missed? How was she to know that Ia was lying?

Did Ia betray her because she is a bad leader? She led them into a trap, yes. But she could have had a better battle plan. She could have taken time to calculate the risks before rushing in. She was too eager to see Ashur dead; even if it was a trap, she still could have come out of it victorious. That was the problem. She could have ordered only half of the battalions into the fortress and kept half back. She could have placed archers on the perimeter and lured Ashur out. There are a thousand different ways she could have snatched victory from his claws. This was supposed to be what she was good at; strategy. But she was impatient, she was reckless.

Ia said his forces were depleted, but that was a clever lie. Or an artful bending of the truth—he didn't need an army when he had half a dozen monsters. And magic, she never mentioned the extent of his magic had grown since their last encounter. The magic Ashur had this time was beyond words. Is it all from the Heart of Aodhe? Does it grow stronger over time? Or is he just growing better at wielding it the more time passes with it in his hands?

Ia had told her that only the Heir of Kyna can wield it. Are there multiple heirs? Could Zisu use it too?

As Zisu lies in bed, drenched in sweat, Sari gently places her palm on her sister's forehead. Her skin is burning with fever, and she can feel the heat radiating from her. Her other mistake was believing the savitus troops could fight as a unit. They are a ragtag band of malcontents and disgruntled qatu. They aren't trained in fighting; they took the isi'tu through means of treachery and sheer numbers. They are not soldiers; why did she expect them to follow orders and fight as if they were? They are amateurs; she expected too much from them. If she had taken the time to actually assess their troops, she still might have been able to put together a successful victory plan. Arishaki would have been able to.

She gets another washcloth and dips it in the basin of clean water, wiping away the sweat dripping down her sister's face. All of these failures, all of these mistakes, are the reason her sister may die.

Her stomach drops and her body goes cold. What had Nanshaie said? If she sought the map to the City of Bec, her sister would die. She had thought she had proven the prophecy wrong, but...

The prophecy never said when Zisu would die, and besides, everyone dies someday. But the string of events leading to Zisu's death can be traced directly back to Sari chasing the bandits for the map instead of getting Zisu to a healer.

She takes Zisu's clammy hand in her own. "Please stay with me, Zisu. Please stay. I can't lose you. I love you too much to lose you now."

On the other side of the room lies Nanshaie. Also unconscious; malnourished and on the brink of death. One of the savitus fighters had managed to free her during the melee and had gotten her out of the fray before Ashur disappeared. Even insurrectionists respected the sacredness of the Oracle and would protect Yshuld's chosen at any cost.

But Nanshaie is still in poor condition. She has been in convalescence since they returned. She speaks sometimes, words that no one understands, in voices that scare many.

Sari has helped the healer feed her, give her water, and bathe her. Yet Nanshaie makes no improvement, and her cryptic words give no clues on how to save her.

Sari has left Kalarah's hut for the first time; she has been keeping watch over her sister, sleeping only sporadically in a chair next to her sister's bed. But now she is seated in the communal sub'tu, again surrounded by the legions of the Amyrdine Bara, the savitus fighers... the insurrectionists. She cannot decide what to call them in her mind, she cannot even narrow it down to 'friend' or 'foe.'

Miramis announces that, finally, the reinforcements that they have all been anticipating are arriving, slowly making their way from various parts of Sua. Sari is shocked at how extensive their network is. It is far more organized than she would have guessed.

She says nothing as she overhears some of the savitus fighters questioning whether she is trustworthy, with the survivors of the attack on Ashur's fort commenting about her spectacular failure as a leader.

"Kegan and Imogen should be—" but Miramis is cut off as Tinanna gasps and clutches her chest, face pale. Leaping across the room, Sari catches Tinanna just as she passes out. Not saying a word to any of the savitus fighters, she dashes out of the sub'tu. She owes Tinanna; Tinanna saved Zisu and regardless of Sari's feelings about her, she owes Tinanna for that.

Kalarah springs into action when Sari barges in without even asking to enter. "On the bed, hurry. Help me get these tight clothes off of her. If it's her heart... I don't know what we will do, but she can't have anything constricting her chest. She needs to breathe."

Sari does her best, anxiety setting her on fire each time her hand brushes across the coarse fur as she assists the healer. Tinanna gasps again, loud and ragged. "Cage," is all she whispers.

Sari squints, confused by what Tinanna said. A cage?

Tinanna pounds on her chest, still gasping for air. "In chest!"

Sari recalls that terrible day she had found Tinanna alone in the desert with a dagger. She had said something similar then, too.

"They caged your heart..." Sari says the words out loud, the words that Tinanna had cried out as she placed the point of a dagger on her chest. "And you wanted to cut it out."

Tinanna nods, eyes closed and breathing shallow again.

The healer takes a pair of scissors to the laces holding Tinanna's corselet and kirtle, pulling away the silken garments and exposing Tinanna's body.

As her eyes scan Tinanna's chest, she catches sight of a striking scar that runs through the center of it. Despite its subtleness, the scar's size is significant. "You mean literally..."

The former assassin nods again. "This cage around my heart can kill me, but it also lets them track my every move. That's how they found me. They'll always be able to find me like this. I won't be free until it's gone, but only they know how to take it out."

"Can you tell when they are tracking you?"

"Yes, I can. And they are. Right now."

Tinanna wheezes again and then passes out.

Sari looks around the healer's sick room. Zisu, Nanshaie, and now Tinanna. All of her companions are in here, and all of them are on the brink of death.

Eighteen

A CONTINGENT OF REVOLUTIONARIES FROM Fayn arrive the next day, a mix of lohyue and calla. The calla of Fayn often renounce their ties to the Suan qatu, claiming that while they are related, they are not the same, often citing the Suan people as bloodthirsty and violent. Sari anticipates clashes, but the calla revolutionaries are overly enthusiastic to show that they want to fit in and will abide by the traditions of the Suan qatu, even if they don't understand them. The thing that really perplexes them is the lack of solid doors. They were used to having a certain level of privacy and security, and the absence of solid doors is something they find hard to understand.

But missing from this contingent is Kegan; the much-promised linguist who could help them decipher the strange book that Sari had brought back from the City of Bec.

"Kegan fell ill when they were at sea and is still recovering. They insist that they be allowed to travel, but they vomited so much on board, they need to rehydrate," a Fayn revolutionary says. This revolutionary reminds Sari of the assassin that had come for Tinanna, the same strange facial features and unnatural way of holding herself and walking. She keeps so still that she might be made of stone, and her gait is fluid like a dancer. Her accent is only barely perceptible, but it is still distinctively different than the Fayn accent.

As they sit down to a meal in the communal sub'tu, this strange revolutionary, Imogen, as she had introduced herself, freezes, more still than a prey caught in the gaze of a predator. "Something is wrong. Something is very wrong." Her eyes are wide, eyebrows raised in a mix of horror and shock.

Does this stranger have the Sight? Sari wonders. Is this how the savitus fighters manage to always stay one step ahead? They have an army full of Sighted from across all of Ahnlisen? But how can that be when Yshuld is said to only gift the qatu of Sua with Sight? "Is it Ashur? Is his army on its way?" Sari slams her hands on the table when the revolutionary does not answer her.

Imogen rises to her feet gracefully and sprints out into the night with an agility that would make even the fa'leen jealous, if the fa'leen could experience such sentiment. Sari gives chase, determined not to be caught unawares, and worried that Ashur's army might somehow know Zisu is here and target her.

Sari's stomach drops when she realizes that Imogen is heading to the healer's sub'tu. *Oh no, please do not let it be Zisu...*

But when Imogen steps inside, she halts, and Sari almost runs into her. Imogen's jaw is dropped, both hands held over her mouth.

"What's wrong?" Sari asks. "What is happening?"

Imogen points at Tinanna, hand shaking. "Is she a savitus fighter?"

"Yes," Sari says. "She's one of the best here, too. But—"

"Oh gods, oh no. Oh gods, no!" Imogen turns away and frantically dashes back out of Kalarah's sub'tu. Sari looks back at Tinanna, sleeping, face contorted in pain, sweat drenching the sheets. Sleeping, but not at all peacefully.

Despite receiving assistance from the healers from Fayn, Zisu's fever has only worsened, resulting in a weakening pulse and increasingly rapid breathing. Nobody has been able to identify the source of her affliction. She had been healthy when they set out for the abandoned fortress. She had been hale, and had even asked some of the savitus fighters to teach her more advanced fighting techniques in the days before they set out. She had been in Ashur's clutches for less than an afternoon. How had she deteriorated so quickly? What had Ashur done to her?, and all without ever touching her?

Sari has been keeping vigil over her sister, staying by her side whenever she is not needed at meetings or trainings. But Kalarah shoos her out of the sub'tu and tells her that she needs to work alone. For the first time in her life, Sari goes into the desert not to hunt but to pray. She prays to Yshuld and Aydras; not sure if they are even listening. She would pray to the Tuyude gods when she was a child, to Efi for strength and battle prowess, to Mayd for the destruction of her foes, and sometimes to Aydras for victory and luck in hunting. But she has never prayed to Aydras for health or healing, not for herself and certainly not for others.

But now she prays to Yshuld, the goddess that blessed her family with the right to rule, and to Aydras, the goddess of healers, to join together and bless the youngest of the royal house.

As she wades into the center of the oasis, she bows her head and closes her eyes, not sure if she is even doing this correctly. She tries to recall the words that the priestess would recite in the isi'tu before formal gatherings, or what the priestess would say during high holidays. She trips over the words, stumbling over the phrases that she may have heard a thousand times but had never meant anything to her. But none of the words relate to healing—just victory, conquest, and domination.

If she wants to beg the goddess to intercede and save someone's life, she will have to make her own prayers.

"Yshuld and Aydras, celestial sisters; goddesses of the sun and the moons, hear me. Please." Please is not a word she has uttered often in her life, at least not sincerely. She's weaponized it to make herself look like less than a threat to those who trade favors in the royal court; a calculated plea to throw them off balance. But she knows she is the one without bargaining power here. All she has is her sincerity. "Please, save Zisu. I dragged her into this, she deserves to live. She deserves to be happy. If someone must pay for my sins, let it be me. Please. Heal her."

She lingers in the water for a long time after her prayers have been recited, unsure if there is something else she must do to ensure that the goddesses respond. But she knows if she tarries too long, the sun will reach its zenith, and she will be risking her own health. "I'll come back at night," she whispers to the wind. "Just in case Aydras only listens when the moons are in the sky." The leaves in the scrub brushes rustle and Sari shivers as she feels a phantom hand run its fingers through her hair.

When she returns to the healer's sub'tu, Imogen is whispering with Kalarah. Sari takes a seat next to Zisu, hoping to see even a hint of improvement; hoping to see a sign that her prayers are being answered. But her sister still labors to breathe, and her eyes still remain closed. She stays next to her sister for hours, wiping away the sweat and changing her robes, ladling soup into her mouth and wondering when she will show signs of improvement. Surely, the goddesses heard her and will intervene. But when?

"Excuse me," Imogen says, fidgeting with a silver ring as the sun sets. "May I ask you to step outside for a little bit? I would like to perform a procedure on Tinanna, and I require privacy."

Imogen's eyes are filled with silver specks. The person in front of her is not a lohyue but a *Ástfríður*, the same as the assassin who was sent to kill Tinanna. "What do you plan on doing?"

"Removing something dangerous in her body."

The cage around her heart. *Another assassin? Is this a more delicate plan to murder Tinanna?* She positions herself in front of Tinanna. "You are not a healer. Tell me why I should trust you to do it."

"Because I am the only person who can. I do not wish her harm. I am a friend."

"Then why can't I be in the room for it? I am her friend, too." A lie; Tinanna is not a friend. Not yet, not unless... But Sari needs to protect her—she owes Tinanna that much.

Imogen fidgets again with her ring, glancing at Tinanna. "Well..."

Another thought occurs to Sari. Perhaps the savitus fighters believe that Tinanna is now a liability, a burden, no longer valuable to them. They are pruning the withered branches. Sari might have done the same thing; there were plenty of times that she left soldiers behind because they could no longer fight. If Tinanna had been one of her troops, she might have left her behind.

But that was before... Before what? Before she knew how skilled Tinanna was? Or before Tinanna had saved Zisu? Before they had spent a night alternating between fighting and fucking, hurting and worshiping each other in equal, ecstatic measure?

"It is a delicate procedure," Imogen says. The softness in her voice finally convinces Sari that Tinanna is not in danger. "And it takes a lot of concentration."

These revolutionaries are strange; they have a spy that could die at any moment, a spy that can lead their enemies right to their nest, and yet they value her life still? She is a liability to their whole movement, and yet they protect her and ensure her safety? Maybe she is more valuable alive, maybe she offers something so important that they are willing to take the risk. Maybe this is strategy, and Tinanna has more to offer than they have let on. Sari wishes, for the first time, she had not grown up in the isi'tu, with it's plotting and intrigue, with lethal gossip and deadly courtiers. Would she be weighing Tinanna's life with as much coldness if she had been raised elsewhere?

"Please," Imogen says, lip quivering. "I need privacy to do this procedure."

Sari nods, picks up a flask of water, and departs from the sub'tu, the chilly night air doing nothing to calm her nerves. She will not be left in the dark; she leaps onto the thatch roof, landing without a sound. She knots her hair into a bun between her ears, grateful for the cloudy night, both moons obscured. She lies flat on the roof and leans over, peering through the window.

Imogen uses a small, sharp blade to slice open Tinanna's chest. Just watching it makes Sari want to vomit. Imogen closes her eyes and takes a deep breath, placing her hand, palm down, on the open flesh.

Sari holds her breath, eyes open wide, not wanting to miss a single second, ready to barrel through the window to save Tinanna if needed.

Steadily, Imogen raises her hand from Tinanna's chest, a stream of copper rising up to follow it as if pulled by a string. The revolutionary bites her lip, and sweat beads on her forehead. She turns her palm up, and the liquid copper pools into her hand. She smiles before collapsing to the floor.

The next evening, Sari returns to the healer's sub'tu after her prayers to Aydras. Neither Nanshaie nor Zisu have awakened, but Tinanna has. She is sitting upright, sipping on cool fikiru. "I prefer it plain," she says as Sari approaches and hands her the cup. "Kalarah mixed in fruit. You can have it."

Sari shrugs and finishes the tangy drink in one gulp. "Are you feeling better? Did Imogen do... whatever she said she would do?"

"I don't want to talk about that."

"Why not?"

Tinanna slumps against the headboard. "It wasn't successful."

Sari raises an eyebrow; she'd seen Imogen remove the metal, or at least that's what she thought she saw. "That's not what I heard," she says, unsure how to call out Tinanna on the lie without admitting she was spying.

Tinanna sighs, rolling her eyes. "It was somewhat successful. They got most of the cage out, but there is a fragment of it that has grown into my heart, and removing it is impossible. It's embedded in it, it will stay in me forever; they will always be able to find me."

"What will happen now?"

"They can still track me, but at least I'm not at constant risk of death anymore. I'll never be truly free, but at least this won't kill me."

Sari has no idea how to respond to Tinanna. *I'll never truly be free, either. Not while Ashur lives.* "Do you want me to get you some water?"

Tinanna nods. Sari gets up, taking the empty tin cup from Tinanna's bedside and dipping it into the bucket of fresh water near the hearth.

"And me, too..." Nanshaie says.

Sari drops the cup and rushes to the Oracle's side. "You're awake..."

Tinanna joins them, her breathing strained but steady. Nanshaie sits up, carefully propping herself up on an elbow, and Tinanna engulfs Nanshaie in a tight embrace. Nanshaie winces as Tinanna's arms wrap around her, but she does not push her away.

A strange tightness grips Sari's chest; some emotion she cannot name fills her heart. The two have known each other for years at the temple, but they had acted like strangers until this point. Why are they affectionate now? Why does it bother her? "I'll go get the healer," Sari says, turning away from the two qatu still locked in an embrace.

"No, wait," Nanshaie says. "I have something important to share."

Sari halts, turning around as the two disentangling themselves, Nanshaie's hands shaking.

"I learned a lot of things while Ashur—" She bites her lip. "The Heart of Aodhe, their plans, I need to tell you now."

"No, you can do that later. You need medical attention now," Tinanna says, moving a damp strand of hair out of Nanshaie's face.

"It has to be now," Nanshaie says, extricating herself from Tinanna's arms.

"Very well." Sari sits back down next to the Oracle, stomach in knots as she prays to Yshuld that Nanshaie's information will be useful.

"The Heart of Aodhe is an energy source with the power to bring about a perpetual paradise, but it can bring about a terrible cataclysm as well. Only those belonging to your mother's bloodline can wield it, though."

"Ashur, myself, and Zisu are all that remain," Sari says. "Its power might be lost forever if we—"

Nanshaie nods. "The power to end the world will be lost forever if you destroy it."

"That is not what I meant," Sari says, wringing her hands.

"But it's what you needed to hear." It's not just Nanshaie speaking; Sari recognizes now when Yshuld chooses to speak with Nanshaie's voice.

Sari shifts in her chair. "But the power could be used—"

"That power—magic—used to exist all across Ahnlisen, plentiful and accessible. There are rumors that it is returning to the land in Fayn. Ia believes that the Heart is the key to releasing even more of that magic."

"And why should we prevent that?" Sari does not understand. It's a recourse, one with consequences but one that can be used, just as fire.

"With that magic loose, Ashur plans to destroy the world." Yshuld says.

"That makes no sense, though. Ia sided with him, she has been talking of nothing but bringing about paradise! Why would she let Ashur destroy the world? Why choose him and not..." Not her. Not Sari. A doomed world is better than a paradise with Sari. Why?

"She believes the world needs to be cleansed, that paradise cannot exist in the world as it is now. She says that she will build her paradise on our ashes." It's Nanshaie speaking this time, sorrow and loss in each word.

"That makes no sense," Tinanna says, looking out the window. "I've been her guard for years, and she's never expressed any of these opinions."

"I do not understand it, either." Nanshaie twirls a stray lock of hair. "She kept explaining it to me, and sometimes it would almost make sense, but others... She believes the world as it is now is on the path to complete annihilation, nothing left to rebuild on. Nothing can stop our predetermined demise. But using the Heart would leave it fertile, capable of growing her paradise after the flames have died."

"When?"

"Ashur and Ia plan on bringing about this destruction on the next Gamasittuum Buuli."

"That's less than a month away." Sari glances out of the window, both moons low in the sky. Gamasittuum Buuli, the night when both moons are new, is a holy day for those who follow Mayd, the goddess of destruction.

Nanshaie buries her face in her hands. "What I've been seeing this whole time; those scenes of destruction; it's this cataclysm. The terrible nightmares. All of them are what will happen on the Gamasittuum Buuli if we don't stop Ashur and Ia."

"That's impossible," Tinanna says. "He might have the power to change soldiers into beasts, but destroying the whole world? With nothing left? That kind of power cannot be possible."

Nanshaie's body shakes as she burst into tears, her sobs echoing through the sub'tu. She leans into Tinanna, leaning into her chest. As Nanshaie cries, Tinanna winces in pain, but she does not push Nanshaie away. She puts a hand on the Oracles had, gently rubbing circles with her thumb between Nanshaie's ears.

Sari reels at the revelation. She is not special; Ia had not chosen her for any reason aside from her being a royal and easy to manipulate. Ia needed someone of royal blood to wield her weapon. Would she have gone along with this plan if Ia had stayed loyal to her? Would she have destroyed the world if she was promised she would rule it after?

Ia had knelt before her, pledged herself to Sari's cause, promising eternal loyalty. In that moment, if Ia had told her to destroy the world, she might have. She might have done anything Ia asked in repayment for that loyalty.

No, there is no 'might have.' Sari's stomach drops. She *would have*. She would have done as Ia asked. She would have let that oath of fealty cloud her mind, believing every lie Ia might whisper in her ear. She would have done it if it meant beating Ashur, finally winning the Sitnu, freeing herself from the iseru only to rule over a kingdom of ash.

Her dreams of reclaiming the crown, of being the hero that saves her people from the insurrectionists, have warped into a nightmare where she is the villain cursed by survivors. She would not have needed to use the Heart to turn herself into the kahbush'a of her own story.

"I have to stop him," Sari whispers, not meaning to say it out loud. She springs from her chair, staggering to a window, needing fresh air—the faces of her dead troops flashing in her mind. Belu. Ditanu. Tanit. Even Yangi. "I had to, I had to—there was no other choice. But if I don't take out Ashur... I can't be... I'm not the monster. I'm not."

"Sari?" Tinanna's voice is shaky. "What are you talking about?"

She needs more air. There is not enough air in the sub'tu. She needs to go outside. She crosses the room, making for the entrance, not wanting either of her companions to see her face. "I will tell Miramis about this."

Nanshaie pulls away from Tinanna. "Who is Miramis?"

"She's a leader for the Amyrdine Bara, the savitus fighters."

"Savitus? Is that who you—Those weren't mercenaries?"

Tinanna laughs but then coughs and winces in pain. "No, Sari has turned coat and is working with the savitus fighters now; the so-called insurrectionists whom she had vowed to destroy."

Sari's hand instinctively reaches for the royal seal still hidden under her tunic. She wants to correct Tinanna, she wants to point out that they are working together but that does not mean her loyalties have shifted. *I don't want to be the villain...*

Regardless, Ashur and Ia must die; and she can think of many delicious ways for them to die.

Nineteen

THE SUN IS SWELTERING DESPITE THE autumn day, and Sari wrings out the cloth in the basin before dipping it again in the bowl of clean, cold water. She hums as she lightly brushes the cloth against her sister's arms, an old lullaby she would sing when they were still young qits in the royal nursery.

"Please come back," she whispers as the last note ends. Tinanna and Nanshaie have both recovered enough to leave the healer's sub'tu, yet Zisu remains unconscious. "Please come back."

Sari can't help but recall the way she and Zisu would chase each other around the nursery when no one else was there, taking turns playing monsters and warriors. Their time as qits might have been stained by the Sitnu, but the few times that Sari had smiled had always been with Zisu.

Someone touches Sari's arm, and she jumps out of her seat, hand instinctively reaching for the sword she no longer wields; the sword she could not wield even if it were still in her possession.

But it is only Nanshaie. How long has she been there? What has she seen?

The Oracle smiles. "May I help you?" But she does not wait for Sari to answer; she finds a cloth and rolls Zisu on her side, washing sweat from her back and neck.

"By the way," Nanshaie says after they finish bathing Zisu. "I came to let you know that Kegan has arrived."

"So they overcame their seasickness?"

Nanshaie laughs, rising to her feet and holding out a hand to Sari. "She arrived last night, but was not feeling well. From what I heard, they were scowling at everyone and when Miramis asked if they were ready to meet you, Kegan said they still weren't feeling well and it would be best for everyone if they had another night to recover."

"Fayn calla are weak." Sari says.

But Nanshaie squeezes her hand and leads her away from Zisu and out of the healer's sub'tu. "I wouldn't say that. Miramis warned everyone once Kegan was locked in their room not to disturb them if they enjoyed having their heads still on their shoulders."

"Kegan is violent?" Sari might be willing to respect this Fayn revolutionary after all.

"Kegan apparently said 'I have no desire to bite anyone's head off, but I will not be held responsible if I do.' Enough people took the warning to heart." Nanshaie holds her hand all the way across the streets of Izmyri and into the headquarters of the savitus fighters.

The calla from Fayn is laughing when Sari and Nanshaie enter the communal sub'tu. But the second the calla's eyes fall into Sari, they stop, scowling.

"What's wrong with them?" Sari asks Nanshaie. Nanshaie shrugs, pulling her veil over her face—assuming once more the position of Oracle.

"Oh, good, you're here," Miramis says. The smith has been kind to Sari, showing concern for Zisu and the mending of Sari's hand, but the begrudging respect that had once shown in her eyes has vanished since they returned from the disastrous attack on the ancient fortress. "Kegan, this is Saritrah and the Oracle."

Sari nods at the calla—annoyed that Nanshaie was introduced with her title, while she was not. *But I do not have a title, not according to the revolutionaries or insurrectionists.* Nanshaie folds herself into a low bow. "It is an honor," Nanshaie says, her cadence taking the formality of her office, "to meet someone so well-learned. I look forward to discussing much more than ancient texts, professor."

The calla laughs. "I am no professor."

"You did not study at a university?" Nanshaie does not let surprise creep into her voice, but Sari recognizes the small backward step Nanshaie takes.

"I taught myself." Kegan shrugs.

"An even more impressive accomplishment." Nanshaie inclines her head again.

Kegan laughs, tail swishing. "I wish Aine were here for this. Never been mistaken for anyone respectable." Their words trail off and the laughter leaves their voice.

"Anyway," Miramis says, clearing her throat and interrupting Kegan. "Let's get to the matter at hand." Miramis gestures for Sari and Nanshaie to take a seat at the table.

"Now I feel self-conscious," Kegan says, plopping a bag on the table. "Being called smart, but I can't give you as much as you probably want."

Miramis scratches her chin. "What do you mean?"

"I can't translate everything. I tried, but some of the pages are too faded, some pages are missing entirely. And the strangest part is sometimes the words re-arrange themselves on the page as I'm reading them."

"Rearrange themselves?" Miramis raises an eyebrow.

"What starts out as valuable information transforms into a very dull paragraph on the migration patterns of birds." Kegan lets out a breath and runs a finger along the rim of a mug.

"I never saw anything like that," Nanshaie says, smothing out the folds of her robe as she takes a seat. "But I did not have as long to read it as I would have wanted."

Miramis reclines in her chair, lacing her fingers together behind her head, ignoring Nanshaie. "Were you able to learn anything useful?" Miramis asks.

"Yes, and no. It is a history book, for the most part. It details a very bloody war."

"The era of Isidoran invasion?" Nanshaie asks.

Kegan shrugs. "I might know languages, but not history that well. Is that a country or a person?"

"A country with imperialistic goals. Garcelon now inhabits much of what used to be Isador, but if it does not mention it, I suppose we can assume it wasn't."

Miramis sighs. "It doesn't matter if it doesn't help us. Go on, Kegan."

"There was someone named Aodhe that helped end the war. She invented something called a 'Heart,' if I am translating that correctly."

"Was it a weapon?" Sari asks, terrified of the answer.

"Not originally. But it was used as one."

"What happened when it was used?" Sari leans forward, trying to keep her anxiety in check but needing confirmation of what Nanshaie had told her already.

"It destroyed everything within hundreds of mitus of it."

"Everything?" Sari asks, tail flicking. "A large weapon is used that destroys everything and there's no evidence of that today? I don't care how long ago this was. We'd see some sort of proof of that. Ruins, some mention of it in history books, scars across the continent. Something!"

"If I had to guess," Kegan says, tapping their chin. "I would say that the proof is the Esiri desert."

Sari's heart sinks as she recalls the abandoned fortress. The Esiri desert seems eternal, endless. Beautiful in its infinity; it's hard to imagine that it once might not have existed.

"But if it destroyed everything, what about the city? Everything was still standing in Bec, that's where we got the book in the first place. It was still standing," Sari says, not sure if she's trying to convince herself or explain something to Kegan.

Kegan shrugs. "Couldn't tell you. I'm just translating what is on the page."

"What you say lines up with what I learned while being held by Ashur and Ia," Nanshaie says, voice still that of an Oracle.

"If this isn't about Isador," an older woman asks, "does it at least say who the combatants were in this war? Forgive my curiosity." The woman glances at Miramis and lowers her head.

Miramis rolls her eyes and shrugs. "Go ahead, Kegan. Answer my mother's question."

"Two religious orders. The Araelta and the Blodheimr Hjart. It seems that Aodhe's home—the City of Bec—was caught in their crossfire. A neutral state with the misfortune of being located between two warring powers."

"I have never heard of those orders before," Miramis's mother says. "Does it say what region they are from?"

Miramis buries her face in her palms. "I cannot wait for your sabbatical to end."

"No," Kegan says. "I do not think so." But Sari hears the hesitation in Kegan's voice. There is something the Fayn calla is not saying.

"How do you know that's what it says? If this is an ancient language," a savitus fighter asks. "And this book mentions cities and people we've never heard of before, how come you know it?"

"I've seen this language before, in Fayn." Kegan reaches across the table to pull the pitcher of water closer, refilling the mug and taking a long sip. They frown, gaze flickering between the glass in front of them and the pitcher. "I've encountered people who claim to be descendants of these Araelta and Blodheimr Hjart." They bring the pitcher to their lips and tilt it back, drinking the rest of it all of it at once. "And they were intent to bring about destruction again."

"What were they doing in Fayn?" Miramis asks, glaring at her mother.

"The Blodheimr Hjart were secret backers of the monarchy. Or rather, the Folas were their puppets."

"Fuck," Miramis keeps her gaze fixed on Kegan, but Sari can feel the eyes of everyone else in the room assessing her. "Do you think they manipulate other monarchies?"

"I've never heard of them before," Sari says, for some reason wanting to defend her parents—they were strong, they were warriors, they were made of fire and steel; they would never have allowed themselves to be manipulated! They were not puppets to anyone. *Oh. Oh no.* It's midday, but she shivers as if it were the dead of night. "Although, Ia claims to have been working with the Araelta."

She tried to manipulate me; she tried to manipulate Ashur.

"The Araelta had tried to sway over many of the court to their side when I was there," Kegan says, hands clasped in front of them, staring into the distance. "Not openly; I doubt anyone truly realized what was going on until the very end. But it makes sense they would now seek out the same kind of favor here."

"You said that the Araelta destroyed the City of Bec?" Sari asks, rubbing her forehead.

"It does not say which side of this war caused the destruction of the city; just that the two were trading blows and Bec was caught in the middle."

"It was not a city that the Araelta lived in?"

"I don't think so, it does not seem like it from what I can read. But there are many pages missing, and I cannot translated everything."

Sari rubs her temples. None of this makes sense. Ia had made it seem like she wanted to bring about a civilization like Bec; the way she had spoken of Bec made it seem like she idolized it, like she held it up as a pinnacle of civilization; the zenith of society; an example for all to aspire to. And yet she has aligned herself with the Araelta; the people who were at least partially to blame for destroying Bec.

"The good news, I suppose, is that I believe I know where Ashur and Ia might be heading next. Or, I think I have it narrowed down to three locations. I want to read a little more and also was hoping someone here might have some other historical books on hand to cross reference."

"I don't know about any tomes here in Izmyri, but I can recite all of the historical epics. Even the more obscure ones," Nanshaie says.

"That would be useful," Kegan says, smiling and refilling their mug once again.

"I would love to help, too," Miramis's mother says. "I am Professor Amata mar Iltani, Head of the Department of History at the University of Khadima Alama. You may call me Matty, though."

Miramis stands up, a silent dismissal; adjourning the meeting.

Sari storms out without another word, clenching and unclenching her left hand, determined to learn how to wield a weapon again despite her injury.

Kalarah had not exactly promised that she would regain feeling in the remains of the last two fingers of her left hand, but she did say it was possible. Some feeling has returned, and some mobility has returned. But not enough to wield weapons as skillfully as she once had. Her face burns. If she had been a soldier in her own army, she would have been considered a burden, dead weight. Such a minor injury, one that could be overcome with time. But the kind of leader Sari had been just half a year ago would not have seen it that way.

She lunges with the practice spear, extra force being applied with her left hand on the shaft, her right hand clutching it more tightly. She still has not figured out how to keep the weight of it balanced while she gathers momentum.

She misses her mark; but she backs up and tries again, imagining that the red mark she had painted on the rock is her brother's face. She has only a few weeks to stop him; the Gamasittuum Buuli is in less than three weeks and Kegan wants a few more days to figure out where Ashur could possibly be.

She's never been one to believe in fate or destiny; the only fate she's believed in is the one she can snatch with her own claws. Throughout her life, she has consistently believed that fate and destiny are illusions. The patron goddess of Sua might be Yshuld, goddess of many things, but the most important of her domains are prophecy and fate. Sari always discounted the last of Yshuld's yokes, even while paying lip service to Her Seers. And yet she is hurtling towards a future that seems to be foretold already.

"Do you mind if I join you?"

Sari spins around to see Nanshaie approaching, a practice spear strapped to her back.

Sari laughs. Nanshaie is not the person she would have expected to come to find her. "Sure, I can give you some pointers if you want."

"I feel like I can give you a few, too."

"Mine hurt, though. I don't want to hurt you."

"Oh? So, you do care about hurting others. What I saw with your sister was not a fluke." Nanshaie, without warning, lunges towards

Sari; the tip of the spear aimed directly at her heart rather than the rock behind her.

Sari, caught off guard, ducks to the ground and rolls to safety, her heartbeat filling her ears. Nanshaie had claimed to learn what she knows of fighting simply from watching others; she had been of little use as they fought their way to the pinnacle of the tower in Bec, and yet the level of prowess she now displays surpasses even well-trained soldiers.

Sari springs to her feet again, flexing her toes in the sand as she tries to find a new center of balance for her spear. Nanshaie circles her like smilodon—intimidating and hungry. Sari watches her opponent's calf muscles, waiting for Nanshaie to give away her next move.

Dodging Nanshaie's strike, Sari spins around to smack the back of Nanshaie's knees, but she missteps, falling into the coarse, burning sand with a yelp.

Nanshaie offers her hand. "Do you want to call it a draw for now?"

Sari laughs, getting back to her feet. "Sure." She grabs her satchel and pulls out a flask of water, taking a sip before handing it to Nanshaie.

Nanshaie sits down beside her, pulling out her own pouch and offering Sari some dates.

Sari takes one and nibbles around the pit, mulling over her thoughts. There is something that she has been wanting to ask Nanshaie, something that has been eating away at her. "In any of your visions, did you see a future where the Heart could bring about paradise?"

"I saw destruction regardless of who got the Heart of Aodhe. I just saw worse destruction if Ashur had it. I never saw paradise; I only ever see nightmares. Remember?"

A knot forms in Sari's stomach. If she tries to take the throne and wield the Heart, will she just end up leaving destruction in her wake? Is she destined to destroy her own kingdom—even as she tries to save it? Is this why people are not loyal to her? Is there something fundamentally wrong with her, and everyone else can see it?

Is she too broken—too battered and bruised from all of her fights in the iseru—for people to follow? Too scarred for anyone to love?

Sari sighs, knowing the answer to her silent questions already. She is too broken for anyone to be loyal to, or for anyone to love. Her parent's made sure of that. Her parents struck her like a hammer on hot iron; they forged her into a weapon. Weapons can do nothing but destroy. "I am tired," Sari says, sitting up. "I am going back. Do you want to come with me?"

"No, I'll stay here for a little longer. I would like to pray."

Of course she would not want to accompany me, Sari thinks. She slings her satchel over her shoulder and straps her spear to her back.

She is no more than ten steps away when she hears Nanshaie. "Hey wait!"

Sari's heart leaps and she turns back.

"But it doesn't matter," Nanshaie says, approaching her. "It doesn't matter what I saw in my visions. Because you aren't going to try to take the throne—you said you gave it up. Right? So, it doesn't matter what I saw if it was based on you claiming the throne, because it won't happen. Right?" Nanshaie gives a hesitant smile, the face of the Oracle replaced by that of someone far too inexperienced—to naive—for the mess she is in.

Sari smiles back, stomach dropping. "Right. Yes. I need to get back, though. I want to check on Zisu."

Even though they are not traveling in the desert, the people of Izmyri still observe nialsamsu on the hottest of days. Sari has set up a cot next to Zisu in the healer's sub'tu. She cannot sleep. Every few minutes, she wipes sweat from Zisu's brow and holds her hand, pleading with her silently to wake up, to get up. Eventually, she drifts off to sleep beside her sister, holding her close like she used to do when they were children.

"Sari?"

She is shaken awake, springing to her feet and reaching for a weapon before realizing it's her sister. Awake. Moonlight streams in from the open window, illuminating her sister in a soft glow. "Sari? Where are we?"

She cannot find the words she wants to say; she pulls her sister in, squeezing her to her chest and breathing in deeply, thanking Yshuld and Aydras for returning her sister to her.

"Oh, thank you. Oh thank the gods, you're alive. I have been so worried," she says.

Her whispered words are drowned out by screams from outside. It's Nanshaie. Nanshaie is crying out; the scream of someone still caught in a nightmare.

Knot in her stomach, Sari rushes outside, leaving her sister alone and confused still, only to witness Nanshaie forcefully banging her hands on the ground and running her fingers through the sand. "We have to get out! We have to get out!"

"What's wrong?" Sari asks, taking Nanshaie's hands in her own, pretending she does not see the blood on them. "What is happening?"

"Something terrible!" She tries to pull away from Sari, struggling to free her arms from Sari's grip. "Fire in the sky and waves of sand; the end of the world, the end of everything. Monsters will roam the desert in search of prey and death shall stalk behind. And then..." She shudders, eyes rolling back. "Someone too terrible to remember shall be freed to prowl again. Shackles cast off; she will seek her quarry."

Nanshaie's voice takes on that same ancient timber, delicate and harsh at the same time, far away yet everywhere. Her eyes are wild; fear racing across her face, her lips quiver and her ears are flat against her head.

"Who will be freed?" Sari asks, struggling to contain the flailing seer.

"She'll never stop..."

"Who? Who won't stop?"

"We have to go, we have to! The old woman... She showed me where we need to go. We need to leave. We need to go now. If we don't leave now..." She pulls against Sari, kicking up dust and sand as she tries to get to her feet again.

A crowd has gathered around them. The people of Izmyri call out for Kalarah, some of them sink to their knees and chant for Yshuld—fear and awe woven into their song. But the revolutionaries from Fayn look on with skepticism, some of them even laugh.

"Can we round up the village?" Sari asks as Miramis shoves her way through the crowd. "Can we get everyone out?"

The smith runs her hand through her hair and sighs. "Maybe a few, but I doubt we can convince everyone."

"Why not? She's the Oracle, she just said—"

"The Oracle is not universally respected anymore," Miramis says, crossing her arms.

"But she's necessary, she's blessed by Yshuld, she sits above even the sahre'danus."

"And no one here recognizes the sahre'danus. Get what I am saying? And besides, there's no way the Fayns here would listen, they don't even believe in Sight."

"But we have to! Just, please trust me." Sari wants to hit Miramis until she listens, but she can't risk letting Nanshaie go.

"Alright. I believe you. But I'm not gonna force that on the rest of Izmyri." For a second, Miramis looks almost sympathetic. Sari knows that this savitus leader trust the Oracle, but her own principals won't allow her to issue strict commands to her fighters, let alone the people just living in the town.

"The old woman says we must leave, it will be here before twilight!" Nanshaie repeats, eyes wide, seeing something terrible just behind Sari.

"I know, I know." Sari takes Nanshaie's face in her hands. "I know."

"We can't let the harbinger walk among us..." Her eyes roll back, and she goes limp, collapsing into Sari's arms..

"Nanshaie," Sari whispers, catching the Oracle before she hits the sand. "Wake up."

Laughter rises from a gaggle of Fayn lohyue to their left. Sari wants to sink her teeth into the jugular of the Fayn lohyue who is imitating Nanshaie's speech with condescension in every word, mocking the holiest figure in Sua.

Just as Kalarah rushes up to them, Nanshaie opens her eyes again. "What is going on?"

"I don't know. You came out here screaming about some tragedy," Sari says.

"I did?" Nanshaie says, not noticing those gathered around them. "I don't remember... How long have I been out?"

With a quick and calculated movement, Ahati mat Gamalet adeptly sidesteps to the left, narrowly evading Sari's spear. Sari curses, dropping her weapon and wiping away the sweat on her forehead. "I still can't get the weight right," she says.

"I keep telling you, switch hands. It's not as hard as you think," Ahati replies. Ahati had arrived with a unit of troops from Arrinhu. Ahati mat Gamalet. Sari had recognized her name immediately; daughter of Gamalet mat Ettu, the sahre of Arrinhu. The largest vassalate in Sua, and always Ettu was threatening to leave Sua and start her own empire. And yet, Ahati had gone against her mother, supporting first Sumalika and later Sari.

"But I've always used my right hand." She flexes her fingers; the remnants of the last two barely move. *Why did I allow myself to get injured so badly?*

In the end, Miramis could not convince anyone to flee, and with Nanshaie forgetting all about her prediction, Sari had to chalk it up to just a bad dream. Not a prophecy of disaster, just a regular nightmare that can happen to anyone. As the days passed and no disaster struck, Sari could not even argue with Miramis about it any further. Still waiting for Kegan to finish their translations, she does the only thing she can think of: training.

"So did I until I was injured. I had to relearn with my left hand, sure, but I learned it the right way the first time. No bad habits to break first. I'd say I'm better than ever now." Ahati stabs her spear back in the sand and sits on the blanket at the edge of the training fields, rummaging through her pack for food.

Zisu wanders over, a flask in each hand. She offers one to Sari. "Are you almost done?"

"Almost." Sari has thanked the goddesses every day for Zisu's recovery, but she can't help but feel like she is missing something. Like the goddesses will reconsider and decide to take Zisu away again; like she has not done enough to *deserve* her sister's good health. She cannot pinpoint why she feels this way, and she's too afraid to ask Nanshaie, who might be able to answer questions about divine bargains and prayers.

"Great, I think I'm going to take one more go with Tinanna."

Sari grimaces as Zisu wanders away, a Fayn sword in hand. She still isn't sure how she feels about Zisu fighting. The little sister she had tried so hard to keep sheltered from violence is now wielding weapons adeptly. Zisu swings her sword with precision as she moves through another set of exercises. Sari is not sure if she should be horrified or proud.

"Mind if I join you?" A calla from Fayn approaches. "Just one round."

Sari takes another sip from the flask Zisu had given her and nods.

"By the way," the Fayn calla says, "what was up with that other companion of yours?"

Sari stows the flask in her bag and rises to her feet, spear firmly gripped in her left hand. "She's the Oracle. Yshuld's Chosen."

They each assume a fighting stance, tapping their feet to count down.

"She seems a little mad. Tighten your grip in the back," the Fayn calla says before unleashing a whirlwind of thrusts and parries in the Fayn fighting style.

Sari strikes back, concentrating on keeping her hands steady as she fights her own muscles and habits. Gritting her teeth, she lashes at the calla.

"She's chosen by a goddess. Do not insult her." She snakes the spear under her opponent's, its point grazing the calla's neck.

The calla drops her spear and raises her hands in defeat.

Without warning, the sky darkens; the darkness of night without any of the guiding lights of stars or moons.

"What the—" She is interrupted by her brother's laughter in the wind, drowning out the sounds of metal and wood clashing in the training yard, punctuated by a crack of thunder.

"I didn't know you get thunderstorms in Sua," the calla says.

"We don't," Sari hisses as a sheet of freezing rain and hail is unleashed from the skies, flooding the landscape. "We need to get to safety! Cover your mouths and nose!"

The rain stings, the hail sharp enough to leave cuts along Sari's exposed skin, as she flees with the rest of her training companions. She unties her sash from her waist and wraps it around her head. She searches the eyes of those retreating in panic, looking for Zisu's.

"Sari!" Zisu finds her, panting, a veil pulled over her head, her sword dragging point down in the sand. "Are you alright?"

Sari nods, grabbing her sister's hand and dragging her along. "We need to get somewhere high. Now."

They climb the curving path carved into the side of the plateau, making it back into Izmyri's gates, and pandemonium has broken out within the town's walls. The howling winds whip through the town, carrying away everything in their path; a handful of small trees, canvas and leather awnings, and worst of all; sand. A wooden plaque careens through the air, crashing into Zisu. The small qatu doubles over, gasping for air.

Before Sari can stop her, Zisu removes the veil over her face, and inhales a mouthful of sharp sand.

"Let me help!" Nanshaie says. She throws one of Zisu's arms over her shoulders, lifting her back to her feet. "I know where to go. Follow me."

Sari reties the veil, hoping her sister did not inhale too much sand. She does not need to ask Nanshaie how she knows where to go. The Oracle foresaw this. *If we had just listened to her,* Sari thinks. *We would have had time to get away. If I had told people to believe her, we would already be somewhere safe. Why didn't I try harder to make the Fayn believe? Why was I so quick to accept it was just a regular nightmare?*

Nanshaie leads as many people as will believe her out of the walls of Izmyri, promising that the only safe place is in the desert. As they leave the gate behind them, the earth lurches. Sari looks back to see even the sturdiest of sub'tus shaking and crashing into the ground.

Zisu collapses, sliding to the ground between Nanshaie and Sari. Sari lifts her up, throwing her over her shoulder, and takes off into the desert, Nanshaie rallying the survivors to keep following her. As they near two buttes, Nanshaie points to an outcrop of rocks that look like stairs carved into the side, and at the top is a small cavern. "Into that cave! We'll be safe there!" Her voice takes on the tone of prophecy.

The survivors, panting and exhausted, follow Nanshaie's lead. The wind continues to mock them, and the rain continues to pelt them; the only bit of hope lies in the fact that at least the rain has made the sand so wet that it no longer flies through the air.

The survivors scramble up the carved steps, Nanshaie waiting at the bottom, encouraging people to climb. "Go," Sari tells her. "I'll make sure the rest get up. Just take Zisu."

Nanshaie shakes her head. "I must see everyone up."

The Oracle says she must stay at the bottom until all are safe—not Nanshaie. Sari nods; she would insist if it were Nanshaie she was speaking with. But it isn't, not right now. She hoists Zisu into her arms, ready to climb the butte.

"Zisu? Wake up. We're almost there, we'll be safe soon."

Her sister coughs, sand spraying out of her mouth. She coughs again before opening her eyes and wiggling out of her sister's arms and walking into the storm, grabbing a sword laying in the sand. "Zisu! Wait!"

She chases after her sister, her screams drowned out by the wind. But despite the lack of moons or sun, her sister glows; standing out against the darkness, a beacon in the tempest. Sari can barely see her through her veil and the sands, but that glow—so similar to the bright glow of the moon Yludi—continues to shine, engulfing her sister as she raises her sword above her head as if she were about to strike down a foe.

The laughs of her brother dissipate as the bright light of her sister flares brighter than the sun. A different voice meets her ears; her sister's voice. "Aydras, help me!" A prayer, a plea. And then, softer. "Goodbye for now, my sister. We'll meet again."

"Zisu, no!" Sari runs towards the light even as she closes her eyes against the pain. She trips to the ground and her hands do not meet sand, but the smooth silk of her sister's robe. Feeling around in the dark, she lifts her sister into her arms and turns back around, needing to get her sister into the cavern. As she runs, she realizes that though the howl of the wind continues, a strange barrier has settled over the area. It's not dissimilar to the barrier over the ancient City of Bec. It holds back the fury of the storm, allowing the last stragglers from Izmyri to make it into the cavern in the butte.

It feels like a sanctuary, a refuge from the calamity outside, when she steps inside herself. Sari finds a small alcove and sets her sister down. "What were you thinking, Zisu?" But her sister does not respond. "Zisu?" She shakes her and then pulls her mouth to her ear, listening for even a shallow breath. "Zisu, please. We're safe now. We're safe."

But Zisu still does not respond. Sari checks her sister's pulse, but finds none. She shakes her head. *No, no. Not now, after everything... Not now.* She leans down, her ear on her sister's chest, but there is no heartbeat. She holds a hand just above her sisters mouth, but still no breath passes her lips.

"No, no..." She lays down next to her sister, pulling her lifeless body to her chest, running her hands over her tangled hair. "You can't leave me," she whispers, kissing her sister's forehead. "I told you that you could go to university, remember? You can't go before—" She screams, not caring who hears her, hoping the whole pantheon can feel her fury.

As the hours pass, survivors huddled in their cave, the rain and hail are replaced with fireballs plummeting from the sky. Sari stands at the entrance to the cave, clutching the royal seal in both hands, and watches as each scorching object crashes into the sands, setting the scattered detritus ablaze. The desert is an inferno, and Sari swears she can hear the screams of fright on the wind, carrying from all corners of Sua. Sometimes, she thinks they might be *her* screams. How many times has she grieved Zisu? Thought her sister was dead only to learn otherwise; sometimes it was in the iseru. But then, it was the night she escaped the isi'tu. Long years she grieved, carrying her sisters death like a talisman, a name she would get vengeance for.

But now, she really is gone. Her cold and lifeless body still sits in that alcove, covered in a thing silk cloth. This time, Zisu truly is dead, no matter what she had said about meeting again.

There would not be a tomorrow with Zisu. There will not be joyous days visiting her sister at Khadima Alam as she studies whatever it is her heart wants to know. There will not be days of their qits playing together. A thousand tomorrows that will never come.

When, at last, the nightmare ends and all that remains is ash and sand, Nanshaie leads the survivors in a ceremony to mourn the dead alongside a Fayn priestess of Xana that had joined the revolutionaries. Sari carries her sister outside, searching for somewhere that she can cremate her remains in peace and away from everyone else. It is customary for royalty to be cremated as a showing of strength, of bravery, and courage. Proof that the heat of the desert is no match for the fire that burns in the veins of the royals. But now, that ceremony seems inappropriate. Zisu did not want to be royal. Not in life and certainly not in death.

Nevertheless, Sari lights the flame and sinks into the sand, ignoring the tears welling in her eyes, telling herself that it's the sting of the smoke penetrating her veil and not the grief cutting through her armor.

"May I join you?" Nanshaie says, startling Sari.

Sari glares at the Oracle, an anger in her chest that she cannot describe or explain. "No."

Why didn't I believe her? If I had...

"There was nothing you could do," Nanshaie says.

"How would you know?" Sari lashes out, her claws extending.

"I'll leave you alone," Nanshaie says, her face pale.

Woven over and through Nanshaie's words are Yshuld's: *you are never alone in the desert.*

But she wants nothing to do with gods or divinity. Not when they had given her Zisu back only to snatch her away again.

As soon as she no longer hears the soft footsteps of the Oracle, Sari screams until her throat is sore and the only sounds left inside of her are sobs.

She wants to step into the flame, let it take her, too. Zisu was the only person who had loved her, without reservation, without condition. Zisu had trusted her, relied on her, had faith in her.

And she deserved none of it. If someone handed her the Heart of Aodhe right now and told her that she could have Zisu back if only she spread this inferno across all of Ahnlisen...

She wants to say she would do it. She wants to say she would tear down the sky and uproot the earth if it meant Zisu would return, would smile one more time.

But she knows that if she did that, Zisu's smile would not be for her. Zisu would still love her, but she would not ever speak to her again.

She had chased down the map instead of getting Zisu to a healer. She had chosen her throne over her sister. She had chosen power over the only person who would ever love her.

I am too broken. She runs her claws through the sand, drawing the sigil of Yshuld. Too broken, too shattered. Her soul is a dozen scattered pieces, each worn down so that the pieces do not even fit together anymore.

The few pieces of herself she can still hold onto; resentment, anger, rage... but at the center of all of that is shame. She hates who she is, who her parents made her, who she allowed her parents to make her. She could have chosen differently. Zisu did.

She wants to scream again, but her throat is too raw, too dry. She's too far down this path to turn around, she doesn't know how to be anyone except the ruthless Mar'sahr'dan'i. It is too late to learn how to be anyone but the daughter of Sumalika mat Qa'taru and Balshazzar mar Alshu—an instrument of death, a weapon of destruction, the daughter of devastation.

She is the kahbush'a and always has been. There is no escaping it. A shura can't change its fur.

The sun should be setting by now, but the sky is still filled with red-black clouds. The flames consuming her sister flicker, dancing invitingly. Sari could step into them, accept fire's sweet entreaties. She could join Zisu, make up for all of her sins by accepting the execution that should have found her all those years ago.

She's been running for too long from death, denying Xana what is hers. It would not be accepting defeat, it would not be abandoning her shattered dreams. She has been a chaotic force of smoke and steel, but she can change. She can. Burn away the resentment, sear away the anger, melt the metal into something softer, something brighter. A qatu of silk and sunlight.

She holds out a hand, wanting to run her broken fingers through the heat, wanting to feel the first licks of death; the only redemption available to her now. She holds her breath, frozen at the crossroads of tomorrow.

The sun sets, and she stays by her sister's side as Yludi rises into the sky followed an hour later by Gali. Sari falls asleep as both moons shine down upon the remains of her sister. But before her eyes slip closed, she swears she sees her sister rising from the ashes and ascending to the sky in a shroud of moonlight.

Twenty

S ARI SITS ATOP THE TALLER OF the two buttes, clutching the royal seal tightly in her right hand, the sun just cresting over the horizon, shining onto the desolate desert in a mockery of radiance and hope. Beneath her, the Amyrdine Bara are building a camp between the two buttes; erecting edin'tus and creating makeshift weaponries and smithing furnaces, setting up a mess tent, and establishing an area for the sick and injured to be triaged. They have decided that the cave they have been staying in will be used solely as sleeping quarters, it is too cramped to fit everything that they need.

Some have gone back to Izmyri to search for survivors and pillage the wreckage for supplies. But the screeches that rip through the night sound far too much like the kahbush'a for many to risk venturing too far into the desert without appropriate protections.

Someone is calling her name from behind. She whips her head around to see Kegan approaching.

"They are calling for you," the Fayn calla says, taking a seat the edge of the butte, feet dangling over the edge.

Sari's scowl deepens as she carefully studies Kegan's face. The Fayn calla can run hot and cold, vacillating between emotions, shifting moods without warning.

"Why won't you come down? They're wanting to talk strategy."

"There's nothing to talk about."

"Why do you say that?"

"Our goal was to save Sua from Ashur," Sari says, throat burning. The Amyrdine Bara goal had been to save Sua from monarchs. Her goal had been to save her throne from any threat. She has no right to say 'our' and lump herself in with the savitus fighters.

"So?" The calla asks, tilting their head to the side, eyes wide.

"He destroyed it. Look," she says, sweeping her hand in front of her, the smell of smoke still heavy in the air. "Sua is dead. And her people destroyed."

"And yet the sun rises."

"Must you always speak in riddles?"

"Must you always speak in absolutes?"

Sari leaps to her feet, determined to end this pointless conversation. "I'm not joining them, there is no strategy to talk of, only survival."

"Aren't those the same thing? I'm much better versed in ancient languages, but my handle on Suan isn't bad. I thought 'strategy,' 'victory,' and 'survival' all shared the same root word in this language."

Sari glares at Kegan. "So?"

"Here I thought you were a fierce warrior. I guess I was told wrong."

"And what do you know of war and ferocity? You've spent your life in cushy chairs in comfortable libraries in Fayn."

"My entire clan was murdered. My village burned when I was bare-ly old enough to walk and talk. It was a group of slavers, and when we fought back, they decided we'd be more profitable as pelts."

The calla before her shows no signs of tragedy etched in their eyes, no screams trapped in their throat, no agonizing nightmares replaying in their mind. "You never said anything."

"I don't tell people. I escaped. I lived on the streets until I found someone kind enough to take me in. I lived, I learned. I fought another day."

"So, you escaped a bad situation and got to live a cushy life, must be nice." Sari crosses her arms. "I've been fighting my whole life."

"It's not a competition," Kegan says. "I survived, and then I fought with the Red Front, and now with the Amyrdine Bara."

Sari knows the calla is baiting her; trying to rile her up, make her lash out so she can prove a point. She had teachers who would do the same thing. This calla has some 'wisdom' they wish to impart and want to force Sari to see their point. But she is done with lessons. She knows all that she needs to know in order to survive. Her sister was the smartest of them and she is dead. But she lets Kegan continue, hoping the calla will eventually tire of the sound of their own voice.

"The woman who took me in, Aine, she died." Kegan pauses, look-ing at Sari expectantly, but Sari gives them nothing. Kegan sighs and continues. "Our hideout was found, and she created a distraction to allow me to escape. I watched her hang on the gallows a few weeks later. But that kinship with her, it reminds me even though she is gone, that there is good and love and kindness in this world."

"She was your—?" Sari relents just a little. She remembers the name 'Aine.' Kegan had wished that Aine was here when Nanshaie called them smart. She remembers the hint of sorrow still in Kegan's voice. The Fayn revolution had been a decade ago, and Kegan still grieved for her lost companion.

"It was not romantic, but our bond was just as deep as any romantic partnership. We were committed to each other in every way, lifelong partners. I loved her. I still love her."

Sari's gaze shifts to the welts on her left hand. "The only love and kindness in my life died, too."

"It's hard," Kegan says, leaning back and crossing their feet at their ankles. "Recovering from the trauma of the past. It's hard and it never ends. I still have nightmares of the night my village was burned. I still wake up thinking I will smell burnt coffee and need to scold Aine for overexerting herself and making her condition worse. I still live with one foot planted in the past. You live with two in the past. You have to learn to forgive."

"Forgive? How? How do I forgive my parents for what they did?" Her chest tightens and her head spins, her voice rising with every word until she is no longer shouting at the edge of a butte but screaming into the empty iseru. "They pitted us against each other! They made me maim and murder my siblings, they made us fight until we were almost dead, they made us all have sexual relations with their advisors or other people in power to gain favor and information. They saw us as less useful than pawns on a chequ board. At least they cared if they lost a pawn on the board; if they lost a mat'sarh'dan, they could just make another. Having more qitus is easy. How can I forgive them for that?"

"It is not your parents that you have to forgive; you have to forgive yourself." Kegan's words are slow and soft. "You have to forgive yourself for believing what your parents said; you have to forgive yourself for internalizing what they told you, and you have to forgive yourself for the ways your own actions hurt you more. You are someone who is worth loving and who deserves love, but you can't keep pushing people away."

"You aren't angry? The world was cruel to you, yet you harbor no anger?"

"I do have anger," the calla says. "Lots of it. And sometimes it explodes out and my friends get caught in the blast. I've had to learn how to hone it, how to wield it like you wield a spear; only aiming it where I want to direct it. I try to use it constructively, to motivate me to make a better future, not shackle me in the past."

"I can't forgive my parents for what they did." She pushes away the memories of their glares, their words, their claws slicing down her back.

"And do you deserve forgiveness for what you have done? The crimes you have committed? Should your friends forgive you for not trusting them? For the people you've killed?"

"That's different."

"How? Because you are 'damaged'?"

Sari swallows.

"It's not different. Where do you think your parents learned how to do what they do?"

"From their parents..." Sari says.

"Do you want to continue the cycle or break it?"

"I can't forgive them." She crosses her arms and turns away from Kegan; both wanting to run away from this calla who can somehow read her thoughts and wanting to push them over the edge of the butte.

"I'm not telling you to. But you have to forgive yourself for trying to gain their approval. You were a child. But you aren't anymore. Don't forgive them, don't forget what they did. But make a promise to be better in the future and maybe you will find a spark of love in yourself and you can nurture that love instead of resentment."

Sari sits in silence, thinking of all the things she did as a qit to gain her parents approval; all the terrible things she did. She thinks of all the reprehensible things she has done since in an effort to gain the crown; to earn the loyalty of the people in the only way she thought she could. She chokes back a sob. "I don't deserve forgiveness."

"Maybe not right now. But you can work toward it." Kegan does not refute her, but their words are still gentle and encouraging.

Sari frowns; Tinanna had said something similar. "Maybe. How?"

"Joining us for the strategy meeting, you daft fool." Kegan gently smacks the back of Sari's head.

Sari nods. Join the Amyrdine Bara and truly bring an end to the sahres and isiaqs. An end to the cycle of qitus being honed into ruthless weapons, an end to the cycle of innocence being wrung out of the young, and an end to long nights of children yearning for a small acknowledgment, pleading for an iota of love from the parents who treat them as disposable tools.

Kegan stands at the front of the gathering, two Amyrdine Bara holding up a large map for the rest to see. The sun is slowly setting, and the screeches of scavenger birds and the kahbush'a echo across the sands. The strategy meeting has gone on for hours, and Sari has felt useless for most of it. Much of it has been reports on efforts to tend to the wounded, updates on supply missions, and long speeches about issues Sari does not understand. But now Kegan has the floor. Kegan has marked several points on the map. "I believe that Ashur and Ia have gone to the Arkae Ar'a."

"What's that?" Miramis says.

"The Arkae are ancient sites of historical power or significance. Eoi was built on the Arkae Mi'ia."

Sari recalls her political education. Eoi is the capital of Fayn. But she had never heard of it being built on anyuthing ancient, let alone anything powerful.

"Never heard of that either. *Aga,* come here." Miramis gestures towards her mother, who had seemed just as bored by the meeting until Kegan took the floor.

Amata ambles over. "You need something?"

"Have you ever heard of the Arkae? Arkae Ar'a? Arkae Mi'ia?" Kegan asks the historian.

Amata crosses her arms and taps her foot. "No, I can't say I have. Does that book say something about it?"

"Not directly. There were some papers I translated that did."

"Do you have them with you?"

"Unfortunately, no. They are in the archives in Eoi."

"After this is all over, I must insist that you visit the university here. We have an amazing linguistics department, and I am sure that we can scrounge up some grant money—"

"*Aga*, not now." Miramis's tail flicks in annoyance.

"My apologies." But the qatu does not seem the least bit apologetic. Sari wishes Zisu had survived; this professor would have been an amazing resource for getting her admitted into Khadima Alam.

But aside from her grief, Sari does not care about any of this. It does not matter how they got to this point. What matters is finding Ashur and Ia so she can kill them or die trying. She is willing to die to atone for her crimes, but Kegan has given her an idea for a different way to do it. If she must die, she is taking them with her. End this all before the cycle can repeat again.

"I believe that the same is playing out again here. This High Priestess, Ia, is using whichever royal scion she believes can be bent towards her agenda in order to unlock the power of another Arkae for the Araelta."

"What kinds of powers do they have? How do you unlock that power? What are they used for? Are you saying that one was unlocked in Fayn? Do you know how? When did this happen?" Amata sits down, pulling a folded piece of parchment from her pocket and snatching a piece of coal from the fire to write with.

"I do not know. The texts that I have access to are vague on those points. But it is believed that they were successful in unlocking the Arkae in Fayn in the chaos of the revolution, although currently that location is heavily guarded."

"Why do you believe that that is the location of this 'Arkae Ar'a'?" Amata asks.

Kegan's ears flatten, and their tail flicks, glancing at Imogen. "Clues from the other documents."

Sari rolls her eyes. They are lying; she doesn't know why this is something that the Fayn revolutionaries would lie about. She doesn't have any choice, though. They are still the best lead she has on Ashur and Ia.

"You say these are points of power? What kind of power? Do the scholars studying the one in Fayn believe that it is something we could harness? And use for good?" Amata does not look up from her parchment, scribbling in the worst handwriting that Sari has ever seen.

Sari recalls earlier conversations about the Heart of Aodhe; a weapon that was not originally a weapon and wonders where it fits into all this.

Kegan takes a deep breath, shoulders sagging and tail twitching. "The events of the other night? I believe that that was them opening another Arkae—I do not know which one, though. I suspect Nu'ra'na. The same thing happened, to a lesser extent though, the night they broke the Arkae Mi'ia in Fayn."

"What do you think will happen if they break Arkae Ar'a? Tell me; can this power be harnessed for good? Can we get it first and use it against Ashur?" Miramis asks, trying to reel her mother back in. But the professor will not be deterred.

"How many of these are there? Where is Nu'ra'na? And they are going to open a third—do you think it will be worse?" Professor Amata continues to ask her questions, but Sari guesses the questions are not asked out of a need to create a strategy and more because the professor is now a hunter honing in on prey: knowledge.

Kegan points to the map, the delta of the Alleghenaie River. "I would guess here is where the Nu'ra'na Arkae is at."

"That's the old fortress," Sari says, steeling her mind against the flood of memories. "He was hiding out in there. But he left after we tried to engage him in battle."

"Guess he went back after we cleared out," Miramis says, reclining and putting her feet on the table. Sari can hear the dismissal in Miramis' voice; she must surely be remembering the crushing defeat her troops suffered under Sari's deplorable leadership. But regardless of what she is thinking, she presses on. "And if he opens a third one?"

Before the Fayn calla can say anything, Nanshaie screams, her terror slicing through the tension. "They are coming!"

Everyone turns to look at the Oracle; Sari notes that this time even the Fayn looks at her in reverence and not suspicion. Her tragically correct premonition has instilled in the Fayn a respect for her and the "mysterious" ways of the Esiri desert.

"Who is coming?" Tinanna says, rushing to Nanshaie's side and placing a hand on her back.

Nanshaie screams again, cradling her head in her hands. "They will kill you! Tinanna, they want to kill you. They will... You will die..."

Sari pushes through the crowd to join Tinanna, kneeling next to Nanshaie. "Who is coming?"

"I can't control it!" Nanshaie shouts. "I can't control my visions. Why are you asking me who is coming? I can't see that!"

"Just focus on the details you can see. What are they wearing?" Sari says, trying to ground Nanshaie any way she can. She has no idea if it will work, but she has to try.

Nanshaie closes her eyes and covers them with her hands. "No, I don't want to see more. I don't want to see any more of this. I can't watch them kill you, Nina. Not again."

Tinanna places a hand on Nanshaie's back, rubbing it up and down. But then she screams, too, clutching at her chest, struggling to breathe.

Sari wraps Nanshaie in a tight embrace. "Just focus on the details. What exactly do you see? You are safe in the present. Just tell us the smaller details of your vision."

Nanshaie gulps. "They aren't dressed as typical soldiers, but they are all wearing some sort of armor and move very precisely. The sun is high; I think it is probably midday. They keep whispering, 'Silla', but I have no idea what that means. The woman leading them is tall, bright green eyes, and they keep calling her 'Silla.'" Nanshaie frowns, shaking her head again as if clearing away the vision. "Does that help?"

Sari tightens her embrace. "Yes, that helps immensely. See? You do have some measure of control over them."

"I know who that is," says Tinanna. "Silla is a high-ranking member of the Siúlóir Scáth. They are coming for me."

"Can you try one more time to remove the metal?" Tinanna asks Imogen as they settle around the bonfire for dinner, the smell of roasted fa'leen lingering in the air.

"I can try," Imogen says, moving a bit of food around on her plate but seeming uninteresting in actually eating. "I do not know if it will work. I told you before you might die if I try."

"I do not want to be a burden on the group. Those assassins are advancing on our camp because of me. If you succeed, I am no longer a liability. If I die, I am no longer a liability."

Imogen pushes her plate to the middle of the table and stands up. "Fine. But we do this now. Before I change my mind. And it needs to be alone."

"I want Nanshaie and Sari, too. If I am going to die, I would like for it to be surrounded by friends."

Sari's heart thumps in her chest. Friends? Since when are they friends?

"This is not how you die, Nina" Nanshaie says, placing a hand on Tinanna's shoulder. "This is not how I foresaw your death. You will survive this."

Tinanna blushes and looks away. Sari wonders at this new nickname; when did the two get close enough to establish names of endearment? Her stomach turns over. Now is not the time to examine this strange jealousy. Not when she should be happy enough that Tinanna considers her a friend. Not when her *friend* might die. Not when she might lose two people she cares for in as many days.

"Fine," Imogen says and straightens her back until she towers over all of the qatu . "Fine. Come along. All of you. But you must never speak of what you are about to see. Ever. Or the Siúlóir Scáth will be the least of your troubles."

They follow Imogen to a secluded corner of the medical edin'tu, and Kalarah obliges in providing a privacy curtain. Imogen instructs Tinanna to lie down, and without a word, Sari and Nanshaie take a seat next to her, Nanshaie reaching for Tinanna's hand and clasping it tightly in both of hers.

"You promise that I will not die here, Shay?" Tinanna says, drinking some tea meant to calm and sedate her.

Tears in her eyes, Nanshaie nods. "I promise, Nina."

Sari is prepared for what comes next, but Nanshaie pales when Imogen slices Tinanna's chest, tracing the crimson incision left from the previous procedure. Instead of the lengthy cut from the previous time, however, this cut is much smaller, almost a quarter of the size. Imogen takes a deep breath and sets down the knife. "Don't fight it," she says to Tinanna, but the former assassin does not respond, eyes fixed on the canvas ceiling of the edin'tu.

Imogen holds her hand over the incision, the blood somehow held at bay. She grimaces, eyes squeezing shut in concentration. Long seconds turn into agonizing minutes, and beads of sweat form on her brow, glistening in the dim light of the edin'tu.

"What's she doing?" Nanshaie whispers.

"I do not know," Sari replies.

The tension falls away from Imogen all at once, and she sags. "You need to stop fighting this!"

This time, Tinanna responds. "I do not know what you mean. Fight what?"

"You did this last time. You are holding onto it! Some part of you wants to be on this leash. That is why I cannot remove it." Imogen quickly bandages Tinanna up without another word and then storms out.

Sari's hand reaches for the royal seal, still tucked beneath her tunic, completely at a loss for words.

The sun is just starting to rise, and the camp is slowly starting to come alive again. But Sari has been awake for hours, her spear in hand. She thrusts and spins and springs back so that she can thrust again. Practicing the same move over and over, willing her muscles to learn faster.

Sari can't shake the nagging doubts that plague her thoughts. Are her actions to blame for the constant betrayals? Has she pushed people away by never allowing herself to trust others? Is it her own mistrust that causes others to decide it's not worth the effort to try and bridge the gap? She has always been closed off. Is this the reason no one has ever trusted her?

Sari thinks about her distrust of others. The walls she's built around her heart have become fortresses, protecting her from pain but also preventing others from truly knowing her. Could this self-imposed isolation be why others are hesitant to trust her?

She had once thought others stayed away because she was Sari-trah mat Sumaika; a royal princess, an heir to the throne. But now she is only Sari. Even here, where she is just another fighter, just another soldier, she cannot figure out what about her pushes others away.

She plops down onto the ground, wiping the sweat from her eyes and re-wrapping the strips of leather around her palms. But does that mean she must trust everyone? That does not sit well with her. She tried to trust Ia; she thought she trusted Arishaki. Does she want to trust Tinanna and Nanshaie? She did trust Zisu, and now Zisu is ash. She predicts betrayal around every corner, and yet she knows she must learn to do otherwise. But how? Where is the line between recklessness and caution?

She puts the stopper back on her flask and stands to begin her practice routine again, only to find the sharp point of a spear aiming at her throat. She looks up, Tinanna standing tall with the sun directly behind her. She looks every bit the assassin she once was, cloaked in lethal darkness.

"You should not be climbing walls and swinging spears with a hole in your chest," Sari says.

The former assassin shrugs. "I've had worse. Get up. Let's see how much you've learned."

Sari leaps to her feet, light on her toes. "Never thought you would ask for a rematch, seeing as you had no reason to."

"And I'm in even worse shape this time, so if you lose, well..." Tinanna grins and raises her spear. "Ready?"

Sari stands with her spear at the ready. Across from her, Tinanna raises her own weapon, a smirk playing on her lips. The two qatu circle each other, their eyes locked. Sari's mind races as she tries to anticipate Tinanna's moves. Sari knows that her opponent is slower than usual, but she can't underestimate her, not again.

Tinanna lunges, her spear flashing in the morning light. Sari dances back, her own weapon coming up to block the attack. The two women exchange blows, their spears clashing with a metallic ring. Sari's palms scream in protest as she struggles to keep up with Tinanna's forceful blows.

Despite her injuries, Tinanna is still an unnerving opponent. She moves with a grace and precision that Sari can only dream of. But Sari is determined to win this fight—she's not going to lose twice. She grits her teeth and pushes forward, her spear darting in and out like a snake.

But sweat drips down her back as she struggles to keep up with Tinanna's relentless assault. Suddenly, Tinanna stumbles, her spear slipping from her grasp. Sari sees her opening and strikes, her weapon slicing through the air like a bolt of lightning. Tinanna falls to the ground, her chest heaving as she struggles to catch her breath.

Sari stands over her opponent, her spear pointed at Tinanna's throat. A strange mix of triumph and shame in her chest. She offers her hand to Tinanna, helping her to her feet.

"Not bad," Tinanna says. "You fought well but not as beautifully."

"What does that mean?" Sari asks.

"When you fight, you fight with fire. I can see it in your eyes, and sometimes I swear I can see smoke trailing behind you. There is a flame in you, a burning desire. Sometimes it overwhelms you, and that is where you falter. It makes you unpredictable. But you fought more precisely today, less predictably but with less passion."

"Well, I didn't want to hurt you."

"No," Tinanna says, sitting down and placing a hand on her chest as she catches her breath. "It's not that. You didn't want to hurt me before, either. Even though you hated me during that fight. It's like whatever has been fueling your fire is gone. It's like you don't have anything to fight for anymore."

Sari does not know how to answer Tinanna; or more accurately, she doesn't want to know. "Your fighting was sloppy today."

"I know."

"You were preoccupied with something; your focus wasn't there."

"I should have expected this, I criticized you after all. Go on, tell me more about my shortcomings."

"There is no more to tell. Where you see flame in me, I see nothing in you."

"Thanks." Tinanna sighs.

"But today is a different 'nothing'. Before, I saw nothing because you kept things so tightly guarded. Now, I see nothing because you've allowed yourself to be hollowed out."

"Silla."

"That's the one coming to kill you, yes?"

"I miss her."

"You know her?"

"She was my mentor, the one who taught me. I was assigned to her once I completed my initial training. Usually, we operate alone. But there is a brief period where we are apprenticed. It is our mentor who bestows on us our title. But once we are titled, we work alone. She gave me my title, and I never saw her again."

"You miss her?"

"I think I loved her. I thought I did at the time, anyway."

"What was she like?"

"Awful. She was strict and cruel. Nothing was ever good enough for her. But occasionally, not often but sometimes, she did praise me.

I lived for that. Pushed myself past my limits just hoping to hear her say 'good job' or 'well done' one more time."

"That's more than my parents ever said to me," Sari says. "I don't know if I am jealous of you or thankful for that."

"Why thankful?"

"You lived with false hope. I knew my parents wouldn't love me. I never clung to them and wondered why they couldn't love me."

Tinanna bites her lip. "She wasn't my mother, I never thought of her as a mother. Sometimes she was just a mentor, but sometimes she acted like a lover. Regardless, she was the only family I had, or that I was allowed to have. I am so stupid."

"Why do you say that?"

"The metal in my heart. Some part of me has hoped she would track me down one day, find me again."

"And now she is, but it's to kill you."

"Yes, but for some reason, I had thought that if she did track me down, it would be to take me back. To leave the *Scáth*, too. And we could work together again. Why do I still want that? I don't want to die."

Nanshaie approaches them, as quiet as a shadow. "Here you are," she says, sitting between them, a flask in each hand. "Drink." She presses a flask into each of their hands. "You aren't going to die."

"But you saw it in your vision," Tinanna says. "You've never been wrong."

Nanshaie holds up a finger, silencing them.

Tinanna empties her flask and sets it down. "If I am going to die tomorrow, I want to spend my last night with you." She looks be-

tween Sari and Nanshaie. She puts a hand to her chest. "Will you...
Both of you..."

Nanshaie moves before Sari realizes what Tinanna is asking, wraping her arms around Tinanna as she straddles her, pressing her lips to Tinanna's cheeks. All traces of the Oracle fade away, and there is just a scared but determined qatu in her place. "Come on, Sari. I know you want to."

Sari is thankful for the darkness of the night as her face burns with both denial and need. She had been hoping that her fight with Tinanna would lead to another night of exploration. She had not thought that Nanshaie would be part of it, but once she realizes that Nanshaie wants this, too, she grabs Nanshaie and pulls her in for a kiss, too.

It's sweater than any fruit she has devoured, it's more delicious than any night she's ever spent in the arms of others. For the first time in recent memory, she feels safe. She feels secure. In the middle of the Esiri with the people she had thought of as enemies, she feels at home. She feels wanted, she feels loved.

She does not know whose hands cup her breasts, whose fingers enter her sex, or whose tongue brings her to the edge. But she feels a fire reignite inside her. She has something to fight for again. She has people she needs to protect. People for whom she wants to survive, to be her best self, and to whom she must prove she can be a better person. She will show them that she is worthy of their trust; that she is more than her past sins.

She relishes in the feel of her hands along their bodies, making sure that she pays equal attention to each of her partners. She has no idea what tomorrow will bring, what they will be to each other once the sun rises. But tonight, they are hers. Tonight, she is theirs. They exist outside of the ending of the world, no longer shackled to their pasts; only bound to each other.

She cannot stop the sunrise, but as she sleepily blinks at the dawn, she knows how she can save Tinanna from the foretold death.

"I think I have an idea." Sari kisses each of her companions and disentangles herself from their arms, ready to do whatever it takes to keep her partners safe.

Sari holds up a telescope, an amazing contraption brought by the contingency from Fayn, and scans the horizon from her perch on the smaller butte. The Scáth approach, all mounted on beautiful war horses—beautiful, but not meant for the desert. She says nothing as they parade into the empty camp. Empty except for Tinanna, who lays in a pool of blood next to the larger butte, the word 'traitor' etched in the sand next to her, her shirt torn open and an angry and red gash across her chest.

They do not see her at first. Instead, their leader, Silla, directs them to the other side. The rider next to Silla has an otherworldly look, with skin that gleams like Imogen's. An *Ástfríður*. The *Ástfríður* points to one of the open crevices in the side of the smaller butte, and the cadre of assassins spans out. Sari grins and lowers the telescope.

Silla nods, and her soldiers rush in. But then Silla looks to both sides, checking the area before entering, and sees Tinanna.

Silla approaches slowly, and freezes completely once next to Tinanna, taking in the sight. Sari wishes she could see Silla's face and could hear her thoughts. She desperately wants to know what Silla is thinking as she gazes on the lifeless form of her former apprentice.

Slowly, Silla gets on her knees, careful not to touch the blood in the sand, and leans over, holding an ear to Tinanna's mutilated chest. So swiftly that Sari does not actually see the action, Tinanna grabs onto her former mentor and plunges a dagger into her back.

"Now!" Sari screams. The Amyrdine Bara cheer and lean over the side of each butte, the savitus fighters raining down arrows on the Scáth riders trapped in the open crevice.

The battle is not even a battle; it is a swift and merciless blood-bath—a mass execution. One by one, the *Scáth* riders fall, bleeding out from a dozen arrow wounds before being impaled upon the sav-itus spears. Sari watches it unfold from her perch on the butte, rel-ishing in the carnage she has ordered upon those that wanted to harm Tinanna.

When the last of the Scáth are dead, Sari finds Tinanna at the end of the crevice, pulling a small bit of copper out of the sand. She holds it up, the last rays of sunlight reflecting off of it. "What should I do with this now?"

"Get rid of it somewhere far from here," Sari says.

Nanshaie appears with wet rags. "You looked just as you did in my vision," she says, wiping the animal blood off of Tinanna's chest. "I can't believe it."

Tinanna places the metal in her satchel and takes Nan-shaie's hand and Sari's in each of hers. "Come with me tonight."

"For what?" Nanshaie asks.

"To get rid of it. Find somewhere in the dunes to bury it."

Nanshaie blushes. "Of course."

Sari nods, wondering if this is the start of a new family.

Twenty-One

KEGAN DROPS A TALL STACK OF papers and books on the table and lets out a sigh. "I've finished."

Miramis claps, and the rest of the Amyrdine Bara follow her lead. Kegan plops into a chair and pushes a strand of hair out of their face. "There's a lot in here that I cannot read or understand, but I believe that I have a basic understanding."

"Anything useful?" Miramis asks, leaning forward.

"The Arkae were made with the Heart of Aodhe, and that is what I believe Ia and Ashur are using to break them."

"Makes sense, but can we stop it?"

"There is a Blade of Kyna mentioned, and from what I can put together, this can be used to destroy the Heart of Aodhe."

"I have a question," Amata says, raising her hand. "I am just a historian, but if they need the Heart of Aodhe to break the Arkae, how did they break the one in Fayn? Or did someone else have the Heart of Aodhe before Ashur acquired it?"

Kegan looks away, ears swiveling back. "A blood sacrifice."

"That is all? That seems a lot more simple than obtaining this artifact."

"A very specific kind of blood sacrifice, one that is not easy to obtain," Imogen says, the shine of her skin dull and her eyes lackluster.

"Ia told me that only someone of the Suan royal bloodline can use the Heart of Aodhe," Sari says, hating that she even has to speak the traitor's name. "Do you think this means that only a Suan royal can use the Blade of Kyna?"

Kegan taps their chin. "I am not sure. None of these books say anything about either being tied to any one bloodline. Although…"

"Yes?"

"Both of these secret orders were very interested in the blood of the Fayn royals. Why do you ask?"

"I think I know what the Blade of Kyna is. It's Katynna. It is said to be a gift from Yshuld herself given to the Suan's royal family as a sign of her divine will and blessing our rule." She realizes only after the words leave her mouth that a group made of people who do not believe in divine right might not take kindly to her proclamation. "Or rather, that is what my parents told me. It might just be a sword."

"And where is this blade?" Kegan asks, squinting, lips pressed into a tight line.

"Oh," Sari says, shoulders sagging. "I lost it. At the old fortress when we tried to take on Ashur. But I can go get it."

"We don't have long. Gamasittuum Buuli is only two weeks away," Tinanna says.

Sari grins, her hand instinctively reaching for the royal seal, secure under her tunic. "I feel a fire burning inside of me. I can do this."

I can get my sword back, and with that and the seal, I can use the insurrectionists to take out Ashur and then claim the throne. They won't see it coming. But even as the words echo in her mind, a knot forms in her stomach, and an unfamiliar emotion takes root in her hollow chest. She glances at Nanshaie and Tinanna, a war inside her between Sari, their lover, and Saritrah, princess of Sua.

The desert night envelops Sari, its cool breeze whispering secrets through the dunes. Sari throws the saddle over the back of the camel and cinches it tightly. Two half-moons provide a measure of illumination as she prepares for the journey back to Ashur's now-destroyed base, hoping her sword is still among the wreckage.

"I thought you were waiting until morning," Nanshaie says, stepping out of the shadows.

"Well, time is not on our side, is it?"

"Please do not go," Nanshaie says, wringing her hands.

"Why not? We need the Blade of Kyna to stop this."

"I've had a vision."

"It will be fine. You had a vision of Tinanna dying, but we were able to turn that around, right? This could be the same thing."

"Please, do not go. We can stop Ashur another way."

"But I need the blade!"

"Why? Why is it that important?"

Sari bites her tongue.

"Fine. I am going with you then."

"Not without another camel," Sari says, resigning herself to a companion on her journey.

Precious minutes are wasted waiting for Nanshaie to retrieve her own mount, and Sari is tempted to leave without her. But she knows that Nanshaie will chase after her, and she can't allow the Oracle to be alone in the desert, not with her brother having set monsters loose upon the Esiri. And she does not want to risk whatever is blossoming among her companions and herself. She wants this... whatever it is. Possibly more than she wants a throne. She squashes the war in her chest. She just needs to get this over with; she can sort out her feelings once she has her blade again.

"I brought my own water, too," Nanshaie says, leading her camel to the gates.

Sari nods and kicks her camel into motion.

They do not speak as they set out into the dark vastness of the desert. They do not speak as they crest dunes and slide into the valleys, alert for any predators that might mistake them for a meal. They do not speak as the sun rises and the winds pick up.

"You know that your Katynna is not the Blade of Kyna," Nanshaie says as they halt their journey for nialsamsu.

"But it is," she says. "It has to be. And if it were not, you would not be accompanying me."

"I am with you because I must be. There is something I am seeking, too. But I am at least honest with myself."

"What does that mean?"

"Why are you doing this?"

"Because I need to stop Ashur and Ia."

"But you do not need the sword for that. So why do you want it?"

She wants it so she can reclaim the throne, take her crown, and... And what? "I'm going to sleep." She sets up her edin'tu and ignores Nanshaie.

Just a few days ago, she had been resolved to die, to remove herself from the world, to remove herself from temptation, to atone for her past crimes, and to ensure that she could not commit any future transgressions. And then she spent one glorious, incandescent night with Tinanna and Nanshaie again; she wanted to live and would have been content with a quiet life with them.

But the first hint of an opportunity for her to again have a shot at the crown, and she's racing towards it.

Their camp in between the two buttes is much closer to the old fortress than Izmyri was, and they make it there in only a few days, not held back by marching troops and heavy weapons. In the short span of time since they'd last been here, a century of destruction seems to have taken place. None of the walls still stand, no remnants of furniture or tapestry are strewn about. It's as if the fortress had existed outside of time, and now it's being bombarded with centuries all at once. Perhaps Kegan is right; this was the location of an Arkae, and with it broken, the fortress lacks protection.

"Do you truly believe that you will find your sword here?" Nanshaie asks, leaping off of the camel and grabbing a flask from the saddlebag.

"I have to try."

But as they shuffle among the ruins, moving aside rocks and debris, her hope dwindles. "Is this what you saw?" Saritrah asks Nanshaie. "Me, not finding anything? If so, you really should have said something."

"No, I didn't see anything about whether or not you got the sword. And I tried, I tried to focus on certain parts of my vision to get any clues. But—"

"There!" At the very center of the ruins, Saritrah sees a flicker of light: the sun reflecting off of steel. "I am going to get it."

"Be careful," Nanshaie says. But Saritrah does not even register her companion's warning. She steps over and around heaps of broken rocks and cracked stones, advancing to the sword with a single-minded determination. It's buried; only a tiny bit of the blade is visible. The rocks are large, but she is confident that she can move them.

Her fingers tremble slightly as she lifts rocks, moves stones, and digs through shattered bricks. Piece by piece, she clears a path toward the sword, forgetting about the world around her entirely. Only a few more large rocks remain and then she shall have her reward.

Saritrah is almost done when the ground shakes and a chasm opens up beneath her feet. She leaps backward to safety, distantly hearing Nanshaie scream. Her heart sinks as the sword disappears into the abyss, tumbling into the chasm, potentially lost to her forever. She wants to dive headfirst into the gaping hole, determined to retrieve what is rightfully hers. But Nanshaie screams again. She turns around; a large kahbush'a is advancing on them, its eyes locked on Nanshaie.

She looks back down at the chasm. The sword is sitting right on top of a large rock. She could dive in, get it, and climb back out. The roar of the kahbush'a brings her focus back to Nanshaie, brandishing a spear at the kahbush'a, mouth set in a thin line of determination, but her footing is unsteady.

The ground shakes again, and more rocks plunge into the chasm. If Saritrah doesn't get the sword now, it will be buried forever, beyond her ability to retrieve it. And if she loses the sword... She doesn't want to think about it. She doesn't want to think about a world where Ashur and Ia are free to unleash chaos and calamity.

She plants her feet on the ground as firmly as she can and pulls the spear out of the sheath on her back. She springs into action, leaping in front of Nanshaie and hurling the spear into the kahbush'a's left eye. It staggers to the side, a deafening roar echoing through the air. The creature thrashes, its massive form teetering dangerously close to the edge of the chasm.

Sari leaps on top of a boulder and then jumps onto the back of the beast, pulling out her spear and then burying it deep in the other eye.

It rears onto its hind legs, flailing in pain. She grips her spear again and rends it out of the beast before leaping back to the ground. The kahbush'a loses its balance as it lurches side to side and plummets downward, disappearing into the abyss. Dust and debris fill the air, obscuring the view of the chasm's depths as silence settles over the ruins.

Sari stands there, her heart pounding in her chest, wondering if she made the right decision. There is no possible way to retrieve the sword now. It's gone. Forever lost. Perhaps, in a thousand years, another lost royal will take a journey here and brave perils unknown, as she did in Bec, searching for a way to bring about a better world and end a reign of terror.

But not her. It won't be her.

"Do you have the sword?" Nanshaie asks, appearing at her side.

"No, it's lost. Even more lost now than before."

"Where is it?"

"Down in that chasm."

"But…"

"I could have gotten it, but I chose to save you."

"Why?" Nanshaie crosses her arms and raises an eyebrow.

"Because you're more important." Sari lets out a breath slowly, realizing the truth of her words only as she says them.

"Because I'm the Oracle." Her shoulders sag, resignation in her eyes.

"No," Sari says, taking Nanshaie's hand in her own. "Because I feel like a better person when I am around you. I like who I am when I am around you, I like who you inspire me to be. I do not want to lose you."

"And that's more important than saving the world?"

"You said it yourself. We can find a way to stop Ashur without the sword. But—" She bites her lip. She wants to hold the words inside, but they push against her throat. "I don't know if I could keep trying if you weren't at my side."

Nanshaie pulls away, turning her back on Sari and heading toward the camel.

"What's wrong?" Sari says, chasing after her.

"I've seen the atrocities you have committed and the ones you might commit in the future. The way you have chosen your throne over and over again, prioritizing it before all else."

"But I didn't this time," Sari says.

"What's under your tunic?"

Sari touches the royal seal, fingering the outlines of the crest engraved on it.

"It's something that you can still use to claim your throne, even without the sword. So the loss of the sword isn't such a huge setback. That is why you came here. Isn't it?"

Sari's shoulders droop in defeat. "You can see right through me."

"Yes, but that is why I stay at your side. Because I also see your capacity to change, your capacity for love. I saw it every time you looked at Zisu. You can change; you can atone for your atrocities. But that's a choice you have to make wholeheartedly. I can't make it for you. But I can keep hoping you will eventually see..." She lowers her head and turns away from Sari.

The word batters about in her mind. Atone. How can she atone for what she has done? That night, when the insurrectionists stormed the palace, she killed one of her brothers. She could have escaped with him, but she killed him to eliminate a rival. She took advantage of that night and gave the insurrectionists one less royal to worry about.

The look on his face, his eyes wide as the blood sputtered out of his neck, his desperate attempts to stop the flow of it, to choke out a few last words...

Her troops. Ditanu and Tanit. Belu knew the second she sipped the wine. Belu, of all of her troops, would have realized what she just drank. The betrayal that burned in Belu's eyes as she took one last look at Sari, the question 'why' frozen on her lips. She justified it as necessary, and done at Ia's request, so was she really responsible?

She did not even ask her troops why they had those tokens from the insurrectionists. Arishaki. He always collected trinkets from those he slew. A ring, a necklace, a broach. Trophies of his major kills. Reminders of his might. Is that why he had the coin with the savitus flower on it Is that why any of them had the coins in their possessions? One of her soldiers was certainly a traitor. But she killed half of her army without even questioning them or attempting to determine the truth.

Her stomach churns.

All the people killed in skirmishes as she fought to reclaim towns and villages... All the people she has killed. All the people she was willing to kill if it meant getting her claws on the crown. Is she really any different than Ashur? Is she truly capable of making up for that?

The flimsy justifications of the past fall away, leaving her with only one reason for why she committed those crimes. She could lay the blame at her parents' feet, say that they molded her, shaped her to be that way. But she could have been like Zisu. Zisu did not become a monster. Zisu was wounded, broken, and maybe shattered, but she did not hurt others.

"There's no way," she says, breaking the silence.

"What was that?" Nanshaie says, startled out of her own thoughts.

"There's no way that I can atone for what I have done."

"But are you willing to try?"

Sari does not know how to respond. "Let's take a break. It's almost time for nialsamsu anyway."

Nanshaie's feet have not even touched the ground before she screams, falling into the sand, that far away look in her eyes. "We need to go," Nanshaie says, her voice commanding and ancient.

"Alright, we can break later. Let me help you."

"I can't control it," she says, her voice less distant. "I'm trying I—"

Nanshaie rolls to her knees, hands planted firmly in the sand. "It's not optional. We need to go back to Bec. Now."

"Let us take our break, first, the sun is too high," Sari says.

"No, we must keep going. We don't have time. We need to—"

"Fine. At least have some dates and drink some water first. We're more than a day away if my guess is correct."

Sari is exhausted when they reach the entrance to the cave that will lead them back into the ancient city of Bec. Nanshaie has slept off and on, her camel tethered to Sari's, and sometimes she mumbles in her sleep; words that Sari does not recognize. But Sari has not slept at all, and her patience for her companion's sleep-talk is waning. "Wake up, we're here."

Nanshaie startles awake and wipes her mouth. "Oh, who is that," she says, pointing to the entrance of the cave.

Sari had not seen her at first, but an old woman stands at the center of the entrance.

"Wait," Nanshaie says, voice full of awe, eyes wide with devotion. "That's the goddess."

"Are you sure?" But even as Sari asks, she realizes there is no way it could be anyone else. The woman is ancient, but her eyes are eternal—a glow surrounds her that burns like the sun.

"My dreams..." Nanshaie says, leaping from the camel and slowly approaching the woman. "It was you—that night in the desert—I saw you as the city fell... Everything has been leading to this moment. You have been guiding me here, haven't you?"

Sari follows, a few steps behind, cautiously.

"Yes," the woman says, holding out her hands. Nanshaie, without hesitation, takes them. "My child, my chosen daughter. The gods have gained the ability to once again walk upon the earth and speak with those who live on it."

"Oh, thank goodness, for this world is desperately in need of your help," Nanshaie says, falling to her knees.

"No, my beloved." The goddess brushes a strand of hair out of Nanshaie's face, a gesture so maternal that Sari briefly wonders if the goddess once had children of her own. "That is not a good thing. Our time has passed; it passed long ago. Our presence is not a blessing. We should not be here."

"I don't understand." She shakes her head.

"You must destroy the Heart of Aodhe. It can be used to wrought terrible destruction. Once, it was used to shepherd in an era of peace and prosperity, but some in the world still wanted more," Yshuld says. For being a goddess, her voice still holds a quiver of desperation, and her eyes are filled with a very mortal fear.

"Can it be used as a weapon?"

Yshuld shivers. "That is the least of it. It can cause and has caused more destruction than you can fathom. It must be destroyed."

"That is what we are planning to do," Sari says. "But we lost the Blade of Kyna."

The goddess shakes her head. "You have not lost it."

"But the sword," Sari says. "It's buried."

"That sword is not the Blade of Kyna. You will find it if you stay the course and confront your brother. But even I cannot foresee if you will have the strength to wield it."

Sari's hand reaches for her royal seal, and a curse forms in her throat.

The goddess smiles and nods as if answering a question, but Sari does not understand what the goddess could possibly mean. And just as suddenly as she appeared, she is gone again.

TWENTY-TWO

KEGAN SOMEHOW KNOWS THEY ARE RETURNING and is waiting at the entrance to the camp, leaning against the rocky side of the butte, tapping their foot. They do not even wait for Sari and Nanshaie to dismount from the camel before they start their tirade. "Where did you go? Where is the sword? Why have you been gone so long? Do you even know how worried Tinanna was when you were missing? She's been—"

"We don't have the sword," Sari says, pushing past Kegan.

The hairs on Kegan's tail stand on end, and they ball their hands into fists. "What?! You said you could get it; you said you would get it quickly! Now what are we supposed to do? It's almost Gamasit-tuum Buuli and we have no plan now! I can't deal with this. I'm going to my quarters. Don't come looking for me unless you have a plan!"

Sari rolls her eyes and the Fayn calla storms off, tail flicking and ears pressed flat against their head. "I wonder if they are always like that."

"They are always like that," Imogen says, silently approaching. "But they are right, Tinanna has been worried. Why did you leave without her?"

"I just wanted it to be me, but Nanshaie found me and tagged along without my permission."

"I see. I'll go let her know you are back. Her incision is healing well, and she's had no issues with her heart since."

"Thank you," Sari says. "I think we must go speak with Miramis."

They find the savitus leader scrubbing dishes in the mess edin'tu, whistling.

"I recognize that," Sari says. "I used to sing that one to Zisu..."

Miramis drops the iron bowl into the pot of water and jumps. "Oh, it's you. Do you have the sword?"

"No," Sari says, face burning. "But we found out that the sword is not the Blade of Kyna."

"And how'd you learn that?"

Sari glances and Nanshaie, and the Oracle explains.

"The goddess herself? Not what I was expecting. She told you that you already have what you need? What does that mean?"

"I do not know. She told me to stay the course and keep going."

"So, just like last time, we are gonna march up to Ashur completely unprepared because you trust the words of some woman you met in the desert who speaks in riddles?"

"Well, not exactly."

"Yes, exactly." Miramis tosses her rag into the dirty water basin. "We're less than a week away from Gamasittuum Buuli, and if Kegan is correct, we are at least a week's march away from Ashur's location on the far eastern side of Sua. And you expect us to follow you based on a prophecy? Here in Sua, yeah, that can fly. But our fellows from Fayn? They don't follow Yshuld. Half of them think Nanshaie is a con artist."

"Oh," Nanshaie says, shifting her weight. "I am sorry to cause trouble."

"Don't worry, sweetheart, I know you're the real deal. But even after what you've done saving us several times, they still think it's just luck." Miramis takes a seat and gestures for Sari and Nanshaie to join her at the table. "So, what do we do?"

Sari hangs her head.

"Should we at least start marching toward Ashur's location? The Arkae Ar'a?" Nanshaie suggests.

Miramis nods. "I'll talk to the rest of the troops. Best get ready to leave at dawn. We will probably be moving out."

The sun is setting, casting a golden glow over the vast expanse of the Erid steppe as they approach the Avon River. Miramis had pushed them hard, marching across the Esiri and making it to the Erid steppe far more quickly than should have been possible. "We have a goddess on our side," is all she says when Sari comments on their speed.

The Arkae is on the western side of the Avon, but they cannot reach it without crossing the white river to the east, traveling some ways north, and then crossing back over again.

Which is what they must do now. Standing on Garcelonian soil, she looks across the river back at Sua—her home, her kingdom... *Hers.*

Nanshaie taps her on the shoulder. "Are you ready?"

Saritrah closes her eyes, breathing in the scent of the rushing river and the vegetation found in abundance on its eastern side. Yshuld had told her to stay the path—and she has. As she rushed across the breadth of her kingdom—*hers*—she waited for some signal, some sign that the Blade of Kyna would reveal itself, make itself known, present itself to her. She stayed the path as they marched through sandstorms, freak thunderstorms, hail, and fire. The world was ending all around them and she stayed the course.

The first stars blink to life in the night sky, and not a single moon outshines them tonight. She had stayed the course, and still she has no weapon with which to strike down Ashur and destroy the Heart of Aodhe. "No," she says. "I am not ready. But we do not have a choice, do we?"

The Arkae is built on a ledge halfway up the western cliffs, easy to miss even if you are looking for it. It looks so similar to the fortress at the delta of the Alleghenaie River; similar materials, design, and construction. It also seems to exist outside of time. She knows she's been near this area before, but never saw it. Maybe it only appears if you are looking for it.

"We do not, but we await your signal." Tinanna grabs her hand and squeezes it tightly.

Sari raises a hand, fist clenched, and the troops advance, the bridge creaking under their weight as they cross the raging Avon River. It is not long before they hear the sound they had all been dreading.

From somewhere deep in the ancient fortress, the kahbush'a do not wait to add their own cries to the cacophony.

Sari grits her teeth and crosses behind the troops, shoving through them when on the other side so that she can climb the cliffs first. She ascends, scaling the crag along a thin pathway carved into the rock, the wind wiping through her hair, and ignoring the beasts that now gaze down at them from above, leering with too-intelligent eyes. She glances back just as the last of the savitus fighters make it across the bridge.

The kahbush'a attack without warning, somehow coordinated.

The beasts careen down the path, leaping over each other in their haste, the stench of decay thick in the air. Their roars are frenzied, their snarls wild. While the eyes speak of an intelligence, they do not fight as the previous ones did. Their attacks are random, uncoordinated, and lacking in tactical calculations. These were once regular people, Sari realizes. These are not Ashur's soldiers. She catches sight of a stray scrap of cloth still clinging to the monster and the embroidered shepherd's hooks on it. Re'u. Ashur captured a Re'u caravan and twisted every one of them into a beast. The growls of the beasts are drowned out by Ashur's laughter echoing from all sides.

Thunder claps overhead and against the cliff, and the night sky is banished behind clouds of fire and smoke. Sari chokes, her grip on her spear loosening, still not able to fight with her right hand as dominant. But she has no choice. She pushes on, hoping that the Re'u can forgive her. Yet another massacre at her hands. More lives she must eventually atone for. What was it that Tinanna had said? Keep trying and hope it will be enough...

While the exterior of the Arkae Ar'a had resembled the ancient fortress, the interior of Arkae Ar'a looks too similar to a Temple of Yshuld. Kegan had said that the Arkae in Fayn had been hidden in the dungeons beneath the royal palace, forgotten and decrepit. Yet the building before her is most assuredly a temple, as pristine as the day it was built, untouched by time.

She shakes out her hands, hoping to get feeling back in her fingers before they enter, frozen as a cold rain pelts them. Her left hand twitches, muscles sore. She should have practiced more; her left hand is still not suited for wielding a weapon, and her right hand has not yet learned how to compensate. They have taken out the last of the kahbush'a, she hopes. All that remains is to take this temple, find Ashur and Ia, kill them, and destroy the Heart of Aodhe.

Except, she still lacks the Blade of Kyna. Had Yshuld lied about it?

Tinanna claps her on the back, jolting her out of her thoughts. "Let's go."

Sari glances at the sky one last time before following Miramis and Tinanna inside. Gamasittuum Buuli. An event that is associated with the goddex Mayd. Sari chuckles. This is also the month of Maydarhi, named after the goddex of destruction hirself. Ia could not have picked a better day.

They rush in. The air is heavy with an eerie stillness, as if time itself is frozen within this forsaken place. For as old as it is, not a single mote of dust dances in the air. The room glows, illuminated by some hidden light source, this ghostly flame reflecting off the stained glass decorating the walls. The polished marble floor is littered with lifeless bodies, all drained of color, faces sallow and eyes hollow. Sari does not want to know how long those bodies have rested upon the floors of this temple, nor which god they were protecting or attacking. She can see no signs of any of the Tuduye pantheon, no sigils or crests that would identify one of the twelve gods as having dominion over this sacred space. A Re'u god, perhaps. Or an old one. She shivers.

As Miramis' gaze sweeps across the myriad doors leading from the circular antechamber, uncertainty flickers across her face. "Where now?"

Sari grits her teeth, a knot in her stomach. She strains to hear, ears pricked forward, hoping to hear distant footsteps or chatter that might point her toward Ia. Even the growl of a kahbush'a would be welcome; at least it would be a clue.

"This way," Nanshaie says, pushing past them as if she knows these halls, as if she's walked them, not stopping to gape at the ancient splendor nor at the slaughter at their feet.

She leads them around winding passages and chilly corridors until they reach a room that looks eerily like the Sanctuary of the Oracle; the room Nanshaie had found herself ensconced in only a few short months ago. Standing at the center, over a slab of marble serving as an altar, are Ia and Ashur, the moat around them red with blood. Neither look up as the savitus fighters file in.

Ashur holds the Heart in his hand, and Ia holds her hands to the sky. The vaulted ceiling of the sanctuary disappears, and a gust of cold wind rushes through the chamber. Above them, the skies have cleared, and every star twinkles crimson against a maroon sky.

Ashur and Ia are both chanting; a language that Ia speaks flawlessly while Ashur stumbles over each word. Tinanna hurls one of her daggers toward the two harbingers of destruction, slicing through the air with deadly precision. Sari's heart races as she charges down the aisle, prepared to leap over the moat and spear Ia's heart.

Ia's eyes fixate on Sari, and with a wave of her hand, Sari is thrown backward, crashing to the ground, dropping her spear. When she looks back, Ia is holding the weapon, a wicked grin on her face.

Tinanna throws another dagger, but Ia deflects it. The room erupts into chaos as the Amyrdine Bara all hurl their spears and aim their arrows at the two figures on the dais at the center of the room. But without even a sign of strain, Ia deflects them before they even cross the moat.

"Charge!" Miramis cries. "She can't repel all of us at once!"

But Ia does.

The room is filled with a blinding light and Sari covers her eyes. When she opens them again, Ashur is engulfed in blue flames. "Gamasittuum Buuli! Mayd," he shouts. "Bless us! Aodhe! Walk these sands once more!"

The smoke is heavy, thick, and dark. She cannot breathe; her lungs protest against the searing pain. She is lightheaded, and sure that she will die having failed in her mission. She closes her eyes, hoping that when she opens them, the nightmare will be gone. Instead, she sees the Amyrdine Bara rising to their feet as if pulled by strings, and one by one, they writhe in pain, suspended in the air, while their bodies crack and break and shift into the forms of beasts.

She will never atone for her crimes, no. She will only go on to commit more horrific ones—now tied to Ashur's leash. Her body rises from the floor, whatever spell he is weaving taking hold. She can feel it inside her, in her stomach, in her lungs, and in most horrifically in her mind. *Kill. Destroy. Slaughter.* His voice punctures her thoughts and she knows she cannot refuse his orders; will not go against his commands. She will be his servant, she will be his kah-bush'a, she will carry out his will.

She closes her eyes, bracing for the pain, but just as she loses consciousness, she sees a shining light before her and the silhouette of Nanshaie bathed in gold.

Twenty-Three

"Get up." Tinanna's command cuts through the air, a sharp sword that pierces Sari's consciousness. Her breath catches as she inhales sharply. She opens her eyes, revealing a shadowed yet unmistakably qatu face of Tinanna, a far cry from the beast Sari expected to see.

But then she looks past Tinanna. Behind her stands Nanshaie, her arms stretched out in front of her as if pushing against a wall. Beyond that wall, on the other side of the sanctuary, is an army of screaming, howling kahbush'a. Each one is pawing and clawing at the invisible barrier that keeps them at bay.

"I've created an opening. Use it! Break the Heart!" The Oracle's words echo with divinity.

Sari struggles to stand, her muscles throbbing and her hand rigid. The once pristine sanctuary lies in ruins, baring the scars of both age and violence. Ashur, exhausted and gasping, leans against the fractured altar, his body trembling.

Sari takes one step toward her brother and then another. He looks up, a predatory smirk on his face, tail jerking back and forth. He holds the Heart up and opens his mouth. But no words come out, and he jerks as if struck by lightning. "No matter. I can still take you out."

"Look what you've done," Sari says, disgusted with herself and with him.

"I've taken out the insurrectionists, Sari. Now it's just you and me. I've eliminated the only thing standing in the way of our last battle."

"You've created beasts that you can't control," Sari says, gesturing to the monsters still braying at the barrier. "How is that a victory?

"And you've grown soft. I will say it was a stroke of genius tricking those ingrates. I didn't see that one coming, sister dearest," he says, still gripping the altar tightly. "But that doesn't change the fact that you're weak. And everyone knows it. Everyone can see your weakness; that's why all your soldiers were so willing to be mine. By the way, where is Tanit? Belu? I was hoping to see their pretty faces today—and perhaps more."

Sari takes another step, picking up a spear. She doesn't know whose, but it's lighter than the one she usually uses. She tightens her right hand around it, testing the heft, hoping she can adjust. The point is iron, not the steel she is used to, and the pole is thin, made from a softer wood. Mostly likely from Fayn. It will have to do. It's not the Blade of Kyna, but it will have to do.

"What happened to Zisu? I didn't see her here with you. She stayed home? Not up for the fight? Still willing to let her siblings do the fighting for her? And here I had thought she might have actually grown up."

"Shut up," Sari says, cold and low, jaw tight and fangs ready to tear.

His sneer widens. "Ah. There's that fire. There's that anger."

Fire. Anger. Kegan's words, Tinanna's words echoing in her mind. Within her and Ashur, anger rages like a relentless inferno, engulfing them in its searing embrace and consuming them; they breathe out smoke and spit out ash. His voracious anger has hollowed him out, burning away all other desires, feelings, and wants.

If she gets her hand on the Heart, her anger will do the same to her. It will control her, manipulate her—she will be at its command.

Was it during her first match? Was that when the fire was lit within her? Was that when her anger took root? Or was it slower, coal by coal, kindling building up over time before that first duel provided the spark? All the times her mother scolded her, all the times her father hit her, all the times they demeaned her, calling her worthless after every loss. Were those more logs stacked on the flame?

Was it her fourteenth summer, when she not only had to participate in the Sitnu, but also parcel out favors on behalf of her parents by spending nights and mornings with isiaqs and advisors?

But Kegan said that she could hone it, channel it, use it constructively. A gift of power. She just has to be strong enough to use it the right way.

She leaps across the crumbled moat, hurling her spear at Ashur. He dodges it, spinning and rolling over the altar to avoid her. "Just like in the iseru?" Sari says, balling her hands into fists.

"No weapons. No other rules," he says, and Sari hears their father in his voice. He says the line, the line that they've both heard far too many times, with the same cadence and inflection. And when did Ashur find his flame? When did the smoke turn into fire? What atrocities at the hands of their parents did he suffer? Atrocities their parents told them were for their own good, to make them stronger.

No, what she endured did not make her stronger. *She* made herself stronger. She refuses to credit her parents for her efforts.

Their efforts made her and Ashur crueler, meaner. Right? Or was that also a choice?

"For the glory of Sua," she says, and the flicker of recognition that passes over Ashur's face tells her that she imitated their mother perfectly.

"The land of perpetual twilight; for the sun shall never set," they say in unison.

The Suan people had witnessed the downfall of numerous dynasties abroad due to the fact that the eldest offspring did not possess the qualities of brightness, strength, or wisdom. Being born first does not automatically ensure the necessary attributes for being a great leader. Hence, many centuries ago, the Suan royals established the Sitnu. Being a warrior society, it was only logical that their leaders should be selected based on strength rather than inheritance. As Sari's fist connects with Ashur's nose, she ponders if this is what their ancient ancestors had envisioned when they conceived the idea of the Sitnu. However, these Sitnu—the monthly matches, the points, the scores, and the tallies—were deliberately concealed from the Suan people.

In a sudden move, Ashur seizes her wrist, twisting it, causing her to lose her balance. She breaks free from his grip and stumbles away.

Only the nobility, only the vassals, and their closest advisors knew—for they could also offer their own children to the Sitnu. Being able to match a mar'sahr'dan'i could win you larger domains, the right to keep a larger army and a chance at a seat on the council. Sometimes, rarely, you could overthrow a dynasty by taking out all of the Sahre'Danu's offspringin one match.

Ashur hisses as she lunges into him, her shoulder connecting with his stomach. She pins him to the ground. "Akitu." *Akitu*; *I win*; the final word; the declaration of victory.

He laughs. "You wish." His hand snakes free and swiftly reaches up.

She leans back, throwing her arm up to keep him from grabbing her neck. But his fingers close around the thin leather strap at her throat, and he yanks, laughing as the royal seal slides from the necklace and into his waiting hands. A wicked grin spreads across his face as he is distracted by the seal in his palm.

Sari sees her chance. She grabs the Heart, weighing it in her hand. In a flash, she sees all of the carnage that he has committed. Not just when he had the Heart, but over his whole life. Almost thirty years of wickedness. She watches as he brutalizes their siblings, committing horrors on the bodies of their sisters and depravity on their brothers; the torture of his troops; the massacres of the villages he conquered, the unapologetic savagery he visited upon any who challenged him.

The power of the Heart sings, humming through her veins, and she knows that the Heart must be destroyed. If she keeps it, she will become undone—her tenuous grasp on morality unraveled, for she is too similar to her brother not to give in. They were carefully sculpted by their father, and slowly molded by their mother. Every day will be a battle to hold onto that flicker of goodness she has held. She knows she would eventually lose. But now—just for this moment, she needs the power.

Ashur realizes that she is not fighting him for the seal and pounces, but the Heart increases her dexterity and enhances her reflexes. She dodges him before his feet even leave the floor, and she stops him with one hand around his neck.

"Goodbye," she says, squeezing his neck and ending his life. "Tell Mother and Father that I don't miss them."

The battered sanctuary, once echoing with the clash of steel, now reverberates with the roars of the unleashed kahbush'a. Nanshaie, exhausted but conscious, collapses, her divine power depleted. The ferocious creatures are released once again.

The Heart whispers to her, telling her what she must do next. *Take control of the kahbush'a, create an army; march to the isi'tu. Claim your throne.*

"No," she says to the Heart. She raises her hand, and the advancing kahbush'a all freeze in place. She chuckles. Her eyes lock onto Ia—once a guide, now a betrayer—lying sprawled on the cold floor. Anger, a tempest, demands retribution. The desire for revenge claws at her insides, an insatiable hunger. Approaching Ia, Sari's grip on the Heart tightens.

Saritrah raises the Heart, the silent whispers guiding her through her first brush with magic; channeling her anger, she envisions an inferno engulfing Ia. Smoke curls around the former high priestess. The scent of burning fur permeates the sanctuary, and screeches of torment clamor off the walls. Sari laughs, savoring every twitch of pain, every spasm of anguish, the Heart relishing in all of it.

The world around her blurs, and the echoes of reality fade. In the grip of the Heart's control, Sari is lost, her vision narrowed to the figure lying vulnerable before her. Her only desire is to see others suffer as she has suffered. She wants—she needs—every single person to scream as she wanted to scream as a child—the world let her suffer, and she would make the world pay.

Kill her, kill her... Her voice, the Heart's voice, their voice in unison. She picks up a spear, cackling, the need to see blood gush from Ia's throat rising in her chest. She raises it, eyes wide as she takes aim, but a firm hand grips her wrist before she can skewer the priestess.

"She needs to die!" Saritrah snarls, not willing to let her prey go.

"Let me do it," Nanshaie says.

"Nanshaie," the high priestess says through gritted teeth. "Help me, please."

"I am not saving you. I just wanted the honor of being the one to kill you." Nanshaie's voice is that of a wounded child, hurt and betrayed but unwilling to endure the pain any longer.

"But I have done so much for you, ever since you arrived at the Temple—"

"I never asked to be the Oracle," Nanshaie continues, her words dripping with the bitterness of unspoken grievances. "You insisted, trapping me in a role I would never have chosen."

"And it was worth it. It will be worth it. The Arkae has been opened, and even if I fall here, the Araelta will be victorious. We shall destroy this world and remake it anew, just as it was in the City of Bec."

"You're wrong," Nanshaie retorts, her voice a storm gathering momentum. "The City of Bec was built by Escneans, not the Araelta. It was your precious sisters that destroyed it, not remade it."

"No, that is not what Namu said, she told me my visions—"

Saritrah's patience snaps. "Playtime is over, Nanshaie. Kill her now."

Nanshaie shakes her head. "I'm not done yet."

Saritrah hisses, grabbing the spear from Nanshaie again and plunging it down. But seconds before the spearpoint can touch the high priestess' neck, Ia raises her hands, and Saritrah goes flying backward.

The hard stone altar beneath Sari is unforgiving as her body crashes against it, pain throbbing through her head. Pain that grants her a brief moment of clarity, but breaking her focus—the kahbush'a are once again free and rushing at an exhausted Tinanna.

"I can grant you the power to end this," the Heart murmurs. "All at once, kill the beasts, kill the betrayers..."

"No," Sari retorts, her voice a resolute whisper. "The kahbush'a are not beasts. They are innocent people. We can't kill them. We can change them back, right?"

The Heart, relentless, tries again. "I can give you the throne you desire. The power to rule."

Sari shakes her head, trying to hold onto that flickering flame in her soul; the flame that longs to make a new family, have a new life, and be with Tinanna and Nanshaie as they all try to atone for their pasts. Together. "I don't want the throne anymore. It's not worth the cost."

"Zisu can return." The Heart refuses to give up. "The beloved little sister you lost can be brought back from the dead."

Sari's heart skips a beat at the mention of Zisu. Could it truly be done? Could she bring Zisu back? She said she would tear down the heavens and uproot the earth for her... if all she had to do was let the Heart rule her, control her... A small price for Zisu.

She digs her claws into her palms. *No.* "That's impossible. Zisu was cremated, and the rites of death were performed."

The Heart, undeterred, offers again. "I was crafted for this purpose—to resurrect the dead. Aodhe made me so that she might travel between the worlds of the living and dead. All other powers are secondary. I can bring Zisu back. I can find her soul and bind it to a body. Any body that you want for her."

Any body... A strong body, a body that can fight back, a healthy body... Never would Zisu have to worry about being overtaken...

"Sari!" Tinanna screams, her voice like a splash of cold water. "Destroy it!"

That's right, Sari reminds herself, her heart racing in her chest. Sari knows she is here to destroy not just Ashur and Ia but the Heart, too. The Heart, with its tempting promises of power, its sweet lies and delicious temptations, cannot grant her redemption for the blood she has already spilled. It needs to be destroyed. But how?

Her head is throbbing with a relentless pounding and every muscle in her body screaming in protest. Slowly, she brings the Heart closer to her face, examining its intricate details and ignoring its clawing voice in her head. The Heart seems to be both solid and liquid simultaneously, glowing like faint starlight. And then, in that ethereal glow, she notices it—a barely perceptible mark. Time has eroded its once-prominent lines, but it is there. A sigil—a symbol, faint but undeniably the same symbol that embellishes the royal seal—a perfect circle with crossed lines through it. All her life, she had been told it was a representation of claw marks. Maybe that was a lie.

She glances at Ashur, his hand still gripping the ring. She has no idea if she is about to make everything worse or save the world, but she snatches the ring and presses it against the Heart of Aodhe, hoping that *this* is the Blade of Kyna.

The Heart of Aodhe and the royal seal explode in a blinding flash of light. Sari falls to her knees, her ears ringing and her vision blurred. She is certain that she has doomed the world rather than saved it.

But as the light fades, she realizes that she is still alive. She looks around, her vision slowly clearing. The sanctuary is in ruins, the altar cracked and broken. The Heart of Aodhe is gone, and her royal seal is nothing more than a pile of melted metal.

Sari feels a wave of relief wash over her. She has done it. She has destroyed the Heart and saved the world from destruction.

Heart pounding in her chest, Sari stares at the pile of molten metal that used to be her royal seal. She reaches out a trembling hand, touching the remnants of her heritage. The metal is still hot, and she pulls her hand back with a hiss. She gazes at the burn, the pain barely registering through the haze of disbelief and confusion.

Who am I without this? she wonders. The last tangible link to her royal lineage has been destroyed before her eyes. She's no longer the Mar'sahr'dan'i, no longer the rightful heir to the throne of Sua. She is no longer Saritrah mat Sumalika, princess and winner of the Sitnu.

She's just... Sari.

But who is Sari? She's been running from her past for so long, trying to reclaim what was stolen from her. She's fought and killed and bled for her birthright, and now...

Now it's gone.

There is a hollowness in her chest, a gaping void where her identity used to be.

The once frenzied beasts, the kahbush'*a*, now lay still, their monstrous forms shifting before Sari's eyes. She watches in awe as the creatures' bodies shrink and morph, until finally, the unconscious forms of the Re'u people or savitus soldiers they once were are revealed. Sari lets out a sigh, grateful that she does not have to worry about how to save them.

Saritrah watches in stunned silence as Ia—somehow still alive—rises up from the floor and leaps across the empty moat. The woman's robes are torn and dirty, but her eyes still gleam with a fanatical intensity. Without a word, Ia makes to flee the sanctuary.

Nanshaie, her face a mask of fury, springs into action. She gives chase, her spear drawn and her movements swift and sure. She catches up to Ia and drives her spear into the woman's back. Ia lets out a guttural cry, but she does not slow her pace. Nanshaie matches her stride, keeping the weapon embedded in Ia's flesh as she tries to drag her to the ground.

"Why, Ia?" Nanshaie demands, her voice trembling with emotion. "Why did you manipulate me? Why did you think the end of the world was necessary?"

Ia's steps begin to falter, but still, she presses on. "Nanshaie," she rasps, "my dear Oracle, you had a greater purpose. But you were blinded by your own torment. I had to manipulate you in order to get you on the right path."

Nanshaie's grip on the spear tightens, and she forces Ia to the ground. "You lied to me. You twisted my visions for your own gain. People *died* following the visions you fed to me!"

"It was for the greater good," Ia insists. "I had to make you see the truth. I was preparing you to join us. You belong among the stars. You belong with the Araelta."

With a final, anguished cry, Nanshaie plunges the spear in again.

"I am ready," Ia whispers, staring into Nanshaie's eyes, her voice strangely serene. "I will take my place among the stars, content in the knowledge that I achieved my goal. Magic is again awake in Sua. Namu, I am coming home. My sisters, I am coming."

The light fades from Ia's eyes. Nanshaie stands over her, tears streaming down her face.

Twenty-Four

THE HOT BREEZE DOES NOT SEAR THE SURVIVORS as they take their leave from the ancient temple. Like the fortress that Ashur had commandeered, it too crumbles to dust almost instantly, the weight of centuries crashing down on it all at once. Sari takes one last look over her shoulder at the ruins before they vanish, engulfed by dawn and distance. She spares a thought for whatever god or divinity once called the temple home; but something in her tells her that the god was already dead when Ashur took command of the temple.

Miramis leads the few survivors back to Izmyri. She has bags under her eyes, and her hair is matted, blood still dried and streaked across her face. But her hard-set jaw and narrowed eyes hide none of her emotions, as much as it is clear that she is trying to hold onto them.

Sari wants to ask what it was like to be at the whim of Ashur's control, if she remembers her time as a kahbush'a, but she knows she does not want to hear the answer. She experienced just a few seconds of it, she does not need to know any more. Their victory may be complete, but the Amyrdine Bara are wilting in the sun, their numbers significantly diminished and demoralized despite their victory.

A strange feeling gnaws in Sari's chest. Guilt. This is her fault. She came up with this plan, just as she had for the ancient fortress. So many lives lost.

But why does she care? They weren't her troops, not even a little bit. She did not mourn or feel guilt when she lost troops previously, and those *had* been her troops. She did not mourn the ones lost at Antalyza except for Arishaki.

Her hand reaches for the royal seal, but it's gone.

She's not royal anymore; she can't be blameless anymore. Her decisions can be questioned; her decisions can be wrong. She can make mistakes now. Was it a mistake to take on Ashur? No, it wasn't. But the way that she did it? Maybe.

Miramis places a firm but gentle hand on Sari's shoulder. "You did what you had to do, Saritrah," she says.

Sari shakes her head, tears welling up in her eyes. "Just Sari, now, please. And maybe I did what had to be done. But at what cost?" she asks. "How many lives were lost because of me?"

Miramis looks around at the remaining survivors, who are watching the exchange with a mix of fear and admiration. "You cannot bear the weight of every life lost," she says. "You cannot be responsible for every decision made by others—Ashur is responsible for what happened here. But you must be responsible for your own actions, too."

"Execute me," Sari says.

"Excuse me?" Miramis raises an eyebrow.

"I want to be executed. I should have died on the night of the insurrection all those years ago. I do not deserve to live."

Miramis snorts. "No."

"But I have to pay for what I did."

"I know. But execution is the quick and easy way out. It requires very little of you; it does not make you change your beliefs, your behaviors, your habits."

"Then what shall I do?"

"I don't know. That's something you have to figure out, Sari. But if you would like somewhere to start, why don't you publicly renounce your throne, renounce it for yourself and all future descendants of yours."

"That is all?"

"Oh, absolutely not. But that will be enough for me. Renounce the throne and tell the isiaqs and sarhes to embrace democracy."

The air is not heavy with the smell of alcohol and sweat, and there are no cries or screams beating against the hard stone walls. The iseru is silent; never again shall a Sitnu disturb the peace of this underground arena. Sari runs her hand on the half-wall that separates the spectator seating from the battlefield at the center, and her eyes linger on the two large thrones at the northernmost point.

"Don't heroes usually return triumphant?" She does not expect an answer. "To parades and celebrations? I can never go back home, even if I was returning as a queen, too much has changed, and I have changed..."

She can almost feel her parents glaring at her, judging her from a top their perches. She can almost hear her mother's disdainful sighs and her father's disgruntled huffs. If she strains, she might even hear Ashur's laughter.

She runs her finger along the etched symbols, ones that she once puzzled over, and even her teachers could not explain their meaning. *This is an ancient place,* they had told her when she asked. *The iseru has existed for as long as your family has reigned.*

An ancient place. She spins on her heel, taking in the whole of the iseru at once. This underground fighting arena was built below the royal isi'tu, below the royal palace. "Or maybe the isi'tu was built on top of it," she says out loud.

"What was that?" Nanshaie asks, breaking the silence that she and Tinanna had agreed to observe when they acquiesced to Sari's request to accompany her into the remnants of the hell she once lived in.

"How old do you think this place is?" Sari asks Nanshaie.

The Oracle closes her eyes. "Do you really want to know?" There is a hint of both mischief and sorrow in Nanshaie's voice.

"This is part of the real Bec, isn't it?" Sari says. She does not need Nanshaie's answers. Ever since she touched the Heart of Aodhe, she's felt something below her skin. It's night Sight, but it might be similar. Even with the Heart shattered, she still feels something else lurking in her bones.

"This was the seat of the Elpacean, government and the main building of their university." Her eyes remain closed as she says it, but she moves as if she is still looking at the structure, taking it in as she cranes her head and spins around to get a better look.

"So the City of Bec that we explored…"

"A beautiful, and tragic dream. An illusion made manifest by Ia," the Oracle says.

"But how?"

"Ia did not have visions of the future, but of the past." It is the voice of the goddess, not Nanshaie. "The paradise she saw in her visions will never exist in the future. Its time has come and gone." The voice of a goddess with a very mortal sorrow.

"And she did not realize that?"

"The Araelta made sure she never would. A victim of their manipulations, even as she carried out their orders."

"So, this is part of the true City of Bec?"

"Yes." The crack of grief in the voice is too haunting for a goddess.

Sari clenches her fist and turns back to Nanshaie, to the Oracle. "And we've been desecrating it with violence."

The Oracle nods, lips tight, eyes bright and welled with tears.

"Sumalika and Balshazzar," Sari says, hands behind her back as she gazes again at the head of the iseru. "The last rulers of Sua. The last of the Qa'taru house. The last to sit on the Kashtu thrones. Aishah, Ashur, Rahbani, Tudiya, Alaparos…"

Nanshaie comes up behind her and takes one of her hands.

"I don't remember the rest," Sari says, voice breaking. "I know I had more siblings; I know I did. But I can't remember their names. I was the second to last, and then Zisuthra. But I had others; I can't remember who, though."

Nanshaie gently squeezes Sari's hand. Sari's brows furrow in frustration, and her eyes well up with tears that threaten to spill over.

She clenches her fist, trying to summon the missing fragments of her past.

Each forgotten name is another piece of her identity slipping away. Her frustration intertwines with a sense of guilt, as if she has betrayed her own family by failing to remember them.

Nanshaie moves closer, wrapping her arms around Sari in a gentle embrace. Sari jerks away, not wanting sympathy or pity. "I wish I could remember," Sari whispers. "Their names, their faces... They were a part of me. We hurt each other, tormented each other, hated each other, and yet... I never want to think of them again."

The lost city of Bec, and the lost scions of Qa'taru; ghosts that will stalk Sari through the dawn and into the dusk. Specters that will linger in her thoughts come twilight, living on the edge of night, living past the setting of the sun and the rising of the moons.

"I have just a flicker of magic from Yshuld," Nanshaie says. "Would you like for me to destroy the iseru?"

Sari closes her eyes, imagining the arena set ablaze and remembering the feeling of magic from the Heart of Aodhe. "No," she says, not opening her eyes. She imagines the heat radiating toward her as the curtains on the dais ignite, the smell of smoke wafting in the air as the wooden seats catch fire, and the crackling as the flames lick and bite at the metal beams holding the ceiling firmly in place.

"Sari," Tinanna says. "We need to go."

"I know, just one more moment."

"No," Nanshaie says, pulling at Sari's hand. "We need to get out."

Sari opens her eyes, and the vision she had of the burning iseru is still in front of her. "But—" She looks at Nanshaie, who shakes her head. Terrified, she flees, running back outside and sealing the hidden stone door tightly into place.

"You didn't do that?" She asks Nanshaie.

"No, that was you."

"Magic..." Ia's words ring in her head. *Magic flows in Sua.* Can anyone use it? Or can she only use it because she had touched the Heart? If anyone can use it, how will that shift power in Sua? Will another Ashur rise up to abuse it? Will the new government attempt to regulate it? The savitus speak of equality, of not using power to oppress people, but they could never have imagined one of those powers being magic. It, like the kahbush'a had been relegated to myth and legend.

Sari signs her name with a shaky hand. A signature in exchange for her life. Acknowledge the legitimacy of the newly elected government and her crimes shall be pardoned. She glances around the room, meeting the eyes of Tinanna and Nanshaie, standing next to her, holding hands. Each of them offers a small nod, but Sari can sense the unspoken question hanging in the air: what now? Will she abide by the document she has signed renouncing all claims to the throne and promising to live her life as a private citizen?

She looks down at the parchment in her hand, feeling both relief and emptiness. She is adrift without a clear purpose or direction. She ignores the voices of her parents calling her weak and cowardly, a mark of shame in the royal line. She thinks about Zisu and how she would have reacted to Sari's choice. She hopes Zisu, at least, would understand. Maybe her sister would have been proud.

Miramis takes the paper and reads it out loud for all in the hall to hear—the last of the Suan royals giving up without a fight. As she sits there, lost in thought, she feels as though she is missing a piece of herself. One of those shattered pieces has disappeared, but she doesn't know which one.

"Let's go," Nanshaie says, holding out her hand. "The next part—"

"I know," Sari says, refusing the Oracle's hand and following the new government officials out of the office and down the hall.

The crowd in the plaza is rowdy and restless as Sari observes them from behind the curtains on the balcony. She wrings her hands. She's dreamed of this moment since she was a child, it's everything and nothing like she imagined.

In her dreams, she would be walking out onto the iti'su balcony triumphant. Holding Katynna aloft, cheers and shouts from her people, her name being carried on the wind, parents holding their children high to catch a glimpse of the new Sahre'Danu. People rejoicing that they have been liberated from the tyrany of the insurrectionists, celebrating that a new dawn is rising for Sua, and hopeful that Saritrah will lead them into a future so bright they will forget the nightmare the insurrectionists had inflicted upon them. All would be certain that there was much to look forward to under the leadership of Saritrah mat Sumalika, the mightiest of the Qa'taru dynasty.

Today will be a day that the people of Sua, not *her* people, will remember, and when the children here today become grandparents, they will tell their children about the day that the violent and oppressive sahredom of the Qa'taru officially came to an end and an era of peace was ushered forth, delivered to them by the Amydrine Bara and their savitus fighters.

Sua liberated. Freed. Unshackled.

Liberated from her. Unshackled from her family. Freed from their domination. She is here to tell them that they are liberated from her: her rule, her power, her authority and might. Free of the oppression she would have wrought upon them just by Saritrah existing. Her chest tightens and she tries to steady her shaking hands.

She is free of herself, too. She is free to do as she wishes, no longer bound by her parents, their desires, and their expectations. Liberated to explore who she is and who she could have been if her childhood had not been marred by neglect and abuse.

Nanshaie grabs her hand and pulls her out of the shadows, pushing her towards the podium. Miramis has just finished giving her own speech, and one interpreter steps forward to relieve the other, shaking out their hands and cracking their knuckles.

She has a speech prepared, one she practiced in front of the mirror and with Tinanna and Nanshaie a dozen times the night before, but it is all forgotten now. She takes a deep breath. It doesn't matter; she just has to say a few sentences.

The interpreter nods to her, ready to convey her message, waiting for her to start. "I am here today to announce that..."

She halts, frozen, all of the words missing. Announce that she is giving up her dream? That she is forsaking her quest? That she is renouncing her entire identity? Who is she if she is not clawing for the throne?

The crowd quiets, murmurs of anxiety the only noise. Nan-shaie takes her hand and squeezes it. "Say whatever you need to say."

Sari nods. "Sumalika mat Qa'taru and Balshazzar mar Alshu died six years ago, struck down by revolutionaries dedicated to bringing justice and equality to the land of Sua, inspired by the movement in Fayn."

She swallows, glancing one more time at Nanshaie. "They were ruthless, they were cruel. They believed in ruling through fear, through violence, and through intimidation. And that is how they taught me, their only surviving daughter, to rule, too."

A year ago, she would have said that with false pride, it would have been a boast. A show of strength. Today, she just feels like she has exposed every weakness for everyone to gawk at.

"They were pitiless, without remorse, believing that it was the only way to keep Sua strong, to keep Sua safe. The tradition of the Sahre'Danus goes back generations. But just because something is tradition, doesn't mean it is right."

Her hand reaches instinctively for the small ring on a thin cord around her neck, but it isn't there. The comfort of the past is gone. "You can always choose to break the cycle; your children do not need to inherit your pain; your scions do not need to suffer in your chains. Shackles are not things that should be passed to the next generation."

The wind picks up, and she cannot tell if the crowd before her is cheering or laughing at her. But she continues; words that she is saying to herself but the world is overhearing. "One of my few friends, Etana mat Alaru of the Susan'i clan, later the elected leader of Eluuti, used to be a feared sahre, with a cunning and shrewd army. She was always claiming new territories as her own. But one day, she and her army put down their arms. They took up plows and sickles. I asked her why, and she told me of a dream—she was going to create paradise. They would still work, they would still contribute their share of labor. But it was always with an eye toward fairness, letting none go hungry no matter what. Each did that which was within their abilities to help all meet their needs."

She takes a deep breath, not wanting to rush the next words, hoping that if such a thing as ghosts exists, Etana is here, listening. "That fledgling dream was shattered by Ashur. But she told me to remember her, remember Eluuti and what she and her people tried to create there."

She will not cry, she will not shed a tear. But she has no idea how she will prevent them flowing as she moves to finish her speech. "My final act as a royal scion is to call upon the isiaqs and sahres to put down their own arms, to surrender peacefully to the tides of change, to choose a different path than their parents. We can choose who we want to be. My sister, Zisuthra mat Sumalika, chose to be kind. And today, I formally choose to abdicate any claim I or my descendants might have to the crown. No more shall a Sahre'Danu sit on the Kashtu Throne. For now, the people will reign."

Her heart is beating so fast that she cannot hear anything except for the blood rushing in her head, and she is glad for it. She does not want to hear the crowds, she does not want to hear their cheers or their jeers, she does not want to hear their response to the death of her identity, her dreams, and her future.

She has no place to go now, this isi'tu is no longer her home, and she has not been offered any by the new government officials. She folds her parchment and places it in her pocket, bowing quickly to the crowd before she races off of the balcony, not ready to face anyone, not wanting to see her reflection in anyone else's eyes.

She ignores the calls from Tinanna and Nanshaie as she races out the back of the isi'tu through the old servants quarters and flees past spectators and observers still gathered on every street. She runs until she reaches the city gates, the merchant's way, and darts into the desert.

She runs until she is sure that she will no longer be able to hear the crowds, the music, the celebrations; sure that she will not be able to hear the fireworks that Miramis said were planned.

She collapses into the soft sand, digging her hands into it as if she could find water just below the surface.

"I want to thank you," someone says.

Sari looks up to see a young woman before her. The woman can hardly be past her twenty-fifth summer. She's never seen this woman before, and yet she gets the feeling that she has. "For what?" Sari spits out the words, voice dripping with bitterness. Is this someone from the crowd? Someone come to gloat over Sari's demise? Someone hoping to revel in Sari's downfall?

"For destroying the Heart of Aodhe," the woman says.

"How do you—Oh. Oh. You aren't as old anymore," Sari says to the goddess.

"No, you destroyed the Heart of Aodhe, but the seal on the Arkae Ar'a was still broken. Three of the Arkae have now been unsealed. I can walk this earth again and take any form I desire."

"I'm glad for you. I guess a lot of people have won their freedom."

"Nay, as I've said before, it is not a good thing that the gods can again walk among mortals. But while I can, I do want to thank you.

With the Heart of Aodhe broken, it will be harder for the secretive forces to advance their mission."

"Is this the part where you send me on a quest? You want me to keep fighting?"

"No, for I have no way to direct you. Our friends, both the Araelta and the Blodheimr Hjart have done a good job of keeping a low profile. I would not even know where to send you."

"So, some other quest then?"

"Is that what you want?"

"I don't know what I want except to be rid of the guilt. I have no idea who I am anymore, what I want, or what I should do. A quest would at least be a start. Isn't that what gods are supposed to do? Send heroes on quests?"

"Do you want to be a hero?"

"I don't know!" Sari reaches for her spear, but her hand touches nothing. She stomps her foot. "I don't know. And am I still supposed to be able to use magic? I destroyed the Heart."

"I do not know. Before the Arkae were sealed, anyone could use magic. It was a skill; some were more proficient than others. Some practiced hard, and others never studied but could still put on spectacular shows."

"Why was it locked away?"

"You know the answer, the details are different but there are always those who will turn tools into weapons." The goddess turns her head to the west, to the direction of the destroyed temple where she had killed Ashur.

"So, I shouldn't use it?"

"You have to make a choice of how to use it. I do have a gift for you, though. Hold out your hands."

Sari does as the goddess tells her, and as soon as she does, she sees another shining, ancient city. No, she doesn't see it. She is transported to it. The city stands tall, its glistening spires reaching towards a marble sky.

"This doesn't look like Bec," she says.

"It isn't. But it was a contemporary of Bec."

"Why are you showing me this?"

"Find it, find the ruins of this city, and within its crumbling walls, you shall find the answers to your questions."

Sari blinks, but the goddess is gone, and the desert is silent.

A quest, then.

She does not tell even Nanshaie about her conversation, although she guesses that Nanshaie somehow knows about it anyway. And Nanshaie still somehow knows that Sari is leaving, despite telling no one.

Nanshaie and Tinanna are waiting for Sari at the gates to the city, each with a bag slung over a shoulder and the reins to a camel in their hand. "Took you long enough. You oversleep?" Nanshaie asks.

"What are you doing here?" Sari should know better by now; a Seer will always know things before anyone else.

"Waiting for you." Tinanna says.

"Where are you going?" Sari asks them both, wondering if she will ever get used to them knowing things without her telling them.

"You tell me. I thought you had a plan." Tinanna feeds a small seed to her falcon and puts him on a perch on the back of the camel.

"Well, you aren't coming with me, and I don't have a plan."

"What do you mean?" Nanshaie asks, head tilting to the side.

"You can't come with me," Sari says, wishing she could say otherwise. She wants to make a family with these Seers, if she can convince them somehow. But they have obligations to Yshuld, and without Ia, the Temple will be in disarray. She cannot ask that of them.

Nanshaie squints. "But I want to."

Sari wants to ask Nanshaie to come along with her. But she doesn't know where she is going, and she doesn't know if she could keep the Oracle safe. Even with Tinanna with them, she doesn't know what dangers await on this quest. She had assumed that Nanshaie would be returning to the Temple. She gave her blessing to the new government and informed the crowd that the goddess welcomed this new era for the Suan people. Sari had assumed that, with her job finished, Nanshaie would return home. "I can't protect you. I think I've proven that time and time again."

"I don't need your protection. I learned how to fight my own battles. I'm not plagued by nightmares anymore, and the biggest threat in the desert used to be you. And look at you now."

"Nanshaie..." Sari gulps and glances at Tinanna, wondering if the other Seer will step in, help her get Nanshaie to understand.

Nanshaie steps closer toward Sari and brushes a stray hair out of her face. "Let me come with you."

"Why?"

"Because you need someone to keep lifting you up, and I need someone to keep me grounded."

"I'm a monster, and I need to atone for what I've done. My journey is not yours, and I will not take you down this path with me. I need to do this on my own, or else it doesn't count."

"I won't help you then. You slay those monsters on your own."

"Nanshaie. I mean it when I say that I wish you and I could..."

"Could what?"

"I have to do this on my own. I can't be with anyone, even you and Tinanna, until I know who I am and what I am. Maybe one day I will be a whole person and not some hollow shell. But until then..."

"I see," Nanshaie says, sagging. "I understand. Tinanna and I shall be waiting for the day that you have found yourself."

Sari looks at Tinanna again, and the other Seer nods, too. Some selfish part of her hopes that her journey is quick and Nanshaie and Tinanna do not have to wait long.

The goddess had told Sari to venture into the desert to find a lost city yet again. That is where her answer lies, she tells herself.

She had sought answers before, hoping that the love of her people would be enough to fill her hollow self. But she has a hole in her heart, and that must be fixed before she can hope for anything more with anyone.

She had mistaken loyalty for love and love for loyalty too many times to know what either truly looked like. She needs to learn—and to remember. Arishaki. Etana. Zisu. What had made their love or loyalty special? Different? And what had she done to take it for granted?

As she rides away, she can feel Nanshaie's and Tinanna's eyes following her onto the horizon. If she were not so broken, maybe it could work. But would she suspect Nanshaie of betrayal within the year? Or a month? Would she beg Nanshaie over and over for reassurance the way she had with Ari? Would she yell and scream at Nanshaie when doubt crept in like she had when she and Etana were young? Would she lash out at Tinanna and challenge her to endless fights? Would she wake up in the middle of the night and demand Tinanna prove her loyalty?

The answers to those questions could never be discovered without causing Nanshaie and Tinanna pain. Not unless she finds a way to heal her wounds first.

Twenty-Five

Y SHULD HAD GIVEN HER NO FURTHER clues on the location of this ancient city—not a name that she could inquire about, not even a hint of the direction. So she rides to the first place she can think of that might offer a clue. The location of the spectral city of Bec; the version of the city that somehow had manifested from dreams and nightmares. A vision made real, a memory made manifest by Ia's ability to see the past.

But it is not there. She finds the fissure they had traveled through, but she meets a dead end. It is not as if it has been walled off, but rather the fissure narrows the further in she travels, as if it had never once opened into a cavernous city.

As she crawls back out, she finds there is someone waiting for her. A qatu bathed in the glowing light of sunrise.

"You look different again," Sari says to the goddess. "Here to give me a hint?"

"Excuse me?" The qatu asks, stepping closer to Sari, the glow fading. "Do I know you?"

"Oh," Sari says, cheeks burning as she realizes it is not Yshuld before her this time. "I thought you were someone else."

"Do many people come this way?" The qatu places her hands on her hips and looks up and down at the face of the butte.

"I'm not sure," Sari says.

"But you were meeting someone here."

"Not really. I've been here before," Sari says, not sure how to continue. The qatu has white, long hair and silver facial markings and looks too pale and delicate to be a desert dweller.

"What was it you found before?"

"Nothing," Sari says. "The echo of a memory."

"Interesting. I had heard a rumor that there were ancient ruins here, and I felt compelled to come find them. But if you say they are not here," the qatu says. "Sorry, I never introduced myself. I am Professor Shirat Khannah, from the University of Khadima Alam. I specialize in ancient history, specifically around the times of the Isidoran invasion of Nin-Imma and Ku-Aya."

The qatu has a Suan name, but she looks far more like Kegan and the other Evenstar calla from Fayn. "That's truly ancient history," Sari says. "And you think there still might be ruins here? I thought Ku-Aya was in the Erid steppe, and Nin-Imma was located much further north."

"I think there was another nation at the time, though. One that might have been inconsequential, small, and I think it existed somewhere here."

"Interesting theory," Sari says. "But all that exists here is sand and dust."

The professor frowns, crossing her arms. "I can see that. I suppose I wasted yet more university funds. Oh well."

"Where shall you go now?" Sari asks, still convinced that maybe there is a clue to be had here.

"I don't know. But not back to the university. I'll be the laughing-stock if I return now with my tail tucked between my legs this soon."

"So, you'll just wander the desert?"

The professor shrugs. "I suppose so. I'll figure it out. I need to find at least something to take back with me."

Sari bites her lip.

"I just can't shake the feeling that there's something here, though. Maybe around the other side..." The professor removes a backpack and rifles through its contents, tossing research equipment that looks rather expensive into the sand without a care. "Ah! Here's the map."

Sari can't help but stare as the professor unrolls a long piece of parchment and smooths it out on the sand. It's a map of Ahnlisen, but one that is also somehow not.

A pang of sympathy tugs at Sari's chest. "I think I know a place that you could look."

"Oh?" The professor says, not looking up from the map.

"Here," Sari says, picking up one of the professors' tools and using it to draw in the sand. "The main entrance is on the grounds of the old isi'tu. But there's a hidden passage, it leads out to the north..." Sari closes her eyes, the memories of that night flooding back. Her frantic escape, her desert flight from her home, from her family, from her life, hoping the insurrectionists did not know about the iseru, or at least did not know about the other entrances to it.

"And you've been inside?"

"Far too many times. But—" But she set it on fire last time she was there. "It is not in the best condition." Oh well, it would still be something for this eccentric to take back to her colleagues and impress them with. And it would be far safer, too.

"You have given me a great gift. And I haven't had the manners to ask your name, either."

"Sari," she says without thinking, but immediately regrets it.

"Like Saritrah? The lost princess? Huh. You know, I heard she abdicated. Did you hear that? Here I thought she'd never give up."

"Just Sari. And I hadn't heard. Imagine that."

"Strange times we live in. Exciting times. Times that historians will write about and study. Someday my descendants might stand in this very spot and wonder if Sua even existed, or if it was a myth. Maybe they will not even remember the name, just speculate that maybe, once upon a time, there was a nation in the desert, and wouldn't it be nice to know what life was like for those people? History is a cycle; we pass our stories on and hope they survive. Our children's children will inherit only the impression of us until even our names are lost. They will still have inherited all of our struggles, but all of our progress, too."

"You're a professor of history, not philosophy?"

"Ha, forgive me. Anthropology. But sometimes, I feel like I am far older than I am, and I have lived too many lifetimes. Can't thisprofessor ramble a little?"

"Of course," Sari says. "I was not planning on heading toward Erzurumei, but if you would like an escort that way, I would be happy to help you out."

"Nah, I know I look like some fragile flower, but I promise I'm tougher than I appear. I can make it. But thank you."

"I wish you well, then."

"What is it that the people here say? *Sen'en'dai?*"

"The Re'u say that."

"Ah, my mistake."

"No, I think it's appropriate. May the gods be with you, too."

It has been a month since she left behind Nanshaie and wandered into the desert in search of answers, and yet she has found none. All she has found so far are ghosts. And today she comes upon another.

The remnants of Etana's paradise. Eluuti. It has been months since it was attacked, burned, and ransacked. But when Sari closes her eyes, she can smell the smoke, hear the clash of weapons, and feel the screams of the dying reverberate in her bones as if the battle were still being waged.

Etana had bid her to remember what they were trying to create. An attempt at paradise. Not the kind of paradise that Ia had dreamed of; not one free of labor or work. The people here had worked, tended crops, kept the livestock, built sub'tus and cooked and cared for one another. Is paradise a lack of unmet needs or a surplus of abundant wants?

Is that what the Amyrdine Bara are trying to build? In Izmyri, people still had to work. But the elderly, the disabled, those unable to work for whatever reason were not left to die. No one goes without food; no one goes without shelter. But is that enough for it to be a paradise?

The goddess had warned her of using magic, and for the first time since she accidentally burned the iseru, she decides to use it again.

She uses her magic to erect a stone monument, tall and sturdy. On it, she etches, "Here are the remains of a beautiful dream and the brave souls who dared to make it into a reality."

A beautiful dream. Is that not what Nanshaie once called the spectral City of Bec? Another version of paradise that could not withstand the violence that the world seems utterly infested with.

Another two months pass, and during that time Sari finds no clues about the city that the goddess has told her to find. But as she packs her tiny camp after an unseasonably chilly nialsamu, she sees something in the distance.

Sari's heart sinks as she recognizes the caravan of a Re'u tribe, the one that had helped her when Zisu was ill. The familiarity in their eyes makes her stomach churn with guilt as they approach.

"Ah, the *Bah'en'rita*," Artaxerxes says. "Where is your sister?"

As she looks into the concerned face of the healer, she knows she can't hide the truth. With a heavy sigh, Sari musters the courage to share the devastating news. "I'm so sorry, but Zisu is no longer with us. I couldn't keep her safe, and I deeply apologize for failing her." The words hang heavily in the air, and Sari braces herself for the chastisement she is sure will follow.

"My apologies. She was a beautiful soul. I am honored that I was able to meet her. Tell me, where do you plan to journey next?"

"I do not know. I am searching for something—answers—but I don't know where to look. I wish to atone for the wrongs I have done, but so far all I have done is wander."

"You are Suan, not Re'u, but your people and mine, we were not always at odds. We wander because even though our cities were destroyed, this is still our home. Perhaps it is selfish of me, but if you would help me, I think you might find answers."

"I am not sure I understand," Sari says. "But I will help. It would give me something to do."

"Our goddess and yours, I think once they were one, the same, a whole. Our holy sites, yours, they share too much. But we do not let you see them."

Something stirs in Sari's chest at the mention of the goddess.

"My sister, Shirin'a, she went to one such site. Many moons ago. She has not returned and has not sent word."

"You want me to find her?"

"Yes, *Bah'en'rita*. This site is very hard to get to. My bones are too old and my back is too stiff to make the journey to find her. None of the rest of our tribe can be spared to find her."

"Can you tell me where it is? Do you have a map?" She hopes he will not be like Yshuld and give her no further clues.

When Artaxerxes spoke the name of this sacred site, she knew that, at last, she knew where Yshuld wanted her to go. Enheduanna, the capital of Ku-Aya. Ransacked and destroyed by Isidora thousands of years ago during their conquests as they expanded eastward. Ancient history, apparently not so ancient. The Re'u are the descendants of those who fled as the gates were breached and their city invaded. But the Isidoran empire fell, and when it did, the cities they once occupied were left to rot.

Out of respect, and a little bit of fear, the people of the Erid steppe rarely venture into these crumbling ruins. As she approaches the cliffs that line the eastern side of the Avon Riven, she wonders what the Janeuqi, the cousins of the Ku-Aya people who lived in what is now Janeuq, do with the ruins of Nin-Imma. The Janeuqi are descendants of the Carathounians, just as the Garcelonians are—another nation conquered by Isidora—but they fled west when the Isadorans invaded, forcing the people of Nin-Imma and Ku-Aya out of their homes. Do they view their ruins, the ruins of the people they drove out, with the same trepidation? She doubts they treat them as anything sacred.

The city of Enheduanna was carved into the cliffs, and even if they weren't avoided by the Suans out of a sense of superstition, the most adventurous of qatu would think twice about the treacherous journey to get inside the ruins. One wrong turn, one misplaced step, and the would-be explorer would be sent crashing into the raging Avon River, swallowed by the white rapids, screams lost in the wind.

Sari inhales the scent of moss and mud, having decided to approach the city from below. The roar of the Avon River drowns out any other sounds, and the sun is hidden behind the towering cliffs, the ominous shadows reaching to entwine with the white rapids.

She tries not to think about the last time she was on the edge of the Avon—only a little farther south are the ruins of the Arkae Ar'a. Or what is left of the ruins. She wonders if the Arkae Ar'a was created by the Ku-Ayan people; was it one of their gods who resided there?

She shivers, returning her thoughts to the present. The only known entrance to the city is a small cave halfway up the cliffs, with only a narrow path winding back and forth across the cliff face, carved out by researchers at least two decades ago, but since worn away by wind and rain.

The ill-fated research expedition from Khadima Alam had infuriated the Re'u, and it's unknown if those researchers met a tragic but accidental end inside of Enheduanna, or if something far more violent had happened.

But Sari has not just permission but the blessing of the Re'u to seek out their lost matriarch.

She removes her sandals and ties rough leather with embedded rocks around the balls of her feet, stepping up the slick and narrow path, the rocks adding much needed traction. She leaves her packs and camel behind but does bring a medical pack, not sure what sort of state she might find Shirin'a in—if she finds her.

Halfway up the sheer cliff, there is a fissure just wide enough for someone to fit through, and she slides in sideways. She is just beginning to think that she picked the wrong crack in the cliff, convinced that she is only ensuring her demise by continuing when it suddenly opens up.

The city is strange; the architecture is similar to that of the phantom-Bec, but it also has some similarities to the architecture common in the few cities that do inhabit the Erid steppe. There is no sky, the rock of the cliff is suspended above her by the roofs of the tallest buildings. There is a strange illumination throughout it, as if the moss growing across the whole city is luminescent, giving off a bright enough glow to make the city visible without need for candles. It's like the city was carved out of the stone, rather than constructed and then buried.

The buildings are granite, not marble or limestone. But they are no less imposing, no less miraculous. There are not as many or as dense as Bec or Erzurumei. There are even fewer buildings here than in Antalyza. But that does not make it less awe-inspiring that such a wonder could exist. As she steps into the street, she searches for the seams between the buildings and the ground and finds none.

It truly was carved into the cliff.

She takes a deep breath, steadies herself, and listens, her head and ears swiveling as she steps lightly, straining for any noise that might betray the location of the lost qatu.

She expects to   hear   breathing, sighing,   or perhaps even singing in this supposedly holy site.

But then she hears the scream of a qatu. "From the north..." she says before sprinting off, forcing herself to focus only on the sound of the Re'u in need. It has to be the Re'u; who else would be here? She picks up her pace as she hears the cry again, followed by a cackle. Low, cruel, but wild in a way that her brother never was. "Let's see how many more of your claws we can remove before you tell us where the artifact is."

She leans forward, hoping to gain even a little bit more speed. She does not have the medical supplies needed to reattach fingers... Her own broken fingers on her hand ache just at the thought. How many times has this happened now? Being able to fight off the attackers but not save the life of the victim? Arishaki, Tinanna, Zisu… Unable to do anything while hoping to reach a healer in time…

The only option is to hope she gets there before any mortal damage is inflicted.

She turns a corner, chasing the sound of the screams, and finds three people—two lohyue and a qatu—assaulting the Re'u. Her heart almost stops when she notices that all three of the attackers bear that strange chalice and tree symbol worn by the Blodheimr Hjart that had briefly allied themselves with her brother.

What artifact are they after now? Another item that would end the world? Her fist lands on the face of the eldest attacker before they even hear her approach, and her foot quickly connects with the hands of another.

They are not trained fighters, they wield their weapons poorly; it's clear that the knives they have are ceremonial and not made for use in combat. She disarms them easily, the three meeting quick deaths. She had not meant to kill all of them, but they had been weaker than she anticipated. Her last blow against the qatu had only been meant to incapacitate them so she might question them later, but it's too late for that now.

But while their knives were not made for combat, they were still deadly, and Shirin'a barely clings to life.

Bruises are forming all over her body, and her fingers have all been declawed, the last knuckle in each hand missing. But the worst of it is her throat, and the long but shallow slashes across it.

Not enough to kill her quickly, but definitely enough that if it isn't addressed quickly, she will bleed out slowly. She wants to ask the woman a thousand questions, but there isn't time.

No time to ask the questions, and no time for her to find a healer. This ancient city will soon have four more ghosts walking its streets.

Sari screams, helpless. Why is is that she is so good at taking life, but can do nothing to save it?

The only thing she can do is hold the hand of the dying qatu. Yshuld told her that she would find the answers to her questions in this city. The answer to who she is, the answer to what she is.

And that answer is a killer.

Why can't she be something else? Why can't she choose another path? She remembers the way Kalarah in Izmyri worked tirelessly to treat her patients, and the way Imogen, while not a healer, was able to use magic to save Tinanna's life.

"Magic?" she says, not realizing she spoke the word aloud. "What if—" She takes a deep breath and closes her eyes, trying to remember what she did when she set the iseru on fire. Trying to recall how she drew upon the magic to erect a monument. Could she do more than manipulate matter?

She feels it: warm but not burning. It starts at the center of her chest, tingling and quickening her heart—a flame, her flame. She has no idea how to control it, if there is such thing as too much or too little, how to direct it to do what she wants... With the Heart of Aodhe, she could have just spoken her desire to it, and it would understand. It had a sentience. But this...

This is me. A fire burning around a heart of steel.

She focuses on the source of that warmth and bids it to travel from her chest to the dying qatu before her. "Please... heal her..."

The magic obeys. It knits skin back together, it grows bones and claws, it creates blood and gives energy to the qatu's heart.

But as it does so, Sari grows dizzy, lightheaded, as if it were taking life from her to give to Shirin'a. Some part of Sari realizes that that is exactly what is happening. She hears the qatu take a deep breath, and just as her vision fades, Shirin'a speaks. "Who are you?"

Sari and Shirin'a trudge through the sandy Erid steppe for several days, and then through the sandy dunes of the northern Esiri desert for several more, the harsh sun beating down on them. Shirin'a is weak and still recovering from her wounds, often leaning heavily on Sari for support, but slowly recovering with the help of Sari's dabbling with magic.

"How much farther until we reach your people?" Sari asks, adjusting the woman's arm over her shoulder.

Shirin'a squints against the glare. "I'm not sure. What time of year is it again?"

"Spring. I believe the month is Efirhi."

"The clan should be camped near Nakur dunes, but we passed them already, didn't we?"

They walk in silence for a while longer, the sun sinking lower on the horizon. Shadows stretch across the sand. Sari is beginning to worry they won't find the caravan at all.

Just as the last sliver of sun disappears, a shout carries over a dune ahead of them. Sari tenses, ready to defend Shirin'a if needed. But as they crest the dune, she sees a small camp nestled against a tiny oasis, two palm trees swaying gently.

Several Re'u emerge from barar'tu as Sari and Shirin'a make their way into camp. A man with a thick, braided beard breaks from the group, eyes wide.

"Shirin'a!" he cries, rushing forward to embrace her. She collapses against him.

Artaxerxes slowly emerges from his own barar'tu, now using a tall walking stick. The bearded man steps away, allowing the siblings to be reunited.

Sari steps back to give them space, a lump forming in her throat, thinking of her own sister, Zisu, and glancing away.

After a moment, Artaxerxes looks up, tears glistening. "Thank you, Sari, for returning my sister to me. You cannot possibly know how much she means to me."

Sari shakes her head, not sure how to respond. She does know. She knows exactly how much a sister is worth.

Shirin'a pulls a small box from her pocket and presents it to her brother. He takes it with reverence, his eyes widening in surprise.

"You found it? After all this time?"

Shirin'a nods, a tired smile on her face.

Sari is intrigued. Shirin'a has been tight-lipped about why she has ventured to the ancient ruins of Enheduanna alone. After Sari had come back around, she had asked Sari to wait for her as she disappeared into the city and come back later with something clutched tightly in her hand. Despite all of Sari's requests, she recieved no answers.

Sari resists the urge to ask about it again. She has already pried enough into Re'u affairs. Still, her curiosity is piqued.

Artaxerxes handles the box gently, as if it were made of the most delicate glass. "I cannot believe you managed to retrieve this sacred relic. You are far braver than I, sister."

Shirin'a shakes her head. "If not for Sari, I would have perished there and never found it. She saved my life."

Sari shifts, uncomfortable with the praise. She has only done what anyone would do. And she had failed to protect her own sister, Zisu. Saving Shirin'a cannot make up for that, but perhaps it is a small step.

Artaxerxes approaches Sari, box in hand, and presents it to her. "You have done our people a great service. This box contains something that I believe is meant for you."

"For me?" Sari says, taking it.

Sari's breath catches in her throat as she peers into the small box Artaxerxes has placed in her hands. Nestled inside is a ring, and not just any ring. Its design is intimately familiar, an exact match to the royal seal she has worn around her neck for so many years. But that is impossible. The royal seal had been destroyed along with the Heart of Aodhe in that fateful battle against Ashur. She had watched the ring melt.

Yet here, resting innocuously in a sacred Re'u relic box, is its twin. Sari lifts the ring reverently, examining it from all angles. The metal still holds a soft glow, as if it had just been freshly forged. The insignia is unmistakable, the geometric symbol of the royal house of Sua.

"How... Where did you get this?" she asks Artaxerxes, her voice hushed with awe.

He smiles. "It has been passed down among our people for generations, its origins lost to time. But we have kept it safe, waiting for the day it would be needed again."

Sari's brow furrows in confusion. She thinks back to her conversation with the goddess Yshuld in the ruins of Bec. Yshuld had said she would find the Blade of Kyna if she stayed true to her quest to stop Ashur. Sari had assumed that referred to her family's ancestral sword. But perhaps Yshuld had instead been referring to this ring, this strange echo of the destroyed royal seal.

"Needed for what?" Sari asks.

Artaxerxes placed a hand gently on her shoulder. "My sister's visions showed that you would come to us and that this relic was meant for you. We do not always understand the will of the Bah'ren, but we listen, and we obey, just as you listen to your Oracle and Yshuld, yes? This ring is yours now, Heir of Kyna."

Sari's thumb traced the cool metal. After a moment, she slips the ring onto her finger, feeling a strange warmth spread through her hand. The royal seal had always symbolized her claim to the throne, her family's divine right to rule Sua. Now, this ring is touched by divine hands in a different way. Not as a symbol of authority but as a guide on her continuing journey. Wherever it led her next, she would not face it alone. Heir of Kyna. Not heir of Sua.

"Thank you," she says.

They invite her to stay the night, which she happily accepts. As she hears their stories around the fire, she understands why Zisu chose to live among these people. They have created yet another version of paradise. Community, responsibility to one another, each individual considering how their actions affect the whole. She realizes she could be happy among them, too. Maybe this is the place that Yshuld meant for her. Perhaps here is where she would find her answers.

It is with great reluctance that she leaves the next morning. She hears a call on the wind, the song of Yshuld. She thanks her hosts, smiling as she turns back one last time and sees Artaxerxes and Shrin'a holding hands.

But she is being beckoned, and she cannot ignore the call.

Heir of Kyna.

She does not know where she is riding, she simply listens to the call and follows it until it is almost time for nialsamsu.

Sari squints against the harsh glare of the midday sun, shielding her eyes as she scans the endless dunes of sand. The call had led her here, though to what end she does not yet know. As the camel plods onward, she spots a figure in the distance, wavering like a mirage.

At first, it is just a speck. But as she drew nearer, Sari's breath catches in her throat. The graceful stride, the glint of sunlight on dark hair, the gentle smile... it is Nanshaie.

But how can that be? Nanshaie should be back in Antalyza, unless... This is no ordinary traveler.

"Yshuld," Sari murmurs as the goddess stands before her.

A soft laugh, so achingly familiar. "Yes, child." Those eyes—Nanshaie's eyes—light up. "I have come to check on you. Did you find the answers you sought?"

Sari's heart quickens. After months of wandering, unsure of her path, she still does not know the answer to her questions. "No," she says, looking to the horizon, spinning the ring on her finger.

Yshuld steps closer, placing a hand on Sari's shoulder. "The Heir of Kyna shall find her way."

"What does that mean?"

"The emblem on this ring was originally the sigil of Kyna."

"But who is Kyna?"

"Kyna was a kind healer and a powerful sage who dedicated her magic to caring for those who needed assistance; a leader in the City of Bec, much admired and respected."

Sari stares at the ring on her finger, its surface glinting under the unrelenting sun. The symbol etched into the metal, which once felt familiar, now seems distant, holding the weight of a history long forgotten.

"She used magic? But you warned me not to." Sari winces as she recalls the moments of weakness that overcame her while she was healing the Re'u woman.

"I warned you of using it for the wrong reasons. You are particularly adept at using fire magic—a magic of destruction, but also rebirth. This ring should help to keep your flame from flickering out—or raging out of control."

"Heir of Kyna. Is Kyna an ancestor?" She does not want to linger on thoughts of destruction, of uncontainable infernos.

Yshuld's expression softens as she meets Saritrah's gaze. "No, Kyna has no descendants," Yshuld replies, her tone carrying a note of finality. "But she had friends who carried on her legacy."

"I have my answers," Sari says. A legacy of healing... Flames of rebirth... And a past she must atone for. She runs a finger over the sigil again.

Yshuld's eyes—Nanshaie's eyes—crinkle with warmth. "What are they?"

Sari hesitates, her gaze shifting to the horizon. "I will be a healer," she says, her voice barely audible over the desert wind. "I have spent too much time taking life. Perhaps I can preserve it."

"Do you have a plan?"

"I've heard that there's a terrible winter in Tsvetokrasa, and many people are sick from the cold. I want to help them."

"Is it wise for someone so full of fire to travel to a land of winter and ice? You shall be so far from the warmth of the sun," Yshuld says. Yshuld, goddess of prophecy, but also the goddess of the sun, something that Tsvetokrasa has very little of.

"People dying from the cold are the ones who need warmth the most," Sari says.

Yshuld smiles, her eyes sparkling with approval before she fades again, her final words a whisper on the winds. "I have faith in you, Sari, Heir of Kyna."

Sari turns her back to look one more time to the south. Days or weeks of hard riding stands between her and the Oracle by the sea. She wonders if she should send a letter to tell Nanshaie where she is going. But she has a feeling that the Oracle already knows, and that she will find the Oracle sooner rather than later. Tinanna and Nanshaie are already waiting for her north of the mountains. She will meet her lovers again soon, this time as a Sari forged with her own fires, and not anyone else's.

Two daggers

Thank you for reading SMOKE AND STEEL. Sari's struggle with anger and resentment and her journey to healing and peace were very difficult to write. I wrote all of it during NaNoWriMo, but it was difficult to sit with these emotions. Nonetheless, I think it is valuable to have books with not just redeemable villains but villains that heal, too. The best way to make sure that books find their way into the hands of readers who need them the most is to leave **an honest review**. I would truly appreciate it if you took the time to do so on a retailer or reader site of your choice. Thank you so much.

If you want behind-the-scenes extras, bonus content, early access to WIPs (including WIP Draft Access to SHACKLES & SECRETS), my ongoing serial following the life of Kyna and Aodhe, CROSSROADS OF FATE, and other exclusive stories set in the world of Ahnlisen, consider joining **Dax Dreaming**. It is free to Follow, and I make tons of content available to Followers. If you want even more, consider joining one of the paid tiers.

https://dreaming.daxmurray.com

The Qatu With No Name

ONE HUNDRED *DIAMS*, HE had promised her. More money than she has made in her whole career. Enough money to make sure *aga* always had the medicine she needed. She hasn't been able to send money to her parents in at least a year. Maybe it would finally be enough for them to stop hating her for choosing this profession.

Nina peeks around the corner, ears pricked for any clanking of the guard's sandals. She is trying to maintain her focus on her mission, but her mind just keeps replaying the conversation with her former mentor, Silla. Nina had not met with the client directly, so she only had the information her mentor chose to share. One hundred *diams* per kill, he had said. But she only needed to take out one of the mat'sahr'dan to get enough to ensure her parents never worried again.

She had been trained until she was a finely honed spear; forged into a dagger that can pierce the hardest of hearts. She is as lethal as the venom of a qaboon, but she kills fall more quickly.

But she had nothing on the mat'sahr'dan. They had been fighting—and killing—since they were no more than three summers old. Only the strongest can reign over a nation of fighters.

She hugs the wall of the *isi'tu*, ignoring the tightness in her chest. She's been ignoring it since the day she was officially made a full member of the Siúlóir Scáth. She only has the fuzziest memory of that day; but she doesn't need to recall the details to know that what they did to her cannot be undone, and this pain in her chest is a constant reminder that they can always find her, or worse, kill her. So she has learned to live with the pain, ignore it while she slinks through the night, taking lives and stealing secrets at the behest of any who can pay the price for their services.

But this high of a mark is usually not allowed. That was one way the Scáth ensured that the royals wouldn't try too hard to find them, root them out, and destroy them. But Mat'sahr'dan Ashur was offering the Scáth far more than money. He was offering them sanctuary. If he became the Sahre'Danu, then the Scáth could openly operate out of Sua.

Most of her assassin siblings are vying to be the one to take out the youngest mat'sahr'dan, Zisuthra. Mat'sahr'dan Zisuthra is not just young, but she is also weak; and worse, she does not want to fight. One of the easiest marks, had she not been ensconced in the royal *isi'tu*.

While several of her fellow Scáth have already made attempts on the lives of the royal offspring, none have been successful. Nina has been careful, taking her time, observing from the shadows, watching her colleagues fail.

The issue with trying to assassinate Mat'sahr'dan Zisuthra is the fact that Zisuthra is always accompanied by Mat'sahr'dan Saritrah, her older sister. Saritrah is nowhere near the top of the list of contenders to take the throne; she is slower than Ashur, less clever than Anenlilda, not as strong as Aishah, and not as bloodthirsty as Alaparos.

But what she does have is anger. And when she becomes angry, she can easily defeat anyone; even her mother. And threatening Zisuthra makes her very, very angry.

Which is why Nina has chosen Saritrah as her mark. Wait until she is separated from Zisuthra and take Saritrah out. That might leave Zisuthra easy prey for any of the other Scáth members, but Nina only has to take out one royal. Let the others fight among themselves for the rest of the kills. She just needs one.

A guard crosses the garden and enters the servants wing through a small door. Nina darts from her hiding place, sliding a piece of parchment between the door and the frame just before it closes, and then she holds her breath, hoping the guard won't notice as he turns the key to lock it. She hears a gruff curse and then the clanking of sandals down a stone floor.

She slips inside, and her stomach groans as she smells the roasting of *fa'leen* meat seasoned with ripe *undu*. The laundresses gossip loudly, their voices carrying down the corridor as they finish their chores for the day. She creeps into the servants staircase, imagining the map she's stared at for hours, hoping she remembers which turns to take. She creeps through the *isi'tu* until she finds herself standing on the other side of a hidden door, peering through a peephole at the fiery royal. *Time to douse your flame.* Nina grins; she doesn't care about politics, which *issiaq* is in favor, which *sahre* has attacked another, who is on top in the games that determine who sits on the Kashu throne. She doesn't care who will replace Sumalika mat Qa'taru. She does not care about Sua.

She cares about her *aga*.

She slides her finger down the wall, searching for the small latch for the door. Just as she inserts the tip of her claw into the seam, a rough hand covers her mouth.

"What might you be doing here?"

Caught. Another failed Scáth unless I can get out of here. She struggles against her captor, sinking her teeth into one of the fingers and stomping on one of their feet before elbowing them in the stomach.

The guard releases her, and Nina races through the hidden servant's passages until she reaches a dead end; the only escape is a window. She hears the guard clamoring after her. She'd rather take her chances with landing wrong. Nine floors above the ground, and the hard stone garden won't be fun to smack into, but it's her only chance. She leaps out, rolling as she hits the stone, suppressing a groan.

She clamors up the garden wall, and just as she is about to spring down to the other side, to safety, someone grabs her tail.

No amount of training could have prevented her from letting out a yowl as she tumbles back to the ground.

The guard again puts a hand over her mouth. "I want to talk. If we can have a chat, I will let you go and forget your face."

Even if she wanted to talk, she couldn't. If the Scáth found out, she'd be dead before dinner. They have ways of killing the traitors without touching them, without seeing them, without being near them. It has something to do with whatever they do when they slice their chests open; something inside of them that can somehow be tracked and also used as a weapon against them.

But if she can get the guard to ease their grip for just half a second. Nina nods.

"We're on the same side," the guard says.

Nina's muscles are tensed, ready to run. But the guard's words catch her off guard.

"What?" She searches for any sign that the guard is telling the truth. Only one of the moons is out that night, and despite it being the dead of the night, the heat still lingers. Try as she might, Tinanna searches the guard's neck or collarbones for any of the scars that might give them away as Scáth.

"You know the rose?" Nina asks, needing to be sure.

"What? No, I mean. Perhaps. It depends. Name a place to meet, and I will be there."

"Just outside the eastern city gates." She can run if she needs to. She'll have a camel waiting. "When both moons are out."

It won't be for another two nights, and Nina expects the guard to say no. "Very well. I will be there. Now get going."

* * *

Nina has not dared go back to the *isi'tu*, not even to observe her colleagues fail. By now, there must at least be some suspicion that the uptick in assassination attempts was not random. For two days, she does not leave the room at the inn. She reflects on the entire situation; the guard gave her the choice of meeting place, the time, and was even content to let it be a few days in the future. The guard wanted Nina to feel in control; but why?

She's still not sure this is a good idea, even as she ties back her hair and pulls on a cowl, checking to make sure her own scars are hidden. She pads down the alleyways of Erzurumei barefoot, the sands no longer scorching. The fine hairs on the bottom of her feet allow her to feel subtle shifts in the air currents, as do those covering her palms. Qatu are prized by the Scáth for these features—she was able to sell herself to them for 40 *diams* when she was only five summers. But most Qatu reside in Sua, either as vassals fiercely loyal to the Sahre'Danu, or as the nomadic Re'u in the northern deserts, who are loyal to none but themselves.

In a way, Nina is no different than her Re'u family. Loyal to only herself in that she let herself become an exile from her people. *But it was worth it. Aga is still alive. But I have to complete this mission for her to stay that way.*

The guard is already there, waiting patiently, leaning against the wall, tail swishing idly.

"I am Belu," the guard says, holding out a hand. "Nice to meet you."

Nina does not take the hand, weary that it might be a trap of some kind. She nods.

"I know you were trying to kill Sari," Belu says. The way the guard says the mar's name—one syllable, no title—rankles her. On the same side? Belu sounded like she was one friendly terms with the mark. "And I get it, I want her dead, too."

That catches Nina off-guard. Twice so far this week, and by the same person. "Then why did you stop me?"

"It's too soon, you see."

Nina cocks her head to the side.

"I'm with the Amyrdine Bara," Belu said, as if that should explain everything.

Nina raises an eyebrow, determined not to give anything away.

"We're new, but we're hoping to achieve here what the Red Front did in Fayn."

Nina sighs and slinks away. "This is a waste of time."

"No, come back! You don't have to work alone anymore. We're all working together now."

Nina closes her eyes, taking a deep breath, steadying her heart rate—ignoring the pain that comes with each beat. "I am sorry; I do not do what I do for political reasons. This is not a cause for me."

"I knew it," Belu says, snapping her fingers. "I knew it. Was it Aishah? Or Ashur? Which of the mars paid you? How many others are there that are paid?"

She was determined not to let anything slip, and yet. She was tricked.

"I will say nothing more. I hope whatever information you have gleaned you determine equal to the courtesy you gave me."

"No, no. Still not done." This time, the guard does reach for her, but the ship spins and leaps out of the way, and Belu grabs only empty air.

Nina has to give some measure of grudging respect to the guard for their determination. She crosses her arms. "If you would like to give me the whole political speech, fine. I'll listen, but I'm not joining."

"Why not? Because you're trapped by something? Someone? Caged? Just as the people of the world are caged by oppressive governments?"

Nina rolls her eyes but does not reply. Her heart won't stop racing and she struggles to keep her senses focused on her surrounding and not diverted to the pain. *The sand is cold, the sky is obsidian, I can the chirps of insects...*

"I can tell, something has you shackled. We can't pay you whatever Ashur or Aishah would have paid you, but we can give you freedom, which is infinitely more valuable."

"Why do you work at the palace? Did you start there as part of this Bara organization?"

"No, I started there because it paid well, but then my father got ill, and I couldn't take care of him and keep my job. But the Amyrdine Bara? Fellow members watch him while I am at work, and I use my position there to get information out. You see why it's too soon for Sari to die? She dies, I don't have a job, we don't get the information we need. So, for my father's sake, please pick a different mar."

Belu would not last a day in the Scáth. She gives away her secrets without worry, she asks for things instead of demanding or just doing. "I will not say anything more."

"I know you won't, but you do, anyway. Here," Belu says as she fishes in a pocket and holds out a piece of folded parchment.

Nina stares at it and shakes her head.

"It's not laced with poison or whatever else you are thinking. It's an address. If you do decide you want to be free of whatever chain you're in, go here, and tell them you wish to purchase a falcon. Please just take it."

"Show it to me."

Belu unfolds the parchment and holds it out so that Nina can read it. "Can you remember that?"

"Won't have to. It was kind and stupid of you to let me go, but I am glad nonetheless. I shall consider your request, but I make no promises."

"That's good enough for me."

* * *

It has been three months since Scáth was tasked with taking out all but one of the royal *qits*. No one has succeeded. Nina does not share her opinion, but she is starting to believe that perhaps this was a set up. But the leaders of the Scáth have ways of ensuring clients do not go back on their word and Nina has often wondered if it is the same way they ensure their assassins do not turncoat.

It has only been one month since Nina met with Belu, and in all of that time, she has not made any more attempts to enter the *isi'tu*. She has taken on some reconnaissance missions, a few hits on those who didn't pay their gambling debts, and a few on those trying to collect on debts. She has not earned more than two *diams* at most. Half she uses to pay her inn tab, and half she sends home.

No, not home. Not anymore. And beside, even when she was Re'u, the Re'u do not have homes. They have communities, and they always said that was worth more.

But tonight, she will try again. This time, she will not get caught. Although she has not gone to the *isi'tu*, she has been following Belu. She knows the guard's schedule and daily patterns. She knows that tonight, Belu's father is the worst he has ever been, and she is staying home. The guard most invested in the mar's survival is otherwise occupied.

Nina knows that Belu's father will recover by tomorrow afternoon; it was only a mild poison he was slipped. Nothing lethal, just uncomfortable.

She creeps through the streets, more silent than a spider. Both moons illuminate the night, but the Scáth requires its members to forsake their families and instead become children of shadows.

It is easier, somehow, to ignore the pain tonight. She dreamed last night; not a normal dream. But the Dream of Sight. It does not happen often, she doubts the Temple of Yshuld would have accepted her had she been presented to them after she had her fight vision at three years old. But it doesn't matter. She was born Re'u. Re'u believe in the *sen'en,* not the twelve *tuyude,* so they do not believe in Yshuld. But if they did, maybe she would be in Antalyza right now; and her mother would be dead.

She shakes her head, realizing she's stalked through the night more quickly than she planned and is already a mere block from the *isi'tu'*s imposing walls. Her dream last night... A falcon visited her, and she was smiling. There was someone else there, and she was laughing.

"I shall have to introduce you to my *aga,*" she said in her dream.

She does not care what the falcon means, she does not care who the other person is. A future exists where not only is her mother alive, but speaking with her—and somehow, she isn't leashed anymore to the Scáth. She is certain that tonight is the night she will kill Saritrah and from there, everything will be set in motion.

The thought of that future is enough to make the pain in her chest fade away. She smiles as she digs her claws into the cracks in the sandstone walls and scales it.

Once perched on top of the walls, she waits; scanning the courtyard for any clue that something is not as it should be. Belu is at home, which might through off the rest of the guards' schedule, but she is prepared and won't be caught this time. As she studies her surroundings, she sees a single *bara* flower, growing out of the crack in a marble stone. Many consider these to be weeds, not flowers. They can survive a rainy season, and they can survive without water at all. They grow in the most unlikely of places and are almost impossible to kill.

Nina grins. *What is Belu's group called again? Something Bara? I wonder if this is where they got the name.*

Determining that she is safe, she places her hands flat on the wall and readies herself to pounce.

But another vision starts. She has never had two in a single year, let alone two in just as many days. She leans back, placing her hand on her heart as she watches herself be forced down onto an execution block, but then a member of the gathered crowd holds up an open hand before clenching it tightly, and in that very second she feels her heart squeezed with such force that it explodes before the axe can slice through her neck.

She blinks as the vision fades and hears shouting below. The guards are pouring in as one of them holds down a squirming figuring, shouting for help. The trapped figure tries rolling to their side, attempting to throw off the guard pining them down. As the captive does, their eyes meet.

She knows him. She trained with him. She beat him up more times than she could even try to guess at. He was recruited from another Re'u tribe, but he clipped his ears and had his tail removed after; he said he wanted to cast off not just family, but birthright. He thought doing so would make him truly a child of the shadows.

But he lost the keen senses that would have given him an edge over lohyue or Ástfríður. He might have been fine in Garcelon, Fayn, or even in the bitter cold of Tsvetokrasa. But in Sua, where almost everyone is *qatu,* he was at an extreme disadvantage. He never should have taken this mission. She turns away, unable to watch as the guards drag him out unconscious.

That would have been her if she had not had her vision...Even if she did not mess up and do something to alert the guards, she would have still been visible when *he* did.

She went through all the trouble with Belu's father, and now...

Belu will most likely be back here tomorrow, someone from the *Bara* attending her father. He might still be a little worse than normal, but on the mend.

She leaps back to the ground, safe outside the *isi'tu* walls, ready to go back to the inn.

But then she wonders, do the *Bara* watch her father because of how valuable she is to their cause? She's risking her life to provide them with something valuable. Is that why they watch him? Or would they help even if she was a member and her only contribution was keeping their files organized?

If she joined them... Would they help with *aga*?

She shakes her head, hand touching her chest, the pain starting to seep back into her consciousness. No, there's no way to cut the leash she's on. Leaving the Scáth means death; they will hunt her until they know she is just a rotting carcass in the desert.

* * *

"Excuse me? *Tu'erebu?*" She's circled the block seven times, trying to decide. "Excuse me, is anyone here? I'm here to buy a falcon."

The door opens and a qatu woman with bulky muscles and singed fur answers the door. She is wearing thick leather pants and her bare arms are speckled with burn marks.

"Is that so? Who told you I sold those?" The woman laughs.

"Belu," Nina says. The more she looks at the woman, the more she feels she's seen her before. Not in last night's vision, but perhaps, in one of them... Long ago.

"*Tu'sala*. Very well, might as well come in. Sit down over there if you like."

Nina does not sit, but she does follow the qatu further inside. "I am considering, well, buying a falcon. But I am in a delicate situation."

"Please, you think you're the first royal defector? Isn't Belu proof enough we can figure these things out?"

"I am not a royal defector," Nina says. "Are we... alone?"

"You're skittish, you running from someone? You think there's someone hiding in the shadows or something?" The qatu sits down, leaning back and again gesturing for Nina to take a seat.

"This is a bizarre question, I know. But before we say anything more, would you mind showing me your neck and collarbone?"

"Buy me dinner and I'll show you more than that," the qatu says, laughing.

When Nina says nothing, she sighs and pulls on the hem of her camise. "No *qaboon* bites, if that's what you're worried about. Damn, you really are scared of something."

Nina bites her lip. *No marks. She's not with the Scáth.* It might be safe; but if she's wrong, she's dead. "I would defecting from the Siúlóir Scáth."

The qatu purses her lips togeher, brows furrowed. "If you hadn't responded to every one of my jests with nothing but a silent scowl, I would think you were put up to this as some sort of prank. But you're serious."

"I am serious. "

"This would complicate things." She scratches her chin, looking Nina up and down.

"Is there a way to stop them from finding me?" Nina wants to take back the words as soon as she says them. This random qatu probably doesn't even know that whatever it is that is done to them is done at all. If she saw Nina's scars, she would probably assume they were acquired while fighting, not during a drug-laden initiation ritual. So how would she know any more than Nina?

"There might be. But it would require that you become someone else entirely, new name, new life story, if you pass by the innkeeper for the place you've been staying, no you didn't; you never stayed there and never seen them before. Got it?"

"I have done that once already in my lifetime," she says. But she hasn't. Even if they don't write back, she still writes to her parents. That... That's something she can't do. "But I do have one condition on that."

The qatu chuckles. "Name it."

"My... There are two people that I want assurances will be taken care of. Without my income... One of them has a complex medical condition..."

"I see. It will be done. My name is Miramis, by the way. We're figure out yours along the way."

"Let me grab my things from—"

"No! We leave now. This moment." Mirami's mirth is gone, and her eyes are cold and commanding. "We are going to Antalyza and we are leaving for there tonight."

"That's on the other side of Sua! That's a journey of weeks! I can't leave without even—"

"We will figure it out."

Nina puts her hand to her heart, the pain the worst it has ever been. She wonders if, somehow, the Scáth knows. If somehow they can tell, if somehow whatever they put in her chest lets them listen to her conversations.

"Silla," Nina says.

"If that was your name before, it isn't now, I just told you." Miramis rummages through a trunk in the corner, pulling out two long cloaks, each are finely embroidered with the intricate patterns usually seen in Fayn clothing. "Put this one."

"No, that was not and is not my name. I just... Wish I could say goodbye to her."

"Your mother?"

Nina shakes her head. She has tried to not think of Silla; her mentor, and then something more. Something deeper. But once one becomes a full member of the Scáth, they are never to see their mentor's again; unless their mentor's hunt them. If she defects, it will be Silla that they send to kill her. She thought she was dying on that last day they had together. But now... "No, not my mother. But someone I loved, yes."

"Well, now you've never known her at all, so she should not matter to you."

"You're right," she says, taking one of the cloaks from Miramis. She feels like she's lost grip on reality; is she really defecting now? And riding off with someone she just met to the other side of the nation? As she pulls the cloak around her shoulders, she remembers this moment. It was her very first vision; she had been so confused by the green embroidery and didn't recognize herself in the vision. But now, would this lead to the happy vision of her laughing with someone or to the future where she is executed?

Without another word, she follows Miramis to a stable, and they leave Erzurumei without incident. As night passes, and dawn approaches, the woman without a name asks, "Why Antalyza?"

"The Scáth do not recognize monarchs or laws, but they do acknowledge the gods. You are to be my eyes and ears in the Temple of Yshuld. You can join even if you do not have the Sight. With your combat skills, I know they will take you as a guard."

But I do have the Sight... "I see."

"But once you enter, you cannot leave the Temple. We will find ways to communicate with you. But you are safe in those walls; they will not enter it. But if you ever step outside, even one single step, they will take the opportunity to kill you."

"Belu told me you hoped the free people from cages, not shove them inside one," the woman without a name says. She wasn't finding a way off of the leash; she was just being put in a cage. But there was no going back now. It wasn't going to be 100 *diams*, but her *aga* will be taken care of.

"Is that how you see it? Hmm. I suppose you might be right. But I will find a better solution. What do you think of the name Tinanna?"

"That is fine," Tinanna says.

"And one more thing, Tinanna," Miramis says. "Once you are there, you never met me, either. Even if you should come across me on the street, it will be our first time ever seeing each other. Anything and everything that happened before you stepped foot in the Temple never happened."

"I understand," she says. She has no *aga,* she has no Silla.

"I will leave you to craft your backstory, I am sure you are good at that sort of thing with your former line of work."

"Yes, I was. I've been so many people with so many pasts. What's one more?"

Acknowledgements

I started brainstorming this story in 2021 and procured a cover by 2022. But it was not until 2023 that I started outlining it during Preptober at events hosted by the Campfire Community. I wrote nearly all of it during NaNoWriMo alongside my NaNo Team, The Court of Magic and Mayhem, and I owe a lot of thanks to the team members: AJ, Bryar, Beebopia, Kei, Tloz, and Saurocorn. Thank you so much for the encouragement, cheerleading, and tea! Thank you to the Campfire Community, overall, for hosting the best NaNo & NaNo-Adjacent events; special shout out to Emory!

I also owe a debt of gratitude to my fellow Writing Forgers: Ingrid, Liz, Ka'ua, Danny, Emma, Kirsten, Y.R., Eliza, and Jessica! Thank you for all the shenanigans. I mean help. Thank you for the help.

I also have to shout out my amazing supporters on Ream! Thank you to the Arcanists, Hannah and Eric, and the Enchanter, Nahum! I am so grateful—words cannot do it justice! I hope you enjoy this story and all the rest that I have planned. A hearty thanks to the STRW team, too.

While not directly involved in the creation of this book, I also have to thank Angry Succubus Noises Static for providing an amazing and supportive escape to take on different challenges—rat extermination and bee control. Thank you, Rebecca, Ashley, Proto, Shu, Fin, Corey, and Sol! I'm so excited to continue the unending journey with you in Dawntrail.

Thank you, Masayoshi Soken, for writing the best music to write to. Thank you, Shadow, for all the interruptions. Thank you, Stormy, for all the spilled coffee. Thank you, dear reader, for joining me on this journey. I hope you will join me for the next one. SHACKLES AND SECRETS is scheduled for release in 2026. Sign up for my newsletter if you want to know more as that date approaches!

And thank you to my partner—you believed in me when I couldn't believe in myself. Also, thank you for all the fish!

Also By Dax Murray

Stand Alone Stories

A Lake of Feathers and Moonbeams
The Magic Surrendered
Birthing Orion

Serials

The Last Page
Crossroads of Fate

SCIONS AND SHADOWS

Crossroads of Fate
Shades and Silver
Stars and Soil

Scorched Scars

Shrouded Sight

<u>Smoke and Steel</u>

Coming Soon:

Shackles and Shards

Join my newsletter to get a free copy of SCORCHED SCARS and SHROUDED SIGHT, as well as regular updates, bonus content, and more!

<u>https://www.daxmurray.com/newsletter</u>

About the Author

Dax is an award-winning author of sapphic, revolutionary fantasy that focuses on trauma, healing, and political advancement. After realizing their dream of being a curmudgeonly hedgewitch in the woods of Western Pennsylvania was not possible due to the construction of an outlet mall, Dax took up a new form of sorcery, where they whispered to rocks in arcane languages and taught them how to spy on you, colloquially known as software engineering.

But Dax left that all behind and today, they can be found waiting on the god (i.e., the cat) who has allowed them to live in their abode and use their word magic to make others cry.

Dax studied political science and creative writing at Allegheny College in Pennsylvania and is a member of the Editorial Freelancers Association. When not writing, they can be found at the Crystarium in Norvrandt.

If you are interested in the *Scions and Shadows* series, the best place to find all of the books plus the plethora of bonus content is on <u>Camp-fire,</u> a unique reader experience with tons of modules for characters, maps, location and lore pages, and more. One low price gets you not just the novel but every short story and bit of bonus content, even those released after you purchase the book! Dax regularly adds new bits of bonus materials, so check back for updates!

Dax also has a membership platform where they are releasing episodic serial fiction stories, lore articles, character profiles, short stories, and more. It's like Patreon meets Substack but using a (dax-modified) version of Ghost CMS. You can subscribe for as little as $1/mo to get access to bonus content or $5/mo to get access to *The Last Page* and *Crossroads of Fate.* Visit dreaming.daxmurray.com to learn more.

Let's Connect

Website

daxmurray.com

Newsletter

newsletter.daxmurray.com

Sign up for Dax's newsletter for exclusive announcements, behind-the-scenes looks at the WIPs, and sneak-peaks! Subscribers are also frequently given opportunities to join her ARC Team and get her new releases before anyone else! Sign up today for cat pics and updates! Join today to get a free copy of the novella *SCORCHED SCARS* and the short story anthology *SHROUDED SIGHT,* both set in the *Scions and Shadows* universe.

Serial Membership Site

dreaming.daxmurray.com

Like a mash up of Substack and Patreon, Dax used the Ghost CMS platform and modified by hand it to create a unique reading experience specifically with readers in mind. It is here that you can find deleted scenes, bonus short stories, and on-going serials such as *CROSSROADS OF FATE and THE LAST PAGE.* Sign up for as little as $1/mo! Higher tiers get access to new novels before anyone else! Use this special link to get 50% off your first year.

50% Off: dax.ink/dreaming

BlueSky

dax.ink/bsky

Elsewhere

dax.ink

Kraken Reads

At The Kraken Collective, we know how frustrating it can be to reach the end of a book and want more. Within the following pages, you will find books with a similar feel to help you scratch that reading itch and why we're recommending them. We hope our suggestions will help you find your next favorite read!

The Kraken Collective is an alliance of indie authors of LGBTQI-AP+ speculative fiction, committed to building a publishing space that is inclusive, positive, and brings fascinating stories to readers. Looking for your next great read? Check out these other sci-fi and dystopian titles from Kraken Collective authors!

Kraken Reads: City of Strife

Claudie Arseneault

If you're looking for more political back and forth underpinned by deeply personal stories, check out _City of Strife_ from Claudie Arseneault! City of Strife is a mosaical, epic novel with a large and majorly queer cast, a web of political intrigue and personal narratives, and a heart of gold. In it, an elven noble's attempt to stop imperialist wizards from taking over his city will have repercussions on its inhabitants, from its richest towers to the homeless shelter at its bottom.

Fans of elves, magic, and crisscrossing storylines will find everything they want within this story.

Kraken Reads: Party of Fools

Cedar McCloud

If you're looking for more sapphic representation and a rag tag group with aspirations of revolution, you'll want to pick up *Party of Fools* by Cedar McCloud.

Resistance members Reed Thorley and Gladys the Destroyer can't believe their luck when the Immortal Emperor herself wanders into their favorite bar, unguarded and playacting an ordinary citizen. This is their chance to give the rebellion the upper hand against the Empire—after a few pints, of course. The middle-aged halfling musician and his elderly barbarian partner are seasoned enough to know that when Emperor Vallora invites them to join her worldwide food tour, their best bet is to say "Yes, chef!" and wait for an opportunity to strike.

But hot as a greased griddle behind them comes Captain Andromeda Stagge, Vallora's personal bodyguard, intent on returning the Emperor to the palace. She's only doing her job. She isn't pissed off at being left behind. It's not as if the Emperor is her only real friend, given the difficulty of fitting in when you're a 200-year-old autistic elf from a lower-class socioeconomic background. It isn't that at all!

Vallora's worldwide food tour hinges on her ability to escape the capital city with Reed and Gladys without being caught. The Emperor isn't supposed to be sampling local cheeses in the company of commoners. Though why the most powerful person in the Endless Empire needs to be under lock and key in Zenith Palace is anyone's guess...